PLEASE
TELL
ME

OTHER TITLES BY MIKE OMER

Zoe Bentley Mysteries

A Killer's Mind
In the Darkness
Thicker than Blood

Abby Mullen Thrillers

A Deadly Influence
Damaged Intentions
A Burning Obsession

Glenmore Park Mysteries

Spider's Web
Deadly Web
Web of Fear

PLEASE TELL ME

MIKE OMER

THOMAS & MERCER

Text copyright © 2023 by Michael Omer
All rights reserved.

Published by Thomas & Mercer, Seattle

www.apub.com

Amazon, the Amazon logo, and Thomas & Mercer are trademarks of Amazon.com, Inc., or its affiliates.

ISBN-13: 9781662509377 (paperback)
ISBN-13: 9781662509360 (digital)

Cover design by Faceout Studio, Molly von Borstel
Cover image: © Mariya Kolyago, © Yellow Cat, © Squeeb Creative, © Chizhenkova Svetlana, © Lucie Lang / Shutterstock; © Jenny Milner / ArcAngel

Printed in the United States of America

PLEASE TELL ME

Chapter 1

Kathy limped alongside the road in the dark, hugging her doll to her chest. The doll was scared, because of the shadows, which was why Kathy clutched her so tightly. Sometimes, when you're scared, the only thing that helps is a hug.

It had started raining a while ago. Stinging drops that pelted her face and soaked her ripped pajamas. The doll was cold and wet. So was Kathy.

Kathy's feet hurt. She was barefoot. She remembered that once, long ago, she'd used to have shoes. She'd wear her shoes when she went outside to play. But those shoes were a distant memory, hazy and confusing. She remembered she sometimes didn't like to put her shoes on. She'd argue with Mommy about it. Which now seemed strange. Kathy would have loved to have shoes.

She hadn't worn shoes for so long. For weeks . . . or months . . . she wasn't sure. Maybe even a year.

It was hard to decide where to step. If she walked on the road, the rough asphalt hurt her soles. Walking on the grass to the side of the road was easier, but when she did that earlier, a thorn sank into her heel. She cried and had to stop and take it out, which hurt really bad. The doll kissed Kathy's foot where it hurt, but it didn't help much.

By now, after walking for so long, both her feet felt raw. She sat down under a streetlight and looked at the bottom of her feet and saw that the skin of her soles was peeling, and there was blood.

But she couldn't stop for long. So she stood up and kept walking.

Sometimes, bad men could follow a trail of blood. Kathy knew that. She'd seen it happen. She stepped in the running water at the side of the road and let it churn around her ankles, washing the blood away. Her teeth chattered, and she shivered. She was so cold.

Sometimes when people were too cold, they could freeze and die.

She started walking again.

The houses around her were big and rectangular and scary. They didn't look like hers at all. She still remembered her home, even though she'd been gone for so long. It had a nice yard, and a white fence, and a red roof, and during Christmas, Daddy would put little blinking lights all over the house.

She wanted to tell her doll about the house, but when she tried, the words didn't come. They got all confused in her mind, and then they melted away, like they always did. So instead she clutched the doll tighter to her chest and kept walking. She needed to leave those scary buildings behind her.

Sometimes, when little girls walked around scary buildings at night, bad things happened to them. Kathy knew that.

There was a noise. A loud roar. Kathy tensed and whirled around, and it was getting hard to breathe because she knew what that noise was, she'd heard it before and now she could see it, the gaping wound, the screams of pain, and the blood was running, so much blood, and she shut her eyes and crouched, covering her ears, but even then she could still see it, and she couldn't move, couldn't breathe, the shrieking . . .

The noise faded away.

She stayed where she was, hugging herself. She could hear her own heavy breathing, and her teeth chattering, and the rain washing the street, but nothing else.

Maybe that noise had just been a truck driving somewhere nearby. But it was sometimes so hard to tell which noises were the really bad ones, and which weren't.

Onward. She needed to get home, where it was . . . safe. Where there were no bad men, and where Mommy and Daddy could hug her and her doll.

She wanted to tell the doll about Mommy and Daddy, and hugs, and safety, but she didn't have the words.

It was becoming harder to walk. She was too cold. And tired. Her eyes shut as she took another step. And another. The steady patter of the rain floated away. She wasn't too cold anymore. She was getting warmer. Perhaps warm enough to lie down for a—

A sudden sharp noise.

Her eyes popped open, and she whirled, saw the two bright lights just behind her. And that noise, that sharp angry noise, almost like the screams of torment, and the images filled her mind. Blood and pain and fear, and she was stumbling backward and now she was screaming, her mouth open wide, a hoarse screech that didn't even sound like her—

"Hey. Hey!"

A car door opened, a man leaped out, ran toward her. Sometimes men did terrible things to girls who walked alone at night. Kathy knew. She fell and landed on the rough asphalt, the jarring jolt snapping her mouth shut, and the taste of blood filled her mouth.

"Hey, kid. Uh . . . Are you all right? Do you need me to call someone?"

Her doll had dropped from her hand, she couldn't see her anymore. She had to get away. She scrambled back on her hands and feet, keeping her eyes on the man. He got closer, closer, tried to grab her. She shrieked again, jerked away. He retreated, eyes widening. Her shrieking became coughing, and she couldn't move anymore, she was coughing hard, could hardly breathe. Blood filled her mouth. She'd bitten her tongue.

"Hey." He raised his hands, taking a step back. "I'm not going to hurt you, okay?"

Her coughing slowly stopped. She sat on the road, trembling, her eyes flicking left and right, trying to figure out if she could get away.

"What's your name?" he asked, crouching slowly.

The trembling became worse, and now her teeth chattered. Her name was Kathy. But she didn't know how to tell him that. The words wouldn't come.

"I'm Ian. Who are you?"

He didn't look like a bad man, but sometimes bad men didn't look like it. Kathy knew that.

"Are you from around here?"

Was she? She wasn't sure. She wanted to go home. She was trying to walk home.

"Listen, uh . . . do you want to get in my car? You should get out of the rain."

She began crawling backward again, breathing hard, her heart thudding in her chest.

"No, no, okay. Don't . . . you don't need to get in the car. Here." He took off his coat and leaned forward, holding it to her. "Put this on."

She stared at the coat. Maybe he was trying to trick her. To get her close enough so he could take her and . . . and . . .

"It'll keep you warm." He let the coat fall to the road, just within her grasp.

She once used to have a coat. She loved that coat, it was pink, and its inside was fuzzy. She wished she had her coat right now. But maybe this coat was fuzzy inside too. And it would keep her warm.

She snatched the coat away and scrambled back a bit, until she felt she was far enough from the man's reach. Then she put the coat on. The sleeves dangled half-empty. It wasn't fuzzy inside. But she felt slightly less cold.

"Okay," he said softly. "Don't . . . uh . . . don't go anywhere. I'm calling someone, okay?"

She looked at him as he took a phone from his pocket. Maybe she should run. But she realized that she couldn't even stand. She noticed her doll discarded on the road. She should go get her doll.

"Hello? Yes. My name is Ian, and I just found a girl walking alone in the middle of the road? She's really young . . . I don't know what age. Six, I guess, or seven?"

She was nine years old. She wanted to tell him that. But she didn't have the words.

Chapter 2

Robin Hart watched little Laura as she played with the plastic make-believe kitchen. The kitchen was one of the more elaborate toys Robin had in her playroom—it had a small sink, an oven, and even a fridge on the side. Pots and pans hung above the oven on tiny hooks. Thinking of the pile of dishes and cups in the sink of her real kitchen, Robin wished it was as neat as the one she let kids play with in the playroom.

Laura held a plastic egg, miming cracking it on the side of the pan.

"You're frying an egg," Robin said. "What sort of egg are you frying?"

"Sunny-side up," Laura chirped. She put the plastic egg aside and moved the pan around.

"Mmmm. It looks really tasty."

"I'm making it for you."

"For me? Thank you. It's my favorite."

Laura seemed very calm today, as she'd been for the past few weeks. When Robin had first seen her, a year before, she'd been tense and withdrawn, and the undercurrent of fear had followed her in everything she did. But a year of play therapy with Robin had done her a lot of good. Laura's mother, Beth, had told her the usual nightmares had disappeared almost completely. Soon, Robin knew, she would need to tell Beth they could end the sessions. She felt a pang of sadness. The therapy sessions with Laura were among her favorites.

Laura handed her a plastic plate and a fork. "Here you go. I also put some Tater Tots there."

"Oh, yum." Robin mimed eating from the plate. "This is very good."

Laura grinned at her and turned away from the kitchen, looking around her. Robin followed her eyes as the girl examined the playroom she already knew so well.

The room's walls were cream colored, the wall-to-wall carpet a very light blue. A draped window let the sunlight filter in. All this was meant to soften the room as much as possible. On one side of the room, rows of plastic toys lined four shelves. The other side of the room had the small pretend kitchen, a plastic doctor's table, and a simple dollhouse. A sandbox and a small yellow table stood under the window. Papers, crayons, and watercolors were all placed on the table.

Laura went over to the sandbox. "Can we play a bit in the sand?"

"If that's what you want," Robin said. As always, she wanted Laura to know that in the playroom, she was in complete control. That feeling of control and power was crucial for her healing process.

Laura knelt by the sandbox. "What should we play?"

"Well . . ." Robin walked over to the sandbox. "Do you want to play before and after?"

"How do we play that?"

Robin sat down next to Laura. With her sitting and Laura standing, they were about the same height. Looking at the girl up close, Robin was reminded of a photo of herself that her mother had framed and placed in the living room. It was a portrait, Robin's face still round and chubby, her hazel eyes large and full of wonder, her red hair settling on her shoulders. These days, of course, the baby fat was all gone, though her mother claimed she could still "work on it," whatever that meant.

Laura stared at Robin, expectant.

Robin drew two lines in the sand, splitting the sandbox into three parts. "Okay, this is how we play before and after." She pointed at the section on the left. "This is the before. I want you to get some toys and place them here to show me how you were before Kathy disappeared."

Laura looked at the sand thoughtfully, then marched over to the shelves of toys and examined them. Robin watched the girl as she selected figures one after the other. In the past year, Robin had had four kids from Bethelville who came to see her as a result of Kathy Stone's disappearance. Five, if she included her niece Amy, who'd been one of Kathy's best friends. Like the rest of Bethelville, the kids struggled with fear and confusion in the wake of the girl's abduction. But unlike the grown-ups, the children had only very vague ideas of what had happened. One day Kathy was there; the next she was gone. Parents and teachers were hazy when talking about it. Since the girl had never been found, explanations were inconsistent. Some parents told their children she was dead; others said she'd gone on a trip, or that she was lost. And then the kids would talk about it in class, the versions intermingling, creating only more uncertainty and fear. The abductor had never been caught, turning him into a dark bogeyman that could always return, hiding under kids' beds and inside their closets.

Laura returned to the sandbox with a pile of figurines and placed them in the sand.

"These are the kids from school," Laura explained. "This is me and Kathy." She placed two plastic figures of little girls next to each other, doing her best to position them so they held hands.

"The little girls look very happy together," Robin said.

"They are best friends. They like meeting in the park, and they have sleepovers at each other's house."

"The rest of the kids look like they're having fun as well," Robin said as Laura positioned other figures around. Since Robin had only eight plastic boys and girls, Laura supplemented the group with a few additional toys—SpongeBob, Donald Duck, and Peter Pan joined in.

"They're playing catch," Laura said. "They're all happy because they don't know yet."

"What don't they know?"

"That sometimes really bad things happen to children," Laura said softly.

She placed a fireman and a ballet dancer at the edge, one by the other. "Those are my parents."

"They are also holding hands."

"Yeah. They never fight, and they don't worry about bad men, or about the virus."

Like many of Robin's patients, Laura thought of the global pandemic and Kathy's abduction as intermingled, even though the pandemic had started a year before the girl's disappearance. Those two catastrophes had swept over the town's residents like tidal waves, leaving everyone reeling.

Laura stared at the little figures. She nudged the two girls closer to each other. Then she leaned back.

"I'm done," she announced.

"Okay," Robin said. She pointed at the middle section of the sandbox. "Here we should place toys that show how you felt when Kathy disappeared."

Laura glanced sideways. "Can I use the figures from the before part?"

"Sure, if you want."

She plucked the dolls of the fireman and the ballet dancer, who represented the parents, from the sand. Then she hesitated, looking at the two little girls. "I don't want to break them apart."

"It makes you sad," Robin said.

"Yeah."

After a second she got up and scrutinized the shelves.

This was a big part of what Robin's playroom was for. Adults could talk about difficult and painful events, processing them through conversation. But young kids weren't as verbal. Saying "My friend Kathy disappeared, and no one knows where she is" wasn't enough to communicate how they felt. The sense of loss. Lying in bed, wondering if the same thing could happen to them. The frustration with their parents, who couldn't give them a straight answer.

Robin gave them a place where they could communicate those feelings in the way that seemed most natural to them—playing an imaginary game or drawing a picture. And as they did that, she very gently nudged them in the direction she wanted them to focus on.

Laura came back with a tiny plastic baby and a fence that belonged to a toy farm set. She placed the baby in the middle of the sand and surrounded it with the fence.

"The baby looks very lonely there," Robin said.

"Yeah." Laura adjusted the fence. "She's all alone, and she cries all the time."

"It must be scary, being there by herself," Robin said.

Laura placed the parent dolls outside the fence, on opposite sides.

"The parents keep her in," Laura said. "It's for her own good. She needs to be kept inside because there are bad men looking for her. And she can't play with the other kids because there's a virus."

"Her parents want to protect her," Robin said.

"Yeah."

"But they're not holding hands anymore."

"No. They're sad all the time. And they keep fighting. The mommy wants to move somewhere else. And the daddy says the little girl should be allowed to meet her friends, but the mommy doesn't agree. The mommy cries sometimes. And the little girl misses her friend. She doesn't know what happened to her."

Laura lapsed into silence. Robin was about to speak when the girl got up and went to the shelves. She picked up the Skeletor toy, from the He-Man series, a green skeleton man wrapped in a purple robe. Robin had several scary-looking toys on her shelves. Kids needed those as well. An abusive father could become a plastic ogre. A bullying sister could be replaced with the figurine of a warty witch. And those figures could be manipulated, used, even punished. They could give the kids the feeling of control they lacked in their own lives.

Laura placed Skeletor at the corner of the designated area in the sandbox.

"That's the bad man," Laura said.

"The little girl is scared of the bad man," Robin said.

"Yes. He wants to take her too."

Robin waited. Laura raised her eyes. "I don't want to do this part anymore."

"Okay." Robin nodded. The fact that Laura had even agreed to do this at all was a huge step forward. It had taken many sessions before she even agreed to talk about Kathy, not to mention the girl's disappearance. Even during their recent sessions, Laura preferred to avoid the subject. But today she was unusually open to it.

Robin pointed at the third part. "Let's make something new here. Show me how it feels now. After the bad dreams stopped, and after we talked about Kathy a few times."

Laura moved the parent figures to the third area and placed them near each other. Though now they weren't close enough to hold hands. She then brought another figure from the shelves—a plastic toy of Wonder Woman. She placed it near the parents and grinned at Robin mischievously.

"Oh, the girl grew up," Robin said, smiling at Laura.

"She's braver now. She knows the bad man can't hurt her. And she meets her other friends again." Plucking child figures from the *before* area in the sandbox, Laura placed them around Wonder Woman and her parents.

"And the daddy and the mommy doll seem happier."

"Yeah. They don't need to come to her bed every night, so it's better." Laura carefully took the farm fence and placed it half-open next to the Wonder Woman figure.

"There's still a fence next to the girl," Robin said.

"Yeah. Sometimes she goes there. When she misses her friend and feels sad."

"Yeah," Robin said gently.

Skeletor, happily, did not make an appearance in Laura's third scene.

They played with the figures in the sand. Robin asked Laura to choose a toy for her, and Laura chose a purple troll figure and then broke into a fit of giggles. Then she said Robin didn't *really* look like that and chose a Barbie doll instead. Barbie and Wonder Woman and the two parents all had a nice lunch.

Then Robin suggested they do something else, and Laura decided to draw a picture of Kathy. She did that quite often lately, drawing Kathy smiling somewhere nice, a pair of angel wings on her back. Laura had told Robin several times that Kathy had died and was now in heaven. This seemed to reassure her, and Robin was pleased that Laura found peace in this.

The doorbell rang a few minutes after Laura began drawing.

"That's probably your mom," Robin said.

"But I'm not finished," Laura said, coloring angel-Kathy's hair.

"You can have a few more minutes. I'll go talk to her."

Robin opened the playroom's door, and a large blurry shape barged in, squirming past her.

"Menny!" Robin shouted at her dog. "Out!"

Wagging his tail, the large American bulldog went over to Laura and sniffed her. Laura giggled, shying away. "That tickles."

"Come on." Robin grabbed Menny's collar, dragging him out. She wasn't worried about leaving him alone with Laura—her dog would never hurt anyone. She was more worried about the toys in her room. Menny had a penchant for stealing toys and chewing them to oblivion. He had a weird specific fixation with the doctor's plastic stethoscope— Robin had had to buy a new one three times.

She closed the door to the playroom and let go of Menny. Then she opened the front door. Beth stood in the doorway. The woman looked a lot like the plastic ballet dancer that Laura had chosen to represent her—thin and wiry, with black hair pulled back in a bun.

"Hey, Beth," Robin said. "Laura is in the playroom. She wanted to finish a drawing."

"Oh, okay." Beth took a step back as Menny sniffed her ankle. "How was she today?"

"Good." Robin smiled. "She seems much better."

"She *is*." Beth exhaled. "She hasn't had a nightmare in eight days. That's a new record. She's been talking more about Kathy these past few days, though."

"That's a good sign," Robin said. "You remember when she first came to see me, she wouldn't even say Kathy's name. She avoided it because it triggered her anxieties."

"Yeah, trust me, I remember. Still, I don't love talking to her about it. I don't want her dwelling on Kathy's death. It's bad enough they did another active shooter drill in school last week. And the kids keep talking about COVID all the time."

"Well, it's part of their life," Robin said.

"Still . . . they should be talking about cartoons and birthday parties at this age. Not about social distancing and school shootings. Oh, and did you hear about that video that got around at school?"

"What video?" Robin asked.

"Some kid had a video on his phone about that murder of that poor girl? The one in the news . . . Haley something."

"Oh yeah. Haley Parks." Like many others, Robin followed the case closely. Two weeks before, hikers found the body of twenty-year-old Haley Parks in Clark State Forest, in southern Indiana. The girl had been a relatively popular influencer on Instagram, with over forty thousand followers, which was enough to make the crime national news. There were plenty of videos of her from the days before her death.

To make the murder even more unsettling, Haley had been stabbed and then hanged. Robin had glimpsed one unsettling photo, and even though it had been pixelated, it still haunted her.

"That's right, Parks," Beth said. "Anyway, that video had some very vivid descriptions and a few photos from the crime scene, with bloodstains and all that. A lot of kids saw it before the teachers caught on."

"Oh no. Did Laura see it?"

"No, but she heard kids talking about it. She was very scared."

"Well, it hasn't come up in today's session," Robin said.

"Oh, okay. Well, if—hey, sweetie!" Beth's face morphed as Laura showed up behind Robin. "You ready to go?"

"Yeah," Laura said. She handed her drawing to Beth. "Look, Mommy. I drew Kathy."

Robin scrutinized the drawing as Beth marveled at it. Like in all the other pictures, Kathy had angel's wings, and in this one she had a halo as well. Laura had drawn shoes for Kathy—little pink shoes. And a shiver ran up Robin's spine as she thought of those shoes and where they'd been found.

Chapter 3

Jimmie's Café was almost full, most of the patrons sitting outside, taking advantage of the pleasant afternoon. Robin approached the café, scanning the tables, Menny on a leash. She should have known not to be on time. Whenever she met Melody, it was best to be at least half an hour late, because that would mean she'd wait for only fifteen minutes until her sister showed up. Now she'd have to sit alone and order a coffee and—

Oh, hang on. The woman talking on the phone at the leftmost table was none other than Melody.

"Look who it is!" she told Menny.

Menny wagged his tail happily, drool dribbling down his jowls. He licked his lips noisily.

Robin walked over to the table. Melody noticed her and waved her over while still talking on the phone. She was wearing a loose black dress, her eyes hidden behind her enormous sunglasses. Her shoulder-length brown hair was smooth and immaculate as ever. When she waved, the sun reflected on the rings that adorned her fingers.

"No, it's not in the laundry basket, it's in the closet in their room on the third shelf. The third. From the top . . . Fred, are you listening? I don't care. Tell him to shut up and listen. The third shelf. No, you can't just send them with their regular clothes. Because Little League has uniforms, that's why. Yes, it's your problem, because you don't want the coach to tell them off just because you couldn't be bothered to look. The third shelf from the top. And make sure Sheila does her book report before her friend comes over. What's that noise? Why are they playing with the vacuum cleaner? Yes, the third shelf from the top."

Robin leaned back in her chair, gazing at the street as her sister talked on the phone. Jimmie's was right across the street from the Sunny Beauty Salon, which used to be Ethel's Beauty Salon when she was a kid. Their mother would take Melody and Robin every couple of months to Ethel's and Jimmie's, for a haircut followed by hot cocoa and chocolate cake. Ethel had died eight years ago, and Robin had heard her mother bemoan the "lack of character" of the new salon more times than she could count. Right now Robin glimpsed two women getting haircuts inside, neither of them seemingly bothered by the location's lack of character.

"No, Sheila can't go hang out with her friends, Fred. Tell her that I said . . . no! She has to finish her book report. It's due tomorrow. What do you mean she already left? Okay, I'm hanging up now." Melody tossed the phone on the table, looking disgusted. She turned to Robin. "Men are worthless."

"That they are," Robin agreed, sitting down. "Is Fred home today?"

"Yup. His job lets them work from home two days a week now. We're trying a new thing. It's called sacred-Tuesday-for-Mommy-or-we-get-divorced."

"Catchy name. Menny, stop that. Sit. So what happens on sacred Tuesday?"

"Every Tuesday Fred stays home and looks after the kids." Melody scratched Menny's thick neck. He shut his eyes in pure bliss. "And *I* get the full afternoon to myself."

"Oh, nice." Robin took her phone from her bag and placed it on the table.

"We started it last week, and I assumed I'd manage to take a nap, but it turned out to be impossible. The kids kept barging into the bedroom. So today I figured I'd meet you here instead. Doesn't stop them from calling me."

"So *that's* why you showed up on time."

"What do you mean? I'm always on time." Melody pulled her hand away from Menny after he covered it with a healthy dollop of drool. "Ew."

They sat across from each other, enjoying a momentary companionable silence. Robin wished she could leave it that way. Just an easy frictionless morning with her sister. But of course she couldn't. There were matters to discuss.

"Listen," she said.

"Oh, God," Melody moaned.

"What? I didn't even say what I wanted to talk about."

"You didn't have to. Whenever you use your therapist voice, it's always about *Diana*."

"I don't have a therapist voice," Robin protested.

"Yeah, you do. It sounds like you're a teacher at school, telling me that I really need to apply myself."

"I don't . . . it's not my therapist voice. That's not how I talk to my patients."

"Oh, it's just for me?"

Robin folded her arms. "Well, you're right, I was about to talk about Mom."

"What does she want?" Melody asked.

"You need to call her."

"What are you talking about? I talked to Diana a few days ago."

Melody always insisted on calling their mother by her name, an act of rebellion that had started when they were teenagers. It drove their mother insane. Even worse, now Melody's four kids all called her Diana instead of Grandma. Weirdly, in Mom's twisted world, this became Robin's fault, for not having kids of her own who could call her Grandma.

"A few days ago is not good enough. When you don't call Mom, she takes it out on *me*. You know that."

"It's not like you call Diana every day."

"No, but I go *see* her."

"Well, she won't let me see her."

Robin picked up a napkin from the table and tore it to shreds. "Don't even *try* that excuse on me. The only reason she won't let you see her is because she thinks you didn't vaccinate your kids!"

"So?"

"Melody, you vaccinated your kids months ago!"

"Yeah, but she doesn't need to know that." Melody leaned back in her chair, smirking.

Robin rolled her eyes. "How long are you going to keep that up?"

"Just a while longer," Melody said defensively. "Look, I can't handle visiting Diana right now, okay? We have a good thing going. We talk on the phone every few days. It really works better when I don't have to see her face to face."

"Works better for *you*." Robin crumpled the leftovers of the napkin and placed them on the table. "Call her. Today."

"*Fine.*"

The tranquil feeling from before was gone, as Robin knew it would be. Tranquility and Mom could not coexist.

Jimmie, the café's owner, ambled over to their table. "Well, would you look at that. The two Hart sisters sitting together in my very own café."

Robin raised her eyes and smiled at him. Jimmie had owned the café for as long as she could remember. When she was a child, this was where her parents had taken her to celebrate her birthdays. She and her friends used to come there after school. She had a phase when she'd been *obsessed* with Jimmie's hot fudge chocolate cake, a staple local dessert that practically every Bethelville resident had eaten at least once. And these days, Jimmie's tar-colored coffee was what helped her get through the day.

Jimmie had a thick mustache, unruly eyebrows, and a bushy mane of hair, all gone gray with age. That combination, along with his spectacles, made him look uncannily like the Disney character Geppetto.

"Did I hear Diana's name just now?" Jimmie asked. "You should invite her to join you. All *three* Hart women in my establishment. Now that's something I haven't seen for a long time."

Robin kept her smile fixed on her face, despite his horrific suggestion. "Yeah, we should do that sometime."

"Definitely," Melody agreed, her tone flat.

"You both have your mother's voice, you know that?" Jimmie said.

"Really?" Robin asked. Jimmie had told her that about a bazillion times before.

"Diana has the voice of a nightingale," Jimmie said with a dreamy smile. "I miss listening to her."

"Don't we all," Melody said.

"Jimmie, I was about to take their order." Ellie, Jimmie's niece, walked over. She'd recently finished college and was working at her uncle's café part time. She was a cheerful girl, almost always smiling. She wore a black tunic over a horizontally striped shirt. When Robin was Ellie's age, it had been almost unthinkable for a chubby girl like Ellie to wear horizontal stripes, which, everyone back then agreed, made you look fat. But Ellie seemed like she couldn't care less.

"It didn't look that way." Jimmie grunted. "Robin has been sitting here for a while. And Melody's cup is empty."

"I was *literally* on my way when you swooped over."

"Well, it seemed like you were busy on your phone. You millennials are so obsessed with your phones, you forget what good service is."

Ellie rolled her eyes. "For the thousandth time, I'm not a millennial. Millennials are like . . . old people." She glanced at Robin and Melody. "No offense, you two."

"None taken." Robin grinned.

"So now you're insulting our clients," Jimmie grumbled.

Ellie ignored him. "Robin, what can I get you?"

"Just coffee, thanks."

"Okay. Melody, you want another cappuccino?"

"Yeah, thanks."

"Would you like *regular* milk in your cappuccino?" Jimmie interjected.

"Oh, for God's sake," Ellie said.

"Um . . . Do you have any other kind?" Melody asked.

"If my niece here had her way, we'd have all kinds of milk," Jimmie said. "We'd have almond milk. We'd have soy milk. We'd have pasta milk—"

"Pasta milk is not a real thing," Ellie pointed out.

"She wants me to serve my customers these milk impostors. Can you imagine? How do you even milk an almond? It must have really tiny udders."

Robin let out an uncontrollable snort of laughter.

"Literally every other place in the country serves milk alternatives, Jimmie," Ellie said. "You think you're funny, but some people are lactose intolerant, and some are vegans—"

"Maybe that's what they served to you at that college of yours while you wasted your time writing screenplays and filming artsy movies. But here in the real world, they can drink real milk. Or if they don't want to, they can drink black coffee, like Robin here! Milk is healthy. It has calcium."

"Um, it has been scientifically proved that it's unhealthy. And milk alternatives also have calcium."

"Your generation is the reason that the dairy industry is falling apart."

Ellie massaged the bridge of her nose. "Okay. So one cappuccino with *regular* cow milk, in support of the American dairy industry. And one black, right?"

"Yeah, thanks," Melody said, amusement etched on her face.

"And what would the gentleman want?" Jimmie asked, looking at Menny.

Menny panted happily at him.

"Some water in a saucer?" Ellie told Menny. "Coming right up, sir."

"And give him some dog biscuits," Jimmie said, already striding away. "We have some in the back in the—"

"In the top cupboard, I know," Ellie said. She crouched by Menny and scratched his head. She glanced at Robin. "You know, I've heard that almond-udders joke seventeen times in the past two days."

"It was a dangerous move, suggesting that Jimmie change anything on the menu," Melody said.

"*Once.* I told him *once* that we could have soy milk. And now I get these speeches literally all day long."

Melody's smile evaporated as she saw something behind Robin. Glancing over her shoulder, Robin immediately realized who it was.

Claire Stone was approaching the café.

Claire had always been quite thin, but in the fifteen months since her daughter's disappearance, the woman had become skeletal. Her haunted eyes were sunken in her pale face.

"Hey, Claire," Melody and Ellie said together.

"Hey," Claire said, nodding, a smile stretching on her face. Her entire demeanor was of someone who remembered how people talked to each other but couldn't quite perform it correctly. She raised her hand weakly.

"Hi," Robin said, contributing to the awkward nonconversation. She bit on the words that came next: *How are you?* They felt wrong. How was Claire? The answer was plain. She was not well.

The three of them wavered, each with her own connection to Claire. Melody was probably closest to her—Melody's daughter Amy used to be best friends with Claire's daughter, Kathy. Melody had often tried to talk to Claire after the disappearance, to help her as much as she could. Ellie's and Robin's relations with Claire were more tenuous. Ellie had babysat Kathy a few times. Robin had gone to school with Claire, and Robin's ex-husband, Evan, was a good friend of Claire's husband.

In their town of five thousand people, many knew each other. But ever since last year, *everyone* knew Claire. And they knew her for *the thing that happened.* Kathy's disappearance, which dominated the local discussions—both the public ones and the hushed, whispered gossiping that hid behind every door. Everyone had their gruesome theories, their "if I were her" suggestions, their "it couldn't have happened to me" claims. The gossiping worsened when it became apparent that the police were looking at relatives and friends—there were no signs of struggle. Kathy appeared to have gone with her abductor willingly.

At first, Kathy's disappearance was a collective trauma, something that brought the town together. Every resident took part in the searches, shared posts on social media, tried to help Claire and Pete in whatever way they could. But as hope for finding Kathy evaporated, as did the grim hope of finding the girl's remains, Claire became a walking reminder of a dark event in Bethelville's past. Unlike her husband, who managed to more or less resume life, Claire seemed to be stuck in that horrible day, reliving it. And those who saw her relived it too. They all had that "What were you doing when you heard about Kathy?" story.

Claire gave the three of them another faded memory of a smile and then brushed past them, stepping into the café.

"She hardly ever comes here," Ellie said in a low voice.

"Probably can't stand the stares," Robin said.

"You know," Melody murmured, "Pete left this weekend. Moved to Indianapolis."

"I heard," Robin said, her eyes following the figure of her former classmate as she leaned on the counter, talking to Jimmie.

"He told Fred he couldn't take it any longer," Melody said. "That he needed a fresh start. In a place that didn't constantly remind him of Kathy."

Pete played pool with Fred, Melody's husband, and Evan, Robin's ex-husband. Small town. All the husbands apparently had to stick together.

"I can't imagine what it feels like," Ellie said.

Melody sighed. "Fred told me that Pete couldn't even drive by Thirty-One Forest anymore. He drives all the way around it if he needs to go that way."

Thirty-One Forest was the unofficial name of the woods on the western part of US Route 31 leaving Bethelville. Robin was sure the woods had an actual name, forgotten due to nobody caring. The woods had been generally ignored by Bethelville's residents, since the local parks were much nicer to visit. However, Thirty-One Forest claimed a new notoriety soon after Kathy's disappearance. It was where the police had found her shoes.

About a mile south of Bethelville, there was a small dirt road leading into Thirty-One Forest. It was often half-hidden by foliage and was easily missed if you didn't know to look for it. The road led to a long-deserted, decrepit farmhouse. Bethelville's teenagers had sometimes gone there to drink alcohol they stole from their parents or to smoke pot while sitting around a small fire, enjoying their first taste of independence. An occasional syringe and bullet casings found in the dilapidated house hinted at other, less innocent activities.

Four days after Kathy disappeared, the police found her shoes, covered in mud, discarded in that house. There were various rumors as to what they also found in the place—a pedophile porn mag; a bloody knife; a long, thick rope. Robin had heard many versions and theories regarding what had happened in that broken-down farmhouse. But the only thing everyone knew for sure was that the shoes were found there. And that was the last clue to Kathy's whereabouts. The most common theory about Kathy's location was that she was buried somewhere in Thirty-One Forest, though the police had searched the place with K-9 dogs and found nothing.

"Claire could probably use a fresh start too," Ellie said. "I wonder if she considered leaving with Pete."

They looked at each other in silence. The afternoon sun slid behind a cloud, the bright day becoming dim, as if Claire had infected the weather with her despair.

"She would never leave," Melody said hollowly. "She's still waiting for Kathy to come back."

Chapter 4

Everything Claire needed to do required so much effort.

It sometimes puzzled her how blind people were to the sheer volume of tasks their lives demanded of them. For example, she'd be sitting in the living room with Pete, and he'd say that he was going to the bathroom. And Claire would want to tell him he wasn't just going to the bathroom. He needed to stand up, and then walk all the way to the bathroom, which could be sixteen steps if he was in the living room, and then open the door, and then close the door behind him, and lock it, and . . . not to get too graphic, but there were a bunch of actions, depending on what he needed to do in the bathroom, and then he would flush, and probably wash his hands, and unlock the door, and open it, and go back to where he'd been before—which, if it was the living room, was another sixteen steps—and sit down. And Pete called it "going to the bathroom."

Of course, that was back when Pete was there. With her. Before he'd left.

Claire didn't go to the bathroom often anymore. Once a day was usually enough. And she shaved off a few of the things other people did when they went, because she couldn't really bother.

She recalled a time when it had been easier.

Not just going to the bathroom but *everything*. The number of things she did during the day was astounding. Even after Kathy had disappeared, Claire would spend the day printing flyers, and calling the police, and reaching out to private detectives and that distant relative who had a friend in the bureau. And as time passed by, she found more people to talk to—journalists and psychics and experts and . . . and . . .

What was she thinking about? She lost her train of thought. This was something else she didn't really have anymore. Focus. She'd walk somewhere and pause, not knowing where she'd gone. Like right now, she was standing in the doorway of her bedroom with no idea what she came here to do.

She stared at Pete's nightstand—empty except for a forgotten phone charger. Pete always had dozens of those everywhere, often three or four tangled hopelessly together. She had no idea what he needed them all for or where they had even come from. Did he buy them? Why would he buy more than one? The very thought exhausted her.

After Kathy disappeared, Claire had been a tornado of emotions. Guilt, and sadness, and anger, and hope (always followed by plunging disappointment), and determination . . .

How long could one person sustain all that?

For Claire, it had been seven months.

Maybe she could have held out longer if she had had support. But slowly, one by one, she saw people conclude that Kathy was dead. First, people around her in town. Then the police. Then family. And finally, the biggest betrayal, Pete. She heard the term *moving on* more and more often. Just "move on" from the belief that your daughter was alive to the conclusion that your daughter was dead. Easy, really. Everyone else was doing it; why couldn't she?

Because it would be a betrayal. That's what Pete didn't get. It would be unfaithful. *If* their daughter was alive, then she needed someone to believe in it. To be looking for her. Otherwise she *was* as good as dead. And as long as Claire thought there was any chance at all that Kathy was alive, she couldn't lose faith.

She could run out of energy, though, which was what had happened.

Back in the kitchen, the landline rang. All the way back in the kitchen. The room farthest from the bedroom.

She had a physical reaction to the phone ringing these days. A sort of clenching, and revulsion. Because of all those times in the past when the phone rang . . .

And she would feel it, that tiny hope that *maybe* this time it would be someone calling with news about Kathy. No matter how she'd try to temper those hopes, her mind would still treacherously conjure them. And she'd walk to the phone, just a bit too fast. Answer just a bit too breathlessly. Hello?

And it would be a call from the bank. Or Pete's mother. Or a wrong number. Followed by a crushing disappointment.

So by now her brain linked the phone's ring with the feeling of hopelessness and loss. It had rewired itself to *hate* the phone and its shrill ringing. As if the phone was a predator and her brain was warning her of its impending danger.

She listened to it ring, knowing that by the time she trudged back to the kitchen, it would have stopped anyway. As she listened to it, she stared at the closet, where just a week before Pete had packed his suitcase.

He'd invited her to come with him. And she said for the hundredth time that she couldn't leave, because if Kathy was found, Claire had to be there, at home. Kathy would expect her old room. Claire didn't want her coming back to a different house.

They argued one last time, Pete telling her that Kathy was gone, and Claire shrieking at him that she didn't know how he could give up hope.

"Hope?" Pete snorted. "Is that what you feel right now, Claire? Hope? Gotta tell you, it doesn't show."

He was right. Hope wasn't the right word. What was the word to describe the feeling of existing in a reality that had all colors sucked out of it? Of sometimes realizing four hours went by without a single coherent thought? Oh, she was sure therapists would call it depression, but that couldn't be right. She wasn't depressed.

She just needed her daughter back.

The phone stopped ringing.

She let out a long breath, slightly relieved at the silence. She considered lying down and going to sleep. It was already late in the evening.

It started ringing again.

She clenched her teeth and turned around. She dragged herself all the way to the kitchen and reached for the phone. It would be the bank. Or one of her few remaining friends, calling to ask how she was doing now that Pete had left.

She picked it up.

"Hello?"

"Hi, is this Claire Stone?" A male voice. A bit formal. The bank, just as she'd thought.

"Yes." She leaned against the wall.

"Uh . . . Are you the mother of Kathy Stone?"

She blinked. For a second, she almost didn't know how to answer.

"Yes," she finally blurted.

"I'm Officer Perez, from the Jasper Police Department. Mrs. Stone, we found your daughter."

Chapter 5

For Robin, stepping into her mother's house was like stepping into the worst kind of time machine imaginable. It wasn't one of those useful time machines, where you could go back to the eighties, attend a live Queen concert, bet on a few football games and buy a bunch of Microsoft stock, and then live your life as a millionaire. No, it was a time machine that only dragged her psyche back in time, turning her back into an anxious fourteen-year-old who mumbled when she talked.

It had been much better when Dad was alive. He would always ask her about her job, about her relationships, as if anchoring her to the grown-up woman she'd become. And besides, he was Dad. Dad had always been the easy part of having parents in the Hart family.

"Hey, Mom, it's me," she said, shutting the door behind her.

"I'm in the living room," Mom called.

Robin walked down the brightly lit hallway, past two vases with flowers. Her mother always had fresh flowers around the house. Robin once wondered aloud how she could afford so many flowers, and she had coyly hinted that she was not the one buying the flowers. And then she'd asked Robin if she was so worried about her future inheritance.

Mom sat on the couch in the living room, flipping through a photo album. Robin instantly recognized which album it was. It was her wedding album.

An irrational part of her suspected this was intentional. That Mom was pretending to look through the wedding album just to hurt her, and to start a fight. That this was her punishment for Robin's transgression—four days since her last visit.

But of course that was insane. Robin didn't call before coming, which would mean that Mom, upon hearing her car parking out on the curb, dashed to the living room; searched the cabinet, combing through the albums to find Robin's wedding album; and sat down, then opened it in the middle as if she had been looking through it all along. No one would do that. It made Robin feel guilty for even suspecting her of something so deranged. She was looking through photos, like she loved doing. And the fact that it was Robin's own wedding album was a coincidence.

"Hey, Mom, you look really pretty today," she said, trying to be extra nice, because of her sudden guilt.

"You two looked so happy together," Mom said sadly. "He's such a handsome man. You were so lucky."

Shots fired. Each sentence masterfully crafted. Mom had shifted from past tense to present tense, and back to past tense. They *were* so happy. Unlike now. He's *still* a handsome man, indicating that if Robin ever came to her senses, she could still get him back. Robin *was* so lucky, but then decided to throw that luck away.

Or a random observation. With her mother, it was impossible to tell.

"It was a very nice wedding," Robin said naturally. And then, trying to avoid a fight, added, "You looked gorgeous in that blue dress. Do you still have it?"

A tiny quirk of a smile in response. Maybe the compliment had been enough. Crisis averted?

"I think I gave it away," Mom said heavily. "Too many memories."

"Oh. That's too bad. I brought you the mail—"

"I just talked to Evan's mother, Glenda," Mom said, flipping a page in the album. "She said he still hasn't found anyone. He's dating, of course."

"That's good for him."

"She thinks he's still waiting for you. You know, if you try to make amends, he might agree to give it another try."

"Mom, I'm not going to get back with Evan."

"You could go to counseling. Evan would do that for you, he's so considerate—"

"It's never going to happen!"

Mom's lips trembled. "I don't know why you're shouting. I just want you to be happy. It's all I ever wanted. You come in here after I haven't seen you for a whole week, and you immediately start shouting at me." Her eyes teared up.

"I . . . I didn't shout . . . I'm sorry." Robin sat by her mother and put her arm around her shoulders. "I didn't mean to upset you. And it hasn't been a week. I was here on Saturday."

"It felt like a week. Your visit on Saturday was so short."

Robin clenched her jaw, trying to physically block the words from coming out, but they spilled out of her mouth anyway. "I'll make it up to you. Today I have the whole morning available."

"It's just that Evan is such a lovely man. He could have any girl he wanted, Robin. Absolutely anyone. And *he* is really successful. If you two got back together, you wouldn't need to worry about your lack of clients anymore."

"I'm actually doing pretty well," Robin said. She tried to ignore the irony. When Evan was starting out as a photographer and Robin was the one with the stable income, Mom gushed about how Evan didn't compromise and tried to make a living doing what he loved. Now that he'd had his big break, in Mom's mind, it meant Robin could live with him and stop working entirely. It never occurred to her that Robin loved her own job.

"Are you really doing well? Because Melody told me . . . never mind. It doesn't matter."

It was difficult, but Robin didn't take the bait. She knew from experience that Melody's words, whatever they were, would be twisted into barbs, losing their original context and meaning. When they were teens, Mom would orchestrate fights between her and Melody that could go on for days. Now they were both grown . . . and she could still manage it, but not as often.

Mom flipped another page in the album and smiled. She touched a large photo of herself and Robin's father with a single finger. "Look at him. He seemed so healthy."

"Yeah." Robin looked at her dad's smile. He *did* look healthy. And happy. She'd danced with him, and he'd kept joking with her.

"Then, one day, a heart attack, and he's gone, just like that." Her mother let out a shuddering sigh. "And during the *pandemic*."

For some reason this always seemed to get stuck in Mom's craw. That while people all over the world were dying of COVID, her husband had the audacity to die of a heart attack. Leaving his wife alone with this mundane widowhood.

"At least it was fast," Robin said. Weird, how many times she'd said that sentence and how many times she'd heard it from doctors, and friends, and family. As if the fact that Death was particularly efficient that day could make anyone feel better.

"That's true." Mom's eyes were still fixed on the photo. "I really was so pretty."

"You're very pretty now too," Robin said automatically.

"Oh, stop it. You don't need to lie to spare my feelings."

"No, I really mean it. You look wonderful. I don't know how you do it."

"In these old clothes? I doubt it."

"I've never seen this skirt on you before. It looks really trendy. It's like something I saw in a fashion magazine."

Here was the crazy part. The practically *bonkers* part. These phony compliments that Robin spouted were a necessary part of talking to her mother. Because she needed to hear those things over and over again. And when she disparaged herself, the *only* possible response was to disagree with her and counter with an additional compliment.

Anything else—changing the subject or trying to tell her that she didn't always need to look perfect, or even saying something like "for your age you still look really good"—would result in a hysterical sobbing scene that would go on for hours. Once, when Robin was eight years old, Mom had asked Dad if he thought her shoes made her ankles look fat. And he gullibly, *stupidly* told her he didn't think so, but if it bothered her, she could try a different pair. So she had *burned* the shoes she wore and accidentally set the drapes on fire. Then, she screamed at him for an entire evening as Robin and Melody hid in Melody's room, under the blanket. Mom didn't leave her room for three days after that, refusing to eat. Robin still remembered her dad begging her at the door. Apologizing profusely.

And the truth of it was, she did look great. Her ash-blonde hair was rich, cascading over her shoulders. Her makeup made her seem twenty years younger. She dressed classy as always. But she would always need another outfit to put on top of her clothing. An outfit tailored out of compliments and adoration.

Satisfied, Mom flipped another page and stared at the photo of Robin smiling in her wedding dress.

"You looked so pretty that day too," Mom said dreamily.

"Yeah."

"I remember Uncle Donald got drunk and kept trying to dance with all your young friends. Do you remember that?" Mom let out a girlish giggle. "That old lecher."

Robin grinned and shifted closer to her mother, looking at the album. "I remember. I thought Aunt Hilda was about to pour a pitcher of water on him."

"Yes!" Mom shrieked in laughter. "She had such a temper. What a strange couple. Your dad was definitely the best in his family."

"Yeah."

Mom touched Robin's photo. "Look at that smile. Remember how I made sure you brushed your teeth for five minutes in the evening? And I always made sure you went to your dental appointments. Thanks to me, your teeth used to be so white back then."

Robin stood up. "I'm going to make some tea. Do you want some?"

"Hmm? No, thanks."

Robin turned away.

"Tea can really stain the teeth," Mom added.

Robin left the room and walked over to the kitchen, where she leaned against the wall and took a few long breaths. She reminded herself that Mom was lonely. That ever since Dad died it had been really difficult for her. And that because of the pandemic, she avoided going to public places, which meant her favorite pastimes—meeting her friends for coffee, or shopping—were now gone.

She made tea, taking her time, rebuilding her mental armor. Some days, Mom's jabs couldn't get past her defenses. But lately, with the return of her insomnia, her exhaustion meant she was much more fragile.

As she returned to the living room, she paused by Mom's bedroom, glancing inside. Her childhood obsession stood there, still as breathtaking and tantalizing as ever.

It was an antique dollhouse, built to resemble a Victorian mansion. It stood on a large table, open to reveal three stories, with three bedrooms, a kitchen, a living room, and a bathroom. Each of the tiny rooms was decorated with intricate and masterfully crafted furniture. All the tiny closets and dressers opened and even contained several tiny outfits and bedsheets. The little piano in the miniature living room could produce musical notes.

It had always been off limits. It was, Mom explained repeatedly, not a toy. It was *vintage*. And expensive. And if she and Melody played with it, they would surely break it. And no matter how much they begged and pleaded and promised to be super delicate, they were denied.

Robin had still played with it, of course, in secret, terrified of being found out. And one time, when she did it, she heard her mother's footsteps and was so scared of being caught, she accidentally *did* break one of the tiny chairs in the small kitchen. And then . . .

Her mind shied away from the memory.

She returned to the living room. Mom had put the photo album aside, thank God.

"You know, when I was talking to Evan's mother—"

"Mom, I don't want to talk about Evan anymore, okay? Please."

"I wasn't about to say anything about Evan," Mom said, her tone hurt. "Not everything I want to discuss is about *you* or about your broken marriage, Robin."

"Okay, sorry." Robin sat down by her mother. "So what were you going to say?"

"Never mind."

"No, really, Mom, what—"

"I don't want you to get all huffy and shout at me again. I was hoping to simply have a nice morning together." Mom shut her eyes and leaned back tiredly. "We used to have such lovely times together when you were a child. What happened?"

Robin knew exactly what had happened. She had agonized about that very same question for years, after each bad visit with her mother, during countless nights in which she lay awake, throughout numerous psychotherapy sessions. And by now she could draw an accurate diagram of what had gone wrong. Or maybe what had never been right in the first place.

"I don't know," Robin said.

Usually Mom would counter that with her own explanation of how it was Robin's fault. Because Robin was ungrateful, or Robin had made bad choices, or Robin wasn't a good daughter like Melody. But this time Mom didn't say anything, just brushed her skirt moodily.

It took Robin a second to catch on. Mom really wanted to tell her about what she talked about with Evan's mother. Not because it was about Evan but because it was what she loved more than anything. It was *gossip*.

And if it was good enough to forestall a discussion of Robin's many faults, it was good gossip. Not some second-rate gossip about a woman in the book club who had started a new diet. Or a couple in town that argued so loudly that all the neighbors heard.

This was pristine gossip. Like an affair that had been exposed, with photos. Or maybe someone was going to jail for fraud.

Robin was *dying* to know what it was.

Not because she craved the gossip. Oh sure, she liked gossip as much as the next person. There was a tantalizing pleasure in hearing something not everyone knew and then an additional jolt of pleasure in passing it along, as if she was a member of some secret club. But it wasn't that. It was that gossip was a firm bridge between Mom and her. When they gossiped, they were the closest a mother and a daughter could be.

But if she asked, Mom would hold back. Curiosity gave her leverage, and she never gave leverage away. So instead she said, "I saw you have new flowers in the hallway. They're really gorgeous."

"Thank you. They're pink roses and lilies."

"And something else, right? What are those fluffier flowers called?"

"When I talked to Glenda," Mom said, "she told me something else."

"Oh yeah?" Robin said carelessly. "What?"

"You'll never guess what happened." Mom's eyes sparkled. She shifted closer to Robin, her voice lowering, as if someone might be listening in. "Claire Stone got some really big news."

Robin suspected this was about Pete Stone leaving, but she didn't say so. Instead she smiled and inched closer. "What?"

"Apparently it was a phone call from a policeman in Jasper. At first, she thought it was a mistake. That's what she told Glenda. Why would a cop from *Jasper*, on the other side of the state, call her?"

"And why did he?" Robin asked breathlessly.

"Did you hear Pete Stone had left?" Mom smiled coyly, stretching the big reveal.

"Yeah, I heard something about that." Robin tried to hide her own impatience.

"Well, he's going to come back." Mom took Robin's hand and squeezed it. "Because they think they found Kathy Stone. And she's alive."

Chapter 6

The drive from Bethelville to Jasper, according to Claire's googling, took about four hours. And she had needed to wait for an additional hour until Pete would pick her up, because he had insisted they go together and that he would drive. So it should have been altogether about five and a half hours. It felt like days.

She'd decided to skip her morning meds, because the only reason she took them in the first place was that life without Kathy, without *knowing* what happened to Kathy, was becoming unbearable. Now that Kathy was back—

Was she?

—she didn't need the meds, right? And besides, once she had Kathy in her arms—

Would she?

—she didn't want the medication to take the edge off. She wanted to be 100 percent lucid.

But after six months of medication, it wasn't necessarily the right call. And riding with Pete, the man she now disliked because he'd given up on her and her daughter, was making it worse.

She spent the drive on her phone, checking the three images and the short video the cop had sent her of Kathy—

Was it really of Kathy?

—scrolling between them over and over again. An image of Kathy sleeping. An image of Kathy eating. An image of Kathy drawing. A video of Kathy drawing. And at first, she just looked at them because, well, because it was what she had. And until she had Kathy in her arms—

If she'd have Kathy in her arms.

—she would have to make do with the photos and the video.

But then the anxiety crept in.

She'd spent the past fifteen months trapped in hell, her daughter missing. And every day, Kathy still wasn't there when she woke up, and still wasn't there when she went to sleep, and it was simply a never-ending sequence of desperation, and yearning, and fear.

And then, she got that call. And for the first time, she felt relief. The relief was so strange at first that she thought she might be dreaming, because she often had these dreams in which Kathy was back. So she bit herself, *literally* bit herself, to make sure she was awake.

And then calling Pete and blubbering about the phone call she'd gotten. They just found Kathy, she was in Jasper and . . . yes, she was alive, of course she was alive, and they had to go get her, because the police could only bring her tomorrow and Claire wasn't about to wait one more damn second. And she bit herself again, to make extra sure.

But then, halfway to Jasper, an insidious thought crawled into her mind. Was it really Kathy?

Because she hadn't talked to her on the phone. That cop said she was still in shock and wasn't really communicating. And she wasn't talking on the video either. And she did look like Kathy, except . . . well, Kathy was always such a happy girl. And the girl in the photos, that pale, thin girl, didn't look happy.

And Claire knew whatever Kathy had gone through in the past fifteen months had left its mark. And like the cop said, she was in shock. But that relief she felt was so bizarre, and the drive was so long, scrolling between the photos repeatedly, that she wondered if maybe it wasn't Kathy at all. Maybe it was another mean trick life was pulling on her, like those other two times people reported seeing Kathy in various places around the country, only to find out later it was a different girl.

Her anxiety got so bad that she texted that cop, and then called him and asked if he could send her another photo. And he *did*, a close-up photo of Kathy—

The girl.

—sleeping again. And yeah! It was Kathy. Or someone who really looked like her.

And here they were at the police station, and Pete was talking to the woman at reception, and she was making a phone call to check. And Claire wanted to *scream*. Hadn't someone told the stupid receptionist they were coming? How could it be that she was in the same building with her daughter—

Or a very similar girl.

—and she wasn't hugging her? How much longer . . .

But now a cop was motioning them to follow him. He was telling them this was really great, that he didn't get to give people good news so often, and this was probably the best day in his job ever, and he opened a door and . . .

Kathy.

Her daughter was sitting on a couch, hands in her lap, looking at the floor.

"Kathy?" Claire said tearfully.

Kathy raised her eyes. It was her; it was really her. And she even smiled, a shy smile of surprise.

And then she was running, sinking into Claire's arms. Claire folded her into a hug, thinking she might never let go. Kathy curled into Claire's body, trembling, crying. And Claire pulled back only to look at her daughter again.

"Are you okay?" Pete asked, kneeling beside them.

Kathy was sobbing, tears running down her cheeks, her chin trembling.

"Are you okay, baby?" Pete asked again.

"She hasn't said anything since she was found last night," the cop said. "The social worker said she's probably in shock. But we figured out who she was pretty quickly with NamUs . . . that's the national missing-people database . . ."

He droned on, but Claire wasn't listening. For fifteen months she'd been asking for endless details about her missing daughter's investigations. But now, with Kathy in her arms—

It was Kathy. It was.

—she didn't care any longer. None of it mattered anymore.

Chapter 7

Robin ran through the house, heart thrumming, knowing she was late. She was so late. Had she already missed it? If it was already over, she was doomed. Where was the radio? She needed to get to the radio. It was in the kitchen, but Robin was somehow lost. Lost in her house . . . no. In her mother's house. What was she doing there? Had she moved back in? She must have, and now she needed to find the radio.

There! The kitchen. And the old radio. Panicking, she turned it on, but all she heard was static. Nonononono . . . she needed to make it work. Mom would be home soon. She turned the dial, but the static only became louder . . . too loud . . . it would wake up everyone . . . glaring headlights outside . . . Mom was home. And the static was so loud that Robin could feel it in her teeth, in her bones . . .

She woke up with a start, her heart already beating wildly, her breathing rapid, panicky.

Her dark room shifted into focus. Not the room of her childhood years. No, her own bedroom in her own home. She didn't *need* to wake up in the middle of the night. In fact, the opposite was true. What she really needed was sleep. But her heart was still pounding, the taste of fear bitter in her mouth. She was having a hard time calming down. Her mind skittered through memories, a montage of identical nights, her sitting by the table, rubbing her eyes tiredly, listening to the radio carefully, every word important. *Crucial.*

She exhaled softly.

What time was it?

Robin plucked her cell phone from the night table. The bright rectangular screen flickered to life. She squinted at it, already regretting her impulsive move. It was seven minutes past two in the morning. She'd been asleep for less than three hours. And now, because of her phone's glaring light, her brain thought it might be morning. To make things even worse there was a notification on her screen—a new email. Maybe a new client. She couldn't afford to ignore it. If she delayed in responding, the potential client might decide to look for a different therapist.

When she opened her inbox, she groaned. It wasn't a potential new client. It was an email from Netflix, suggesting a new show she might like.

With the phone already unlocked in her hand, her fingers developed a mind of their own. Because the Facebook icon had that tantalizing notification mark on the corner. Tap.

The notification she'd logged on to see was that Melody had posted in a dog-lover group they were both in. Only God and Mark Zuckerberg knew why she should get a notification about *that*. Sometimes, she didn't get notifications about people messaging her. She never got any notifications about her best friend from college. But Melody posting in a random group: *that* merited the red alert of Facebook notifications.

It was a cute pic of dogs, though, because there was a large Labrador and a puppy Labrador, and they both had muddy noses, so all was forgiven.

But she was in Facebook now, and her finger knew what that meant. Scrolling.

There were a lot of posts from local Facebook friends about Kathy's return. People gushed, talking about how happy they were to have her back. Each was punctuated with so many heart emoji that Robin's feed looked like a Valentine's Day gone haywire.

It always confused her when people stampeded their way to social media to share their feelings. Robin had been *thrilled* when Mom told her they'd found Kathy. Since the disappearance, she'd agonized end-lessly about the girl and her poor parents. She could hardly imagine the awful torment Claire and Pete had gone through. And having the girl back felt like nothing short of a miracle. But it never occurred to her to post about it. She mostly used social media to post funny pictures of Menny and to share the occasional amusing meme. She almost never posted anything more personal than that. When Dad died, she had refrained from posting anything beyond a general announcement and later thanking all the people who offered their condolences.

And now she found yet again that she was the odd duck, for sharing her thoughts by the ancient art of *speaking*, talking to her friends about it. Instead of posting it on social media for all her 856 friends to see, including the guy who had installed her new sink and a bunch of people from college with whom she hadn't talked for years.

Here was Dennis, who lived down the street, saying, Kathy is one of my favorite students. And Therese from yoga wrote that Kathy's mother is a dear friend. Here was another from Paula . . . Robin had no idea where she even knew this woman from—I knew Kathy from the day she was born. Everyone seemed very keen to mention their own connection to Kathy. Robin imagined what she would write. Claire was in my class, but we never particularly liked each other as kids. No, this was social media, and she would have to selectively tell the truth. Once, in third grade, Claire had loaned her a pencil. Claire and I shared a classroom for twelve years of our lives, and she was there for me when things were dire.

Some posts were aimed to inspire—It just goes to show that if you stay positive . . . or We all prayed for her return and God answered our prayers. Others seemed to mostly be about the person writing the post—When I heard she was found, I cried in relief. I've been think-ing about that poor girl for the past year.

Robin made it a point to like each post, because she didn't want people to think she wasn't liking the fact that Kathy had come back. But she avoided commenting. Commenting was the *real* rabbit hole. Still, she couldn't avoid skimming the comments other people wrote. Praise for each other, mostly. You made me tear up. Or That was beautiful.

Some guy had commented on a post that shared Kathy's return. He wrote, If the mom had been paying attention to her daughter in the first place none of this would have happened.

A magma-like surge of fury burned through Robin. She quickly scrolled down. She would *not* engage with that guy. He was probably a troll, trying to get a response out of people. She would make his life *better* with her angry comment. That's why they said "Don't feed the trolls."

No way she was falling asleep now. She needed to calm down first. She shifted to Instagram.

Apparently, Instagram had joined the Kathy frenzy as well. There were photos of Kathy from before the disappearance, taken from articles online. Screenshots of the news articles discussing her return. People photographing themselves pantomiming hearts with their fingers, with the hashtag *KathyReturnedToUs*.

Was Robin wrong for not posting about Kathy? Perhaps this was what people in a community *should* do. Was she being insensitive?

She logged back on to Facebook and tried to write a post about it. Not too long. A bit emotional. Somewhat plagiarized from another post she'd seen. And she added eight heart emoji. Then she scrapped it and wrote a new one, less emotional, with only one heart. Then she deleted that one and wrote a third one in which she quoted Nelson Mandela: *There can be no keener revelation of a society's soul than the way in which it treats its children.* Then she deleted that one, too, and became disgusted with herself.

She was still furious at that guy, and by now she had the perfect answer for him. A well-formed reply that would leave him ashamed, maybe even force him to apologize and admit he was wrong. She scrolled through her feed, searching for his comment. Where had she seen it?

She couldn't remember. She checked the comments for each post but couldn't find it. What was his name? Something beginning with an *R*.

Okay, this was stupid. She knew he wouldn't feel ashamed. He would be delighted. It was a good thing she couldn't find his comment.

Then, unable to help herself, she tapped the search icon. She didn't even have to type her search query. Her most recent search was for "Evan Moore," her ex-husband.

She'd made a point to unfriend and unfollow him on all social media accounts, which just meant that she kept searching for him. She didn't even know what she was looking for. A new girlfriend? An offhand mention of her? Maybe a post about how miserable he was.

But Evan wasn't the type. His posts were always either pretentious or self-aggrandizing. Sometimes both. Ah, he had joined the Kathy train. He was thankful that the daughter of his dear friend had returned. He had known her since she was a baby. Kathy apparently called him Uncle Evan when she was a toddler. She'd been in his thoughts constantly for the past months. One hundred and seventeen likes and loves, fifty-seven gushing comments.

The previous post was about the prize he recently won for one of his exhibitions—*Poverty and the Pandemic*. Robin scrolled down a bit more but only saw posts she was already familiar with. She hated that she knew all his recent posts. She hated that this was something she was doing in the middle of the night. She tapped the back button, returning to her feed.

There was a post from Claire. She thanked everyone for their kind posts and emails and said she was grateful to have her daughter back and that they were taking the time to heal as a family. That post had over seven thousand reactions. Robin liked it and commented, I'm so happy for you.

She glanced at the time, and it was 2:52. What the hell? Why was she even on her phone?

Putting it away in revulsion, she shut her eyes and turned away from the night table. Took a few deep breaths. Tried to find those lost threads of sleep.

Which was her brain's moment to shine. Because now, amped on forty-five minutes of random digital white noise and the bright light of the phone's screen, her mind was like a three-year-old who just ate a large chocolate sundae. Jumping from one thought to the next, a miasma of images, regrets, memories, anxieties, and fantasies. She shouldn't have interrupted Laura in their last session; it had seemed as if the girl was about to say something important. Laura's mother wore a nice dress: Where did she get it? She should go shopping. When was the last time she did that? A sudden memory of going shopping with her dad as a little girl, and a stab of pain, the grief of his death still fresh. She shouldn't have looked at her phone. She shouldn't have let that guy's comment get to her, but he'd been so infuriating. Most people had *loved* Claire's post, but she only *liked* it. Was that insensitive as well? Did she have an issue with Claire? It's not like they hated each other in school; they just didn't move in the same circles. And Robin had helped when Kathy disappeared. She considered taking the phone, finding the post, and changing her reaction from like to love. But she forced herself not to.

She had to sleep.

Ironically, the fact that she really *needed* to sleep only made it worse, lacing the merry-go-round of her thoughts with that repeated worry. If I don't go to sleep right now, tomorrow will be really difficult. This is the third night in a row I didn't get enough sleep—if I don't go to sleep right now, tomorrow will be torture. It's probably four a.m.—if I don't go to sleep *right now*, tomorrow will be a nightmare.

When Menny woke her up, licking her face, she felt like she hadn't slept a wink.

Chapter 8

The day of the disappearance

When Claire glanced out the kitchen window and saw Kathy was gone, she assumed her daughter was playing hide-and-seek.

Kathy's dolls were spread out on the front lawn—a blonde Barbie doll, the L.O.L. tweens, and that mermaid Kathy got from her aunt for her birthday. They sat around in a circle, except for the mermaid, who'd toppled aside, her face half-hidden by the grass. Something about the way the mermaid had fallen gave Claire pause. Kathy loved that mermaid. It seemed careless.

Claire was cleaning her baking pan, which was hard work, because she'd slightly burned the cake she'd made that morning. The blackened crust clung to the pan's corners, resisting her efforts to scrub it off. When she shifted the pan to try a different angle, the sudsy water pooled in it, trickling onto her long skirt, and she gritted her teeth in frustration. She wanted to finish with this menial task and get back to designing her new necklace. Her custom jewelry was doing really well on Etsy lately, and she wanted to get some new products out there.

She kept glancing outside, her eyes shifting, searching for her daughter. Inevitably, she kept glancing to the road. The traffic in sleepy suburban Bethelville was far from busy, but sometimes they'd get the occasional speeding moron. And if Kathy decided to play by the road . . . but no. Her daughter knew better than that.

Later, replaying that moment in her mind repeatedly, Claire couldn't excuse her next action.

She leaned forward and scrubbed harder.

Kathy was already eight, which meant Claire had eight years of experience as a mother. And here was what she'd learned from all those dozens, even hundreds, of moments in the past years when she didn't know where her daughter was. Kathy was inevitably fine. She always turned out to be in the adjacent room, or in the bathroom, or right behind Claire, or with Pete.

She did feel that familiar trepidation crawling. That anxiety that goes hand in hand with being a parent. Life gave her this child that suddenly was more important than anything else in the world, and then cruelly gave the child a mind of her own. So she could wander away, and play on the road, and climb tall trees, and pick up sharp, rusty pieces of junk, and eat mud. And the only way to make sure those things didn't happen was to watch her daughter every second of every day. Which, of course, was impossible.

Claire was actually one of those parents who tended to hover around their children. She checked on Kathy in the middle of the night to make sure she was breathing. Repeatedly interrogated Kathy's teacher about her day, making sure everything was okay, and that Kathy ate properly, and played with other kids, and wasn't bullied. She did her best to protect Kathy from that invisible new threat that plagued the world, COVID.

Despite all that, she kept scrubbing that pan. Because she was already in the middle, and it had already stained her skirt, so she might as well at least get it clean. And obviously once she was done, she would walk outside and call Kathy and tell her to stay where she could *see* her.

As she scrubbed, the trepidation grew. Because she hadn't heard the front door opening and closing. The hinges always squeaked, despite her telling Pete to oil them, so she would have heard them. Which meant Kathy wasn't in the house. Could she be in the backyard? It wasn't likely. With the thorny rosebushes alongside the path to the back, Kathy always went *through* the house to the backyard. The girl was scared of the roses' thorns and the occasional bee that would buzz around them. And Pete was at work at his accounting firm, so Kathy obviously wasn't with him. And sure, there were dozens of places in the front yard that weren't visible from the kitchen window, and Kathy did love to explore and play hide-and-seek by herself . . . but still, *that mermaid.* Just left there, her face touching the ground. Kathy wasn't one of those kids who left their toys behind for their parents to pick up. And *definitely* not her favorite mermaid.

So Claire scrubbed faster, because she really wanted to get this over with so she could step outside and make sure Kathy was fine, and now she didn't care about the dried burnt crust anymore—it could stay on the baking pan for all she cared—so she turned off the water, and placed the pan to dry, and stepped outside. And even though she was walking, because she'd been a mother for eight years and she knew from experience that her daughter was totally fine, she walked much faster than usual, her breathing short, unsteady.

She opened the door, the chilly winter air stinging and unpleasant. Kathy had worn a coat when she'd stepped outside, but Claire now regretted letting her play outside altogether.

"Kathy?" she called. "Come inside, baby. It's too cold out."

Which was when her daughter should have answered, reassuring her. Her heartbeat would drop to normal, and she would exhale, her breath steadying, and she could go back to the kitchen and start fixing lunch.

Except no one answered.

Which still didn't mean anything, right? Claire often joked that she had the lamest superpower of them all—she was the Unhearable Woman. Almost like the Invisible Woman from that Marvel movie. As in, she could talk, and no one would hear her, particularly not her husband or her daughter. Sometimes she could literally call Kathy to dinner *five* times, finally raising her voice, and then Kathy would whine and ask why she was shouting at her. Claire would say that she had called her five times, and Kathy would tell her she hadn't heard her.

The Unhearable Woman.

She strode over to the backyard, ignoring the rose's thorns that scratched her arm. "Kathy!" She raised her voice, feeling irritated, because this wasn't the time for Kathy to ignore her. It made her worry. It scared her.

"Kathy!" Now she was shouting, and there was no way Kathy couldn't hear her, there was absolutely no way, she was practically shrieking, who cared what the neighbors thought, she wanted to see where her daughter was *right now* because it was getting harder to breathe, and her heart was thrumming wildly in her chest, and she tried to remember when she'd last glimpsed Kathy, was it five minutes ago? Ten minutes ago? Where could she be?

She was running through the house, because yeah, she didn't hear the squeaky hinges earlier, but maybe she hadn't noticed them and Kathy was actually inside. If she was in the bathroom, she might not have heard her mother calling her. Kathy hummed in the bathroom, because she didn't like to be in a small, silent room all alone, and if she was humming really loudly . . .

The door to the bathroom was open, the light off; Kathy wasn't there. Nor was she in Claire and Pete's bathroom. Or in her room, or in any other room in the house. Claire stormed through the house, calling Kathy's name repeatedly, and now the fear was overwhelming, and her voice was laced with tears, and when she found her daughter she would scream at her because it was better to be angry than afraid, and she wanted to feel that staggering relief of knowing where Kathy was.

What if she had gone to the neighbors' house? Once, before COVID, this was a frequent occurrence. The Millers had a daughter a year younger than Kathy, and the girls had loved to play together. Of course, along came that insidious virus, forcing the parents and their children into self-imposed isolation, and just walking next door wasn't really a thing anymore. You had to call first, feel your way around those uncomfortable questions, making sure everyone was *fine*, that no one had a cold or maybe had met someone a few days ago who now, it turned out, had tested positive. This was another thing the pandemic had killed, along with millions of people. It had killed spontaneity.

But maybe Kathy had gone there anyway. And Claire was past worrying about social distancing. She *wanted* to knock on the Millers' door and find out that, yes, Kathy had gone over there.

She didn't so much knock on the Millers' door as pound on it, and then realized she could have called Vera Miller instead of arriving at her doorstep breathless and hysterical, and Vera could have reassured her on the phone—"Sure, Kathy's here, didn't she tell you?"—and they'd have laughed about how kids drove their parents to an early grave. But she didn't know where her phone was right now, and she wanted to see Kathy with her own eyes, and even punish her, which was something Claire never did, because Kathy was such a good girl, and punishments weren't effective and—

"Claire?" Vera opened the door and instantly took a few steps back, in one of those small rituals everyone had developed in the new world of social distancing.

"Hi, Vera." She wanted to sound calm, but her voice was trembling, and she was breathless. She had actual tears running down her face. "Um . . . Is Kathy here?"

"Kathy? No."

Because of course she wouldn't be. Kathy *knew* she couldn't just go to the neighbors' anymore. She would never do that without asking first.

But the alternatives were worse. And now that she knew her unlikely explanation—Kathy was at the neighbors' house—wasn't true, the other

52

explanations clouded her mind like a swarm of angry, malicious wasps. Kathy could have walked off. She could have fallen somewhere and hurt herself. She could have run after a puppy or a kitten in the street and gotten hit by a car.

And that dominant fear all parents held within their chest. That image often appearing in news reports. She could have entered a stranger's vehicle.

A black van, its windows tinted, a shadowy silhouette inside, the window lowered just a crack to talk to her daughter. Her naive daughter, who maybe didn't remember that time when Claire warned her she shouldn't talk to strangers, and absolutely, under *no* circumstances should she step into—

Vera was saying something.

"What?"

"Did you look everywhere in the yard?"

Of course she'd looked everywhere in the damn yard. Claire wanted to strangle the vapid woman. What did she think? Did she think Claire would run here without *looking in the yard?*

"Yes. I . . . I looked in the yard. And in the house. She's not . . ." The tears clogged Claire's throat.

"I'll come over, help you look," Vera said immediately.

"Thank you," Claire whispered, because she was desperate. *Desperate.* Maybe Vera would think of an alternate explanation, replacing all Claire's dark thoughts. Or maybe Vera would search more efficiently than Claire. She'd think of some hiding spot that hadn't occurred to Claire, and just peek there, and there would be Kathy, and this day would shift back to normal, this entire episode becoming nothing more than an unpleasant experience she would tell Pete about when he came home from work.

So they returned to Claire's house together. And they called for Kathy in the yard, and in the house. And it didn't seem like Vera knew of any hiding spots Claire hadn't thought of. And Vera's worried expression wasn't reassuring at all. In fact, it mirrored a fraction of Claire's own fears.

When she had the talk about strangers and strangers' cars with Kathy, the girl had been seven. And although Claire had been very adamant and clear, she also did her best to be vague about the whys and hows. Because she didn't want Kathy to know what "bad men" were. She didn't want Kathy to know about pedophiles and rapists and murderers. And since that one talk, she'd never mentioned it again, because it was a scary subject, and she didn't want Kathy to be scared.

She should have talked to her about it every single day. Before bed. She should have etched that fear into her daughter's psyche, a mental scar Kathy could talk about with her therapist when she was older.

"I should call Pete," she said weakly.

Vera nodded, looking pale. And then said what Claire had feared. The words that would ensure this wasn't just an unpleasant experience that would blow over. "I'll call the police."

Chapter 9

Bethelville had about 5,500 residents. This meant that when Robin went to the post office, the chances she would meet anyone specific there—say, her ex-husband—were very low. Which made it all the more outrageous when Evan showed up, standing behind her in the line.

"Hey, Robin," he said, tapping on her shoulder gently.

He was a head taller than her. Like Mom and some other kind souls had pointed out over the past year, he was incredibly good looking. Thick black hair, wide shoulders, and that elusive quality in men—a taste in fashion. Even his everyday outfit—jeans, a white T-shirt, and a brown jacket—had been chosen well. And he had a kind smile, or at least that's what people said. Robin couldn't think of his smile as *kind*, exactly, not anymore.

"Hey!" Her voice went extra high, as if she was surprised (which she was) and delighted (which she wasn't) to see him.

The woman in the front of the line was arguing with the man behind the counter about the price of mailing her package. Robin was stuck there.

"Isn't it great about Kathy?" Evan said. "I'm really glad for them."

"Me too," Robin said. "So glad."

"I talked to Pete on the phone. He told me Kathy hasn't gone back to school yet," Evan said.

Robin nodded. She'd heard it too. It'd been ten days, and it seemed perfectly understandable to her.

"I think they should send her back to school," Evan said. "The faster she gets back to a routine, the better to overcome her trauma."

Robin was impressed. Twenty seconds into the conversation and Evan was already mansplaining things about her own profession to her and getting them wrong.

"It really depends on the child, and the trauma," she said, smiling politely.

"Well, you should know," he said, conceding the obvious. "Still, I think that would be best for all of them."

"Yeah," she said, glancing at the angry lady at the front of the line. She was now grudgingly paying with coins from a tiny purse. Oh God, they would be stuck there forever. "So, uh . . . I saw your interview last week. About the prize on that exhibition. It was really good."

"I thought I sounded kind of dumb." Evan chuckled. And then paused and waited.

Having grown up with Mom, Robin could spot an attempt to squeeze compliments a mile away. And while with her mother she obliged, she felt no need to do so with her ex. She smiled at him, saying nothing.

Evan cleared his throat. "But yeah, I'm glad I agreed to the interview. I thought the topic of poverty and the pandemic deserved more airtime. I had to cancel a few things to manage it. You know how it is."

"Busy, busy," Robin said dryly.

When they were married, Evan had tried to build a career as a photographer. He did mostly weddings, though he constantly moaned about the uncreative and repetitive work. His big break had come with the COVID quarantine. Sensing an opportunity, he went on a tour across the country, photographing abandoned amusement parks, deserted city streets, dormant subway stations. He also took shots of people trying to cope with the abnormal situation. One of his photos, of three people fighting over a pack of toilet paper, had gone viral, making him visible for the first time, and slowly propelled him to success. Her issues with him aside, Robin never doubted Evan's talent. He had a good eye.

"So how have you been?" Evan asked after a second. "Ever since . . . you know. Finding out about Kathy?"

She frowned, not following. "Uh . . . fine, I guess? Happy for them, and all that."

"Yeah," Evan said. "I just mean . . . you know. With our thing back then. It must have made you think."

A tidal wave of rage washed over her, leaving her speechless for several seconds. How very *Evan* to tie those two things together. And he was looking at her with that expression that perhaps others would call *kind* or *caring*.

She clenched her fists tightly and mustered control over her vocal cords.

"No," she said crisply. "It hasn't."

She turned around and ignored him. Behind her, Evan sighed, sounding mildly exasperated. Robin tried to seem as if she wasn't seething with fury. As if Evan's words had no effect on her whatsoever. He could probably see that her body was tense. Evan could always read her moods.

"Robin—" he started.

Her phone rang. Saved by the bell. Or in this case, saved by her ringtone, which was the chorus of Taylor Swift's "Shake It Off." Perfect for the moment. She glanced at her phone. The name on the screen was Claire Stone.

She hadn't even remembered she had Claire in her contacts list. It took her a couple of seconds to recall that a few years before, she and Claire had talked twice on the phone when Claire organized a high school reunion event.

"Hello?" she answered, trying to keep the confusion from her voice.

"Robin? Hi, it's Claire. Um . . . Claire Stone?"

"Yeah, hi! How are you doing?"

"I'm good." Claire let out a short, nervous laugh. "You know. Really glad that Kathy is back."

"I can imagine. I never got the chance to tell you in person, I'm so happy for you."

"Thanks. Robin, that's actually the reason I'm calling. You work with children, right?"

Robin got out of the line and stepped outside. She didn't want anyone in there to hear this conversation, particularly not Evan. "Yeah, that's right."

"I was wondering if you could meet with Kathy? Like, in your clinic?"

"Sure! I'll be happy to meet with her."

"She . . . she's been having difficulties. She hasn't been talking since she came back. At all."

Robin swallowed. Poor kid. Everyone was so excited the girl was alive that it was easy to forget the tragedy underlining it. That Kathy had been abducted and had spent more than a year captive, away from her parents and her home. Going through only God knew what. "Okay, that's definitely understandable. Does she write?"

"No. She doesn't do anything verbal."

"I see. Does she answer yes and no questions?"

"She does. She can nod and shake her head. But if we ask her more than two or three questions in a row, she reacts badly. It makes her very anxious. Especially if we ask about . . . whatever happened."

"Okay. That makes sense."

"It does?"

"Yeah. I assume she's been through a lot." As far as Robin knew from the news and from gossip, the police still had no idea where Kathy had been for the past fifteen months. "It's not surprising that she has a bad reaction to things that trigger certain memories she has."

"Like what kind of memories?"

"It's impossible for me to tell. Even the separation from you must have been quite traumatic."

"Yeah, I guess you're right. It's really difficult to get her to leave the house. Sometimes she agrees to go to the backyard with me, and we went to the park a couple of times, but she was really anxious."

"Anxious how?"

"She gets really tense, and she grips my hand tightly. She refuses to let go. And every little sound makes her jump. She starts breathing really fast. Um." Claire's voice became hoarse.

Robin's heart ached for Claire. She was probably under immense stress, constantly worrying for her daughter, wondering what had happened to her and how she could make it better. "I see. We could definitely work on that."

"And she needs to be in the same room with me all the time. Like, *all the time*. Even when I'm in the bathroom. Do you think she'll . . . Is it normal for a girl who went through what Kathy went through to behave like that?"

"Kids handle trauma in different ways. Not even knowing the details of what she went through, what you're describing doesn't sound like particularly unusual behavior."

"But will she . . ." Claire's breath hitched. "Do you think she'll get better? That she'll start talking again?"

"In the majority of cases, with treatment and help, kids who go through traumatic events get much better." Robin was careful to keep things vague. She didn't want to promise anything concrete.

"She was such a happy girl . . . Did you ever meet Kathy? Before she . . . When she was younger?"

"I think I saw her at Melody's once or twice, playing with Amy."

"Sometimes I begged her to be quiet . . . she could talk nonstop. And she had this infectious laugh . . ." Claire's words became almost unintelligible as she sobbed.

"Yeah," Robin said softly.

"I'm so glad she's back, Robin. I really started to believe Pete was right, that she was . . . gone. And she's back in my life, and I'm so grateful. But I don't want her to be so . . . unhappy."

"I think therapy is a very good idea. And I can see her tomorrow morning if you want."

"Tomorrow? That would be amazing," Claire said, sounding immensely relieved.

"And I would need to have sessions with Pete and you as well, without Kathy."

"Sessions with . . . Why do you need to see us?" Claire's voice shifted, became wary. Robin was used to that. Parents often expected her to wave her magic therapist wand and fix any problems their children had with a few hourly sessions.

"To really give Kathy the help she needs, she requires constant support. I'm sure you're already giving her the love and reassurance that she needs, but I can give you some professional guidelines to walk you through the trickier parts of handling your child's trauma."

"Oh . . . okay. Yes. We will be happy to receive some guidance."

"Good. And Claire . . . I want you to be prepared. It'll take time. And patience."

"I'm up for it. However long it takes."

Chapter 10

Robin was staring out the kitchen window as Claire's car pulled up to the curb. Her hands tightened around her coffee mug, her heart rate quickening. She shouldn't have felt so nervous. She'd been doing this for years. She received new clients every month. This wasn't any different.

Except it was.

She had no idea what Kathy had gone through in the past year and a half. The extent of trauma could be severe. Robin was usually very confident of her own professional capabilities, but right now doubt was gnawing at her. Was she up to the task? Could she really help this girl?

If Robin had slept better, perhaps she'd have felt more at ease. But the excitement and anxiety about seeing this girl had kept her from getting almost any sleep. And the three cups of coffee she'd drunk since she got up that morning just made her anxiety worse.

It didn't matter. She couldn't let it show. As far as Kathy and Claire were concerned, she would be a rock. A safe haven from the hectic events of the past. And a place where Kathy could start to heal.

Claire stepped out of the car and looked around her, hesitant. Robin was used to it. She didn't have a separate entrance to her clinic, and new clients were often confused by the idea of knocking at her door. She took a quick last swig of her coffee, put it down, and walked outside.

"Hey, Claire," she said, stepping over to the car. "The playroom is inside."

"Oh. Okay," Claire said faintly.

She seemed much better than the last time Robin had seen her, which wasn't saying much. The color had returned to her face, and she had gained some weight, smoothing out her angular face. But the dark marks around her eyes were still present. The sadness that used to hang around her like a cloud had been replaced by worry.

"She has to be in the same room with me," Claire said. "Would that be a problem?"

"Not at all. That's often the case," Robin said. She glanced into the car briefly. Kathy sat in the back seat, her head lowered, holding something in her lap.

"So far, the cops don't know who took her," Claire said. "They don't know . . . anything, really. There haven't been any clear signs of, um . . . abuse. I have a copy of the medical report here if you want it."

"I can take a look at it later. What did you tell her about today?"

"I told her we're going to meet a good friend of mine." Claire shrugged. "That's all. Should I have said something else?"

"It's okay. I'll explain it to her inside."

"I'd prefer if we don't bring up the past year," Claire said anxiously. "She doesn't react well to talking about it."

"We'll have to," Robin said gently. "We can't keep her in the dark about the purpose of this. It'll just confuse her. She'll know we're not telling her something. Kids know bullshit when they hear it."

"Oh." Claire seemed hesitant to open the car's passenger door. "Do you think you'll be able to . . . figure out what happened to her?"

Robin sighed. "That's not the purpose of my sessions. My sole aim is to help Kathy get better. We might get some information during our sessions, or we might not. And today's goal won't be about that at all."

"What will it be about?"

"It'll be about making her feel safe in the playroom. And safe with me. Before she feels safe here, we can't even begin working on her trauma."

"I told her you are a very nice lady and that there was nothing to worry about."

Robin grinned. "Which is nice to hear. But these are just words. And for Kathy, whose world has been seriously shaken, words don't mean too much. Not even her mother's words. Let's start by making her feel safe and work from there."

Claire gave it some thought, then nodded. "Okay." She opened the car door. "Honey, we're here."

Kathy shuffled out into the open and raised her eyes up to look at Claire, and then at Robin.

Robin had seen Kathy a couple of years before, like she'd told Claire, at Melody's place. She hadn't been paying close attention—Melody's home was often full of kids tearing through the rooms, playing and shouting at each other. Kathy had been one of several girls who had been there that day. Since then, Robin had seen Kathy's pictures cycled on the news and on social media. All the photos she'd seen had been *before* the disappearance.

The child who stared at her now looked nothing like those photos.

She'd grown, of course. Fifteen months was a long time for a little girl. Her black hair was much longer, reaching almost to her waist. Most of the photos were of Kathy smiling, and there wasn't even a memory of a smile on her face right now. And her eyes were wide, haunting. The eyes of a deer as it stared, paralyzed, at incoming headlights.

She held a rag doll in her hand. The little toy might have looked cute once—the doll of a black-haired girl in a floral dress. But it was smudged with dirt, and some of the wool stuffing in the doll was escaping through a hole in its cheek. A lot of the stuffing was apparently already gone, because the doll's face sagged, making the top of its head dangle at an unnatural angle.

Robin took it all in, not letting any of her feelings float to the surface. Instead, she kept her expression neutral and gave Kathy a warm smile. "Hi, Kathy, I'm Robin. Let's all go inside."

She led them in. The clinic was to the left of the entrance, so that Robin's visitors generally got a glimpse of the rest of her home—a quick snapshot of her living room. The door to her bedroom was always shut, her line in the sand. And Menny, as was usual when a new kid came over, was in there. After a few sessions, once the kids were familiar with her and the playroom, she usually let Menny walk around freely. But never in the beginning, when they were still on rocky ground, the child wary and on guard.

When they stepped inside, Robin turned around, smiling, watching how Kathy reacted as she took it all in.

Some kids immediately rushed into the room to inspect the toys or play in the sandbox. But Kathy seemed to freeze in the entrance, her eyes darting left and right. She shifted closer to Claire, clinging to her leg.

Robin went over to the door and shut it. "Kathy, this is my playroom. It is completely safe. You can play with the toys here, and you don't have to do anything you don't want to."

Kathy's eyes flickered around the room, but she remained absolutely still.

"Your mom knows that something bad happened to you," Robin continued, her tone calm and gentle. "She wanted you to visit me to help you feel better about what happened."

Robin took a few steps back, giving Claire and Kathy space, and waited.

Claire cleared her throat. "Kathy, do you want to play with something?"

Kathy seemed to shrink, clutching her mother's leg even tighter. Claire shot Robin a desperate look. Robin met her eyes, smiling lightly, trying to project reassurance toward Claire. She walked around the room, doing some minor tidying—realigning a small elephant doll that had fallen sideways, hanging the plastic doctor's stethoscope on a plastic hook, straightening the crayon box on the table. Then she turned to face Kathy again. The girl seemed to be slightly more relaxed, but her face remained alert.

"Sometimes it can be overwhelming to choose from all these toys," Robin said. "Maybe you'd like to play with your mom in the sandbox? Or cook her something in the kitchen?"

Two options. Leaving the power to choose in Kathy's hands but removing the choice paralysis that came with too many options.

Kathy's eyes flickered from the sandbox to the kitchen, and for a few seconds, her expression shifted. The lost, scared girl was gone, and instead, Robin could glimpse a young girl trying to make a decision.

And then she moved, grabbing Claire's hand. She led her mother to the sandbox and knelt by it.

"You decided to play in the sandbox," Robin said.

Kathy ran one finger through the sand, drawing a circle. Then she set her doll aside and plunged both hands through the sand, burying them up to the wrists.

"You hid your hands completely in the sand," Robin said. "Now we can't see them. But you can still feel them. Only you know where your fingers are."

Was that a sliver of a smile on Kathy's face? Or just a twitch in her lips? Tiny movements in the sand hinted that she was wriggling her fingers. She let out a deep breath. Then she pulled back, her hands emerging from the sand. She let the sand trickle from one fist, creating a small mound. Then she took another handful of sand and let it trickle, making the mound larger.

"You're making a hill in the sand," Robin said. "A tall hill."

Every sentence Robin said was completely natural, her tone steady and soft. She was letting Kathy know she was watching. She was paying attention. And that Kathy's actions made a difference. It was the most basic and the most potent tool in Robin's toolbox. Verbal reflection.

For a while, Kathy was content to simply make her mound taller. Robin kept reflecting Kathy's actions back to her calmly and patiently.

Then, after several minutes, Kathy glanced at Robin, meeting her eyes. She held a fistful of sand. She turned sideways and let it trickle slowly onto the carpet.

"Kathy," Claire blurted. "No, don't make a—"

"You are letting the sand trickle onto the carpet," Robin said calmly, raising her voice slightly to interrupt Claire. "The carpet is now sandy."

Kathy frowned at the carpet. She tried to gather the sand and put it back into the sandbox, pinching it between two fingers.

"You are putting the sand back in the sandbox, where it belongs."

There was definitely a tiny smile there this time. Kathy turned back to the sandbox and brushed the mound away.

"You removed the hill from the sandbox. The sand is now—"

A motorcycle went by the house, its engine roaring. Robin hardly paid it any attention; she was completely intent on the girl.

But Kathy leaped to her feet and rushed to her mother, mouth open in a wordless cry. She grabbed Claire, crouching behind her, her breath raspy, erratic. She was visibly trembling.

Claire raised her voice. "Kathy, honey, calm down, it's just a motorcycle."

It was easy to spot the underlying exasperation in Claire's tone. Robin assumed this kind of occurrence happened numerous times every day. Robin could relate: Claire was probably exhausted.

But as much as Claire felt drained, it was nothing compared to the utter exhaustion Kathy was probably feeling. The girl's response to the motorcycle noise, despite her earlier focus on the sand, made that clear. Kathy was always alert, always listening and watching, prepared for danger. This hypervigilance was a clear sign of acute trauma. It almost certainly taxed Kathy, sapping her strength, leaving her constantly drained. It would have to be one of the first things they worked on.

Robin went over to one of the cabinets and retrieved a blue bottle of bubbles from it. Then she turned to face Kathy, who was still clutching her mother, frozen and shivering while Claire was trying to soothe her. Robin unscrewed the wand and blew into it, releasing several bubbles into the playroom's air.

Kathy's eyes immediately followed the bubbles as they hovered around the room, then popped one by one. Her breathing was still erratic, but the bubbles caught her attention.

"I can control the bubbles if I change my breathing," Robin said, crouching next to Kathy and Claire. "I want a lot of bubbles. So maybe I should blow really fast."

She blew fast into the wand, getting two small bubbles and a bunch of foam.

"That didn't work out so well," Robin said, twirling the wand in its container. "Maybe I'll try taking a very deep breath and blow it out much slower."

She took a deep breath and let it out slowly into the wand, releasing a bunch of bubbles into the air. She quickly counted them. "I think I got fourteen. That's a playroom record right there."

After screwing the wand back onto the container, she held it out to Kathy.

The girl hesitated, then snatched the container from Robin's hand. She unscrewed the wand, took a deep breath, and blew into the wand. The bubbles shimmered in the soft light that filtered through the draped window. Kathy's eyes skittered around as she seemed to count the bubbles herself.

"Very nice." Robin smiled. "Do you want to try again?"

Kathy nodded and repeated it again.

On her third try, she managed a cloud of bubbles that hovered everywhere.

"Eighteen," Robin said. "You broke my record!"

Kathy's deep breaths had the desired effect. She had visibly relaxed. She was now popping the bubbles one by one with the wand.

"You know what?" Robin said. "I want you to keep the wand. And you should practice blowing into it every day. See if you can break your own record. Your mom can help you keep track of how many bubbles you made each try. Does that sound good?"

Kathy looked at the wand and then nodded.

Robin turned to Claire. "You should do it in the evening, just before going to bed. And probably once in the morning, and one time around noon. Okay?"

Claire was watching her daughter with wonder as Kathy blew more bubbles into the air. "Okay," she whispered.

Hopefully, the breathing exercises would help Kathy relax before going to sleep and throughout the day. It would be a good start.

Kathy was so engaged in blowing bubbles that Robin assumed she would do it for the rest of the session. It was quite usual for the first session to focus on getting the child acquainted with the playroom and with Robin. The more Kathy relaxed in the playroom, the more she would think of it as her safe place. Ideally, she would think of Robin as safe too. So Robin contented herself with occasionally cheering the girl on as she played with the bubbles.

But after a while, Kathy screwed the cap shut and handed the bubble bottle to Claire. She examined the room. Now that she was becoming familiar with the space, it seemed she was getting interested in the possibilities it offered.

She took her doll from the floor and carried it over to the plastic table. She sat down on the chair, placing the doll on the table in a sitting position, leaning against the wall. Once she was satisfied with her doll's placement, she took a blank piece of paper and gazed at it, momentarily transfixed.

"In this room you decide what you draw," Robin said. "You can decide if you show us the painting or not. You can decide what you use to draw with. I have crayons, finger paint, pencils—"

Kathy took a container of black finger paint and popped it open. She stared at the shiny black surface, then carefully dipped her finger in it. Slowly, she tracked the black paint over the page.

She drew a smiling stick figure. She was hesitant at first, but as she worked, she dipped two fingers, then three, her actions becoming more confident, more intent.

"You are drawing a man," Robin said. "He is smiling. He looks happy."

Kathy paused to consider the drawing. Then she popped the red paint open. She dipped her finger in the paint and smeared a long gash of red across the stick figure's hand.

"It looks like the man hurt his hand," Robin said, her tone natural, calm.

Another gash.

"Now he hurt his other hand."

Kathy's eyes narrowed as she took a large dollop of red paint, smearing it on the page.

"Now he hurt one leg. And the other leg."

Claire made a small sound, and Robin glanced back at her, giving her a tiny shake of her head. It was important that Kathy not feel like her drawing was bothering her mother or Robin. Kathy shouldn't worry about what her mother thought. She shouldn't feel guilty about drawing this or be concerned that her mother might love her less because of it. This drawing should only be about what Kathy felt and wanted.

Claire looked as if she was about to burst into tears. Robin held her gaze until Claire gave her a nod, quickly wiping her eyes on her sleeve. She took a few steps back and turned her face away, taking a deep breath.

Satisfied that Claire wasn't about to cry, Robin turned back to Kathy's drawing. Kathy was now smearing the red color on the bottom of the page.

"The red paint is covering the floor in the drawing," Robin said.

Kathy touched her finger to the black paint and applied it to the man's face. She made his eyes larger. His mouth became a gaping black void.

"The man is no longer happy," Robin said. "He's in pain."

More red paint. And more. Kathy was pouring the red paint all over the page.

"The red paint is covering everything."

Kathy smeared the paint in whirling motions, creating a crimson vortex, the screaming stick man at its apex. As she swirled the paint, the red and black mingled, the man's body disappearing into the spiraling red, until his body was gone completely and only the wide-eyed screaming face remained, twisted and smeared almost beyond recognition. Then it was gone. Kathy kept shifting the red paint onto the page, smears of it staining the yellow plastic table.

"The red paint made the man disappear," Robin said.

Kathy took a shuddering breath and gazed at her palms.

"Your hands are covered with the sticky red paint," Robin said. "It's everywhere."

Kathy began looking around her. She tried to clean her hands on another blank piece of paper, leaving a smear over it, but naturally, she couldn't get it off.

"Would you like to wash off the sticky red paint?" Robin asked gently. "There's a sink in the bathroom right here."

Kathy nodded.

Robin led her to the clinic's bathroom and helped her turn on the water. Kathy put both her hands in the running water and watched as the red paint swirled into the sink.

"The water is washing all the sticky red paint away," Robin said. "It's making you clean again."

She showed Kathy how to use the soap dispenser, and the girl seemed fascinated with the pink foam that emerged as she scrubbed the red paint from her hands. Claire had stayed at the far side of the playroom. She stood staring at the plastic toys on the shelf, probably trying to collect herself.

On the bright side, Kathy didn't realize her mother wasn't in the same room with her. Or maybe she did realize and was fine with it as long as Robin was with her.

Kathy washed her hands for far longer than necessary. Finally satisfied she was clean, she turned the water off and wiped her hands on her shirt, ignoring the towel hanging by the sink. Then she paused, frowning at the red paint still caught under her fingernails.

"Here," Robin said, retrieving a small nail file from the cabinet. She handed it to Kathy. "You can use this to scrape out the leftover paint."

She waited, watching, poised to act if Kathy mishandled the nail file. It wasn't too sharp, and was quite tiny, but could probably still hurt the girl if she applied enough force. But Kathy gently scraped the red paint from under her fingernails until she seemed satisfied. She handed it back to Robin, who put it back in the cabinet.

Kathy returned to the playroom, joining her mother by the toys. She walked back and forth along the shelves, looking at each figure, and then paused. She picked up one of the plastic figures, a smiling woman holding a cake. She examined it and then turned to the dollhouse. She placed the woman in the dollhouse's kitchen. Then she picked up her own doll from the plastic table and tried to put it in the kitchen as well, cramming it inside.

"The girl is in the kitchen with the woman," Robin said. "There isn't a lot of room in the kitchen now."

There really wasn't. The rag doll was too large for the dollhouse and had to be squashed inside. Clearly displeased, Kathy took the rag doll out. She turned back to the shelves and found a plastic toy of a young girl, which she put in the kitchen.

"The girl is in the kitchen with the woman," Robin said.

Now Kathy was getting into it. She turned to the shelves and picked up dolls one by one. The small Wonder Woman figurine. A plastic farmer.

She didn't choose them randomly. She picked up numerous toys, then put them back in place. But whenever she found a figure she was pleased with, she put it in the house.

A ballet dancer. A Monopoly Man, with the mustache and the top hat.

She stared at the array of the dolls in the kitchen, all surrounding the woman with the cake. Then she turned back to the shelves and picked up one final figure.

Batman's Joker.

Robin had bought that figure in a garage sale, and it was one of the creepiest toys that she had. The Joker looked like an evil clown, his eyes large and bloodshot, his smile garish.

She took him back to the dollhouse, and after hesitating, put him in a different room, at the top floor of the house.

That done, she turned around, looking at Claire and then at Robin.

She was pale and exhausted. The tension seemed to evaporate from her body, and for one terrifying moment, Robin thought she was about to faint. But she steadied herself against the wall and looked lethargically around her.

Robin glanced at her watch. Usually, each session was an hour. This session had gone for an hour and ten minutes, and Robin hadn't noticed. It had been much more intense than she'd expected the initial session to be.

"I think that's enough for today," she said, and glanced at the dollhouse. In the kitchen, the toys seemed to be having a party.

And above them, on the top floor, the paper-white evil clown stood, his arms folded, and smiled ominously.

Chapter 11

Robin finished writing a summary of her first session with Kathy, then leaned back, massaging her forehead. She needed some shut-eye. Unfortunately, she still had the session with Claire and Pete this evening. She looked at the clock. She had a bit more time before it started.

That unsettling drawing came to her mind. She'd seen morbid drawings by kids many times before. But there was something in the way Kathy swirled the red paint, and in the void-like mouth of the person she'd drawn, that stayed with her.

And those toys Kathy collected for the dollhouse. There was so much focus and intent there. The hint of a vivid memory, begging to find its way out. Robin should try to get Kathy to play with the dollhouse in the next session too.

Her mind probed at the missing months in Kathy's life. What had happened there? Had her abductor kept her trapped somewhere all that time? If so, did he live in Jasper, where they found her? And how did the things that manifested in the session connect to it all?

She got up and retrieved the medical report Claire had given her from her bag. Sitting by her desk, she flipped it open.

The first few pages were printed photos. Robin's heart lurched when she saw them. She hadn't seen Kathy when she first turned up or in the days that followed. When they'd found her, Kathy had been much thinner, her eyes sunken in her face. A close-up of her back exhibited numerous inflamed scratches.

She flipped to the next page and skimmed through the report. Kathy had been barefoot when she'd been brought to the police station, and the soles of her feet were scraped and bleeding. In addition, her shirt and the top of her pants were stained with blood, which the doctor theorized came from the multiple lacerations on her lower and upper back. Her teeth showed clear signs of neglect. The rest was a list of negatives. No broken bones. No additional bruises. No sign of sexual assault. No physical reason for her lack of communication.

She checked the time again. Her session with Claire and Pete was about to start. Since Kathy wouldn't remain at the house with anyone but Claire, they'd agreed to have the session via Zoom. Robin wished that wasn't the case. For one thing, the session was late in the evening. She did her best to avoid any screens two hours before bed. Her brain would interpret the glare from the screen as something akin to daylight, which would make it all the more difficult to sleep. And she was already suffering from exhaustion.

She opened the Zoom app on the laptop. The app let her know that Claire Stone was already waiting for her. She joined the call. Pete and Claire appeared on screen. The camera was aimed so that Claire appeared at the center of the screen, while Pete's face was on the right side of the screen, his ear cropped out. He seemed fresh and energized, but Claire was obviously tired, her shoulders sagging. They both sat on a couch in what looked like their living room, and Robin surmised that their laptop sat on the coffee table in front of them.

"Hey," Robin said, her eyes darting to check herself in the corner of the screen. She'd pulled her red hair back and reapplied her lipstick an hour before, so she didn't look as weary as she felt. She had decades of experience at hiding her own tiredness. She'd also made sure the space behind her wasn't messy. All Pete and Claire would be able to see of the room was her bookcase, with a bunch of therapy books, and her potted peace lily. The untidy desk was well beyond the laptop camera's range of sight.

Claire and Pete's own living room seemed immaculate. Did they keep some clutter in the unseen parts of their home? The endless Zoom sessions had taught people that you didn't really have to clean up your house when meeting people online. You just had to clean up one segment of one room.

"Hi," Claire and Pete said together.

"Nice to see you again, Robin," Pete said.

Robin had met Pete on a regular basis when she'd been married to Evan. Her ex-husband loved to invite Pete and Fred over for a guys' night. They'd drink beer, and Evan would barbecue some burgers. Evan never told her she wasn't invited to join them; he was too classy to do that. But whenever she dropped by, the conversation would slow down, their smiles becoming forced and pained, until she would inevitably leave and go watch Netflix in the bedroom. It became one of the many minor things she grew to hate. Hearing Fred's braying laugh through the bedroom wall or Pete's know-it-all voice as he lectured them about politics. Finding dirty plates and empty beer cans in the morning and pointedly ignoring them until Evan finally cleaned them up.

Once, she'd asked Evan why they hardly met at his friends' houses. Evan pointed out that he was the only one who didn't have a child, which made it easier to meet at his home. The way he'd said it, belligerently, made Robin feel as if he was blaming *her* for that.

Now she smiled at him. "You, too, Pete. It's worth addressing this before we start. We all know each other, of course. Claire and I went to school together, and Pete and Evan are very good friends, so I saw a lot of you in previous years. But during Kathy's treatment, we should set those previous connections aside. I won't let these things interfere with my time with Kathy, or with our talks."

"Of course," Claire said.

Robin glanced at Pete, who was nodding as well. With that out of the way, she asked, "How's Kathy doing?"

"She finally went to sleep," Claire said. The relief in her voice was palpable.

"Oh, good. Did you do the bubbles exercise?"

"Yeah. I think it helped. She seemed calmer tonight than on previous nights. But then an ambulance went by a few streets away, and she freaked out. So it took a long time to calm her down again. Just like with the motorcycle at your session. That kind of thing happens a lot."

"Is it mostly loud noises that trigger those kinds of reactions?" Robin asked.

"I think so. But there can be other stuff. Like, when we went to the park, some kids were playing with a ball and threw it close to us, and that really scared her. And meeting strangers sometimes gets her really worked up. A detective came by our house two days ago, and Kathy reacted really badly."

"Not just strangers," Pete added. "My brother came the other day, and Kathy wouldn't be in the same room with him."

"Yeah." Claire nodded. "Thomas is a really big guy, and she got really scared when he stepped in the house."

"Still, they know each other back from when she was a baby," Pete said. "I thought . . . well, it was really frustrating."

"I see." Robin said. "I'm sure it's very difficult for you when something like that happens."

"Not as difficult as it is for Kathy," Claire pointed out.

"I agree," Robin said softly. "But it's okay to feel that it's also difficult for you. How do you calm her down when that happens?"

"Well, I hug her," Claire said.

"And we tell her there's nothing to worry about," Pete said.

"I keep telling her we'll keep her safe," Claire added.

Robin watched them both, noticing how Pete tried to include Claire in his sentences, while Claire almost made it a point to distance herself from him. Their approaches to Kathy's anxiety were almost classic—Claire trying to shelter Kathy and offer her safety, while Pete gave Kathy a typical fatherly pep talk.

"Okay. We'll work on some additional exercises to soothe her when she's stressed," Robin said. "And I would be really happy if you worked as a team to help Kathy."

"What do you mean?" Pete asked sharply. "We're working together. I mean . . . I have to go to work, I can't be there throughout the day, but I make sure to get home as soon as possible to be with Kathy before going to sleep."

"I understand," Robin said. "And I'm not talking about that. What I mean is that your approaches are different, and I would like you to discuss them with each other. Different approaches could be helpful—they could synchronize and enhance each other. But not if Kathy feels like you disagree with each other."

"We never argue in front of her," Pete said.

Robin nodded. Kids were much more perceptive than Pete thought, especially ones as fine tuned to every shift in the room's mood as Kathy obviously was. She could probably sense the tensions and disagreements between her parents as easily as reading a book. "What I'd like you to try right now is for you to put yourselves in each other's shoes. Tell me how you feel, from the perspective of your partner."

"Aren't we here to talk about how we should help Kathy?" Claire asked.

"Absolutely, and I think that's part of it. To figure out how we can work together, we need to understand each other better. I would get a better idea of how to approach my sessions with Kathy if I get your perspectives and how you feel about your partner's methods."

A long silence stretched between them. Then Pete cleared his throat. "Well, Claire thinks—"

"Try to talk in first person. As if you were Claire," Robin suggested.

Pete shuffled uncomfortably. "Uh . . . I think *Pete* could call during the day to talk to Kathy. He doesn't do that, because he says she doesn't answer when he talks, but Claire . . . I think she listens and that she takes comfort from hearing his voice."

Robin blinked in surprise. She hadn't expected such self-reflection from Pete, and definitely not so soon.

"And Claire . . . I feel," Pete continued, "that Pete could try and be more understanding of what Kathy is going through." He cleared his throat again, his body tense.

"Okay." Robin smiled. "Claire, what about you? How does Pete feel?"

"I feel," Claire said, her voice crisp, "that *Claire* is pampering Kathy too much. That she's stifling Kathy and making her too dependent."

Pete bristled. "I never said—"

"Let's let Claire finish," Robin suggested gently.

"When we were kids, our parents didn't hover over us, even if we had problems. They let us sort them out," Claire said, her voice shifting, almost a mocking imitation of Pete. "And we should do the same for Kathy. But *Claire* doesn't agree."

Even on her laptop's screen, Robin could see the anger simmering in Claire's eyes and knew it was the first time Claire had allowed herself to fully voice her frustrations. Better out than in, of course. But Robin could already see Claire's anger at Pete would be one of the main issues she would have to tackle during their guidance sessions.

"Right," she said. "For now let's set it aside. I see the advantages in your different approaches to Kathy, and I believe that I will be able to help her more during my sessions, knowing how you both feel. And we'll keep doing these exercises to help you synchronize and work together."

Neither parent seemed particularly pleased at that.

"Let's talk about today's session with Kathy," Robin said, changing the subject.

"You were really great with her today," Claire said.

"I'm glad you feel that way." Robin smiled. "Pete, I don't know if Claire told you about the session—"

"She told me that Kathy drew a creepy drawing."

"Well . . . that's true. That was a small part of the session. In general, Kathy did incredibly well during the session. We got her to lower her guard and enjoy the playroom, and she managed to express herself unusually well."

"She doesn't speak," Pete pointed out. "So there's definitely room for improvement there."

Claire clenched her jaw and turned to Pete to say something, but Robin interjected.

"She expressed herself through drawings and games. With kids who have gone through trauma, talking about what they went through isn't the main way they show their emotions. Imaginary games, and art, are a much better medium to handle the trauma."

"Okay," Pete said. "Can you estimate how long before she starts talking again?"

"It's impossible to know how quickly we'll be able to see improvement, but like I told Claire, it will take a lot of patience."

"And you want to do a weekly session with her, right?"

"We can start there and see how things go."

Pete nodded, frowning. His eyes kept glancing at something off screen, and Robin suddenly had a feeling that there was a TV turned on in the room, in a spot hidden from her. That was something else she hated about Zoom sessions. She would often see people's attention wane as they talked to her. Sometimes they would be typing or moving the mouse, and she wondered if they were on social media throughout the session.

"Robin . . . that drawing she did," Claire said.

"Yeah?"

"Do you think it's something the person who took her did to her? Did he cut her?"

Pete's eyes darted back to the screen, alert.

"We don't need to jump to conclusions. Her drawing could mean any number of things. And as far as I could see, the medical report doesn't mention anything about such abuse."

"That's true," Claire said. "There are no scars or anything like that."

"Her body was really scratched when they found her," Pete pointed out. "By now most of those scratches healed."

"But they didn't look like cuts, right?" Claire told Pete.

"No. I think more like abrasions," Pete said.

"That could be what she was showing us," Robin suggested. "That she bled a lot from those scratches."

Or maybe whoever took her threatened to cut her. Maybe she saw him cut someone else. Or maybe it was something else entirely that they only interpreted as a person bleeding.

"When will we know for sure?" Pete asked.

"I don't know if we will. I realize not knowing must be incredibly difficult. But that's not the point of these sessions."

"Then why do this? Why force her to remember those moments if we can't even figure out what she went through?" Pete raised his voice, sounding exasperated.

"We're not forcing her to do anything," Robin said gently.

"I know, I just . . . I don't understand what you're doing."

"Kathy went through some traumatic events, there's no doubt about that," Robin said. "These memories are lodged in her brain, and they are so visceral that when she accidentally recalls them, she actually *relives* them. This is what probably happens when she hears a loud sound."

"Then we shouldn't make her remember them." Claire sounded aghast.

"That's not possible. She can't avoid thinking about them, and anything could trigger them. Because of that, she's also trying to avoid anything that triggers those memories, which is probably why it's so hard to get her to leave the house."

"Then what can we do?" Claire asked.

"We help her process these memories in a safe environment, like the playroom, where she feels in control. When she processes these memories by playing or drawing them and showing them to us, she slowly gets used to them. We help her desensitize these memories so that when she recalls them, she won't actively experience them. That's my most important goal with her. To help her turn these visceral memories to unpleasant memories, and nothing more."

Claire sagged into the couch. "Oh. I see."

"You sound disappointed."

"I thought . . . we could somehow make her get over those memories completely. I don't want her to think about all those terrible months."

"There's nothing we can do about that," Robin said tenderly. "Those memories are there to stay."

Chapter 12

The day of the disappearance

Melody had been searching for Kathy for the past two hours, along with dozens of Bethelville's residents. In the beginning, she'd call Kathy's name every thirty seconds or so, a hopeful, desperate shout. She'd hear others calling the girl's name too. Now, her voice hoarse, she hardly ever called out anymore. And when she did, her voice no longer sounded hopeful. Hope had been replaced by fear.

The sun had set, darkness settling on the town. Wavering beams of light indicated other people as they looked between trees, behind houses. One of the theories was that Kathy had gone for a walk and then got hurt. Perhaps she lost consciousness due to dehydration or a hit on the head. So people looked for her in ditches or in woody areas.

Melody's gut instinct told her this theory was hopeful nonsense. She knew Kathy, and the girl would never leave the yard without asking Claire for permission. Even Melody's own two rowdy boys wouldn't do that, and definitely not now, during the pandemic.

She took out her phone and called Fred again. Just as before, he didn't answer. Fred had gone to search in the park in the southern part of town, and she hadn't heard from him in the past hour. She gritted her teeth and called Sheila, her elder daughter.

"Did you find her?" Sheila answered breathlessly.

"Not yet," Melody said. "Did your dad swing by the house?"

"No, but Grandpa did earlier. He stayed for a little while."

"Okay." Thank God for her dad. He probably made the kids feel better. "I need you to put the little ones to bed."

"Wouldn't it be better if you came by? They're really nervous. And you should talk to Amy." Sheila was sounding nervous herself.

Melody's gut twisted. "You didn't say anything to her, right? About Kathy."

"Of course not. But someone should."

"We will, once we know where this is going. Just . . . put them to bed, okay? Make sure the boys brush their teeth, because they won't do it if you don't tell them to."

"Okay."

"Thanks, sweetie. Let me know if your dad calls. Bye."

Someone went past Melody on the other side of the road, a dark silhouette, mask hiding the bottom part of his face. They nodded at each other, though she didn't recognize him. Before COVID, she knew almost everyone she saw on the street, but now, with half their faces hidden, it became so much harder. And in the darkness, it became practically impossible. That man could be anyone at all. The sheriff had told them to keep alert for anyone unfamiliar. But the pandemic had rendered everyone unfamiliar. Those masks that helped to keep everyone safe also hid them from each other. And could hide strangers among them.

"Kathy!" she called out.

She'd heard Kathy and Amy talking only yesterday. They hadn't met in the house, of course. The girls hardly met each other in their homes anymore. But they talked on Zoom all the time. Which meant Kathy's voice was a frequent sound in Melody's life. She tried to remember the girl's voice but couldn't. *Had* it been yesterday? The pandemic had turned the days from straightforward distinguishable time units into blobs that intermingled with each other. Yeah, it was almost definitely yesterday. And Kathy had sounded fine, hadn't she?

Melody had no idea what she'd tell Amy if Kathy wasn't found tonight.

Chapter 13

How long had it been since Claire had gone to meet friends? It seemed to her like it had been decades. She hadn't done it since Kathy's disappearance, that was for sure. And even before that, during the first year of the COVID outbreak, going to meet other people at their own homes felt risky. So how long was it? Two years? Three?

And now she found that she didn't remember how it was done exactly. How did she normally dress for an afternoon coffee with friends? What would they talk about? She felt as if she was trapped in a dream in which she got onstage only to realize she didn't know the lines.

Ever since Kathy had returned, she and Pete had been invited for dinners and nightcaps and brunches several times. And she always begged off because Kathy was still recuperating.

But when Melody and Fred invited them over, she found herself saying yes. First of all, unlike others, Melody had stayed in touch with Claire throughout the past year, calling her often, suggesting they should meet. She'd been a real friend.

And second, Melody said Amy really wanted to see Kathy.

Before the disappearance, Amy and Kathy had been almost inseparable. Even when they had to keep social distancing, they talked constantly on Zoom. BFFs, that's what it was called, right? Best friends forever. Or in their case, best friends until Kathy disappeared. BFUKDs.

And now here they were, knocking at Melody and Fred's door. Kathy was dressed in new clothes Claire had bought for her. Her daughter had grown two inches in the past fifteen months but also lost a lot of weight. Her old clothes made her look like a scarecrow.

Claire wore a short-sleeved yellow dress she'd found hidden at the back of her closet. She was worried it smelled a bit moldy from disuse, but Pete told her she was imagining things.

Kathy clutched Claire's hand, her fingers tightening with anxiety. Claire could relate. Her own heart was thumping in her chest. She wasn't sure how Kathy would react to meeting Amy. She *still* reacted badly around Pete's brother Thomas. Was her previous connection to Amy still intact?

The door opened, Melody in the doorway, a large smile plastered on her face.

"Hey!" she said.

"Hey!" Claire responded.

Both their voices sounded strained, high pitched.

"Amy!" Melody called over her shoulder. "Look who's here!"

Daddy had once read a story to Amy where the princess in the book felt like she had butterflies in her stomach, and Amy was really bothered by that description. Because once Liam dared Noah to eat a worm, and Noah did it, and then he said he could feel it crawling inside his belly, and he ended up throwing up. But Daddy said the princess in the book was excited, which was why she felt like she had butterflies in her stomach. It's not like she ate the butterflies. Anyway, it was a dumb way to say the princess was excited.

Except now she knew how the princess felt.

Because she would meet Kathy again. And she'd thought she would never ever *ever* meet Kathy again. Because Daddy and Mommy told her so all that time ago.

When Kathy left, Daddy and Mommy sat Amy down, and they told her that Kathy was gone. And she wanted to call Kathy and ask her where she went to, and they said Kathy didn't have a phone but that her parents and the police were looking for her. And the police were really good at their job, like Uncle Dwayne, and they would find her really soon.

And then Amy had bad dreams where Kathy was lost in the forest and was calling for help but Amy couldn't find her. And she'd wake up and run to Daddy and Mommy's bed every night. And twice she even wet the bed, but she didn't like thinking about that.

And then a lot of days went by, and she asked Mommy and Daddy every day if the police had found Kathy, and if they'd tried to look in Paris, because once Kathy told Amy that if her mom wouldn't buy her a doll she wanted, she would run away to Paris. And finally Mommy and Daddy told her Kathy was gone, and she was never coming back. And she said it would never happen to Amy, because they were really careful, and because Amy was really smart and knew not to get into strangers' cars, and Amy said Kathy was very smart and knew that, too, and Mommy and Daddy didn't know what to say to that.

She had more nightmares after that. And Auntie Robin took her to her cool toy room, and they played together a lot, and the nightmares didn't happen every night anymore.

Now Kathy came back. And Amy was really excited, but Kathy didn't come to school, and when Amy asked to talk to her on the phone, Mommy explained that Kathy didn't want to talk to anyone, not even her mommy and daddy, which was really strange, because Kathy *loved* to talk. And she kept asking every day, and finally, after a bazillion years, Mommy invited Kathy and her parents over.

Which was why Amy had butterflies in her stomach, even if she hadn't eaten the butterflies. She would never, because she wasn't as dumb as Noah.

She went to the door, and Kathy stood outside, even if she looked a bit different. And she was clutching her mom's dress like a little girl.

Amy said "Hi" almost in a whisper because she suddenly felt really shy. And Kathy smiled a little but didn't answer.

Claire stepped into Melody's house, and it was almost like stepping through time. Back to the days when she'd chat with Melody over bagels and coffee while their girls played outside on the swing. She yearned for those times, not only because they'd been happier but also because she'd been a different person. Everything was so simple and easy back then. Her worries were about the neighbor who refused to trim the branch that touched their roof, or whether they could afford the trip to California in the summer.

Kathy's return had been a constant blessing, a second chance, and she still literally woke up every morning with a smile. But one of the difficult things she struggled with was that she hadn't gotten her old life back. She had to build a new life for both of them.

"I got a new bed last month," Amy told Kathy. "Do you want to see?"

Kathy looked at Amy and then up at Claire.

"Let's go see together," Claire suggested.

She went with Kathy while Pete joined Melody and Fred in the living room. Pete seemed like he *had* gotten back his old life. He was meeting friends and going to work, and he spent a bit of time in the evening playing with Kathy, just like he used to do before her disappearance. And mostly, it was Claire who soothed Kathy when she panicked or who went to her several times every night when Kathy woke up crying.

At least ever since the first session with Robin a few days ago, Kathy let Claire go to the bathroom and close the door. She sat outside the door and waited for Claire to be done.

Amy led them to her room and showed them her new bed proudly, explaining she'd chosen the sheets. She hopped onto the bed with a gleeful smile.

"Come on," she told Kathy. "You have to get on. It's so soft."

Kathy hesitated. Claire was about to suggest they sit on the bed together when Kathy let go of Claire's dress and climbed onto the bed, settling next to Amy.

Claire let out a long breath. Amy was prattling about school and about how everyone made a card for Kathy, did she get them? (they did; Claire gave them to Kathy, who showed absolutely no interest in them) and how she would tell everyone she met Kathy, and when was Kathy going back to school?

Claire had spent the past weeks learning to judge her daughter's new, volatile moods. And she now watched in wonder as she saw the muscles in Kathy's body relax slowly. Kathy seemed to listen to Amy almost with wonder as Amy jumped off the bed and showed her the new clothes she'd gotten, and an actual makeup kit, and a necklace she'd made at summer camp.

After a few minutes, Claire hesitantly said, "Kathy, I'm going to the living room to say hello to Melody. Is that okay?"

And her wonderful, amazing daughter met her eyes and then nodded, once.

Back when Kathy talked, Amy sometimes got frustrated because she wanted to say something and Kathy would be talking, so she'd try to interrupt her, and Kathy would raise her voice and keep talking, and by the time she finished, Amy would completely forget what she had to say.

And when she told her mom about that, Mom said that if she forgot, it probably wasn't important, which wasn't true at all because it *was*.

But now that Kathy didn't talk, Amy wished she would start talking again, because Kathy had funny jokes and interesting stories. And after Amy showed her all the things she got since Kathy left, she was running out of words.

She tried to think about what Kathy had missed and told her about important things that had happened at school, which were the one time that Georgia threw up during math, and the Halloween party where Mrs. Pearce dressed as a witch, which was funny because she really *was* a witch, and . . . well, those were the important things.

"Why don't you want to talk?" Amy asked.

Kathy frowned at that, like she was confused.

"My mom said you don't even speak to your mom and dad. Is that true?"

Kathy nodded.

"Where did you go for all this time? My mom said they found you all the way across the state."

Kathy turned her face away and fiddled with the blanket.

Mommy had said Amy would have to be patient with Kathy because she didn't talk and she was still getting over what happened to her. And when Amy asked what happened to her, Mommy said it was bad things, but she didn't say what.

"Do you want to draw?" Amy suggested.

Kathy loved drawing. She and Amy used to draw a lot together, and Kathy was *really* good. She knew how to draw a cat's head that looked really cute with big eyes, and fairies, and a really nice rainbow.

Now Kathy nodded, so Amy took out the pages and her colored pencils.

"I got them at Easter," she said. She lay on her stomach on the floor, and Kathy joined her, lying in front of her with their foreheads almost touching, like they sometimes used to do. When Kathy still talked.

They began to draw. Amy drew a mermaid and a fish, and then she glanced at Kathy's page.

"What's *that?*"

◆ ◆ ◆

"I didn't believe she would let me leave her side." Claire was breathless with excitement.

"See?" Pete said. "I told you. We need to stop coddling her. It doesn't do her any good." He was smiling, raising his beer bottle as if raising a toast.

Claire clenched her jaw to stop herself from answering. This was the constant argument she and Pete had been engaged in for the past two weeks. Pete said that the only reason that Kathy refused to leave Claire's side was because Claire *let* her. He wanted to send Kathy to school. "Let the teachers handle her if she acts up," he'd said. As if Kathy's panic was just an annoying tantrum.

She turned her eyes away, intent on having a good time.

"Amy was so excited to have Kathy over," Melody said, grinning. "She begged us every single day for the past two weeks."

"I'm really glad we came," Claire said.

"And Claire, you look so good!" Melody said.

"Thanks," Claire said. "I feel good. And Kathy is getting better. Robin helps a lot."

"Robin?" Melody asked in surprise. "My sister?"

"Yeah," Claire said. "I took Kathy to see her. She's really good at her job."

"Oh, that's great," Fred said. "She really helped Amy deal with . . . uh . . . some nightmares she had."

"I was really impressed," Claire said. "She's helping Kathy deal with her trauma."

"I wasn't sure about it at first," Pete said. "But it seems to have helped. And we're getting a much clearer picture of what Kathy went through, which is important."

"Oh, she's talking to Robin?" Fred asked.

"No," Pete said. "But Kathy is a bright girl. She's conveying her experience."

"I don't know if it's a clear picture of what she went through," Claire said. "And that's not the point. The purpose is to help her get used to living with the difficult experiences she—"

"Well, honey, you said Kathy showed you some things, right?" Pete said. "Like the drawing and the dolls. She's communicating what she went through. I'm hoping we'll eventually know everything."

"That's good," Fred said. "Did Robin tell you how long it would take? With Amy, she was able to help within a couple of months."

"She didn't really give us a time frame," Claire said.

"Robin is really great at what she does," Melody said. "If anyone can help Kathy get better, it's her."

Amy didn't like Kathy's drawings. There was a person with really big red eyes, and he held a stick and he looked scary, and it made Amy want to look away.

"Do you want to go to the kitchen and see if we can grab some cookies?" she asked. Her eyes were half-shut, but she didn't want to shut them completely because Kathy might think she was scared.

Kathy shook her head. She was drawing a third picture of the same person. In this one he had large teeth.

Maybe it was time to go to the living room and see what Mommy was doing. And maybe Mommy would have an idea for something else they could play. Amy didn't want to draw anymore.

She got up, but then Liam and Noah barged into her room. And usually when they came into her room she yelled at them to get out, but now she was actually happy they came because they always made a lot of noise, and Kathy was just too quiet.

"Woah! What's that?" Liam snatched one of Kathy's drawings.

"It's a monster," Noah said, jumping on Amy's bed. He bounced on it. "A killing monster. Rrrraaaargh!"

"Stop jumping on the bed. Mommy said it ruins it!" Amy shouted at him.

Kathy crawled away from her pages and was now hugging her knees, and her eyes were really wide, and she kept looking at Noah and then at Liam.

"I read a story about monsters who bite off people's heads," Liam said. He waved the page with Kathy's drawing, miming as if it was biting her head off. "Chomp, chomp!"

"Quit it!" Amy slapped the page away.

"Can you draw a monster for me?" Noah shouted.

Kathy shrunk back, and she was making small, weird sounds, like it was hard to breathe.

"Liam, Noah, get out!" Amy shrieked. "You're scaring Kathy."

Now Kathy was looking at Amy like she was frightening her, too, and Amy cried because Kathy wasn't behaving like Kathy at all, and she was making Amy feel bad. Why wouldn't she talk? And why did she draw these weird red-eye men? And why was she grunting like that?

Liam was waving two of the drawings now, making monster noises, and Noah was jumping higher and higher on the bed, and it creaked, and Amy was afraid her new bed would break.

"Get out!" she screeched.

Noah jumped off the bed, right in front of Kathy.

The scream was so loud all of them got up from their seats at the same time. Claire was already rushing to Amy's room, heart pounding. How could she have let her girl out of her sight? How could she have been so stupid? She should never—

Her breath hitched as she reached the doorway.

At first, all she saw was Kathy. And the blood on her hand.

"Kathy!" she gasped. "Are you okay?"

Kathy was moaning, rocking back and forth, eyes vacant and unblinking.

"Oh my God!" Melody said behind her. "Noah! What happened to you?"

Claire glanced away from Kathy, and she realized Noah was the one screaming, lying sideways on the floor. Blood was smeared all over his leg. And as Melody rushed to help him, Claire saw more blood was still trickling from a puncture in his skin.

She looked back at Kathy. A sharp pink pencil lay by Kathy's feet. Its tip was stained red.

Chapter 14

Robin heard Mom talking as she stepped inside her house. Was she on the phone? She walked over to the living room; she spotted the clutter of cutlery. Mom had guests over. For a brief second, she felt relief. She wouldn't have to stay for long, and Mom wouldn't be as vicious as usual.

But as she reached the room, her heart sank. She instantly realized the trap she'd set her foot in.

Mom sat in her usual chair, pouring tea from her china set into small cups. Sitting on the couch in front of her were Robin's ex, Evan, and his mother, Glenda.

"Oh, Robin," Mom said in surprise. "You're already here? I thought you'd be coming much later."

Robin smiled tightly. "I told you when I'd be coming when we talked."

"No, you didn't," Mom said lightly and turned to Evan and Glenda. "I asked Robin to come when she has some time and help me with my phone. It's not working properly."

"I had some issues with my phone as well," Glenda said. "But Evan got me a new phone for my birthday."

Glenda had been Mom's friend for as long as Robin could remember. Dad had once jokingly whispered to Robin that Glenda's parents had named her after Glinda, the good witch from *The Wizard of Oz*, but because they had misspelled her name, they got a regular witch. And

Glenda did look the part. She had extralong fingernails; a long, pointy chin; and a tiny mouth that always settled into a slight frown.

"I can come back later," Robin said.

"No, there's no need," Mom said. "I don't want to trouble you, and Glenda and Evan don't mind. Do you?"

"Not at all," Evan said gallantly.

She would fix Mom's phone and get out of there. Ten minutes tops. Robin went over and sat down beside Glenda.

"Here." Mom poured tea for her. "Try the apple pie. Glenda made it. It's really good."

"Oh, I—" Robin began, but Glenda was already cutting a large piece of apple pie. "Okay, thanks. So what's the problem with the phone?"

"It keeps telling me I need to delete my photos," Mom said, aggravated. "I don't want to delete them. How else would I be able to see my grandchildren?" She handed Robin her battered phone.

"You still haven't seen them?" Glenda asked, her voice thick with compassion. "Oh, you poor dear."

"Well, I can't afford to let them in. Not until Melody agrees to vaccinate them," Mom said. "And she won't change her mind about these vaccines. And of course I won't have any grandchildren from Robin in the near future."

It took all of Robin's willpower to keep her mouth shut. Melody owed her *big time*. She angrily tapped the screen of Mom's phone. It was a ridiculously outdated device, bought ten years before. And it had been one of the cheaper devices back then. Robin had bought her new phones twice, which her mom returned to her, explaining that they didn't work as well as her old phone.

"At least Robin comes over," Glenda said. "We're lucky to have such doting children. You know, I saw Mildred the other day, and she said she's lucky if her kids show up at Christmas."

"Robin and I always had a special bond," Mom said softly.

Some of the tension in Robin's body dissipated. She gave Mom a brief smile.

"You know," Glenda told Robin, "Diana told me once you never missed any of her shows."

Robin cleared her throat. "That's right."

"I would finish my show," Mom told Evan, "and drive straight home. And Robin would wait for me at the kitchen, with the radio still by her side. And we'd talk about the show and how it went."

"Mom would make us some tea, or a jar of lemonade," Robin said, almost tasting the memory of the sweet lemonade in her mouth. "And we'd eat ginger cookies and laugh about the phone calls Mom got during the show, and about the songs she picked. Sometimes she'd let me pick a song for the following day."

"Robin *loved* it," Mom said with a grin. "I think it's one thing for strangers to enjoy your radio show. But if your child loves it, that means it's really special."

"Well, I know I listened to your show many times as a kid," Evan said. "And it was amazing."

"Oh, you flatterer." Mom laughed. "You're just saying that."

"No, I really mean it," Evan said. "Time would fly by when I listened to you."

Robin tried to focus on the phone. The damn thing really was sluggish. She cleared the cache of several apps, knowing that it wouldn't really help for more than a day. The thing needed a more thorough treatment, like being bashed with a large rock.

"So, Robin," Glenda said. "Evan told us that you're treating Kathy Stone."

Robin raised her eyes in surprise. "I . . . What?"

"Pete told me," Evan explained. "He asked me what I think. Naturally, I told him you're very good and that you could really help Kathy get over this entire thing."

Robin clenched her jaw. Evan should have known better. Glenda and Mom were the town's most prolific gossips. By tomorrow half the town would have heard she was treating Kathy.

"I have to say I was a little hurt to hear that from Evan and not from my own daughter." Mom's voice trembled.

"I can't really talk about it," Robin said.

"I talked to Robin about Kathy a week ago," Evan said. "I think what the girl needs is routine."

"You talked to Robin a week ago?" Mom cooed. "She never mentioned it."

"We met by accident, at the post office," Robin said, turning her attention back to Mom's phone. She needed to fix the thing and get out of there.

"That's *interesting*," Glenda said.

"Anyway, the way I see it, they should really send Kathy back to school," Evan said. "Make her feel like she's got her life back."

"School year's nearly over," Robin said briskly. "Kathy will be behind at everything, making her feel even more out of place. Not to mention that kids would constantly badger her with questions about what happened."

"The teachers could manage that," Evan said. "Pete told me Kathy's old teacher said she could do some private tutoring for her. And they could tell the other kids not to bother her. It shouldn't be that hard. But Claire won't do it."

"Maybe you should suggest it in your next session," Glenda told Robin.

Robin smiled politely, considered about a dozen scathing remarks, and said absolutely nothing.

"Evan said you are trying to make little Kathy tell you about what happened to her," Mom said. "I don't know if *that's* a good idea."

"What? That's not what I . . ." Robin stared aghast at Mom, and then at Evan. She forced her mouth shut. "I really can't talk about this."

"The girl should focus her energy on leaving that horrid affair behind. That family has suffered enough," Glenda said.

"It's even worse, now that the police reopened the investigation." Mom sniffed. "I heard they tried to show the poor girl mug shots."

"I always thought it was someone close to the family who took her," Glenda said. "You know, because they say there was no struggle."

"I don't know if that's conclusive evidence," Evan pointed out. "She was a little girl. Anyone could have overpowered her quickly."

"With her mother in the house a few feet away?" Glenda asked.

"*I* heard Claire was on the phone in the bedroom, with the door shut," Mom said. "Anyway, my point is, you don't need to add more stress to the girl's life. It's bad enough as it is."

"Fine," Robin said crisply. She was done with the subject. And with this day, for that matter.

"Didn't you tell me once that some of your patients found the experience of facing their trauma very stressful?" Evan said. "One even quit midtherapy."

Robin's temper flared. "He didn't quit midtherapy; his mother stopped the therapy despite my recommendation. And part of it was that their insurance wouldn't pay for any more sessions. And repressing trauma is a terrible idea—"

Evan raised his hands. "I didn't say she should *repress* her memories. I was just mentioning something *you* told me."

"Maybe the right thing to do is to help Kathy get past that horrid experience," Mom said. "I always figured your job was like a mental shepherd, herding the stray thoughts in the right direction."

"That's a beautiful way to put it," Glenda said.

Mom smiled. "Now that I don't have a radio show anymore, I have only my friends and family to talk to. So I guess it's your gain and everyone else's loss."

"In a way, it's not only Kathy and her family that need to heal and move on," Evan said. "It's our community. The whole thing with Kathy has been very painful for everyone, and now the residents of Bethelville can finally move on."

"I know *I've* felt it," Mom said, striking her chest with her palm. "I thought about the poor girl every day."

"Same here," Evan said. "And I know Robin was *shattered* when it happened."

Robin gritted her teeth, knowing where this was going. "I wasn't shattered. I was very distraught. Everyone was."

Evan raised an eyebrow. "I remember talking to you that evening—"

"You weren't even in town that evening!" Robin snapped. "You were on one of your endless photo-shoot tours."

Evan looked hurt. "I mean, I talked to you on the phone. And I cut my trip short to help with the searches. *Anyway*, when we talked, you were crying uncontrollably—"

"Robin always had a soft heart," Mom said. "She got it from me."

"—and you kept saying how you couldn't even imagine how Claire felt."

"That's not how that conversation went," Robin said through clenched teeth.

"For weeks after that you kept talking about it. How this was the worst thing that could happen to a mother. And, well, I think it had a lot to do with what happened later."

"Say the word," Robin said. She was about to fling her mother's horrid phone at Evan's face.

"What?"

"You always dance around it. Say what happened."

"You know what happened, Robin." Evan rolled his eyes. "Are you making *me* face my own trauma now? Are we in therapy?"

"*Your* trauma?" Robin spluttered. "*I* had a miscarriage, Evan, not you. In fact, you were gone when it happened. As usual. I was alone in that hospital when the doctors told me . . ." Tears clogged her throat.

She wouldn't cry now. Not in this damn crowd. She cleared her throat. "My miscarriage had nothing to do with Kathy's disappearance."

Evan's eyes softened. "You kept thinking about how Claire felt. It scared you. And you were seeing all these other messed-up kids during your sessions. Surely you of all people know how much thoughts and psychology can affect the body. What happened could be your own body trying to prevent your fears from coming true."

"That's definitely possible," Mom said. "Robin, you remember when you used to get headaches at school before math tests. I always assumed it was your body's reaction to—"

"I fixed your phone," Robin snapped, handing it to her. "It should work now. Though I really think you should get a new one. Now I have to go."

"You haven't even eaten your pie," Glenda said. "You should really try it."

"Stay for a bit more, Robin," Mom said. "Don't be rude. I've taught you better than that."

Robin shot to her feet, her temper completely frayed. "No. I see what you did here, Mom. Very subtle, inviting me over when Evan and Glenda are here. Sorry, but I can't play along, I have other plans."

Mom touched her chest, tears instantly springing to her eyes. "I don't know what you're saying. I didn't *plan* anything. I invited Evan and Glenda earlier this week. I didn't even know you would show up."

"It's true," Glenda said. "She called us two days ago."

"And I needed help with the phone." Mom's voice trembled. "I tried to fix it on my own, but it's not easy at my age to learn these things."

All three of them were staring at Robin with a mixture of pity and accusation. This was what her mother did best. She could make Robin feel like a crazy person, accusing Mom of so-called imaginary plots.

"Fine," Robin said. "I still have to go. Bye."

She turned around and stormed out, the familiar mixture of guilt and rage already washing over her. As she stomped off, something caught her eye.

The dollhouse in her mother's bedroom.

Behind her, she heard Mom's muffled voice saying something about all the time and effort she put into raising her.

She gritted her teeth and glanced behind her. No one was coming after her. No one was looking. She stepped into the bedroom and quickly crossed it to the dollhouse.

She snatched the tiny kitchen table and the three small wooden chairs, thinking of how Kathy had placed the dolls in the kitchen. Then she took the double bed from the dollhouse's main bedroom. And as an afterthought, she took the girl's bed from the kid's room as well. Her hands were now full, but she didn't dare stuff the delicate furniture into her purse.

Instead, she stepped back and walked to the front door, furtively glancing behind her, feeling like the worst daughter in the world.

Chapter 15

The media said that Kathy returned "home" after she had been "abducted." They said that Kathy had been held against her will for over a year. They said that she was now healing.

Kathy's so-called abductor read another article about the girl, teeth grinding in fury.

The headlines were all the same. *Missing Daughter Reunited with Her Family.* Or *Girl Kidnapped Aged Eight Miraculously Returned Home.*

Here was a headline suggestion for you. *Girl Returned to Neglecting Family.* Here was another one, more clickbaity, just like you media moguls liked it—*Ten Reasons Why Kathy Stone's Life Is Much Worse after Return to Biological Parents.*

What did they even know? Did they spend the past year with Kathy, giving her the parenting she deserved? Did they care for her when she was sick, read her bedtime stories, cook her meals?

Did they give her handmade dolls just like the one she was carrying when they found her?

The guy who found her was happy to talk to reporters, to tell them how she clutched that doll, wouldn't let it go. Of course she wouldn't, because she loved that doll. She appreciated it because it was special. And she probably missed the second one, the other doll she left behind.

The doll that was right here, on this table. Waiting for Kathy.

Here was another headline for you bastards. *Girl Reunited with Her Second Doll after Being Taken Again from Her Undeserving Parents.*

Because, yes, Kathy would not remain with Claire and Pete Stone. They were a dysfunctional couple who couldn't even stay together for a year without their daughter. Kids shouldn't serve as glue to keep their parents together.

Sure, mistakes had been made in the past year. Exposing Kathy to all that violence hadn't been a good idea. And leaving her alone in that shed . . . well, that was probably the reason she got away. Definitely a bad call.

Next time, it would be better.

But it would have to happen soon. If the girl began to talk again, it would ruin everything. That risk was even greater now, with Robin seeing her. Robin could get her to speak.

Kathy and Robin would have to be watched. Until an opportunity presented itself.

And then Kathy would be taken again. By someone who actually loved her.

Chapter 16

Robin wasn't sure who looked more tired—Kathy or Claire. Both had bloodshot and puffy eyes, their faces pale. Kathy seemed tense and wary, her entire body tight as a spring. Claire, on the other hand, seemed drained, her shoulders slumped.

"Come in." Robin smiled at them pleasantly. "Would you like something to drink? It's really hot today."

She'd heard what had happened at Melody's place, both from Melody and from Claire. The versions predictably differed, but Robin could read between the lines and figure out the chain of events on her own. Kathy had reacted badly to Melody's loud, energetic sons. Triggered, she perceived them as an immediate threat, which made her fight-or-flight impulse kick in. And possibly because she was cornered in Amy's room, she chose to fight, her weapon of choice being a sharp pencil.

Robin could relate. Melody's boys made her own fight-or-flight instinct raise its head.

The rest she'd learned from a tearful phone call with Claire the night before. Pete had shouted at Kathy and yanked the pencil away from her, which made her curl into a tight ball and refuse to move. They had to carry her to the car, and now Kathy refused to leave Claire's side again and seemed to shrink whenever Pete was around her. She hardly slept at night.

Robin gave them both ice-cold water and led them to the playroom.

"Kathy, how's the bubble training going?" Robin asked. "Are you practicing every day?"

Kathy hesitated, then nodded.

"Do you want to show me your skills?"

"We're out of bubble soap," Claire said. "I used some dish soap mixed with water, but it's not as good."

"Oh, okay, I have some refill," Robin said. "And I'll give you your own refill before you leave. Dish soap isn't for professionals like Kathy." She raised her eyebrow at her.

Kathy gave her a tiny, amused smile.

Robin retrieved the refill bottle and filled Kathy's container. "Okay, let's see it."

Kathy took a deep breath and blew softly for a few seconds, filling the room with bubbles.

"Nineteen!" Robin said. "Very nice. Do you want to try again?"

She watched Kathy attentively as the girl blew bubbles twice more. The girl relaxed quickly. She seemed to feel relatively safe with Robin in the playroom, and the bubble breathing exercise smoothed out the wariness she carried around with her.

"Kathy, today I thought we can let your mom rest in the living room while we play here," Robin said. "Is that okay?"

Kathy considered that, then nodded.

Robin glanced at Claire. "You can make yourself some tea or coffee in the kitchen if you want."

"Thank you," Claire said. She was obviously grateful for more than just the coffee. She left the room, and Robin shut the door behind them.

Kathy was already crossing the playroom to the small plastic table. She sat down and picked up the container of red finger paint. She popped the lid open, then took a sheet of paper and poured the red paint on it.

"You are putting the red, sticky paint on the blank page," Robin said.

Kathy let it trickle until there was a large blob of red on the page. She put the container away and gazed at the red splotch, her shoulders tensing up, her breath becoming quicker.

"In this room, only you decide what happens with the red, sticky paint," Robin said. "You control the paint. You decide if you want to touch it or leave it there or just throw it away."

Claire had told Robin that Noah's leg bled after Kathy stabbed him with the pencil. Melody had told her it looked like a slaughterhouse. How did Kathy remember it?

After staring at the paint for a while, Kathy carefully touched the paint with one finger and then gazed at it. She touched thumb to finger.

"You touched the red paint with your fingers," Robin said. "You decided to smear it on your fingertips."

Kathy proceeded to touch it some more, and then, as she had in the previous session, she smeared it on the page with her palms in circular motions until the page was completely covered in a red swirl.

Once she was done, Kathy immediately got up and went to the bathroom and washed the paint off. The intentness of her actions, both earlier and now, made Robin think she had planned to do this before-hand. Smear her hands with paint. Wash the paint away, cleaning her-self. Robin made a mental note to buy a batch of red finger paint. After washing her hands clean, Kathy glanced at the cabinet. Robin opened it and handed her the nail file, which Kathy used to remove the excess paint from under her fingernails, just like last time.

Satisfied, Kathy stepped back into the playroom and, with no hesitation, beelined to the dollhouse. She paused in front of it and then carefully picked up one of the tiny kitchen chairs that Robin had filched. She scrutinized it, her eyes widening with wonder.

"I got some new furniture for the house," Robin said lightly. "Do you like it?"

Kathy put the kitchen chair back and then examined the rest of the house. She ran her finger along the girl's bed, which Robin had placed in one of the rooms.

Unlike her mother's dollhouse, Robin's didn't have enough rooms to have a different bedroom for the kids *and* a living room. So Robin had ended up placing the girl's bed in the living room with the small plastic TV. Kathy looked thoughtful, then took the bed out of the house, placing it to the side. Next, she examined the double bed, which Robin had placed in the room at the top floor of the house, and put it back in the attic.

Then Kathy went over to the shelves of toys. Her movements, again, were very purposeful. She picked up the toys one by one. The mother figure with the cake, the little girl, the ballerina, the farmer . . . all the figures except for the evil clown. She carried them over, placing them in the kitchen. She did her best to place them on the new chairs, once even smiling with delight when she realized that the chair fit the plastic girl toy perfectly. That done, she turned back to the shelves and picked up the evil clown. She held it, her fist clenched tight. Was she worried that the villain might escape?

"In this room, you decide where the toys go and what they do. You decide what happens to them."

Kathy paused for a second, looking at the clown figure in her hand. Then she went over and placed it in the living room of the dollhouse.

"The clown man is alone in the living room," Robin said. "All the others are together in the kitchen."

Kathy shifted the toys in the kitchen, playing with them. She tried sitting them on the different chairs, mimed actions that could have been the toys eating or making food. She seemed to relax as she did so, the corner of her lip curling with the hint of a smile. As Robin had intuited, Kathy was clearly fascinated with the dollhouse, even more now that it was partly furnished with the intricate furniture.

This gave Robin an idea.

"The house is still a bit empty," she said. "Maybe you should bring some toys from home when you come here again, to fill it up. What do you think?"

Kathy seemed to take a long time to think about this suggestion. Finally, she nodded at Robin.

This task would make Kathy think about the dollhouse while she was at home, maintaining an invisible thread between the playroom and the girl. It would help strengthen Kathy's bond with the playroom. And if she really did bring something next time, it could also shed some light on what was on her mind.

After a while, Kathy took a step back and examined the dollhouse. Then she picked up the clown figure again and traipsed him over to the kitchen.

"The clown man joins the rest of the toys in the kitchen."

Kathy picked up the plastic farmer figure. She turned it upside down, and held it with its leg touching the clown's hand, as if he was holding the farmer by his ankle. Then she walked the clown back to the living room, with the farmer being dragged behind him.

Robin contemplated saying the clown man and the farmer were walking together, trying to reflect the scene with a positive spin. But that was clearly far from what Kathy was playacting. Robin wanted, first and foremost, to let Kathy know she was paying attention. And that she could handle anything Kathy showed her. "The clown man is taking the farmer to the living room."

Kathy placed the clown in the living room and the farmer lying at his feet. For a second she seemed uncertain. Then she turned around and scanned the playroom. She paced back and forth along the shelves. Finally she paused by the sandbox. Had Kathy lost interest in the dollhouse? She'd been interested in the sandbox last time.

"Do you want to play in the sandbox?"

Kathy glanced at Robin, frowning. Then she turned away from the sandbox. There was an assortment of buckets and colored shovels near the sandbox, alongside a toy toolbox with plastic tools. Kathy knelt by the toolbox and rummaged in it, coming up with a small light-blue drill. She pushed the drill's trigger switch, and the bulky yellow drill head turned around slowly, whirring.

"The drill head turns whenever you press the trigger. You decide when it works."

Kathy paced back to the dollhouse and manipulated the clown figure so his arm was outstretched. Then she held the drill as if he was holding it.

The drill was even bigger than the clown figure, but that didn't make the scene she was depicting any less unsettling. It looked like he was holding an enormous gun.

"The clown man is holding the blue drill."

Kathy tilted the clown and the drill so that the drill tip touched the farmer's head. It was a complex maneuver for her tiny hands, with one finger on the drill's trigger, but after a bit of effort, the tip of her tongue protruding between her lips, she managed it. Her focus was absolute. Robin wasn't sure Kathy even heard her when she said, "Oh, no, the clown man is pointing the blue drill at the farmer's head."

Kathy pressed the trigger, and the drill head spun, making the farmer topple and drop off the table on which the dollhouse stood.

"The clown man hurt the farmer with the drill," Robin said. "The farmer must be afraid."

Kathy glared at the floor, clenching her jaw. Then, with brusque impatience she picked the farmer up, placing him lying down where he'd been before. Then she repeated her maneuver with the clown holding the drill to the farmer's head, except this time she was careful not to touch the farmer. Then she pressed the trigger again. The drill whirred at the clown's hand, a fraction of an inch away from the farmer's head.

"Poor farmer, the clown man is hurting his head with the drill," Robin said.

Kathy kept pressing the trigger. The drill whirred on and on. After a few seconds, Kathy's hands trembled with the effort of her uncomfortable position, but still she held the drill, breathing fast through her nose.

Robin kept her eyes on the girl, unease growing within her. Over the years, she'd seen many unsettling things in her playroom. But this silent girl's absorbed demeanor as she enacted the violence between the toys drove a chill into Robin's heart. She found herself feeling split. Part of her had to remain calm, to keep showing the girl it was *okay*. That Robin could handle whatever Kathy showed her.

But the other part of her was watching aghast, the jagged corners of the moment scraping against Robin's own mind.

"The clown man keeps hurting the farmer with the drill." Robin kept her tone neutral, almost detached. Injecting a bit of sadness and empathy for the plastic farmer. "What a bad clown man."

She expected Kathy to put the drill down soon, but Kathy kept holding it, the drill whirring. Finally, the drill dipped, touching the farmer, and he skittered to the floor again.

Kathy paused, then picked him up, placing him in the same position. She was about to replay the same scene for the third time. Robin's heart skipped a beat.

"Let's try to think of how we can help the farmer," she said, forcing herself to smile pleasantly. "Can you figure a way to help the farmer so maybe the clown man would stop hurting him?"

Kathy gazed at Robin, looking entirely lost.

"Maybe someone could help the farmer out," Robin suggested.

Kathy hesitantly looked at the toys still lying on the shelves. She put down the clown and the drill and walked over to the shelves. Then, as if on impulse, she picked up the largest toy on the shelf, a two-headed dragon. Then one of a tall wrestler. And a tank. And a big plastic shark.

The figures filled her hands, and she carried them over to the table with the dollhouse, scattering them on top of it. Then she returned to the shelves and selected even more large, threatening toys. A warlock. A barbarian with an enormous sword. A long rubbery snake.

She placed them in a circle and then placed the clown and the farmer within the circle.

"All the big, strong toys came over," Robin said.

What followed was a hectic mess. Kathy grabbed the toys, smashing them into the clown, piling them up onto him. Some fell off the table and were left forgotten.

"The toys are stopping the clown man. He was a bad clown man, because he tried to hurt the farmer, and he has to be stopped."

Finally, the clown was completely covered in a pileup of toys—the shark's head protruding from one side, half the dragon on the other side.

"All the big toys stopped the clown man," Robin said. "He won't be able to hurt the farmer again."

Kathy let out a long, shuddering breath and smiled at Robin, her lips trembling. A tear trickled down her cheek.

"If the farmer wants, he can go back to the party in the kitchen now," Robin said, swallowing. "The big strong toys won't let the bad clown man hurt him again."

Kathy picked up the farmer and examined the dollhouse.

She stepped away from it and went over to the sandbox. She knelt beside it and shoved the farmer deep into the sand. Then she piled more sand on top of it, leaving it buried under a low mound.

It was clear that as far as Kathy was concerned, the plastic farmer wasn't about to come back.

Chapter 17

Ellie held her phone in her hand, heart thudding in her chest. She should make the call. Tell them about him. They would listen, right? After all, little Kathy had disappeared. They would be desperate to hear *anyone* with information.

Anyone? Really?

Even her?

Because she knew what her parents would immediately say. They would say she was making it up. That she was trying to draw attention to herself. Like they repeatedly said throughout her childhood. And other people in town would point out that time at school, with the graffiti. And maybe someone would also mention her ex, Norman, who constantly told vicious stories about her. It had been such a relief to get out of town, away to college, and to see that some people could appreciate her and have her back.

But in Bethelville, everyone had already formed their opinions about her. And she was actually considering pointing an accusing finger at *him*? Mr. Perfect? The guy who practically everyone in town adored?

They would never accept that. And then they'd start to wonder what *she* was doing there, where she shouldn't have been.

Oh yeah, they'd listen to anyone. But they wouldn't necessarily *believe* anyone. And there was no way in hell they'd believe her.

Still, she had to tell someone, right? Time was of the essence. Maybe not her parents. Or the police. She considered telling Uncle Jimmie. He would believe her. He was the only one in town who listened to her. Who took her word over someone else's.

But he would also wonder what she was doing there. And she had no good answer for him. Only bad answers all around.

She pocketed her phone. It wasn't like it would change anything. After all, *Mr. Perfect* hadn't taken Kathy. Even if the police followed up on her information, they'd quickly see that. It was better to stay quiet.

How would it feel? To have your child disappear like that? A perfect, sweet, lovely girl like Kathy? Ellie couldn't even imagine it. When she babysat Kathy, she never let the girl out of her sight. Claire should have done the same. How could she let anything happen to her daughter?

Uncle Jimmie once told her that she shouldn't judge her own parents until she was a mother herself. So maybe she shouldn't judge Claire either.

Though having babysat Kathy several times, Ellie had seen things. Heard things. Claire and Pete were far from the perfect parents.

Chapter 18

The dream started out innocently enough. She was a child again, in her parents' house. Looking at the dollhouse. Marveling at the intricate details. At the gorgeous miniature furniture.

Finally, not able to stop herself, she began playing with it. She placed figurines from her playroom in the dollhouse. Sitting one in a chair in the living room, bathing another in the tiny bathtub. The third she placed in the tiny bed . . .

Which broke. A tiny crack; maybe Mom wouldn't notice . . . but there was a smudge on the bathtub. And the living room chair was somehow missing. Now the entire house was falling apart, floors caving in, wallpaper rotting, furniture peeling. Just because she played with it. Why had she done it? It was not a toy. It was not a toy!

Footsteps behind her. Mom would go in, and Robin knew what she would do when she saw what had happened. She would *hurt* her. She would pull her hair and scratch her face and pinch her arm and—

She woke up, heart lurching.

It was unsettling. Mom had never hurt her physically as a child. This was one of those things that she and Melody disagreed on. Melody claimed that she used to hurt them when Dad wasn't around. Supposedly she would kick them if they were too loud or pull their hair viciously when they annoyed her. Melody claimed Mom did it all the time. She recalled one specific occasion when she ripped off a clump of Robin's red hair.

Robin had no recollection of anything remotely like it. As a therapist, she knew very well how deceptive memories could be. Still, if Mom had done those things, Robin would have remembered at least some of it, wouldn't she?

She checked the time, and it was 1:42 a.m. She had to try to get back to sleep.

◆ ◆ ◆

Well, she hadn't been able to go back to sleep. For the entire night.

All in all she slept for two hours and ten minutes—not even long enough to watch an entire film. Well, maybe if it was a medium-length film. Robin tried to remember the last film she'd seen. Something with that actor, wasn't it? The cute one? She couldn't remember the film's name, or the actor's. Or the film's length, for that matter, though it was longer than two hours and ten minutes, she was sure of that much.

She went shopping because she'd run out of dog food. She'd also run out of human food, if she had to be honest with herself, but she was mostly there for dog food.

The supermarket was not the place to be with little sleep.

The bright fluorescent lighting was vicious, and her vision skittered. Her cart had three working wheels and one that was a free spirit who wanted to escape and tour the world. The cash registers bleeped an endless cacophony of bleeps. Those intermingled with the tantrum a child was throwing in the next aisle.

Robin was close to tears.

She'd jotted down a quick shopping list. And then she'd left it on the table and driven off to the supermarket. And although it had been less than twenty minutes ago, she couldn't think of one item on that list besides the dog food. Milk, maybe? Toilet paper? Pasta?

Well, the kid throwing a tantrum was in the aisle with all the pasta, so the hell with pasta. She could do without pasta for a while.

In fact, she would skip everything. She would grab the dog food, and that would be it.

It took her a few seconds to recall where the dog food was, the thoughts slow, as if her brain was submerged in molasses. She trudged over there at a snail's pace. Her exhaustion made her paranoid. She kept feeling as if people were looking at her as she went past them. And then there was a shopping cart traffic jam caused by a man who placed his in the middle of the aisle as he examined cereal boxes. Men shouldn't be allowed to go shopping in the supermarket. They should be shot on sight if they walked in. Robin hated everyone.

So here was the dog food, and which food did Menny like best? Was it lamb and shrimp? Or duck? She tried to read the labels. Everything was staticky, the letters jumbling together, the cash registers bleeping, a yeasty smell that should have been good but just made her nauseated.

She grabbed the green bag, because maybe that was the color of the bag back home, and tossed it into the cart. On the way to the cash registers she saw the toilet paper, so she grabbed a pack, too, because that was probably one of the items on the list.

The lines for the registers were ridiculous. She could either stand behind a woman whose shopping cart overflowed with produce or get behind three other people whose carts were half-full. Which should she choose? Whichever she chose would be the slower line for sure.

She got behind the three other people. Because that woman with the overflowing cart struck her as one of those people who, halfway through, would recall six different things she forgot to get.

"Hey, Robin!"

Oh shit.

The woman next in line was Tara. Who was nice. Robin liked Tara. They'd done yoga together for two years. And one time they'd bonded because the woman in front of them in class had farted throughout the entire session, nearly killing them. But Robin couldn't handle other people at the moment.

"Hey," she said, plastering a smile on her face. "How are you doing?"

"I'm good! What about you?"

"Oh, great."

"Getting food for Menny?"

"Yeah." Robin chuckled. "You know how it is." Words that made no sense in the context of the conversation. But Tara seemed content.

"How *is* Menny? How old is he?"

"He's seven."

"He's so cute."

Robin nodded. She realized she was still smiling from the beginning of the conversation.

Tara lowered her voice. "I heard you are seeing Kathy Stone."

Was there anyone her mother hadn't told? Robin looked down at her cart. No help there. "Um, I can't really talk about that."

"Patient confidentiality, I totally get it," Tara said. "It's a good thing someone's helping her. Especially after what happened to your nephew."

How had Tara heard about that? Did Melody tell people? Or Fred? No, it was much simpler. Melody had four kids. And they would have told their friends about the pencil stabbing. This was not a story that could be kept silent. Damn it. "It wasn't a big deal. Just a misunderstanding."

"Personally, if I was Claire? I'd want a clean slate. Pete had a job offer in Indianapolis. They could start fresh. It would be good for little Kathy too. Get away from the bad memories."

"I don't know if it's a good solution. And memories aren't necessarily triggered by geography." Robin caught the side glance of a man as he entered the supermarket. He hurriedly turned away when she met his eyes.

A sudden realization bloomed in her mind. She wasn't being para-noid. People *were* looking at her. Because she'd become a player in the number one conversation topic in Bethelville. She'd gone from being nobody to being the therapist who was working with Kathy Stone.

"Um, Tara, what did you hear about—"

"Hey, Tara!" A voice from behind them. "Oh, and Robin! What's up?"

It was Ellie, the waitress from Jimmie's Café. She stood behind them, hugging a handful of items in her hands.

"Hey, Ellie!" Tara's tone shifted, got higher. "What up, girl."

What up, girl? Was Tara trying to act younger for Ellie? Robin smiled at Ellie. "Hey, Ellie. How are you?"

"I'm good. Um . . . this is so stupid . . . Robin, would you mind if I put my stuff in your cart for now? I thought I could manage without a cart, but it turns out I have way too many items."

"Sure." Robin gestured at the cart. "Feel free. All I have here is Menny's food and toilet paper."

"You made it sound like it's Menny's toilet paper." Ellie gratefully put her stuff in the cart. Macaroni and cheese, ice cream, cream cheese, eggs . . . eggs! That was one of the items on Robin's list. She could go fetch some now. Or not.

"You know," Tara said. "I think I haven't purchased toilet paper for over a year. Back when COVID started, I bought like . . . a bazillion packs."

"Oh, it was you?" Ellie grinned. "I had to use coffee filters in the bathroom for a while because the stores didn't have any toilet paper left. I guess I can blame you for that."

Robin laughed, and suddenly, horrified, realized she couldn't stop. Her laugh was hysterical. She didn't even remember what Ellie had said that was so funny, but now she was wheezing, out of breath, Tara and Ellie both staring at her as if she was crazy.

"So how's Jimmie?" Robin asked, wiping her eyes.

Ellie rolled her eyes. "He drives me insane. I'm working on the café's social media pages. *He* asked me to do it. But now every time I snap a picture, he starts moaning about how my generation can't enjoy the moment without posting it on Facebook."

"Well . . . ," Tara said.

"I don't even use Facebook," Ellie muttered.

The supermarket's automatic doors slid open, and a mother holding her daughter's hand walked in. It took Robin a second to realize they were Claire and Kathy.

Kathy's eyes were wide and alert, her head whipping left and right. For Kathy's hypervigilant senses, the supermarket was probably as hostile and exhausting as it currently was for Robin. The girl's eyes locked on Robin, and she froze.

"Hey, Claire," Tara said.

"Oh!" Claire turned to look at them. Her eyes swept the three of them, and she smiled. "Hi! How are you?"

"Good!" Tara said brightly. "Yeah, good."

"Just shopping," Ellie added helpfully. "How are you two?"

"We're good!" Claire said.

She was so different from the Claire who took her daughter to Robin's playroom. That Claire was raw, vulnerable, tired. But this Claire seemed cheerful and full of energy.

Kathy, however, was anything but. Ever since laying eyes on Robin, she had remained frozen, her body tense, jaw clenched tight. Her eyes had widened even more and skittered around like she was an animal desperately looking for an escape. Robin could imagine how the girl felt. Kathy connected her with the playroom. A place where they tackled delicate issues but where Kathy was in complete control. Here in the supermarket, Kathy probably already felt unsafe. Seeing Robin there must have confused her.

"It's nice to see you both," she said pleasantly.

"You too," Claire said. She tried to move on, but Kathy didn't budge, anchoring her to the spot.

"Kathy, let's go," Claire said.

Kathy started and stepped back, toward the exit.

"No, honey, we need to buy some groceries," Claire said.

Kathy was dragging her more forcefully now, her breathing erratic.

"Kathy . . ." Claire's facade slipped, and Robin glimpsed the anxiety and desperation the woman had tried to keep hidden from prying eyes. Claire finally gave up, letting Kathy drag her outside.

"I wonder what freaked her out like that," Tara said.

Robin couldn't really comment on that, but Ellie already realized the reason. "I think she was confused seeing Robin here."

Tara cleared her throat. "Oh. That makes sense. When I met my therapist on the street once, I felt really weird. It must be even more confusing for a little girl."

Tara and Ellie exchanged glances. This incident would supply more fuel for the rumors that zipped around Bethelville. People would talk about how the traumatized girl had a meltdown when she saw her shrink in the supermarket. And how Claire couldn't control her and had to leave the store. Maybe they would say Pete would have been able to control Kathy, because he didn't coddle her like Claire. And maybe that it was Robin's fault for treating a girl who lived so close to her they were bound to meet each other on the street.

She knew the anger and bitterness she was feeling were mostly due to her weariness, but knowing the cause didn't make her thoughts any less frustrating. If her mother hadn't told everyone she was treating Kathy, this wouldn't have been a thing. It was one thing to gossip with her, but when her mother gossiped about her, it drove her insane.

Ellie and Tara were talking about a TV show they both watched, and Robin kept silent. Then Tara reached the register.

"Robin, do you want to go before me?" she asked. "You have only two items."

"Sure, thanks," Robin blurted. Logically, she knew Tara was being nice. But an insidious thought whispered in her ear that Tara let her go first only because she and Ellie were conspiring to gossip about her once she left.

A good rule of thumb was that if her inner monologue came up with the word *conspire*, it probably meant she was being paranoid.

She needed sleep.

She quickly paid for the dog food and the toilet paper. Ellie's stuff was still in her cart, so Robin left it behind, carrying the bulky packages in her hands, as she desperately tried to remember where she'd parked the car. She dropped the package of toilet paper and had to bend down to pick it up, and then a man asked if he could help and she half shrieked at him that she was *fine*.

By the time she got to the car, she was a walking pulsing raw nerve, and it was all her mother's fault. She would go and tell her that right now.

She drove to Mom's place and slammed the car door extra hard when she got out, which was satisfying. Then she marched to the front door and opened it with her key.

Charged with fury, she paused at the entrance, listening. A muffled sound of water running. Her mother was in the shower. She would have to wait for her to finish. She always took extralong showers; it would take her ages.

It occurred to Robin she could lie down on her mother's bed. Maybe nod off; God knew she needed the sleep. Also, a little sane voice inside her brain whispered that arguing with Mom right now, when she was exhausted, wasn't the best idea.

She stumbled to Mom's bedroom, about to drop onto the bed, when the dollhouse caught her eye.

A few minutes later, she walked out the front door, carrying the enormous dollhouse in her arms, a turmoil of vindication and fear in her gut.

Chapter 19

As a child, Robin would stand and stare for hours at Mom's beautiful dollhouse. Her eyes would caress the intricate furniture, the thoughtful placement of each piece within each tiny room. Her mother would sometimes spend days searching for just the right handwoven dollhouse carpet to match the new stamp-size drapes, or for a new hand-carved desk for the study.

Robin was allowed to look, but never to touch. It was a special kind of torture, to be able to scrutinize this thing of beauty without being able to play with it.

Kathy now stared at the dollhouse in a very similar way. As if she couldn't believe she would be allowed to touch it. In her hands, she gripped a closed shoebox she had brought to the session. This box apparently contained things for the dollhouse, as Robin had suggested. Claire had told Robin that Kathy spent the past few days crafting items for the dolls in the playroom. Once Claire had realized what Kathy was trying to do, she took her to a craft shop, and they bought supplies for Kathy's new project.

"You can play with the dollhouse if you want," Robin told Kathy gently.

She'd placed the new dollhouse on a table next to the old one, in case Kathy preferred playing with the one she'd used previously. The two houses looked so strange next to each other. It almost seemed like a poor neighborhood that had been partly gentrified. Robin's own dollhouse seemed like a shithole next to the carved wooden Victorian mansion she'd taken from her mother.

For a while, she wasn't sure if Kathy heard her. The girl kept staring, swallowing every single detail. There were no dolls in Mom's dollhouse. She had never purchased dolls to live in it. As a child, it drove Robin crazy. Why would she work so hard to create this perfect mansion for dolls and then keep it empty?

"Do you want to choose some toys to live in the house?" Robin asked.

Kathy glanced at her, then gazed down at the shoebox in her hands. She placed it on the table between the two houses and then, to Robin's surprise, turned away from them and walked over to the small drawing table. She placed a blank sheet on the table and poured a large dollop of red paint on it. Repeating the ritual from the previous sessions, she smeared red paint all over the page with both hands, then washed them at the sink in the bathroom. A cleansing ritual.

That done, Kathy dried her hands very thoroughly and returned to the dollhouse. She gently plucked a miniature grandfather clock from the living room and examined it, running a finger across the carved edges of the clock. She gasped as she realized she could open the door to the pendulum. She opened and closed it several times, then placed it back in the living room. Then she gently lay her fingers on the double bed in the miniature parents' bedroom.

Robin had done very similar things the night before. Finally, after decades, she could play with the dollhouse without the terror of knowing her mom might catch her in the act. She'd inspected each piece of furniture, marveling at the craftsmanship and beauty. It took her a while to realize she was crying. Partially for the girl who had desperately wanted to do this throughout her childhood. And partly for the grown woman who realized it was too late now, that it just wasn't the same.

She could appreciate the marvelous toys, but she could no longer really *play* with them.

It wasn't too late for Kathy.

After inspecting the house carefully, the girl strode briskly to the shelves and selected the figures. The little girl, the baking mother, the ballet dancer . . . all the figures from before. Except for the farmer, who was left untouched. Kathy took the five figures to the dollhouse and for a while seemed content to just playact with them.

"The mother made a cake for the cop and the little girl," Robin reflected. "It looks delicious. They must be so happy to eat such a tasty cake. The ballet dancer is sleeping in the bedroom. Oh, now the girl went to sleep in the children's room. It must be nighttime. They look so tired."

A small smile hovered around the girl's lips. Her face softened, the tension in her body dissipating. At some point she took the lid off her shoebox, rummaged inside, and removed a small square blanket, which she draped over the girl lying in the bed.

"Oh, the girl has a new blanket with flowers on it," Robin said. "She must be so happy."

She peered into the shoebox, wondering what else Kathy had made for the dolls. A small pillow. A matchbox that seemed to be decorated to look like a bed. Some clothing—Robin could glimpse a dress, a shirt, a long necktie, a pair of pants. The amount of focus and care Kathy must have put into these little items was impressive.

She had also brought a handful of items she didn't make herself—a few marbles, a thimble that could function as a large mug, Play-Doh, a bracelet that was probably intended to be a large necklace, a plastic tree, several stickers. Kathy had filled the box with things she could use for the house.

Kathy turned away from the dollhouse and glanced into the smaller, cruder one that Robin owned. She rummaged in it and took out the small plastic TV. She placed it inside the big dollhouse's living room.

The clunky, ugly plastic toy looked out of place among the handcrafted furniture. Mom would have had a heart attack.

"They now have a television. They can watch it together."

Kathy glanced at Robin. Her expression, twisted in frustration and anger, took Robin by surprise. Was Kathy irritated by the discrepancy between the crude plastic TV and the rest of the delicate furniture? Even if she was, it seemed like the TV was important for Kathy to include.

Now Kathy turned back to the shelves and grabbed the evil clown figure. She took it to the dollhouse and placed it inside the living room. It was too large for the tiny furniture, but Kathy managed to prop it up so that it leaned against the couch.

"The scary clown is watching television in the living room," Robin said.

Kathy removed the Monopoly Man and the Wonder Woman figurine from the living room, placing them in the kitchen.

"Everyone is leaving the room with the clown," Robin said. "They know they should be careful with him."

Kathy rummaged in the shoebox and took out the small bracelet. It looked like something she owned in the days before her abduction—a delicate silver ornament with a tiny dolphin locket. Robin watched as Kathy picked up the little girl. The bracelet would be too large to be a necklace for the small figure.

But then Kathy carefully wrapped one side of the bracelet around the little girl's leg. She encircled the other side of the bracelet around the foot of the coffee table in the living room.

The bracelet wasn't meant to be a necklace. It was meant to be a chain.

"The scary clown tied the little girl to the table," Robin said, controlling the tremor that threatened to invade her voice. "The girl must be very frightened."

Kathy grabbed the clown and traipsed him up to the second floor, where the ballet dancer was lying in the bed. As she did before, she tilted him. She placed his hand on the dancer's leg, then walked the clown away. The dancer dragged behind him.

"The bad clown is dragging the dancer away from her bed," Robin said. "He's hurting her."

Kathy walked the clown and the dancer out of the house, then paused. She put them both down, then peered into the small kitchen. Carefully, she pinched something from the kitchen table and took it out. Robin had to look closer to see what Kathy was holding.

The night before, Robin found out that one of the drawers in the toy kitchen cabinet held minuscule silverware, each piece smaller than her fingernails. She'd placed a few of them on the kitchen table, amusing herself by setting a table for two.

Now Kathy held one of the toothpick-thin knives. She placed it in the clown's hand and viciously raised and lowered his arm, the knife sticking repeatedly into the plastic ballet dancer.

"Oh, no!" Robin said. "The bad clown is hurting the dancer with the knife. That's terrible."

She considered intervening, trying to coach Kathy into playacting a better version of the story. But no, the first phase *had* to be showing Kathy that Robin could handle what the girl was showing her. This was part of what Robin had to be for Kathy. A container for the horrible images etched in Kathy's mind.

After miming the stabbing half a dozen times, Kathy let the tiny knife clatter onto the table.

"The bad clown dropped the knife," Robin said. "Okay. Do you want—"

But Kathy was already rummaging in her shoebox. Taking out the tiny tie she'd made. No, now that Robin could see it clearly, it wasn't a tie, it was . . .

No, there was no way. Ice formed in her chest.

Kathy kept rummaging in the box and took out the plastic tree. A pair of miniature pants clung to it, and Kathy plucked it off impatiently, letting it tumble onto the floor. And then she knotted what Robin had originally assumed was a tie to one of the tree's green plastic branches.

It was a noose.

Kathy placed the tree with the noose next to the dancer and then tried to mime as if the clown was placing the noose over the dancer's head. It was too complicated. The noose kept unraveling from the branch, and the dancer dropped from Kathy's fingers twice. Finally, she put the clown away and looped the noose around the ballet dancer's head.

She let go.

The dancer swung back and forth from the tree's limb.

Stabbed and then hanged.

Just like the influencer, Haley Parks, whose body had been found in the forest a few weeks before.

Chapter 20

From his car down the street, he watched the girl leave Robin Hart's house. She was holding Claire Stone's hand. Robin stood in her doorway, waving at the girl. Smiling. He liked that. It was a good scene. He imagined the scene as it would look on screen. The girl leaving the house, looking back at the camera. A close-up on her fingers as she clutched her mother's hand tightly. And then a shot of Robin standing in the doorway, wearing that thin shirt, the top button open. Her hair fluttering in the wind.

There was no wind now, but sometimes, you had to make allowances for the scriptwriter's creative flair.

He watched Robin until she shut the door. Claire and the girl drove off. He jotted the time in his spiral notebook and flipped it to the passenger seat. He was about to drive after them, then changed his mind. Stayed in his spot, watching Robin's house.

Movement by one of the windows. He watched her as she stood in the kitchen in front of her fridge.

He took out his phone, opened her profile on Facebook, stared at her profile photo. The camera loved her, no doubt about that. He licked his lips. She was perfect for his next project.

Leaning back in the car seat, he watched as Robin moved through the house, turning off the lights. Going somewhere?

The front door opened again, and she stepped out, her dog on a leash. She locked the door and started walking down the street, toward the park.

The pen scratched on the notebook's page as he added another entry, this one about Robin. This scene would be more tense. The camera would follow Robin as she walked down the street with her dog. The camera would zoom in on her from behind, juddering slightly, giving the audience the feeling that *they* were the ones following Robin.

He was breathing hard now, his handwriting becoming sloppy. Watching as she stepped into the park.

Chapter 21

The cloudless sky was indigo blue as Robin walked Menny amid the trees in the park. If she had to be honest with herself, she didn't really walk Menny as much as he walked her. Or rather, dragged her. He had things to do. Trees to pee on. Squirrels to chase. Suspicious rocks to sniff. He was a busy dog. And Robin would have to keep up with his schedule. He pulled her with a steady determination, and Robin half ran to avoid dislocating her wrist.

She hardly noticed where they were going, her mind lost, intent on her session with Kathy.

She was quite sure Kathy had enacted the much-publicized murder of Haley Parks. And the fact that Kathy had brought the tree and the noose with her in that shoebox made it clear this was no accident. Kathy hadn't been simply messing around with the toys in Robin's playroom. She'd had a clear intention in mind.

After she'd playacted through the murder, Robin had suggested they should try and think of a way in which the story that Kathy showed her could have a better ending. And Kathy was happy to do so. This time she found a small rocket ship and mimed it flying with the clown all the way back to the shelves. The ballet dancer was safe from the murderous clown. However, once that was done, Kathy took the dancer's little figure and buried it in the sandbox, like she'd done before with the farmer.

That family of toys Kathy had selected on their first session. It seemed like the killer clown was killing them one by one. At first there were six; now there were four. Did Kathy intend for all of them to die? Would the toys all be buried in the sandbox one after the other until only the little girl remained? Or maybe she wouldn't stop there. Maybe the only survivor by the end would be the evil clown.

Menny led Robin to the park's path. The tree-lined trail was getting dark by this time, the orange sunlight flickering between the branches as Robin stepped deeper into the woods. Menny slowed down, stopping to pee on one tree, sniff the next.

Now that she knew about the tree and the noose in the shoebox, the other items Kathy had brought took on a nefarious meaning. Would the marbles in the box be used to smash a toy's head? Would the thimble turn out to be a mug that held a poisoned drink? Kathy had taken the box with her when she left. Did she intend to bring it next time? Did she want to keep on working on the toy props?

Play therapy was intended to help children work through difficult issues. If Kathy wanted to playact these things, it was her way of coming to terms with her own trauma. And it was Robin's job to gently guide Kathy through it, helping her make sense of her difficult memories. But thinking of Kathy making murder tools for a violent clown at her house made Robin feel uncertain. How should she approach this?

The path led to the Tippecanoe River, and Robin paused for a few seconds, taking in the view. The setting sun's reflection rippled on the river's surface, a ball of molten gold. A trio of birds shot out from one of the trees on the opposite bank, soaring through the sky. Somewhere in the distance, children shouted and laughed.

Robin walked down the path to the riverbank, where a single gazebo stood. She stepped inside and sat on the wooden bench. Someone had carved the names *Jayden* and *Mia* into the wood, with a heart in between. The heart was badly shaped, looking more like an eyeless fox's head. Robin didn't recall having seen this carving the day before. Had this Jayden made his subpar declaration of love today? She wished the happy couple all the best as she fished in her bag for her cigarettes. She placed the cigarette between her lips, then lit it, took a long drag, and exhaled a plume of smoke.

Menny turned to look at her, his eyes focusing on the cigarette in her hand.

"What? Don't judge me." She took another drag of the cigarette. "I'm down to two a day."

He let out a long tragic sigh and settled at her feet, his face a mask of disappointment.

"God, you're so dramatic," Robin said.

How was the Haley Parks murder connected to what Kathy had gone through? The figurine of the little girl had been chained in the living room, where Kathy had been determined to place the television set. Had Kathy been forced to watch the Parks murder reports on the news? It was a conceivable form of twisted abuse. Someone making a little girl watch as the murder was reported. Perhaps hinting that if Kathy didn't behave, the same thing would happen to her.

If that was the case, was the previous session, in which the clown murdered the farmer, also something Kathy had been forced to watch?

Robin could imagine the man who had abducted Kathy as he flipped through the channels until he found this—a news report about a victim of a shooting. And then maybe he hissed in the girl's ear that if she ever tried to escape, he would do *that* to her.

She took out her phone and searched "recent murders on the news."

The results were all over the place, quite literally. She got national reports all over the United States, as well as something in Britain and one thing in France. She decided to google "murders in Indiana" and limited the search results to the past two years.

She quickly learned an uncomfortable statistic. There had been over five hundred murders in Indiana in the past year alone. Some obviously got a lot more press than others. The Haley Parks murder, one of the most prominent murders in 2022 so far, dominated the first page of search results. Many of the other murders had been shootings. Robin skimmed a few headlines, growing more and more upset. If Kathy's kidnapper forced her to watch the news reports about murders, he would face no shortage of them. And nothing even guaranteed he'd only focus on local news.

She registered something as she scrolled through the results. Had she seen the word *drill*?

She scrolled back but couldn't find it now. An unpleasant chill ran down her neck. She'd assumed Kathy had used the drill she'd found in the playroom because it was the closest thing to a gun she could find. But Robin had a few toy soldiers with guns in the playroom. Kathy had surely seen them, but instead she chose the oversize drill. Could that be intentional?

Robin stubbed her cigarette out on the ground. Menny perked his ears, obviously assuming they were about to resume their walk.

"In a minute, buddy," Robin told him. She googled "murder Indiana drill."

There.

It was fairly recent. The body of twenty-five-year-old Gloria Basset had been found floating in the Wabash River. The police originally assumed the victim had been shot to death, but the autopsy uncovered some unusual findings. Those findings were not detailed in the news article, but a police source was quoted saying that "the hole in the victim's cranium was too symmetrical to be the result of a bullet wound. Additionally, no bullet fragments have been recovered." When asked what could cause it, the source suggested an ice pick or a drill.

What if Kathy had been forced to see this news report as well? Robin felt sick. She could only imagine how terrified little Kathy would have been to watch the news report as this was described, and possibly further embellished by her abductor—

No, hang on, that couldn't be.

According to the article, the body of Gloria Basset had been recovered on May 11. That was a full week after Kathy had returned home. It couldn't be related. Robin shook her head and went back to the search results. But all relevant results were related to Gloria Basset's death. Robin ran another Google search, this time omitting the word *Indiana*, and discovered there was something called "drill music" and that a drill rapper had been a suspect in a murder that occurred in London. But that couldn't be related to Kathy's drill scenario.

No, the most logical assumption was the original one, that Kathy had been shown a shooting victim and that she'd used the plastic drill to simulate a gun.

Robin put her phone away. She felt ill. In the past twenty minutes, she'd been exposed to more murders than she had been in the past month. The numerous portraits of victims that popped up in the articles she read all swam together in her mind. She wished she hadn't gone down that rabbit hole. Sure, Robin liked watching the occasional cop show on TV. And when the pandemic started, she'd binged a bunch of true-crime documentaries. But simply reading through recent violent news articles wasn't the same. It was chaotic, pointless, and painful, with no resolution in sight. She felt her faith in humanity waver.

She would have to follow up on her theory, though. If Kathy had been shown news articles, it would be something she'd have to address in future sessions.

Menny leaped to his feet as she got up. They walked back toward the house. The park was even darker than before, and Robin regretted her research yet again. Walking through the shadowy woods was very unsettling after reading about all those murder victims, many who had simply been at the wrong place at the wrong time. Such as a secluded park at night.

She couldn't get Gloria Basset out of her mind. It seemed like a strange coincidence, that Kathy would play out a murder involving a drill after the same thing had been reported on the news. But if the timeline didn't work . . .

There was another simple explanation.

She'd planned to discuss this with Claire and Pete during their guidance session, but Claire had texted her, canceling it. Some emergency at Pete's work. Robin now took out her phone and dialed Claire.

"Hello?" Claire answered her phone almost immediately.

"Hey, Claire, it's Robin."

"Yeah, hi, Robin." In the background, Robin could hear what sounded like the clatter of plates. Claire was probably setting the table for dinner. "I'm sorry we couldn't make it to the session."

"No problem, we'll do it next week. I wanted to ask you . . . Is there a chance Kathy watched the news recently?"

"Watched the news? No, there's no way."

"It's just that the way she played today and in the previous session seemed to be related to—"

"Kathy doesn't watch television *at all*," Claire said, lowering her voice. "The few times I suggested it, she seemed very anxious, so I dropped it. And when Pete once turned on the TV to watch it a week ago, she freaked out, and we turned it off."

"Oh." Robin was taken aback. "You hadn't told me."

"I . . . I didn't mention it specifically. I told you she's afraid of a lot of things. She gets tense whenever we leave the house. Or when there's a loud sound. Or when I turn on the vacuum—"

"I understand," Robin said. "So there's no way she might have seen the news on television. Maybe she saw something online? Or a newspaper headline?"

"Why do you think that? Did she do something that made you think she watched the news?"

Robin hesitated. She didn't want to scare Claire with her suspicions. So far, she'd avoided talking to Claire and Pete about Kathy's imaginary games with the dollhouse. "Some of the imaginary games she played were violent . . . similar to that drawing she drew in our first session."

"Oh, God."

"It's okay. Like I told you, it's her way of processing her trauma. It's a healthy coping mechanism. But some of the things she did seem like they related to a story that has been on the news a lot lately. The one about Haley Parks."

"Haley Parks?" Claire asked, confused. "Who's that?"

That caught Robin by surprise. Practically everyone in Indiana knew about Haley Parks. But then again, before Kathy came back, Claire probably hadn't been very interested in the news. And after Kathy came back, she had had her hands full.

"Haley Parks was a young woman who was murdered a while back, and it's a very prominent story lately. That's why I thought she might have seen it on the news."

"Oh. She might have glimpsed the first page of a newspaper when we were in the supermarket," Claire said. "But other than that, it doesn't sound possible. She's with me all the time. And I don't want her online at all in case she sees something about herself."

"That's smart," Robin agreed. "Okay, then it's probably nothing. Thanks, Claire."

"Was everything all right today at the session? She seemed okay when we came home. More relaxed than usual."

"Yeah, I think we're making good progress. Let me know if you notice anything unusual."

Claire let out a snort. "What isn't unusual lately?"

"Fair enough." Robin grinned. "Anything more unusual than . . . the usual."

"Will do. Thanks, Robin."

"Bye." Robin hung up.

She and Menny had left the woods behind them, to her relief, and were now walking up her well-lit street. She pocketed her phone. So much for her theory. She should have known better anyway. Children's games were usually a mix of imagination and reality. After all, it wasn't like Kathy had been abducted by the actual Joker. The figure of the clown only represented someone Kathy was afraid of. The same person, presumably, who had abducted her. And the plastic drill was a way to demonstrate that person's violence.

But as she reached her home, another explanation occurred to Robin. One that chilled her to her core.

Chapter 22

Detective Nathaniel King was not having a good day.

He recalled that when he showed up to work in the morning, he had been pretty optimistic. The medical examiner had called him to let him know the autopsy report for the Basset murder was finally ready. In Nathaniel's mind this was the moment that things could change for the Basset murder case. They would know what the murder weapon was, which would let them narrow their suspect pool, and Nathaniel could make an arrest. An intense interrogation would follow, and then a confession, and Nathaniel would be able to finally move on. And if he was already fantasizing, the deputy chief might just personally shake his hand and tell him he did a fantastic job, and as a reward he was going on a trip to Hawaii. Immediately after the parade they were throwing in his honor.

Things did not pan out precisely like that.

The final autopsy report did not, in fact, specify a murder weapon. While the ME clearly stated that the hole in Gloria Basset's cranium had not been caused by a bullet, he couldn't be sure what *had* been used. He posited that it had been a sharp, circular, long object. No shit, doc. This is why it took you four weeks to write the report?

This description was too obscure to be of any use at the moment. Nathaniel sighed and went back to what he had been doing for the past two days.

Looking through traffic-camera footage.

Gloria Basset had last been seen at Tenth Street, turning tricks. She had been seen by two of her friends and associates, answering to the names Ginger and Brandy, whose actual names were Adrienne and Betsy. They weren't sure at what time they had seen her, but both said she was jonesing and desperate to find a client.

Unfortunately, there were no traffic or security cameras in the vicinity, so Nathaniel had to scour footage in nearby streets, hoping to notice anything unusual.

He had, in total, 144 hours of footage to look through. And even at double speed, that was seventy-four hours . . . no, hang on. Seventy-two hours. Oh God, his brain was turning into mush. His eyes were dry and irritated; his entire body felt atrophied; his back ached from his bad posture. Yes, he should have sat straighter. But no one could look through traffic-cam footage for an entire day without slouching.

There were a few problems with investigating the murder of someone like Gloria Basset. First of all, the suspect pool. Or rather, the suspect ocean. Other murder victims had a limited group of suspects. The spouse, of course. A jealous ex, perhaps. Maybe a family member. With prostitutes you had their pimps, sure, and maybe an ex or a spouse. But then you had all their recent clientele, *and* all their potential clientele. Which meant, if Nathaniel did the math, a shitload of men.

The second problem with Basset's murder was that no one really cared.

Oh, her parents cared, and her friends. And Nathaniel, who'd had to break the news to her mother, and watched her as she crumpled onto her chair, sobbing. But when it came to the chief of police and the deputy chief, and his lieutenant, and the mayor, and the press . . . they didn't care. She was a prostitute and a heroin addict, and then she died. End of story.

The lieutenant was already grumbling about the amount of time Nathaniel was spending on Basset's murder. He wanted Nathaniel to work other cases. People were dying almost every day in the great city of Indianapolis, and if Nathaniel wanted to spend long hours investigating this one woman who had been asking for it, he could do it on his own damn time.

Oh, and if Nathaniel thought this murder necessitated *two* detectives, well then, he was out of his mind. Yeah, sure, homicide detectives generally worked in pairs, but for a case like this? Burke, Nathaniel's partner, had been taken off the case after three days and was asked to help with a case of aggravated assault. Yeah, it wasn't homicide's job, but guess what, aggravated assault and homicide were both managed by the same lieutenant, and the guy who was assaulted was the nephew of the deputy mayor, so . . .

He watched as one of the vehicles on the footage slowed down. Did it maybe look like the driver was looking for a good time? Yeah, could be. Nathaniel rewound the footage, made sure that the driver was alone in the car, and paused it where the license plate was clearly visible. He ran the plates, found nothing whatsoever, and added the license plate number and the car make to his ever-growing list of maybes. This list wasn't a lead, but if he ever had a potential suspect, he could check it and see if the suspect's car had been there that night.

He leaned back and rubbed his eyes. He needed a break. He grabbed the autopsy report and read through it again. The body had been found floating in the river and was in a bad state of decomposition. Nathaniel had a vivid memory of how it looked and smelled when he showed up at the crime scene. So when the ME wrote that the body was in an "advanced state of decomposition," Nathaniel knew only too well what he was talking about. He'd noticed the hole in the woman's head at the crime scene. Which, he knew from experience, would mean that he'd have ballistics to work with. But when the ME told him there was no exit wound and no bullet, he realized this bullet was different.

And of course, there was the missing hair.

The autopsy report mentioned it—a missing clump of hair on the right side of the cranium—opposite the location of the hole. This wasn't necessarily related to the murder. The clump of hair could have been tangled in an underwater branch and torn off. Also, Basset was a heroin addict, which contributed to hair loss. Except that Basset's hair seemed pretty thick, and the missing hair looked like it had been cut, not torn.

Still, there could be a myriad of explanations—

The phone rang, interrupting his train of thought. He picked it up.

"Detective King speaking."

"Hi." The voice on the other end was feminine. Hesitant. "The man I talked to earlier said you were the detective who's investigating the murder of Gloria Basset?"

"That's right. Who am I talking to?"

"My name is Robin. I think . . . that is, I might have heard something that could be related to the . . . the murder."

Instinct told him not to ask for her last name. This Robin sounded unsure and scared. If he prodded, she might hang up. "Okay, Robin. I appreciate you calling. What did you hear exactly?"

"I . . . Could the murder of Basset be related to the, um . . . death of Haley Parks?"

He hadn't expected that. He'd heard of the Haley Parks murder, of course. Who hadn't? It wasn't their department's case—Parks had been found in a forest, not in Indianapolis, and she wasn't even a resident of the city. Still, if you were a cop in Indiana these days, you talked about the Haley Parks murder.

And of course, there was almost no chance it was related to Basset. The MO was clearly different—one girl was stabbed and hanged; the other had her head punctured and was then thrown into the river. The murders occurred at opposite ends of the state. And the victims were clearly different—one a successful influencer and model, the other a prostitute.

"What makes you think the cases are related?" he asked.

"I may . . . know someone who had witnessed . . . that is . . . someone I know hinted at a connection. She . . . that person might have seen something relating to both murders. But it's not likely, right?"

"Anything is possible. What did this person tell you?"

"She didn't . . . I can't really talk about it. Not without getting permission . . . You know what? I'm sorry, but I really should have checked with . . . I should get permission to talk to you. I'll check and call back."

"Wait—"

She had already hung up.

Nathaniel put the phone back in its cradle and frowned. He picked up his pen and wrote down *Robin*, then copied the number she'd called from.

Could there be a connection between Basset and Parks?

Far from likely. But he could think of some similarities. The last known location of both victims was significantly distant from the location where their bodies were found. That was unusual.

Also—and this wasn't really evidence so much as it was a gut feeling—both cases were bizarre. Usually, the murder weapon was obvious and common. A knife, a gun, a heavy lead pipe. Sometimes people killed with their bare hands. In all his years as a homicide detective, Nathaniel had seen two cases that involved something more complex. One killing had been a poisoning, and the other had been an overdose of heroin.

And here were these two unusual cases—one whose murder weapon was an ice pick or a drill. And the other where the victim had been hanged. Yes, she'd been stabbed as well, but the autopsy revealed that Haley Parks had still been alive when hanged. Strangulation had been the cause of death.

He wanted the cases to be related. That would mean Basset would get the attention and resources that Haley Parks got. And he would be lying to himself if he didn't acknowledge the fact that he wanted to investigate the Haley Parks case.

It took him three phone calls to get a copy of the Haley Parks autopsy report. It was four times longer than Basset's report. The ME working on the Parks case had done his job very carefully. Nathaniel read through it, finding what he was looking for on page three.

A missing clump of hair.

His heart thudding in his chest, he dialed Robin's number. She didn't answer. He tried her three times. Nothing.

Her number was listed, and he now had her full name—Robin Hart. And after a quick internet search, he found out she was a child therapist. She looked cute in her Facebook profile photo—a redhead smiling at the camera, trees in the background. She lived in Bethelville.

Nathaniel didn't think much of therapists. He'd gone to therapy three years before with Imani, his girlfriend at the time. Throughout their sessions, he felt like the therapist constantly sided with her. Imani said that he was frequently consumed by his work. He could be gone for days and distant when he came home. Nathaniel explained that this was part of his job as a homicide detective. Dr. Ellis, a thin man with an aggravating mustache, suggested that Nathaniel set clear boundaries between his job and his personal life. These boundaries were a repeated theme during their sessions. The therapy ended when Imani left him. Nathaniel felt like this was Dr. Ellis's fault. The man had cost him the love of his life.

Nathaniel skimmed Robin Hart's Facebook profile. Who had told her that Basset's murder was connected to Parks's?

She'd said she wanted to ask whoever it was for their permission before she talked to Nathaniel. No, hang on: she'd said she *couldn't* talk to him without getting permission.

A client. Had to be. A child.

He tapped his pen on his desk impatiently. The missing hair wasn't enough to connect the two cases. Anyone in the department he'd talk to about it would laugh their ass off and tell him he just wanted a piece of the real action. He needed to know what Robin Hart knew.

He tried calling her again. Nothing.

He ran a search on "Robin Hart Bethelville" and got two results—one was her website, and one that listed her in a psychologist directory.

Some results came up with Robin's name crossed off—hits for *Bethelville*. All recent news stories.

Stories covering the Kathy Stone abduction. The girl had recently returned to her parents in Bethelville. No one knew where she had been for more than a year.

Now Nathaniel *really* needed to talk to Dr. Hart.

Chapter 23

The day of the disappearance

Frank Hart stepped into Melody's home and called out, "Hello? Anyone home?"

There was no response, but that didn't surprise him. Melody and Fred were both out, which meant the kids knew they could plug into their screens with impunity. There was no parent there to tally their screen time, to later point out that they'd spent hours on their phone or console or whatnot. Naturally, the kids all took advantage of this rare opportunity.

His grandkids were all there. They were just currently zombified.

He found Amy sprawled in front of the TV. Liam and Noah were in their room, eyes unblinking, fingers twiddling remotes, staring at the small screen of their Nintendo. Sheila was in her room on her phone. All the kids mumbled something akin to a hello after he greeted them.

He checked his own phone. A message from Melody, telling him she didn't know when they'd be back. Little Kathy hadn't been found yet.

Frank wasn't too worried. The girl would turn up, eventually. During his own numerous years as a parent, he'd gotten hundreds of hysterical calls from Diana. Telling him the girls had disappeared, or they were very sick, or some other calamity. And things would always turn out fine.

The bond between a mother and her child was the strongest substance known to man. Sometimes, it could be too strong. Especially for someone as bighearted as his wife. And Kathy's mother was probably similar. It would turn out that the girl went to visit a friend and forgot to tell anyone. Or she went to the park and didn't notice the time.

Sheila tottered out of her room. "I'm hungry," she moaned.

"Hi, hungry, I'm Granddad." Frank grinned at her.

Sheila rolled her eyes. He knew that eye roll. Like Diana, this one was. God, he adored her.

"I'm about to make dinner," he said. "Your parents might be late."

Amy got up from the couch. "Why? Where are they?"

"They have a work thing," he said naturally. No need to worry Amy. Kathy was her best friend.

"What kind of work thing?" Amy asked.

"What do you want for dinner?" Frank countered.

"Can we have pancakes with maple syrup?"

Frank knew a dinner consisting of pancakes with maple syrup was a big no-no in Melody's home. "Sure," he said breezily.

That's another thing he'd learned from those years with Diana. Mothers' rules were meant to be broken when they weren't around.

"Dad's not answering his phone," Sheila said. "I need to ask him something."

"You can ask me," Frank suggested.

"The internet is wonky; can you fix it?" Sheila said.

"Probably best if you talk to your dad," Frank amended.

"He probably forgot his phone in his car again. He can be so annoying," Sheila grumbled.

Frank shrugged. He found Fred annoying as well. In fact, when the man started dating Melody, Frank thought he was positively shifty. He'd given Fred the full father-in-law treatment for years, mentioning his shotgun and shovel, ha ha. He stopped after Melody confronted him one day, her eyes blazing. She had Diana's temper, that one. Not like his sweet Robin. So he gave Fred a break. If he had to be honest, the guy was a decent father and probably an okay husband. Frank preferred Robin's husband, Evan, but you couldn't pick and choose for your daughters, right? Well, at least not anymore. Fathers had it much better a few hundred years ago in that regard.

His phone rang. He glanced at the screen and smiled. The caller ID was *Diana, my love.*

Robin had asked him a few months ago if her mother ever got on his nerves. He knew his daughters had an uneasy relationship with their mother. And he'd told Robin that whenever Diana called him, as she did several times every day, his heart still gave a small leap. Because that's how it was when you truly loved someone.

Robin burst into tears when he said that. She could be very emotional, his little one. Just like her mother.

"Hey, honey," he said, answering the call.

Diana was breathless, panicky. "They still haven't found the girl."

"They'll find her soon, love."

"Frank, what if bad people took her? What if they're still around? Claire Stone's home isn't far from ours."

"No one took her, love," he said, lowering his voice, eyeing Amy. "She'll turn up in a bit."

"I need you to come home, Frank. I can't be alone right now."

He sighed. Diana was too delicate for this world. And it was his job to keep her safe. "Okay, love. I'll make the grandkids some dinner, and I'll come right back home."

"Get here fast." She hung up.

He pocketed his phone and opened the fridge, getting some eggs. Pancakes. Soon, Robin and Evan would have a kid of their own, and he'd have another grandchild. And he could make pancakes for all of them. And little Kathy would turn up. Everything would be just fine.

Chapter 24

Robin sat on the carpet in the playroom in front of Daniel, a ten-year-old who'd been seeing her for several months. She listened as he told her about the day before. Daniel talked quickly, and as he often did when he was anxious, he picked at his lip repetitively.

". . . and then Mrs. Mermenstein, she asked *me* what I thought about dis story we read in class, and I said it was interesting, and dat I liked the grasshopper, but then Randy laughed behind me because my answer was stupid, so I stopped talking, and Mrs. Mermenstein, she asked me why I stopped talking, but I just shrugged, and she said I should look at her when she's talking to me, but I din't, so she said she would call my mom later. An' afterwards I cried, because I was worried Mom would punish me, and some girls I din't know looked at me 'cause I was being a baby, and I went home really mad, and I spent all day in my bed, and it was the worst day I *ever* had."

"That sounds like a very unpleasant day," Robin agreed gently.

"It was the worst day *ever* in all my life."

"You said Randy laughed at you. Did he say he was laughing at you?"

"Nah, he was laughing so hard, so I knew he was laughing at me because I was being stupid."

"Did he say you were being stupid?"

"Nah, he just laughed."

"Did Mrs. Mermenstein say you were being stupid?"

"Nah."

"Then who said you were being stupid?"

"I just knew. Because that's why Randy laughed at me." Daniel pulled at his lip viciously.

"So it was something you thought, but no one said."

Daniel let out a long breath. "Yeah."

Robin paused for a second, letting it sink in. Then she said, "And later, when you cried and those girls looked at you. Did they say you were being a baby?"

"Nah, but they were looking at me, like, all the time, and they whispered with each other."

"Then who said you were being a baby?"

"I was crying like a baby."

"But did someone say you were crying like a baby?"

"Nah. They din't need to."

"They didn't need to," Robin repeated. "Because it was already something you thought."

Daniel released his lip and dropped his hands into his lap. "Yeah."

"Let's pretend something," Robin said. "Let's pretend you were going through the same day. But you had different thoughts, okay? Positive thoughts. For example, when Mrs. Mermenstein asked you what you thought about the story, what could you think about?"

Daniel hesitated. "I could think that I like the story."

"That's right, you liked the story. And what else?"

"I could think she wants to ask me what I thought because she was interested in my opinion."

"And what would you think when Randy laughed?"

That brought a longer pause, and Daniel's forehead furrowed in concentration. "I could think he was laughing because I was fat."

"Let's pretend," Robin said. "That maybe Randy laughed because of something that had nothing to do with you."

"But he laughed when I talked."

"But maybe it was a coincidence, right?"

"Nah. I don't think so."

Robin smiled. "But can we pretend it was?"

Daniel rolled his eyes. "Sure."

"So what did you think he laughed at? In our pretend game?"

"He laughed at a joke someone told him."

"Good. And what would have happened then? If you thought he laughed at a joke?"

Daniel thought about it. "I would finish answering, an' I wouldn't get in trouble."

"That's right. And later, when you cried—"

"I wouldn'a cried because Mrs. Mermenstein din't call my mom."

"Okay, but *if* you cried. And those girls looked at you. Can you think of a positive thought?"

"Dat maybe they were looking at me because they wanted to ask me what's wrong."

"And what would have happened if you thought that?"

"I wouldn't have gotten mad. And wouldn't spend all day mad."

"So you changed the entire day, the worst day in your entire life, just by thinking different thoughts?"

"Maybe." Daniel sounded doubtful.

"Okay, let's do this—"

The doorbell interrupted her. Robin frowned and checked the time. They still had twenty minutes left.

"Hang on," she told Daniel. "I'll go see who's at the door."

"Can I play with the trucks?"

"Of course." Robin got up. "I'll be right back."

Menny was already scratching at the door, wagging his tail. It could have been a cannibalistic murderer on the other side of the door, and her useless dog would just wag his tail at him. She peered through the peephole. A man she didn't know stood on the path.

"Who is it?" she called through the door, still peeking at him.

"Dr. Robin Hart?" the man said. "I'm Detective Nathaniel King from the IMPD. We spoke on the phone yesterday evening." He took an ID from his pocket and displayed it.

Oh shit. She opened the door. "Hi. I'm sorry, I can't talk right now, I have a patient here."

"That's fine," he said. "I can wait."

He was much taller than Robin, his hair jet black, his cheeks cleanly shaved. His brown eyes crinkled when he smiled. The gray suit he wore was slightly rumpled. Melody would have said he was handsome—she was a sucker for tall men. Mom would instantly dislike him, partly because he was a cop, partly because he didn't dress immaculately, and partly, if Robin had to be honest, because he was African American, and her mother had a subtle racist streak.

"Maybe we can talk on the phone later," Robin suggested.

"I'd rather talk face to face." Nathaniel's smile remained steady. "I won't take much of your time."

Robin needed to get back to Daniel. "Okay, I'll be finished in twenty minutes."

"Perfect." He shoved his hands in his pockets. "I'll wait out here in my car."

Robin returned to the playroom, anxiety settling in her gut. Daniel was playing with several trucks intently. She looked at him, her mind racing. Why had Detective King come all this way? He'd called her Dr. Robin Hart, though she'd introduced herself as Robin when they talked. Had he checked up on her?

When she called him last night, she'd been in a weird state of mind, after her unsettling research and her scary walk in the dark park. But after sleeping on it, her theory sounded dumb. Kathy had played with her toys, enacting analogies to violence, and Robin had interpreted them literally, jumping to far-fetched conclusions. Now this cop was here and would want to know who'd told her this.

She forced her mind back to her session. She would deal with the detective later. Daniel had some maladaptive thoughts, and he needed her help to learn how to handle them.

She took a cutout silhouette of a gingerbread man. Then she sat down next to Daniel.

"Remember what we talked about from before?" she asked.

"We talked about my thoughts," Daniel said, still playing with the truck.

"That's right." She handed him a pen. "I want you to write—"

"Can I play with the truck a bit longer?"

"Of course," she said automatically. "In this room we only do what you want to do."

"Right," he said with satisfaction, running the truck along the floor.

That cop was already messing with her session. If he hadn't interrupted her, distracting Daniel, this wouldn't have happened.

"But I think this game I thought of could make you happy too," she said. "And if we try it, I can lend you this truck for the rest of the week." Not ideal, bribing him to play the game. She would have to be careful so that it didn't become a pattern.

Daniel considered this. "Okay." He dropped the truck and took the pen and the gingerbread man from her hands. "What do I gotta do?"

"I want you to write bad thoughts on this gingerbread man's arms and legs."

"What kind of bad thoughts?"

"Start with the ones you had yesterday," she suggested.

As he hunched forward to write, she let her mind go back to the detective. She didn't want him talking to Claire and Pete. Things were tense enough there without this mess. The best way to handle the detective would be to play dumb. Would he try to threaten her? She imagined him talking to her like a cop in one of those shows, pounding on the table, telling her she was obstructing justice and he could send her to prison. Well, if he tried that, she could handle him. She knew her way around bullies.

"I'm done," Daniel said.

"Okay." Robin glanced at the gingerbread man. Daniel's writing was close to unintelligible, but she could decipher *I'm fat* on one arm and the word *baby* on the left leg. "Here, give me the pen."

He handed it to her, and she drew a frowny face on the gingerbread man's face.

"Okay," Robin said. "Now I want you to rip off the legs and arms of the gingerbread man. And when you rip them off, you can read aloud what you wrote."

"Okay," Daniel said doubtfully. He picked up the gingerbread silhouette and ripped off one of the arms. "I'm fat."

"Now the others."

"I don't want to read them out loud."

"That's fine, you don't have to." Robin smiled at him encouragingly. "Just rip them off."

Daniel tore off each limb vehemently and let them scatter on the rug. Finally, left only with the torso, he let it drop as well. For a second, an image flashed in Robin's mind. The drawing from Kathy's first session, the man whose arms and legs were cut and bleeding. She pushed the image away.

"What do you think the negative thoughts did to the gingerbread man?" she asked Daniel.

He played with his lower lip. "They chopped his arms. And his legs."

"That's right. They tore him up. That's what these thoughts do to us. They tear us up from inside." Robin flipped the torn limbs. "Now I want you to write *good* thoughts about yourself on this side. What's something you're good at?"

For a few seconds, Daniel looked at a loss. Then he said hesitantly, "I'm . . . good at making my sister laugh?"

"That's a good one. Write it on one of these."

She coached him through writing those positive thoughts while planning her actions with the detective. She wouldn't let him manipulate or bully her. If playing dumb didn't work, she'd tell him she couldn't talk to him because of confidentiality. Let's see him try to get a warrant for that.

When Daniel finished writing his good thoughts, Robin coached him into reading each one out loud. Then, as he did that, she taped the limbs back onto the gingerbread man's body and finally drew it a smiling face. Daniel didn't seem particularly impressed with the result. Perhaps if she had had her head in the game, she could have engaged him more. There was nothing to do about it now. Positive thinking was a habit that needed work, and they would focus on it in future sessions. But it was a start.

By that point Daniel's mother had come to pick him up. Robin escorted them out. The detective was nowhere in sight, and she allowed herself a few seconds of hope. But as soon as Daniel and his mother drove off, the detective emerged from a car parked under a tree.

"Come in," Robin said with a large smile. A chirpy redhead with a wide, vapid smile usually did the trick.

"Thank you." Nathaniel returned her smile.

Robin allowed that Melody wasn't the only person who would find this guy handsome.

"I'm sorry you came all this way," she said as she led him to the kitchen. "It really wasn't necessary. I saw the news about that poor woman, and it got me thinking, you know? Two murders in the same state. I was wondering if they could be connected. Tea?"

"Just water, thanks." Nathaniel sat on one of the kitchen chairs casually and gazed at her, unblinking.

"And when I talked to my sister about it, she thought I might have a point, which is why I called you. But then I realized you probably get calls all the time." She put a glass of cold water on the table in front of him. "I'm really sorry to have wasted your time."

He picked up the glass and sipped from it. Then placed it back on the table, saying nothing. Seconds ticked by.

She knew that trick. She pulled it herself often enough. People didn't like silence. They filled it up with words. But she had no problem with silence herself. She settled herself in front of him, wearing an apologetic smile.

And waited.

He drank half the glass. She let her eyes wander around. Then looked back at him. He watched her, saying nothing. She got up, took a pitcher, and filled it with water, then added a bit of ice. She topped off his glass and sat back down.

"How are the sessions with Kathy Stone going?" he asked.

For a fragment of a second she lost her composure. Suddenly sure that he had been asking about her around town. Someone would have told him, everyone knew that—

Then she let her expression relax into the same vapid smile. "I'm sorry?"

His eyes twinkled, and she knew he'd noticed that slip in her facade. Well, it didn't matter. She wasn't going to involve Kathy and her parents in her own idiotic sleuthing from the day before—

"Kathy Stone. You're working with her," he said, spreading his hands. "Look, Doctor, no offense, but you didn't just happen to see Gloria Basset on the news. Sadly, people like Gloria don't really get a lot of news coverage when they die. And you're not someone who would call the police on a whim. You're brighter than that."

"That's nice of you to say, but—"

"You're a child therapist, and according to the glowing reviews I found online, you're a damn good one. So let's drop the act. Kathy told you something about her abductor. Something that made you think he was connected to the Basset murder and the Parks murder. Am I close enough?"

"I can't really talk about that." Robin folded her arms.

Nathaniel sipped from his water. "I talked to the detective investigating her abduction yesterday. He told me she still isn't talking to anyone. But she's talking to you, right?"

"No."

"The person who killed Gloria Basset could kill again. If you don't tell me what you know and someone gets hurt, that'll be your responsibility."

She could already feel that *need* she had around a person with authority or power. To placate him. Make him happy. Just like she always wanted to placate Mom. Like she'd placated Evan for years. She wanted to agree with him. She could imagine him nodding at the information she would give him. A good citizen, helping the police. Making the right call. He would approve of her. She could almost imagine him as he listened to her, tilting his head and raising his eyebrows in satisfaction.

But you know what, Mr. Cop-Who-Interrupts-Sessions? She was done placating. She couldn't care less if he was happy, or angry, or disappointed with her. And he could shove that so-called responsibility. She had a responsibility to Kathy, which trumped everything else.

"Maybe that'll be my responsibility," Robin said crisply. "Or *maybe* if someone else gets hurt, it's the police's responsibility for not doing a better job."

Nathaniel grinned. "That's fair. So you're saying I should talk to Kathy directly, and not to you."

"It would be better if you didn't," Robin said. "She's gone through a lot."

"But you aren't giving me anything."

"I can't talk about my sessions," Robin said. "But I'm telling you I jumped to conclusions last night. It was unprofessional of me, and I wasted your time. There's no reason to make it any worse."

"What do you normally do in those sessions?"

"I have a playroom. The kids play with toys, or make up stories, or draw, and through that we can process issues that bother them."

"So presumably, Kathy was here and played with some toys, and you jumped to conclusions?" Nathaniel raised an eyebrow. "Must have been a violent game."

"These violent games happen."

"I doubt they happen often. It sounds quite unusual."

"Really?" Robin didn't bat an eye. "Ever see a child reenact the sexual abuse they went through using a Barbie? Or a child playing an imaginary game in which one toy hits another repeatedly for getting a bad grade? Or a kid drawing a picture of Mommy with all the bruises that Daddy left on her? You'd be surprised to hear how often that happens here."

That made Nathaniel lose his know-it-all smile. He put his glass down. "I'm sorry, you're right. I walk around thinking cops have a monopoly on dealing with terrible people. But I guess you get to see quite a lot of that."

"Yeah. And the reason these kids open up to me is because they know they can trust me. And I won't break that trust."

Nathaniel nodded gravely. "So what made you call me yesterday?"

"I was a bit freaked out. That's all. I'd had a difficult day, and I made a bad decision. Like I said, I'm sorry I wasted your time."

"Why do you think you wasted my time?"

"You came all this way to talk to me about a ridiculous theory I made up that connects Gloria Basset's murder to the Parks murder.

Obviously, this is a dead end. I don't know a lot about murder investigations, but I assume every second counts—"

"You're right," Nathaniel interrupted her. "Every second counts. So why do you think I drove over here?"

Robin spread her hands helplessly. Maybe his investigation was stuck. Or maybe he had to check every lead, no matter how far fetched.

Nathaniel sighed. "I think you could be right. That these two murders are connected. There's evidence that could corroborate that."

She stared at him, stunned. If that was true . . . if she'd been right yesterday, it meant—

"If they *are* related," he continued. "And if Kathy Stone hinted at that, it probably means she was a witness to these murders. And that in all likelihood, the murderer was her abductor."

"Um . . ." Robin cleared her throat. "If that's the case, you shouldn't be talking to me. You should be talking to the local cops, and the sheriff. They were the ones who handled the investigation. They're the ones who know who the suspects are and are working together with the Jasper Police Department to locate—"

"I'll definitely talk to the sheriff," Nathaniel interrupted her. "And to the local cops. And I already talked with two officers in the Jasper Police Department. The person responsible for Kathy's abduction is still at large. Which means that we're talking about a very violent individual who will definitely strike again. As a psychologist, you are *obligated* to let the police know if you think a person's life could be in danger—"

"Let me stop you right there." Robin raised her hand. "I'm obligated to report when I think a patient of mine is about to harm themselves or someone else. This is hardly the case. You think Kathy's abductor is the murderer of Gloria Basset and Haley Parks? Fine. Go talk to the sheriff and the local police. Talk to the feds. Do your job. And let me do mine."

Nathaniel stood up and took a small business card out of his pocket. "If you have anything else you want to share about Kathy, don't hesitate to give me a call."

"I'll keep that in mind."

"I might come back later, if I have any more questions," he added, turning to the door.

"If you do," Robin answered, "please call first."

Chapter 25

Claire sat by Kathy, watching her as she hunched over her math worksheet. An atmosphere of tranquility enveloped them like a blanket. They had had a really nice and relaxed day. Claire had started reading *Anne of Green Gables* to Kathy during the morning. Before the abduction, Kathy wasn't particularly interested in books. But then again, Claire had never tried reading anything to her other than short children's books, mostly Dr. Seuss. Now Claire realized Kathy was delighted to listen to her reading more mature stories. *Anne of Green Gables* had been Claire's favorite when she was Kathy's age. So they'd spent a couple of hours lying in Kathy's bed, Kathy's head nestled on Claire's shoulder, with Claire reading aloud from the book. As she read, she even inflected her voice a little, giving Matthew Cuthbert a deep voice and Rachel Lynde a sort of squawky shrill voice that made Kathy giggle.

Throughout the day, Claire did her best to help Kathy study. Pete was adamant that Kathy should rejoin school next year. Claire wasn't sure it was even possible, but she'd agreed to try, and she would do her best to make it easier for Kathy. That meant she would have to catch up on the school she missed.

Kathy was willing. She did her best with the worksheets Claire had received from the teachers at school. However, she struggled with writing even the simplest words, and sentences were practically impossible. She did a little better with numbers, so they could work on her math.

Unfortunately, her focus was fragmented too. She could work for about fifteen minutes straight, but then her eyes would wander; sometimes the pencil literally dropped from her fingers. Or sometimes a loud noise would distract her, and it would take Claire a while to calm her down, by which point Kathy forgot what she had been working on.

Still, she managed to progress slowly throughout the day. And Claire got some time to herself when Kathy worked on her doll accessories. She did that every day now, crafting clothes and furniture and tools, and storing them in her shoebox.

Now Kathy was back studying, struggling with long division. Before the abduction, Kathy had no issues with math. Like Claire and Pete, she'd had a knack with numbers and could easily grasp the things she learned at school much faster than most of the kids in her class. Now, everything came slowly. She'd start working on an exercise, patiently guided by Claire, then pause and raise her eyes, frowning with confusion. Claire would do her best to help her through, but with Kathy's silence, everything became much more cumbersome. Still, Claire discovered if she only repeated the steps Kathy had to follow in a low, soft voice, Kathy would eventually master the subject herself. Overcoming this difficulty became another thing they could share together, bringing them closer, reminding Claire that she had her daughter back.

The front door rattled, and Pete stepped in.

"Hey," he said, smiling and taking off his coat. "What are you two studying?"

Too loud. Way too loud. Claire instantly flinched as Pete talked, knowing he didn't even realize how loudly he spoke and how sensitive Kathy was to it. The girl tightened, eyes skittering, muscles clenched. The tranquility in the room had dissipated, replaced by a tension that crackled like electricity.

He strode into the room, and again, Claire wished he would try to move just a bit slower, a bit more smoothly. Kathy shifted closer to Claire, the sudden movements making her anxious.

Pete had always been that way—full of energy, intense, vibrant. She used to love that about him—how he could command a room, take charge. A natural-born leader. And Kathy used to love it, too, years before. Pete was the cool dad who taught her to ride a bicycle, and played catch with her, and would roar loudly, shouting that the tickle monster was coming to get her.

He'd tried that tickle monster routine two weeks ago. It had been a disaster.

Claire tried to talk to him about it, suggesting that he should try to speak in a softer voice. Be more gentle. He told her he was using his regular voice, which was true, and that she was coddling Kathy. How did Claire expect their daughter to function in life if they constantly treated her like a fragile porcelain doll?

"Oh, long division?" he said, standing above them. "That's a tricky subject. How is she doing?"

That's another thing he did that grated on Claire's nerves. He talked about Kathy when she was in the room as if she wasn't there. Sure, if he asked Kathy how she was doing, she wouldn't answer with words. But she could smile. She could nod. She could shrug. Most of all, she would feel like they were talking. Didn't he see how important that was?

"What do you think, Kathy?" Claire asked. "How is it going?"

Kathy gave her a tiny, hesitant smile. Claire smiled back. "We're getting there, right?"

A tiny nod.

"How was work?" Claire asked. Because it was one of those things she used to ask back then, before their tiny family had been fractured.

"Not bad," Pete said. He went to their bedroom to take off his suit, while telling her something about a meeting. Which meant, of course, that he raised his voice so she could hear him. Which paradoxically meant that Claire stopped listening because she was intent on Kathy's growing anxiety.

"Hey," she whispered to her daughter. "Do you want to take a break from math? Maybe do some bubble practice? Maybe we'll manage to break Tuesday's record."

To her relief, Kathy agreed, and Claire handed her the bubble wand. Kathy focused on producing bubbles, breathing deeply as she did so, slowly relaxing. Claire silently thanked Robin for the millionth time. Even just this little thing—the bubble exercise—had made such a huge difference for Kathy.

"Do you want to order takeout today?" Pete asked, stepping back into the living room. He looked at Kathy blowing bubbles, a smile at the corner of his mouth. "We can get burgers."

"I was planning on making pasta," Claire said.

"Let's order burgers," Pete said.

"Okay." Claire shrugged. She didn't mind making pasta; it took her twenty minutes. But if Pete felt like he was "helping out" by ordering burgers, she wouldn't stand in his way.

Pete fiddled with his phone to order the burgers. Claire set the table, glancing occasionally at Kathy to make sure everything was all right.

The knock on the door caught her by surprise. She and Pete opened it together, standing side by side. The man before them introduced himself as Detective Nathaniel King.

Chapter 26

Claire tucked Kathy into bed. Her daughter was still wide awake, headphones on her ears. Lately, she'd been going to sleep listening to the steady sound of ocean waves. It made it much easier for her to fall asleep. Still, the worry in Kathy's eyes was easily visible. The stranger in the next room made her daughter uncomfortable.

Claire stepped out of Kathy's bedroom, leaving the light in the hallway on and the door open. Kathy needed those things to be able to fall asleep on her own. The fact that she even managed to go to sleep without Claire lying in the bed with her was huge progress.

Claire returned to the living room. Pete and the detective sat by the table. The detective was jotting in his notebook while Pete talked.

". . . scratches on her body," Pete said. "The scratches healed pretty quickly, but we have photos if you want to see."

Claire sat down and cleared her throat. Pete stopped talking, and both men turned to look at her.

"Sorry it took me so long to join you," Claire said. "I had to help Kathy into her bed."

"It's a pretty long process," Pete interjected, talking to the detective. "Before everything happened, Kathy would go to bed all alone. But ever since she came back, we have to help her with everything. Claire's been a champ about it. She spends hours with Kathy every evening."

"I'm sure it's been difficult," Nathaniel said.

"I don't mind," Claire said. "I'm just glad to have her back. But we should talk more softly. She has her headphones on, but she's still awake. I don't want this to upset her."

"Of course, I completely understand," Nathaniel said, his voice becoming much more gentle. "Like I was telling Pete, I might have a new lead on Kathy's case, and I was hoping to talk to you both about it."

Claire had been waiting for this, whether she told herself that or not. Kathy's abductor was still out there, lurking. Sometimes, a terrible thought intruded on her—what if he comes back for Kathy? And her mind would skitter away from it, the implications too horrifying to face.

"Isn't Detective Pierce handling it anymore?" she asked, her voice cracking. Pierce had been their contact for Kathy's case throughout the terrible time since Kathy's disappearance. Claire had talked to him only once since Kathy returned.

"Detective Pierce is still working the case, with some detectives from Jasper," Nathaniel said. "But Kathy's case might be related to a case I'm investigating."

"Not another abduction?" Claire asked, swallowing.

"No, something else entirely," Nathaniel said, raising his palms. "Still, it could provide a breakthrough to Kathy's case as well. And we could really use your help."

"Whatever you need," Pete said. "We'd love to see that bastard rot in prison."

Claire hadn't given the abductor's punishment much thought. Not as much as Pete had. She believed if Kathy knew that whoever had taken her was behind bars, she would feel safer. And Claire herself would feel safer too. But she wasn't enthusiastic enough to promise the detective "whatever he needed."

"Pete filled me in on the day of the abduction and the week that followed," Nathaniel said. "And he was telling me about the days since Kathy's return. I understand Kathy isn't talking since she returned."

"That's true," Claire said.

"She isn't talking at all? Not to you or . . . anyone else?"

"No," Claire said.

"Has she been communicating in any other manner? Like writing?"

"No," Claire said. "As far as I understand, there's no medical reason for her not to talk. She has a psychological barrier when it comes to communicating verbally. And that includes writing."

"What about yes and no questions?"

"She can nod or shake her head, but after a few questions she always freezes," Claire explained. "She reacts badly to questioning."

"Did you try sign language?"

"I suggested it," Pete said.

"We might try it in the future. For now we're focusing on helping Kathy feel safe." Claire kept her tone steady but sent a piercing stare toward Pete.

"How are you helping Kathy feel safe?" Nathaniel asked.

"She's with me all day," Claire said. "And she's seeing a therapist."

Nathaniel nodded. "Okay. And did Kathy give any hints while she was with you, or doing her therapy, as to what happened to her during the past months?"

Claire began saying she hadn't, not really, just as Pete said, "Yes."

"Oh?" Nathaniel turned to Pete. "Like what?"

Claire looked at Pete as well, confused and annoyed.

Pete said pointedly to Claire. "*You* told me about the drawing she did in Robin's first session." He turned to the detective. "That's Robin Hart, Kathy's therapist."

"Lower your voice," Claire said steadily. "Kathy's still awake."

"Fine," Pete barked, hardly lowering his voice. "And didn't Robin say that Kathy was enacting violent memories with the toys in the playroom?"

"She didn't say they were memories, she said they were Kathy's way of expressing her trauma," Claire said.

"Did she tell you what exactly Kathy showed her?" Nathaniel asked.

"Well . . . ," Claire said. "She told me Kathy was playacting violent incidents. She didn't get into specifics, but she said Kathy reenacted quite accurately the murder of Haley Parks. She thought Kathy might have seen it on TV. I told her that it couldn't have happened since she returned . . . we've been very careful. So Robin figured Kathy might have seen it on TV wherever . . . wherever she'd been held."

"So Kathy playacted the murder of Haley Parks . . . ," Nathaniel said. "Did Dr. Hart—Robin—tell you how, exactly? She enacted it with dolls? It's a pretty elaborate game, especially seeing as Kathy doesn't talk."

"She didn't get into the specifics." Claire shuddered. "And I didn't ask her."

"Would it be okay if I question Dr. Hart with you present? About the sessions? Perhaps work in tandem with her regarding future sessions, so that we can get more information?"

Claire answered "No" just as Pete said "Yes."

For a second, they all sat in silence, and then Claire smiled thinly. "Obviously we need to discuss it later."

Pete frowned. "If it helps put that monster behind bars—"

"We'll talk about it later," Claire said again.

The point of Kathy's sessions with Robin was to help Kathy, *not* to help the police catch whoever it was that abducted Kathy. Sure, Claire would love to be able to tell Kathy that the man was in prison, but not if it got in the way of her treatment.

"Okay," Nathaniel said. "Can you tell me about the drawing? The one Kathy drew in that first session?"

Claire told him about it. How she'd drawn the man, and how she added cuts on his arms and legs and turned the entire thing into a crimson drawing. Her voice trembled as she described it.

"She drew cuts on the man's arms and legs?" Nathaniel asked. "Like . . . what? Small cuts? Holes?"

"More like red lines that crossed through the arms and legs," Claire said.

Nathaniel stared at her, frozen, his eyes widening slightly. Then he blinked. He flipped a page in his notebook and put it on the table. "Something like this?" he asked.

He quickly drew a basic stick man, and then crossed the man's arms and legs with short lines.

"Yeah . . . sort of. Except the lines were higher . . ." Claire took the detective's pen from him and drew the lines as she remembered them. "Here . . . and here."

"I see." He seemed distracted as he looked at the sketch.

He asked them more questions about the day of the abduction and about the days since Kathy's return. Recalling all these things again was taking its toll, and Claire's voice quivered as she answered. She had to go to the bathroom twice to wash her face and breathe deeply.

As he was getting up to leave, the detective said, "Would it be all right if I come here with a social worker and talk to Kathy myself? Maybe show her some photos of people?"

Claire answered "No" just as Pete said "Of course."

Claire smiled at both men—the one who didn't know Kathy at all, and the one who spent a single hour every day with her. Her smile was wide and cold, her teeth grating against each other. "I think, Detective, that we will have to discuss this later, as well."

Chapter 27

Robin sat outside Jimmie's Café, enjoying the afternoon's gentle sun, along with a slice of peach pie and a large cup of coffee. She'd had a busy day, with four patients and one parent consultation, and she felt like she'd earned a few hours of relaxation.

Which would have been much more pleasant if she didn't constantly feel people looking at her. And whispering. Was she being paranoid, or was there a lot more whispering than usual? She couldn't help feeling there *was*. And that she was one of the main topics of hushed conversation.

Still, she did her best to ignore it, to focus on her phone, where she was currently scrolling through photos of cute dogs.

The adorable Pekingese she was looking at was suddenly replaced by the unpleasant screen of an incoming phone call. From Mom.

Robin hadn't talked to her yet, not since she'd taken the dollhouse. She had ignored twenty-three incoming phone calls. They'd texted because Robin felt that was safer. In the texts, Robin said she had taken the dollhouse but added that she got the impression her mother had no problem with that. After all, hadn't she said that Robin was doing great work with Kathy? And Robin had been sure she wouldn't have an issue with loaning the house to help the girl.

Robin had learned gaslighting from the best. But Mom was mostly impervious to it. She texted that she wanted the dollhouse back. That if

Robin couldn't afford a proper dollhouse for her playroom, Mom would be glad to pitch in and help her buy one. She'd seen a nice one on the Toys"R"Us website.

Robin had promised to return it. And then didn't. And she hadn't come over either. It had been more than a week. This was a brewing disaster of epic proportions.

She would answer the call now. Let Mom vent. It would be worth it in the long run. Emboldened by the sunny sky and the sugary peach pie, she answered the call.

"Hi, Mom."

She was *already* sobbing. "Do you hate me that much? After all I've done for you? I gave my life for both of you. And now both my daughters won't visit me, even though we live in the same town."

"No, Mom, I don't hate you." Robin lowered her voice. "I've been busy. I'll swing by tomorrow, I promise."

"What?" she wailed. "I can't hear you, speak up. Where are you that you can't talk like a normal person?"

"I'm at Jimmie's Café—" Robin instantly realized her mistake.

"Oh, I thought you were *busy*. Not too busy to sit in a café, apparently."

"No, it was just a short . . . hello?"

Mom had hung up.

Robin pocketed her phone and sipped from her coffee, which had suddenly turned tasteless. She'd planned on sitting at Jimmie's for an hour, or even more, checking social media, maybe reading a book. But now, every minute she would feel guiltier. Every minute would make Mom a minute more right. She wasn't busy. Because another minute had just gone by, and instead of visiting her mother, she was out there doing literally nothing.

She caught Jimmie's eye, and he came over.

"How was the peach pie, Robin?"

"It was great, as always." She smiled at him.

"The secret is the fresh peaches."

"Well, it's really tasty. Listen, can I get the . . ." She paused.

A couple of women went by and stared at her, whispering between them. And she could swear one of them was giving her the stink eye.

"Everything all right?" Jimmie asked.

"I don't . . . Did you see that?" Robin asked. "The way these two looked at me?"

"Eh?" He glanced after the two women. "I didn't pay attention. But I wouldn't worry about it. Just people shoving their noses in other people's business."

"I . . . What? What are you talking about?"

He frowned. "Nothing. Don't mind them. Another coffee?"

"Is this about . . ." She hesitated. "What did you mean when you said other people's business?"

"Are you two talking about the Kathy thing?" Ellie asked, sidling over. "I don't get why everyone is getting all worked up."

"Everyone is getting worked up?" Robin repeated.

"Don't you have tables to clear?" Jimmie exploded at Ellie. "I swear, half the time she's on the phone, and then she goes upsetting my customers. You millennials . . . you don't have an ounce of tact."

"I'm not a millennial . . . and what, all millennials don't have tact?" Ellie asked. "And boomers naturally have truckloads of it. Tact pouring out of their ears."

"We know when to keep our mouths shut." Jimmie folded his arms.

Ellie rolled her eyes. "What's the big deal? Robin should know if people are talking shit about her."

Robin blinked. "They are?"

"Don't listen to her," Jimmie grunted. "Just a few hags. And it's all bullshit anyway."

Robin looked at Ellie, raising an eyebrow.

"It's the Kathy thing," Ellie said, lowering her voice.

"What Kathy thing?" Robin asked. She was feeling sick. She regretted the peach pie now, no matter how fresh the peaches were.

"People are saying that instead of helping Kathy get over her trauma, you're making it worse." Ellie shook her head. "Like, really making her relive it? And everyone is suddenly an expert in child psychology, and they know the best way to treat Kathy. Oh, and someone said you only made Kathy more aggressive because of um . . . your nephew. That she stabbed." Ellie's voice slowly dissipated as she caught the furious glare her uncle was giving her.

"Are you done?" he growled.

"I thought Robin should know," Ellie mumbled.

"I think the kitchen trash needs taking out," Jimmie said crisply.

"Yeah, yeah." Ellie walked off.

"Don't worry about what she said," Jimmie told Robin. "We all know you're doing fantastic work with Kathy. Claire and Pete were smart to take her to see you."

"Thanks, Jimmie," Robin said unhappily. "I think I should—"

The sound of squealing brakes interrupted her as a large green SUV hit the sidewalk a few feet away, one wheel jutting up on it. It just barely missed an astonished passerby, who leaped backward, shouting an obscenity. It took Robin a few seconds of shocked staring to realize it was her dad's car.

The driver's door opened, and Mom stepped out of it.

She seemed larger than life. She really *was* taller than usual. At home, she walked around barefoot or in comfortable dainty slippers. Now, she had five-inch heels on. Her dress was royal blue, her shoulders bare, a long slit showing off her legs. As if on cue, a gust of wind blew, and her thick hair fluttered. It almost seemed as if the sun was hitting her differently than her surroundings, making her look more vibrant.

Mom almost never left the house anymore, fearing COVID. But despite that, right now she had no mask on.

She turned away from the man she had nearly run over and approached the café.

"Diana," Jimmie breathed. "Welcome! I'm so glad to see you here. Are you joining your daughter?"

Oh, God no.

Mom gave him a smile worthy of a queen. "Yes, thank you, Jimmie. And I'll have the usual."

She hadn't been to Jimmie's since the pandemic started. The fact that she assumed Jimmie would know what she meant by "the usual" was ridiculous.

"One croissant, with strawberry jam and butter on the side, and a glass of freshly squeezed orange juice. Coming right up." Jimmie grinned at her like a schoolboy in love. If Robin hadn't still been in shock, she'd be scandalized.

Mom sat down in front of Robin, her smile still fixed on her face, her eyes flinty.

"I don't think you can park here," Robin said weakly. She stared at Dad's SUV that literally jutted into the area of the outdoor café.

"Jimmie?" Mom said in a singsong voice. "Can I park here?"

"No problem at all," Jimmie called from behind the counter.

Considering that she had been wailing and sobbing on the phone only ten minutes before, her makeup was pristine.

"I . . . you didn't have to come over," Robin said. "I know how worried you are about the pandemic."

"You left me no choice." There was a tremor in Mom's voice. "How else would I see my own daughter? You don't come and visit me anymore."

"I was at your home last week."

"You know"—Mom's lips trembled—"not a day goes by that I don't wake up, see the empty side of the bed where your father used to sleep, and feel utterly and completely alone."

Robin sighed. She *knew* her mother was trying to guilt her. But of course, knowing what she was doing didn't prevent it from working. "Mom, I visit you as often as I can."

"I suppose that *now* that you are an esteemed therapist, with such an important patient, you don't have time for your mother anymore."

"It has nothing to do with—"

Mom waved her hand. "How would the police be able to solve the case without the great Robin Hart holding their hand, telling them what Kathy told her during her sessions?"

Robin was floored, both by how close she was to the truth and by how twisted and wrong what she said was. "What? This isn't what's happening at all." How had she even heard about this?

"I don't even care," Mom said. "I taught you better than to take advantage of a family's misfortune to advance your own sense of importance. But it's your life, Robin. I can't live it for you."

"Mom, where did you hear all this? It isn't true."

Mom sniffed and dabbed a tear from the corner of her eye. "I wish your father was alive. Then I wouldn't feel so lonely. And you and your sister would come to see *him*. You always loved him more, even though I was the one who raised you both."

Jimmie came over and placed the croissant and the orange juice in front of Mom. There was a flower decorating the dish. "Here you go, Diana. Anything else?"

"No, thank you, Jimmie." Mom smiled at him gratefully.

"You know, your daughter has your voice," Jimmie said, glancing at Robin.

"Yes, isn't it wonderful?" She gave Robin a long look. "I wish she would have used it. I kept suggesting she study journalism in college. She could have been a news reporter."

"Well, I guess she made her own way." Jimmie grinned. "And colleges these days aren't what they used to be. My niece just finished college, and as far as I can tell, she wasted years of her life studying *art*. What use is *that* in the real world?"

Robin felt like a child, listening to the grown-ups talking about her, knowing she wasn't allowed to intervene and speak for herself.

"Robin definitely made her own way." Mom's voice dropped, becoming cooler. Jimmie didn't seem to notice.

"Well, it's great having you here again," he said. "I hope we'll be seeing more of you."

"How could I ever stay away?"

Jimmie gave her one last smile and went back inside.

Mom turned back to Robin. "So. Did you buy a new dollhouse for your clinic?"

"I . . . I'll do that soon."

Mom frowned. "You know, the decent thing to do was to tell Claire Stone she should take her daughter to a *real* clinic that has the resources and the personnel to give her daughter the best treatment possible."

"Mom." Robin's voice trembled. The hurt and misery that stabbed at Robin surprised her. Even after all this time, knowing what her mother was capable of saying, the woman could still inflict pain upon her. "I can't talk about this, and you know that. But I give all my clients the best treatment—"

"You can't even afford a proper dollhouse for the girl to play with in your small place." Mom took out her purse. "At least let me help. That dollhouse I saw on the website costs one hundred and fifty dollars. I'll split it with you. Here's eighty—"

"I don't *need* your money," Robin said through gritted teeth.

"Funny, you never seemed to mind when I helped you with your college tuition. And that was a lot more than eighty—"

Robin got up.

"You're leaving?" Mom asked, shocked.

"If you don't stop, I'll leave," Robin said. She hated the tears in her throat. The way her mother made her feel so small.

"Stop what? We were just having a conversation."

Robin took a step away.

"Okay," Mom blurted.

The torment was clear on her face. If Robin left her to eat alone, it would be *humiliating*. She couldn't stomach that.

"I won't talk about giving you money. Or about your sessions with Kathy Stone. I can see it's a delicate subject."

Robin sat back down.

Mom frowned at her with pursed lips. Then she daintily picked up her croissant, cutting it in the middle. "So," she said, her voice shifting. "Anything new with your love life?"

Chapter 28

Robin's heart sank when she opened the front door and saw Kathy had her shoebox in her hands.

Ever since her afternoon at Jimmie's the day before, her mind had been churning nonstop, trying to process everything that had happened. Could her mother have a point? Should she refer Kathy to someone who had more experience with the unusual trauma she went through? For that matter, could there be some truth in what people were saying—that she was merely forcing Kathy to relive her trauma instead of getting over it?

But no matter how long she thought about it, she was sure she was doing the best thing possible for Kathy. Giving the girl the opportunity to communicate her trauma within her own absolute control was the best way to handle it. And she wasn't even gently suggesting it—everything Kathy did in the playroom came from the girl herself. Robin only helped by paying attention and empowering her.

To make sure, she consulted with a colleague over the phone—a professor who'd taught her at the university. The professor agreed with Robin that it sounded like she was acting correctly. It was a relief to hear a peer say those words.

And as for the police—Detective King had called Robin that morning, asking if she could come with him the following day and talk to the Haley Parks task force, explain what Kathy had shown her during the sessions. She had adamantly refused.

Robin half wished that they could do something else in this session. Perhaps they could sculpt in clay. Or play together in the doctor's station, with Kathy administering medical aid to Robin.

However, it looked like Kathy had come prepared with her own props. The girl was intent on playing with the dollhouse.

"Robin, can we talk for a second?" Claire asked after saying hello.

"Sure," Robin said, ignoring the growing unease in her gut. "Kathy, do you want to go ahead to the playroom?"

Kathy nodded and hurried to the playroom. It was reassuring to see how relaxed she seemed as she went inside alone. Kathy had fully embraced the playroom as a safe place.

"There's been some progress in the police's case . . . you know, about the abduction," Claire said.

"What kind of progress?"

"There's a new detective involved. Detective King?"

"Nathaniel King," Robin said. "I wanted to talk to you about that—"

"He talked to you?" Claire asked.

"Yes, um . . . I actually called him."

"You called him?" Claire gawked at her in confusion.

"About a week ago." Robin cleared her throat. "You remember when I called you? Asking if Kathy saw the news? So afterward I called him. I didn't tell him about Kathy at all. I just wanted some official information regarding those cases that have been on the news."

"I see," Claire said slowly. "Is that like . . . standard procedure with a case like Kathy's?"

"There *is* no standard procedure," Robin said. "Kathy's case is . . . well, unique. And I wanted someone to fill in the blanks."

"Then why did he come to talk to us?" Claire asked. "Why did he link this to Kathy?"

"He put two and two together." Robin sighed. "He looked into my background, saw I was a child therapist from Bethelville, and connected it to Kathy's recent return. I'm really sorry. I should have talked to you before calling him. But I really didn't think—"

"Yes, you should have." Claire's voice cooled. "But never mind. Like you said, you didn't name Kathy. Did you tell him what happened in the sessions?"

"Absolutely not. I wouldn't break Kathy's confidentiality like that. I made that clear when he was here." Robin swallowed. "And he wanted me to talk to some law enforcement associates of his. I clarified that it wasn't going to happen."

Claire nodded slowly. "Okay, well, I think that maybe you might need to."

Robin blinked. "What?"

"I discussed this with Pete," Claire said. "Detective King is looking for Kathy's kidnapper. And if they catch him, well . . . wouldn't Kathy feel a lot safer knowing that the man is in prison?"

"Maybe," Robin said hesitantly. "It'll probably help. But—"

"Pete wanted the detective to sit and watch the sessions. Or that you film them, and the detective could watch them later."

"That's out of the question." Robin was aghast.

"That's what I said. Detective King suggested you two work together to get the information from Kathy, and I told him no."

"Good. That's not the point of these sessions at all."

"Right," Claire said. "But . . . if you see anything that might shed some light on the identity of the kidnapper . . . something that the cops could work with . . . they should know."

"I don't know if that's a good idea," Robin said slowly. "The things Kathy shows me are abstract. They could be interpreted incorrectly."

"We can leave that for the cops to decide."

"And it could have consequences," Robin said. "Suppose the cops catch someone. The district attorney might need to present

Kathy's confidential sessions as evidence . . . I have no idea where that could lead."

"I want Kathy to sleep a full night's sleep without waking up screaming." Claire's voice trembled. "If the bastard who took her is incarcerated, that could help, right?"

Robin shrugged helplessly.

Claire took a long breath. "It would help *me* sleep better at night too. And it's my compromise with Pete. I told him I would ask this of you, and he agreed that for the moment, we won't do anything more. I don't want cops questioning Kathy or showing her photos. This is the lesser evil, as far as I'm concerned."

"Okay." Robin swallowed. "If Kathy shows me anything clear, I'll let the detective know. And if I'm not sure about it, I'll talk to you beforehand."

"Thanks," Claire said. "Okay, sorry, I took too much time from Kathy's session already—"

"Don't worry about it," Robin quickly said. "I don't have another session after this. Just pick her up ten minutes later."

"Thanks." Claire turned and left.

Robin stepped into the playroom, surprised to see Kathy wasn't there. Hearing the water running in the bathroom, she glanced at the small plastic table. Sure enough, a red-smeared page sat on top of it, paint stains all around it. Apparently, Kathy had started her cleansing ritual without waiting for Robin.

Robin edged closer to the paint-soaked page. In the bottom left-hand corner of the page, Robin could spot Kathy's palm print within the crimson swirl. It seemed so small.

It was possible to guess what the girl was trying to accomplish through these rituals. Kathy had experienced violent encounters during the months she had been missing. She'd apparently seen a copious amount of blood, which was impossible to process for a little girl. This was her way of coming to terms with it. Running her hands through the red paint while she was in a safe place. She decided what she did with it, how much she poured, when and how she touched it. And then she washed it off, watching as it disappeared down the drain. The child was intuitively desensitizing herself to the violent memories.

Now that Robin knew it was possible Kathy had been a witness to murder, the red paint smeared on the page seemed ominous, terrifying. She could almost smell the coppery tinge of blood emanating from the red smears. She struggled with the impulse to throw the thing in the trash and scrub away the blood . . . paint, not blood. It was red finger paint.

She took a deep breath. She would clean up later. Maybe Kathy would want to throw away the page herself. And Robin would not let the girl feel that the things she showed her unsettled her in any way. More than anything, it was important that Kathy feel free to share her feelings and memories with Robin.

She walked over to the bathroom door, which stood half-open. Kathy held her hands in the running water, pink soapsuds dropping from her palms. Robin cleared her throat gently, and Kathy glanced at her, then turned back to the sink.

"The water is washing away all the red paint," Robin reflected. "It's cleaning your hands."

It took a few minutes for Kathy to be satisfied that her hands were thoroughly clean. Once they returned to the playroom, Kathy beelined directly to the toy shelf, finding the toys she always took. Unerringly, she left the ballet dancer and the farmer behind. They were gone.

Kathy placed the toys in different rooms within the house. The Monopoly Man in the bed, the Wonder Woman in the kitchen. The little girl was inside the bathtub, the woman with the cake beside her. The murderous clown came last, as always, sitting in what Robin was starting to think of as his den, in the living room. For a while, Kathy was content to move the dolls around. She delighted at washing the little girl toy with a tiny loofah and brushing her teeth with the toothbrush.

Then she opened the shoebox and took out some new props. A small round rug for the bathroom. Yellow drapes for the children's room, which she taped to the windows carefully. Tiny plates with modeling-clay food, which she placed on the kitchen table. Mom would be horrified at the sight of modeling clay inside the dollhouse.

Then Kathy retrieved the Play-Doh container. Robin tensed, thinking that if Kathy began using Play-Doh props, she might have to tell her not to. But when Kathy popped the container's top, Robin realized it didn't contain Play-Doh at all. It contained what looked like watery muck. It was green-brown in color and had some bits and pieces floating in it.

The girl placed the container in front of the house. If the water in it hadn't been so disgusting, it could have represented an outdoor pool for the dolls. But Robin had no illusions. This wasn't a pool.

This time, the evil clown grabbed the Monopoly Man, dragging him outside. Kathy's eyes narrowed, her breath becoming more rapid as she walked the clown and the dragging Monopoly Man toward the sludge pool.

"The bad clown is taking the man in the suit to the pool with the dirty water," Robin said. "The water looks very unpleasant."

When Kathy got the two toys to stand by the pool, she tipped the Monopoly Man into the scum headfirst. Green water trickled around the Play-Doh container as the toy sank inside it, only his legs protruding out of the barrel. Kathy manipulated the clown's arms so that he held the Monopoly Man's legs.

Then, in an unnerving motion, she rattled the Monopoly Man's legs. It was clearly intentional. She was miming the man's struggles as the clown held him down.

"The bad clown is holding the man in the suit underwater," Robin said. "The man in the suit can't breathe!"

Kathy kept joggling the Monopoly Man's legs a few seconds more and then let go.

The Monopoly Man tilted within the container. The entire thing toppled over, the scummy water spilling onto the table, splashing into the dollhouse's kitchen.

"Oh no!" Robin blurted loudly, grabbing the container. It had been a reflexive gesture, a result of her dismay at her mother's dollhouse being stained with muck. But she moved too fast, her distressed call too loud.

Kathy bolted away from the dollhouse, dashing to the bathroom. She slammed the door shut.

Robin could have punched herself. This wasn't the first time a child had accidentally misused a toy in the playroom. Games in the playroom were often emotional, and toys were occasionally even thrown against the wall. Robin always kept her cool.

It was because it was her mother's dollhouse. That's what had made her react that way. In fact, she'd been tense ever since the moment Kathy popped open the lid of the Play-Doh. She'd been worried that the disgusting muck would somehow stain the pristine house, which, she'd learned as a child, was a sacred temple.

Water trickled from the table, dribbling onto the rug. Robin grabbed a few paper towels and dabbed at the small puddle of scum. Looking closely now, she was half-sure that Kathy had created the water by adding green paint and scoops of dirt to tap water.

That done, she went over to the bathroom and sat by the door.

"No one got hurt," she said, her voice loud enough to be heard through the door. "Nothing bad happened. It was a little accident. Everything is okay."

She couldn't hear any movement behind the door. She mentally reviewed the clinic's bathroom, trying to figure out if Kathy could hurt herself in there. Not likely. The sharpest item in the room was the nail file, and Kathy couldn't hurt herself with it in any significant manner. And the window wouldn't open enough for Kathy to climb out. Kathy was probably safe in there, and Robin didn't need to force the door open. She would let Kathy do it in her own time.

"I cleaned up the water." Robin took care to keep her voice steady and soothing. "If you want, you can come out and see."

After a while she added, "You can stay there until you are ready to come out. There's no rush." She glanced at the dollhouse and the discarded Monopoly Man, his face still green from the painted water. "When you come out, we can think of a way the story could end differently. Maybe someone could stop the bad clown before he hurts the man in the suit."

A shuffle inside the bathroom. The door remained closed.

Robin thought of the props Kathy kept making for the dolls and the dollhouse. "Maybe we could build a jail together," she said. "Where we can put the bad clown when he's acting badly."

The door clicked open. Kathy peeked out with one eye through a tiny crack. Robin smiled at her. "Would you like that? I think I have a small box we can turn into a jail."

She could see Kathy nodding hesitantly through the crack. Robin got up and opened the cabinet, rummaging inside it, until she found a small cardboard box in which she kept some stress balls. She emptied the box and walked back to the bathroom door.

She showed the box to Kathy. "What do you think?"

Kathy opened the door and slid out.

They sat down on the rug. Robin handed a marker to Kathy, suggesting she mark where she wanted the door to be. Kathy drew a rectangle on one side, and Robin gave her a pair of scissors.

"But don't cut all of it," Robin said. "Leave one side so we can open and close the door."

The eye roll she got from Kathy made her grin. It was the closest the girl could get to telling her, "Well, duh."

Kathy cut the door. Then they added a small window at the other side of the jail. Robin also cut a very tiny window in the door, with bars. Finally, they prepared a large strip of cardboard that could function as a bar to hold the door shut. Robin sliced two cuts on both sides of the door and showed Kathy how they could slide the bar through them so that it blocked the door.

"You can write *jail* on top of the door," Robin said. "So the bad clown will know where he's going."

Kathy's mouth quirked in a small smile, but when she held the marker above the cardboard, she seemed to freeze. Writing a word was still too much for her. Too verbal.

"I'll tell you the letters," Robin said gently. "*J* . . ."

Kathy wrote a large *J*.

"*A* . . . *I* . . . And do you know what comes next?"

Kathy hesitated a second before adding the *L* at the end of the word.

"Well done! Now let's find some cops to put the clown in jail."

Robin had three cop figures, but Kathy didn't seem satisfied. Eventually, the cops were reinforced with He-Man and a shark. The large task force came over to the dollhouse in Kathy's arms. There, she piled them all on top of the clown and slammed the shark on top of the pile a few times for good measure.

"The cops and their friends are stopping the bad clown because he hurt the man in the suit!" Robin said energetically. "That's right. He was a naughty clown, and now he's going to jail."

The police force took the clown to the cardboard jail held within the shark's jaw. Kathy thrust him inside and shut the door, and then, with a little help from Robin, barred it as well.

Kathy took a deep breath. Then she went over to the old dollhouse and took a few plastic chairs and a bed from it and piled them all in front of the door. And then put the shark in front of it for good measure.

"The evil clown is not coming out of there for a *very* long time," Robin said.

Kathy peered through the small window at the clown, who lay inside. Then she sat up and gave Robin a big happy smile.

Robin swallowed the lump in her throat.

Kathy spent the rest of the session playing with the dollhouse. She took only one small break to bury the Monopoly Man in the sandbox.

When Claire came to pick her up, Kathy was smiling.

Claire looked at Robin. "How did it go?"

"It was a good session," Robin said. "I think we made a lot of progress. We can talk about it today at length during your session."

"Oh." Claire lowered her gaze. "We have to cancel again. I'm sorry."

Robin clenched her jaw. It wasn't unusual for parents to avoid the guidance sessions, but Claire had seemed more committed to Kathy's therapy. "It's really crucial that we have these sessions, Claire."

"I know! We'll reschedule. Do it in a couple of days. Today we just had sort of an emergency."

Robin sighed. "Okay. Let me know when we can talk."

"Will do." Claire hesitated. "Keep in mind what we've discussed before. About the police? It's important."

"I will."

Robin watched as they drove away. Menny padded over and looked up at her, tongue lolling.

"You want to go for a walk, buddy?"

Menny ran back and forth excitedly.

"In a second. I need to make a short phone call."

She took out her cell and scrolled through the recent calls, tapping the one from that morning.

He answered after less than a second. "Hello?"

"Detective King, it's Robin." She pursed her lips. "I can go with you to talk to your task force pals tomorrow."

Chapter 29

Robin gazed through the passenger window as trees and meadows flew by. It was a two-hour drive to Indianapolis, and she was already regretting riding with Nathaniel King. The day before, when he suggested picking her up, she'd been relieved. She didn't particularly like to drive. It sounded like the meeting with the task force might take a few hours, which would mean driving back in the dark, which she positively hated.

But now she realized she would spend four hours with this cop she didn't know. And with his music taste, which she found slightly offensive.

His playlist started well, with Leonard Cohen's "Everybody Knows," but the next song was by Ariana Grande. Then it was Ray Charles, followed by . . . something digital and high pitched. And then Jimi Hendrix, which Robin could get behind, and then a song titled "Mi Mi Mi," which she definitely couldn't.

"Okay, what is this?" she finally blurted.

"What?" Nathaniel glanced at her.

"The music is all over the place. What are we even listening to?"

"Oh, I'm sharing my playlist with my niece on Spotify. She's ten. So it can be a mixed bag."

"You can say that again." Robin glanced at the next songs on the list. "Oh God, she has 'Baby Shark' here."

Nathaniel waggled his eyebrows. "How do you know 'Baby Shark' isn't one of my songs?"

Robin laughed. "Can we turn the music off?"

"Have it your way. But you'll never hear James Brown warming up to Dua Lipa anywhere else." Nathaniel switched it off.

"Thank you."

They drove a minute in blissful silence.

"So I should probably prepare you for this meeting," Nathaniel said. "There's a task force that's dedicated to investigating the Haley Parks case. Four state cops, two homicide detectives, and a fed. And there's also a task force that's investigating the Gloria Basset murder. And this is a meeting of both task forces."

"Who's in the Basset task force?"

"Well, there's me." Nathaniel paused for a second. "And that's it."

"Are you serious?"

"Extremely serious." He frowned. "I was wondering about that. Why did you contact *me*? You thought you might have something connecting Basset and Parks. Why not contact the people investigating the Parks murder? Obviously, you realized they had more resources."

"I, uh . . . tried," Robin admitted. "They have a hotline. And when I called, they didn't take me very seriously."

"I'm not surprised. They get dozens of calls every day. Every true-crime podcast listener in this state is sure they would be the ones to solve the Haley Parks murder."

"Yeah," Robin said. "I barely got a few words out before the guy on the phone asked me point blank if I witnessed anything or if I have any concrete evidence. Which I didn't."

"So you called me next."

"Well, it took me almost fifteen minutes. I called the IMPD, and they transferred me a bunch of times until I reached you."

"That explains it." Nathaniel exhaled. "Well anyway, with your help and some forensics, I managed to convince someone in the Parks task force that these murders might be connected. So they want to talk to you and hear firsthand about your sessions."

"I can't tell them about—"

"I know, I know." He waved his hands. "Patient confidentiality. But you'll be able to tell them something, right?"

Robin sighed. "Yeah. I agreed with Kathy's mother that I'll tell them things I think are directly connected to the case."

"That woman is crazy tough." Nathaniel said in admiration.

"Who, Claire?" Robin asked, surprised.

"Yeah. Claire Stone. I thought she was about to punch me first time I came over. I just asked if I could sit in on the sessions . . . you shoulda seen the look she gave me. I've faced armed drug dealers who weren't half as scary."

Robin smiled to herself. "Well, good. I didn't know she had it in her."

"I think it's a mother thing, you know?"

"'A mother thing'?"

"Yeah. Like hens that get all big and scary when their chicks are threatened?"

Robin shook her head, saying nothing.

"I get the feeling that what I said was offensive somehow," Nathaniel muttered after a moment.

"Why?" Robin asked sweetly. "Because you generalized all mothers everywhere and compared them to chickens? Or because you trivialized Claire's response, making it a reflexive reaction, like spreading her wings and clucking?"

"Well, when you say it like *that*, it sounds bad. I meant that most mothers have a special connection with their children. And I could see Claire has that, you know?"

"Sure. Whatever."

She stared ahead, thinking of all the different mothers she'd seen as a therapist. About Claire and Kathy. About Melody and her four children.

About those few months when she thought she was about to become a mother.

"So, when I was a kid, some kids picked on me on the school bus," Nathaniel said. His tone was soft.

"What?"

"I'm telling you a story. About mothers. So these kids picked on me on the school bus."

"Picked on you how?" Robin asked.

"They just picked on me, you know? Called me names, threw things at me. I know you look at me now, and I'm big and strong and handsome, but you know . . . as a kid I wasn't as big or strong."

"But you *were* handsome?" Robin grinned.

"Crazy handsome. You better believe it. Anyway, one day, I came home crying. And my mother interrogated me until she got the truth out. Let me tell you, everything I know about criminal interrogation, I learned from that woman." Nathaniel smiled. "So she went to school, and she stormed into the principal's office and shouted at everyone. At the principal, at his secretary, at a teacher who went by . . . just nonstop furious yelling. I was waiting outside in the hall, and kids gathered around, listening to all the screaming. I thought I would die of shame."

He stopped talking, grinning to himself.

"Did it help?"

"Nah, of course it didn't. It only made everything worse. So a week later I came home again, and I tried to hide my tears, because I knew my mother would throw a scene if she saw that. But there was no hiding anything from her. And she told me she would make it better, but until it got better, she would take me to school and pick me up from school. Just so I wouldn't be with those bullies on the bus."

"That's really lovely."

"You have no idea. She didn't have a car. She walked with me to school and waited for me when school ended. It was a thirty-minute walk. And every day when we walked back home, I would tell her everything that happened during school, and she'd tell me about *her* day. And it got to the point that I worried she would manage to fix the bullying on the school bus, and we'd stop walking together, you know?"

"She sounds amazing."

"Yeah," Nathaniel said. "Two years later, sudden growth spurt. No one would mess with me anymore. You know why?"

"Why?"

"Because I was big and strong *and* handsome."

"Right." Robin smirked at him.

"So I rode on the school bus again. I was getting too old for my mother to walk me, anyway."

Robin nodded.

"So what I was saying earlier, about mothers . . . I was thinking of *mine*, you know?"

"Okay. And you're right," Robin conceded. "A lot of moms do have what you call 'a mother thing.' It's just more complicated than . . ."

"Hens?"

"Exactly."

"So what about *your* mother?"

"What about her?" Robin asked.

"Did you have these good moments with her?"

"Yeah, sure, I guess." Robin shrugged.

"You guess?"

Robin rubbed her eyes. "My mother and I have a complicated relationship. But there were great moments."

"Like what?"

"She had a popular talk show on the local radio. Everyone listened to it."

"Oh, that's cool. A local celebrity?"

"Exactly. It was called *Getting Personal with Diana Hart*. It aired three times a week. And every time it aired, at four in the afternoon, my sister and I would sit down by the radio and listen. It was a full hour. We never missed a show. We would both wait for her to come home. And when she got back, we would talk about the show. You know, what we liked, and how she was. It was like our special time with her."

"That's sweet."

"Yeah," Robin said tonelessly. The parts she left unsaid weighed her down. Nathaniel seemed to notice she didn't want to talk anymore and focused on the road instead.

Searching for a distraction, she took out her phone and tapped the Facebook app. She scrolled down, liking puppy pics, ignoring a political rant, reading the first two lines in a post about a scandal in the psychology world . . .

And then she glimpsed her own name.

She only realized it as she scrolled, her mind catching on a second too late, the post already gone. She paused and scrolled back, finding the relevant post. It was one of those posts about Kathy, with Kathy's portrait shot almost everyone used from the news stories. The post was by someone named Sherry Nelson. Robin vaguely recalled the woman. Wasn't she the organizer of a local bake sale in Bethelville a while back? Apparently, they were Facebook friends, though Robin couldn't recall ever having an actual conversation with the woman.

The post started like all those other Kathy posts. How happy she was that Kathy had returned. She'd prayed for months for the girl . . . Robin's eyes flickered onward, ignoring the bland text, finally finding her own name.

> . . . really upset to find out that the therapist
> Kathy is seeing, Robin Hart, is more interested in
> her own fame, than Kathy's well . . .

The rest of the text was hidden from sight by Facebook's "See more" link. For a fragment of a second, Robin almost didn't tap it. She didn't need to *see more*. Seeing more would not make her life any better. Seeing more would not calm her thudding heartbeat or soothe her tense muscles.

She tapped the "See more" link.

> . . . than Kathy's well-being. Robin has apparently been forcing Kathy to relive her traumatic year over and over as some sort of experimental psychological technique. Kathy has suffered because of this, and people close to the family said the girl is in even worse shape than before, lashing out aggressively, and refusing to go anywhere public. If I were Kathy's mother, I would be deeply worried about this. Just my two cents.

"What the hell?" Robin exploded.

"What is it?"

"Some moron is bad-mouthing me on Facebook." Robin stared at the post's statistics in horror. It had thirty-two likes, "sad" reactions, and "hug" reactions. And twelve comments.

"You can block him," Nathaniel suggested.

"It's a her. And even if I block her . . . people are seeing her post!" Robin tapped the comments. She was pretty sure she didn't know any of those people, but the comments seemed generally outraged, with one commenter who wrote "you would be a much better therapist than her."

"Ignore it," Nathaniel said. "It's just Facebook. People talk shit on social media all the time."

"You don't have any idea how this makes me feel!"

"I don't?" Nathaniel looked at her. "Hello? Should I remind you I'm a cop? Do you see a lot of love for my profession on social media lately?"

"But did anyone write about you personally?"

"Sure, a few times. I ignored it. It blew over."

She wanted to respond. She would tell Sherry Nelson where she could shove her two cents.

But she didn't. Nathaniel was right.

She put her phone away, breathing hard. Her jaw clenched tightly, and to her horror she could feel an actual tear threatening to emerge.

"Want to hear a funny story?" Nathaniel asked.

"No."

"It'll distract you from that dumb Facebook post."

"I doubt it."

"Let me try."

Robin exhaled. "Fine."

"A few years back, when I was still in uniform, I got a call. This guy called 911 to say someone broke into his house. So me and my partner went over there. It was this one dude, living alone. And sure enough, someone had broken a window and entered his house."

"So far it's not a very funny story," Robin said distractedly, still fuming. Damn Sherry Nelson. Robin would write her *own* Facebook post about what a dumb bitch Sherry Nelson was.

"Hang on, I'm getting there. So we ask the usual stuff, right? Are you hurt, did you see anyone, is there anything missing. So when we ask about anything missing, the dude starts getting dodgy. Suddenly he's not answering our questions. Now me and my partner exchange looks. We know what this means. This guy probably had his dope stolen or something. So we lean in kinda aggressively, tell him he has to come clean. Finally he says okay, fine, let me show you something. And he takes me to the back room. And you'll never guess what he had there."

"A cow?" Robin said.

"What? No! Why would he have a cow in his back room?"

"Well, you said I'll never guess, so I gave it a shot."

"You're ruining the story. No. What he had there were shelves of My Little Ponys."

"Seriously?" Robin laughed.

"I swear. Like . . . hundreds of the things. Rows and rows of My Little Ponys. And it turns out the guy who broke in stole five of them. But he stole the most expensive ones."

"How expensive? I have a My Little Pony in my playroom. It cost something like ten dollars."

"That's what I asked. I was like, Are they gold or something? So he says nah, but they're super rare, and each cost more than five hundred dollars. The most expensive one, Sweet Scoops, cost eight hundred dollars."

"Oh wow." Robin wondered if maybe she had toys worth anything in her playroom. Rare pieces or anything like that. Not likely.

"Wow is right. So the entire collection is worth almost three grand. So I went to the nearby local pawnshop and was like, Did anyone try to pawn these really valuable My Little Ponys, and he looked at me like I was insane. I guess My Little Ponys aren't pawnshop material. So then I figure, the burglar had to know which ponies are more valuable, right? There were hundreds in that room, and he just happened to take the five most expensive. So I search online and find this My Little Pony expert in Indianapolis."

"Gotta say, you put a lot of effort into the My Little Pony case."

"I was invested by that point." Nathaniel grinned at her. "So we go to see that dude, and he opens the door for us . . . and guess what he's holding in his hand."

"Sweet Scoops?" Robin hedged a guess.

"You got that right! He's holding the eight-hundred-dollar pony, Sweet Scoops. He sees us in our uniforms and bolts, runs out the back door."

"You're making all this up."

"Swear I'm not. So we chased him, right? The dude is trying to lose us in the crowded street, which maybe he could have. Except he's a grown man wearing a pink My Little Pony shirt, and there aren't a lot of those around. So we catch up to him, and Sweet Scoops is gone. He says he doesn't know what we're talking about. He never saw Sweet Scoops."

"He threw it away?"

"Nah, it was much worse. He still had it on him."

Robin let it sink in, then stared at Nathaniel, horrified. "No."

"You guessed it! Dude shoved the thing in his underpants. And it was a hot day, and he was running. Well . . . I guess maybe you don't want all the details."

"No!" Robin was helplessly giggling by this point. "I really don't."

"We found the rest of the ponies in this dude's house. Turns out he was trying to get his hands on Sweet Scoops for years, and when he saw in an online forum that a local had it, he couldn't help himself. So we got the guy's ponies back. But I had to tell him why Sweet Scoops smelled so weird. Let me tell you, that guy wasn't happy."

"You didn't have to tell him!" Robin had tears of laughter running down her cheeks by this point.

Nathaniel considered that. "Nah, I guess not. But I *really* wanted to."

Robin laughed until her stomach hurt, while Nathaniel drove on, smiling. And even after she calmed down, every few minutes, she would think about Sweet Scoops jostling inside the My Little Pony thief's underwear and start laughing all over again.

Chapter 30

The sheriff's department in Bethelville, which Robin had been to a few times, was quite a large structure. During the days after Kathy's disappearance, it had been the hub of the search parties and would often accommodate over sixty people at the same time, which was quite impressive for a town with just over five thousand people.

The headquarters of the Indianapolis Metropolitan Police Department made it seem like a small, decrepit shed.

It was an enormous, imposing building that towered over the street. Robin was glad she was with Nathaniel and didn't have to step through the main entrance alone. Nathaniel led her confidently inside, breezing past the main desk with barely a nod. He summoned the elevator, and when they stepped in, he pressed the button for the fourteenth floor.

He took her to a large meeting room with windows that over-looked the city. Two expansive whiteboards stood against the wall with a few photos taped to them, as well as rows of scribbled notes. Robin recognized one of the photos—a portrait of Haley Parks that had been circulated in news stories. Several were of the crime scene, including a photo of Haley's body as they'd found it, swinging on a tree, her clothes stained with blood. Robin quickly tore her eyes away, feeling as if the photo had been branded into her retinas. Unlike photos she sometimes saw on the news, this one wasn't censored in any way. She had a glimpse of the girl's face, the obvious deterioration of the body. She wished she could unsee it.

They were a few minutes early, so the room was empty, and Nathaniel took a chair facing the windows.

"Do you mind if we sit on the other side of the table?" Robin asked weakly. The height was making her dizzy. Robin didn't really have a fear of heights, but she definitely had some mistrust of them. And if she kept avoiding glancing at the whiteboard, she'd have no other option than staring at the windows.

"Sure." Nathaniel shrugged. "Do you want some water?"

"Yeah." Her throat was dry. She was getting anxious. In a few minutes a group of detectives and federal agents would step into this room, and she'd have to explain why she thought a little girl who played with a figure of a Batman villain could be evidence in two murders.

They showed up quickly afterward. Nathaniel introduced her whenever someone came in, but her mind was buzzing, and she didn't catch most of their names. Out of the seven law enforcement agents she met, only one was a woman, a state cop. Her name, at least, Robin remembered—Officer Tyler.

As they sat down, they talked to each other, the way coworkers often do. Robin caught snippets of discussions that meant nothing to her—one of them talked about an email they'd all gotten, another told his associate in a low voice something about a shift that had gone on for too long, and at some point, the woman muttered about a close call with someone named Abernathy, and two of the state cops chuckled appreciatively. This all made Robin even more uncomfortable, feeling as if she'd crashed an intimate party. Nathaniel glanced at her and smiled reassuringly, and she found herself smiling weakly back.

Finally, one of the homicide detectives—an older, bald guy with a sort of Anthony Hopkins vibe—cleared his throat. The rest slowly stopped talking. He seemed to be the guy in charge. What was his name? She desperately tried to recall. Detective . . . Claflin? Was that even a name?

"So," he said. "Ms. Hart. Or is it Doctor?"

"It's Doctor," Robin said, her voice slightly high. "But you can call me Robin."

"Okay. Dr. Hart, as Detective King probably told you, your information sparked a lot of arguments here."

"He didn't tell me that," Robin said. "He just said you wanted to hear me out."

"Right," Claflin said. "First . . . can you tell us in your own words what Kathy Stone showed you during the sessions that made you contact Detective King?"

Robin repeated what she'd seen Kathy playact with the toys the first two times. This came rather easily—Robin was used to summarizing play sessions. She did it every time for her own progress reports. While she talked, her voice became steadier and more relaxed. This was her field of expertise, and she knew it better than any of the people in that room. Some of the men initially seemed dismissive. But those looks slowly evaporated. Perhaps they didn't think it was actual evidence, but hearing about a nine-year-old girl enacting violent murders with toys wasn't something anyone could ignore outright.

When she finished talking, Claflin cleared his throat. "I have two boys, and one of them has a few superhero figures," he said. "He plays with them, and the games can get pretty violent. So I'm wondering . . . could this be simply a girl playing with toys?"

"It *was* a girl playing with toys," Robin said. "But this was not a typical game. The intention was very clear: she was playacting something very specific, and it was crucial to her that she got it right. Especially with the toy drill, she did it repeatedly. She was trying to process and communicate something that was troubling her."

"Have you ever seen cases like that, in which children playact violent moments they saw?"

"A few times. In cases of domestic abuse. Kids playact difficult moments that they saw or experienced themselves," Robin said. "I also had a case of a traffic accident survivor, and she replayed the crash with toy cars."

"What about the drawing?" one of the state cops asked.

Robin frowned. "The drawing?"

"Detective King said Kathy Stone also drew something for you," Claflin said.

"Oh! I didn't tell him that."

"Claire Stone told me," Nathaniel said.

"I don't know if it's relevant," Robin said. "Kathy drew a man getting hurt in his arms and legs. And then she smeared a lot of red paint on the page, which I assume represented the blood."

"Hurt his arms and legs?" Claflin frowned. "How exactly? Can you show us?" He turned around and picked up a marker from the shelf underneath the whiteboards.

Robin got up, took the marker from him, and approached the whiteboards, her eyes avoiding the photos. She found an empty space and drew the man Kathy had drawn as best she could recollect him. "She drew something like that. And then she took some red paint . . ." Robin found a red marker. "And drew lines across the arms and feet. Like this. And then she drew the blood dripping, and finally smeared the red paint over everything."

"So it doesn't look like the man hurt his arms and legs," Claflin said. "It looks like they were cut off."

Robin gawked at him, stunned. Then she looked back at the picture she'd drawn.

The four lines completely severed the man's limbs.

"That wasn't my interpretation of it," she said. She recalled herself saying the man had hurt his hand, and then his leg. "I think she was drawing a scratch. The drawing is flat, so it looks like it was severed—"

"She could have drawn little holes, or scratches along the limbs," the female state cop said. "But she didn't. She drew them horizontally."

"Why do you think that?" Robin asked. "That's one interpretation. It's not exactly an accurate drawing."

"We think that because it might link this to a third case," Nathaniel said.

"A third case?" Dizziness struck Robin.

"There's an unsolved murder in Kentucky," the federal agent said. "The body of twenty-one-year-old Cynthia Rodgers was found buried in a forest. The specifics of the case seem to match that drawing."

"The specifics?" Robin stared at the drawing. "What specifics?"

"The severed limbs," Nathaniel said after a few seconds of silence.

"You . . . you mean they found . . ."

"Maybe it's best if we don't discuss all the details," Claflin said. "There are things that don't match up, of course. Kathy drew a man, and the murder case is of a woman. So it's not necessarily related."

"Some of the forensics match," the agent pointed out. "The trophies the killer took—"

"Let's discuss this later," Claflin said sternly.

"*Three* murder cases?" Robin said. "Then . . . is this a serial killer?"

Kathy had populated the house with six toys. And the clown killed them one by one . . .

"It might be," Claflin said. "If all the murders were really done by the same individual, which we are not entirely convinced of yet."

"There could be more murders," Robin said slowly.

"What do you mean?" Claflin asked.

She explained about the toys Kathy took away each time. How whenever one was killed, Kathy would bury it in the sandbox. She filled them in on the third toy dying—the Monopoly Man in the barrel. And she explained her thoughts—the six toys dying one by one.

The room was silent after Robin finished talking. She looked at the faces around her and saw skepticism in some. Others, like Claflin, seemed serious and concerned.

"*If* the same person committed the three murders we discussed, it's reasonable to assume he was also the one who abducted Kathy Stone," Nathaniel finally said. "And it's possible she witnessed other murders as well. Like the one Robin mentioned."

"That would mean these murders occurred in the past fifteen months, right?" one of the homicide detectives said. "I don't recall any unsolved murders by drowning in Indiana in that time frame."

"Could be in other states, like the Rodgers murder," the fed pointed out.

"The drowning could have been ruled as an accidental drowning," one of the state cops said.

"Or the bodies might not have been found," Nathaniel said. "It took a while before the bodies of Basset and Rodgers were discovered."

"Even if those three murders are connected, it doesn't necessarily mean they were done by the same person—"

"Oh, come on, I feel like the evidence—"

"*Evidence?* Seriously? Are you prepared to call the Kentucky State Police to tell them we have a drawing of a stick figure matching their murder victim?"

As they talked, raising their voices, no one paid attention to Robin. The adults were now talking. They were done listening to her. And instinctively she nodded as the cops talked. Trying to blend in.

"This doesn't change our approach. We need to focus on Haley Parks."

"It could be just a messed-up kid playing weird games, with all of us wasting valuable time," Officer Tyler said, annoyed. "I mean, it's not a lot to go on, right? A little girl playing with some plastic figures? Joker killing the Monopoly Man?"

Robin gritted her teeth, feeling that new voice growing inside her. The one who took the dollhouse from her mother's home. The one who wouldn't bend when Detective King pressured her. Why the hell did they even bring her all this way if they didn't intend to involve her?

"There's the trophies linking the murders together," the fed said. "There were no other deaths in the past two years in Indiana in which hair had been taken from the victims. We've checked that."

"Oh, come on, missing hair. These were all violent deaths. The hair could have been torn off during the struggle. And the MO of these murders is vastly different. Don't serial killers usually kill in the same manner?"

"Not always," the fed said. "There's the signature and the MO, and—"

"Excuse me," Robin said sharply.

All of them turned to look at her.

She cleared her throat. "I don't know if this is a serial killer or a coincidence. But whatever the case, it's my professional opinion that Kathy Stone was witness to an actual violent crime. And she's doing her best to convey that to me, and to process it. So it's *not* just a little girl playing with plastic figures. This is not something you can ignore."

Nathaniel nodded. "I agree. It deserves our attention."

"I'm not arguing that the girl didn't go through some horrible shit," Tyler said. "The question is, Do we abandon our leads on the Parks murder to focus on this new angle? Because that's a huge gamble. Haley Parks deserves justice."

"So does Gloria Basset," Nathaniel said sharply.

"I agree! And we don't know if we can give them that by chasing this wild theory," Tyler said, folding her arms. "We can't know if this is what the girl even really saw. She doesn't talk, right?"

"No," Robin said. "She doesn't talk. Not since she came back."

Chapter 31

The day of the disappearance

History was full of great artists who weren't appreciated in their time. Evan didn't plan on being one of them.

How had Vincent van Gogh felt, knowing how incredible his art was without anyone else to appreciate it? Evan could imagine it. Occasionally he'd post an image on Instagram and get a handful of likes and a couple of comments. That was how poor Vincent must have felt.

In fact, maybe it was even worse. Vincent was lucky there was no Instagram back in his day. Imagine posting *The Starry Night* and getting seven likes and one comment from your cousin saying it was "very pretty." With a smiley with hearts for eyes.

It was enough to decimate the soul.

Well, Evan wasn't planning on keeping things that way. After years of frustration, with Robin being the main breadwinner and him sometimes supplementing their income with dreary jobs photographing weddings, he'd seen his chance and grabbed it with both hands.

For almost everyone, the pandemic was a curse. For Evan it had been a blessing. His art was already becoming known. And after this project was done . . . the sky was the limit.

And this photo shoot . . . it was his best yet. Daring, unusual. No one had ever done anything like this before.

He took another photo of his young model. The last rays of the setting sun, filtering through the clouds, lit her face just right. It took his breath away.

When his phone rang, he ignored it. But the ringing kept on, incessant, intrusive. Killing the moment. Gritting his teeth, he took the phone out of his pocket. It was Robin.

"Hi," he answered. His tone just a bit sharp.

"Evan . . ."

He cleared his throat. "Yeah, is everything all right?"

"Pete Stone's daughter disappeared."

For a moment, he didn't say anything, his phone clenched in his hand. Finally, he lowered his voice, glancing at his model. "What do you mean, disappeared?"

"They can't find her anywhere. There's a search going on . . . I thought you'd want to know. Maybe Pete would appreciate a phone call."

"Yes . . . yes, of course. Thanks for letting me know."

"You should come back sooner. Pete might need support. And I'm . . ." Her voice wavered. He could hear the tears in her throat. "I'd appreciate it too."

"Sure." He frowned. "I'll do my best."

"Thanks," she whispered. "I'll let you know if they find her."

He said goodbye and hung up.

"What happened?" his model piped.

His voice was slightly unsteady. "It's nothing. Let's finish this up. Just a few more shots and we're done."

Chapter 32

Robin sat in her kitchen, drinking red wine. She knew she shouldn't. She had been getting almost no shut-eye for the past weeks. And alcohol only made her sleep worse.

But the past day had so many jagged edges to it, and she needed something to smooth them away. She'd always had a visual mind, and that meeting with the task force had supplied it with horrific fuel. Throughout the ride back, she kept recalling the photo of Haley Parks. And if she tried to push that memory away, her mind would conjure images of other women. Gloria Basset with a gaping hole in her skull. Cynthia Rodgers, the details of her death too horrific to dwell on. And maybe other victims, their bodies not yet found.

Nathaniel had tried to distract her, but even if she tried to listen to him, she would lose track of what he was saying midsentence, the unseeing eyes of a dead woman staring at her.

So when she reached home, she opened a bottle of wine and poured herself a big glass. And after drinking it, she poured another one, welcoming the heaviness that came with the drink, the slight fuzziness in her head.

Still, it wasn't enough. Those imaginary fragments kept scraping at her, a constant looming terror.

She tried to distract herself, scrolling through her phone. She opened Facebook and saw that toxic post by Sherry Nelson. It had garnered a few more likes and even a share. She tried to get worked up about it, to replace her fear with anger. But she couldn't. It seemed so inconsequential. A woman ranting about her on social media. That flimsy replacement for actual human connection. Robin saw the words that woman wrote for what they literally were—stored bits of data in some server somewhere on the globe. Alongside trillions of other bits. And all those likes and comments were the same. Just bits. Ones and zeros. They weren't tangible. They weren't real.

Somewhere out there, a man was murdering women in vicious and horrendous ways, and poor Kathy had been a witness to his actions. It didn't get any more real than that. Who cared about Sherry Nelson and her ridiculous two cents?

In fact, nothing on Facebook managed to distract her. She needed a real human connection.

She dialed.

Melody answered after a few seconds. "Hey." She sounded exhausted.

"Hey." Robin's voice trembled. "Um . . . are you . . . doing anything?"

"What's wrong?"

"I could really use some company."

"You want to come over?"

Come over. Robin glanced outside. The street was rife with shadows. "I can't drive. I drank some wine. And . . . I don't want to walk in the dark alone."

There was a short pause. "I'm on my way," Melody finally said.

It took her ten long minutes to show up, and Robin felt a wave of relief when Melody's headlights finally shone through the kitchen window. She went to the door, Menny already there, wagging his tail.

"Hey," Robin said as she opened the door. And then she started crying.

Melody's arms enveloped her, pulling her into a warm hug. Robin let her sister lead her back inside, Menny circling them, nearly tripping them twice. They dropped to the sofa, Robin leaning against Melody's shoulder.

"I think I got snot on your sweater," she said, wiping her eyes.

"It'll blend well with my kids' snot," Melody said.

"Thanks for coming," Robin said. "I just . . . didn't want to be alone."

"Okay," Melody said gently. "Can I get us drinks?"

"Sure. I already started."

Melody got up and went to the kitchen. She returned with the wine bottle and two glasses. "Almost half is gone. Am I right in guessing that you drank all of it this evening?"

"It's been a rough day."

Melody poured them both a glass. "Less for you. I don't want to replay that night in high school with the cranberry vodka."

"If memory serves, *you* were the one who made a mess that night."

"Um, no. I distinctly remember cleaning the vomit in my room, praying Dad and Diana wouldn't come in to see what the noise was."

"Oh yeah." Robin smiled. "Your room smelled like sick for two whole days."

Melody raised her glass to toast. "To cranberry vodka."

"May we never drink any again." Robin clinked her glass with Melody's.

"Speaking of Diana . . . ," Melody said.

"What about her?"

"You have to visit her, Robin. *And* return her damn dollhouse. She's been driving me crazy. Calling several times a day."

"Why don't *you* visit her?"

"I can't," Melody reminded her. "She won't let me, because she's afraid of COVID."

"I can't believe we're talking about this again. There's nothing preventing you from going there. You vaccinated your kids, Melody!"

Melody sipped from her glass. "Diana doesn't know that. Anyway, we're not talking about me. We're talking about you and your little rebellion."

"Don't do that." Robin raised her finger. "Don't you pull a Mom on me."

Melody's eyes widened. She looked stricken. "I didn't pull a . . . you can't compare me to Diana. I'm not *anything* like her."

"What you just did is exactly the sort of thing Mom would do. Reflecting the blame on me. This is very much your doing, just like it's mine."

"I don't know how it's my fault. I didn't steal Diana's precious dollhouse!"

"I can't hold the fort alone, Melody. You need to start visiting her."

"Don't be so dramatic. I talk to her all the time on the phone. It's not like I disappeared from her life."

"That's not the same as going to see her, and you know it." Robin gritted her teeth. "I won't do this again."

Melody snorted. "*Again?* What are you going on about?"

"It's like when we were kids. With the radio show—"

"Oh, come on. That was your stupid decision. Don't act like a martyr."

"I did what had to be done!" Robin was shouting at this point. The memories started flashing in her mind. Waking up in the middle of the night, the alarm blaring. The radio, she had to get to the radio . . .

"What had to be done, or what Diana wanted?" Melody demanded. "Those aren't the same things, Robin."

Robin was about to strangle her sister. "I'm not having that argument again. That radio show—"

"That radio show was just another way for Diana to torture you."

Listening to the radio, to every word, memorizing the details, every moment important . . . crucial . . . she couldn't talk about this. Not now, after the day she'd had. She pushed the memories away and folded her arms, jutting her chin. "If you don't tell Mom your kids are vaccinated, *I will.*"

"You wouldn't." Melody looked genuinely shocked.

"Yes, I would. She'll find out anyway at some point."

"Give me a little time, okay? Summer vacation is about to start—"

"I can't, Melody! I'm falling apart. I'm not sleeping, there's some shit going on with my job, Mom is driving me insane, and I'm done. I'm done!"

They were both breathing hard. Robin's face was flushed, her heart pounding. She and Melody almost never shouted at each other. Sure, they would fight occasionally, give each other the icy treatment. But this was something else.

"Fine." Melody was the first to break the silence that stretched between them. "I'll tell her. I'll even go visit her, okay? And if she calls me about the dollhouse, I'll say you told me you need it for a few more days."

"Thanks." Robin let out a shuddering breath. She sipped from her wine, doing her best to steady her trembling hand.

"I'm sorry, I didn't know things were so bad," Melody said.

"It's fine. Well, it's not. But it'll be fine."

Melody nudged closer to her. "So what happened today?"

"I don't think I can talk about it."

"This is the shit going on in your job?"

"Yeah."

"Is it related to Kathy?"

Robin hesitated. "I can't talk about it."

Melody nodded grimly.

"Are you going to tell me I should stop treating her too?" Robin asked.

"Do you want to stop treating her?"

"No."

"Good." Melody took another sip. "I doubt they'd find a better therapist than you."

"I really needed to hear someone say that." Tears filled Robin's eyes again.

"You know . . . when I got here you seemed totally freaked out."

"I was a bit scared."

Melody exhaled. "Back when she was abducted, I was scared all the time. And we kept worrying that whoever took her might be living nearby. I kept having nightmares about the kids. That I'd lost them, and I'm calling them, and they won't answer me."

Robin rubbed her eyes. "I was scared too. But it must have been terrifying for you. Especially with Amy."

"I couldn't sleep for days after the abduction," Melody said, swirling the wine in her glass. "Fred would hug me at night to get me to stop trembling."

"I wish I could say the same."

"You wish Fred had hugged you at night?" Melody quirked an eyebrow.

"I wish Evan had." Robin shook her head. "He was gone most of the time, on his photo shoots. The night after Kathy was abducted, I let Menny sleep in our bed so I would feel safer. Evan bitched afterward that he could smell the dog on our sheets."

"Yeah, he wasn't a great catch, that guy."

"Tell that to Mom. You know, he was gone all the time. Everyone all over the world was staying at home for once. Maybe it wasn't by choice, but people stayed put, with their families. But not Evan. Because it was such an opportunity."

"Well, a shitty man he may be, but he was right about it being an opportunity for him," Melody pointed out. "That was his big break."

"I needed him here, Melody. And when Kathy was gone and I was pregnant, I needed him more than ever. But even then, he would come home for a couple of days at a time and leave again."

"I know, sweetie." Melody put her arm around Robin. "I, for one, am glad you kicked his ass out. You deserve someone who would take care of you."

"Yeah." Robin snuggled closer to Melody. "Well, I have you."

Chapter 33

He sat in his car, waiting for the woman to wake up.

How would this scene be scripted? The tension should be unbearable. The viewer should know that something terrible was about to happen.

> *EXTERIOR—WOODS*
> *Sounds typical with wood nightlife—chirping, rustling in the bushes. CAMERA PANS TO SHOW A CAR PARKED BY THE TREES.*

Perhaps in the movie script, the woman would already be awake, shrieking in the trunk. Not in real life, though. Right now she was unconscious. He'd made sure of that.

He didn't like drugging them. It felt almost like cheating. But he had to do it. He'd learned it with the Parks girl. Sure, they all looked harmless enough—he chose them that way. Small, thin, the perfect victims. But scare them enough, get that adrenaline surging, and they could fight. They could hurt him. They could even escape. Parks nearly got away, *after* she saw his face.

It was a thin line to walk. He needed them awake, just enough that they could struggle. But he also needed them weak and groggy so they didn't struggle too hard. So he drugged them and then waited patiently until they started waking up.

The night was so dark, he couldn't see two feet ahead. He'd turned off his headlights, of course. The last thing he needed was some patrolling cop to wonder who was out there in the car by the trees. So he sat in the inky darkness, his phone in his lap, passing the time. Waiting.

He opened his photos and scrolled through the recent ones. He knew them by heart. The photos of the girl in the front yard with her mother. The woman never taking her eyes off the girl, constantly vigilant. In the past weeks he'd spent days watching the girl's house and following the girl and her mother around. Kathy was *never* left alone. And he saw her mother checking the windows in the evening, turning on the alarm. The front door had a big new lock on it. The woman had learned her lesson.

He swiped the screen. He had to get to the girl. But it wasn't as easy as he'd first expected. He would have to bide his time, wait for the right moment.

He kept scrolling through the photos, reaching the new ones. A few other women he was monitoring.

Not everyone realized, as Kathy's mother did, that the world was dangerous.

Take the woman he had in the trunk of his car right now, for example.

He had a bunch of photos of her jogging in the park. Alone. Maintaining the same schedule, the same routes. Two days a week in the early morning, and two days late in the evening. He looked at the last photo he took of her, her hair in a ponytail, white shirt, short pink yoga shorts. All her shorts were either pink or purple. Old-fashioned girly colors. He liked that.

Watching her photo on his phone, he could feel the stiffening in his pants. He considered relieving the stress, then shook his head. No. Not yet. He could wait just a bit longer.

Instead, he flipped until he reached Robin's photos. Walking with her dog in the park. Standing in her kitchen, framed by the window. Standing in line at the local supermarket. Soon. His next project.

A sudden thump from his trunk.

Ah, she was awake.

He turned off the screen and stepped out of the car. He stopped for a minute to savor the moment. Imagine the script.

The man is dressed in a gray hoodie, facing AWAY FROM THE CAMERA.

We hear MORE THUMPING.

A desperate cry for help.

He circled the vehicle and popped the trunk open.

The woman lay inside, eyes wide with terror.

He showed her the knife.

"If you behave, I won't have to cut you," he said. "You will behave, right?"

A brief, terrified nod.

He wasn't even lying. He had no intention of using the knife. The script was completely different this time.

Chapter 34

The stench of death was distinctive as Nathaniel made his way down the narrow trail leading to the crime scene. Ordinarily, this part of the park probably smelled of wet earth and trees and moss. But murder had transformed it. It wasn't just the smell. It was the fluttering crime scene tape tied around the trees. The broken branches and muddy footprints marking the arrival of the detectives, the forensic team, the medical examiner. It was the red and blue lights of the squad car behind him, flickering on the surrounding foliage.

An angry caw made him raise his head. Two crows, sitting on a branch, eyed him with vehemence. One of them quirked its head and cawed again.

The path took a sharp turn to the right and opened up to a clearing by a stream. And there they all were, processing the crime scene. Nathaniel's eyes swept across the things he'd gotten too familiar with. The yellow evidence markers placed on the ground. The flash of the police photographer's camera. A crouching forensic team member scooping something into an evidence bag.

The medical examiner was kneeling by the decomposing body of a young woman. The barrel of murky water they'd found her in stood nearby.

"Sir." A uniformed cop with a clipboard approached him. "This is a crime scene. Please—"

"Detective Nathaniel King." He flashed his ID. "Detective Lopez is expecting me."

"Let him in," a tall man in a trench coat said. He stood a few yards away from the barrel, jotting in his notebook. Unlike his associates, he seemed almost like a man snatched from that era of noir movies, where detectives drank whiskey in their dark offices while women in red dresses told them about their woes.

Nathaniel signed the crime scene log that the officer held in his hand and strode over to Detective Lopez.

"You showed up fast," Lopez said.

"Unfortunately, I've been expecting this phone call for a few days now," Nathaniel said.

Lopez nodded. "So they told me. So you think this is a serial killer?"

"It might be." Nathaniel noticed a few more crows perched on the surrounding trees. Their beady eyes scrutinized the scene with interest. "What do we have?"

"Victim is Mandy Ross. Her driver's license is in her purse, which we found discarded in the bushes over there. Officer Cole was the one who found her. As you probably know, we had officers canvasing the nearby forests for the past three days. Cole reported it at eleven thirty in the morning. She was found inside the barrel, only her legs visible." Lopez gestured at the trees. "A few crows were pecking at her."

"I see we have some footprints."

"Yeah, we have a good print. The ground was muddy." Lopez walked over to where one of the forensic technicians was kneeling by the mud. He was filling a boot-shaped hole with a gray plaster. "See? Once we find a boot to compare it with—"

A sudden shout by one of the technicians made Nathaniel whirl around. The man chased a crow that was fluttering away. Other crows were cawing loudly, sounding as if they were laughing mockingly.

"Stevens, what's the matter with you?" Lopez snapped.

"The damn crow flew away with one of the evidence markers!" Stevens said, staring at the treetops.

"For God's sake . . . get another one."

"I don't know the number on it."

Lopez gave him a hard stare.

"I'll find it," Stevens muttered, trudging away.

"Make sure it matches the crime scene photos. I don't want any evidence from the scene ruled inadmissible because you were outsmarted by a bird." Lopez shook his head, returning to Nathaniel. "Those crows are driving me crazy. And every few minutes some smart-ass mentions that it's a *murder of crows*, or that he's about to *murder a crow*, like he's the first person to ever come up with that."

Nathaniel, who *had* just been about to say it was a murder of crows, decided to keep quiet.

Lopez pointed. "You see that groove in the mud over there? That's probably where he dragged the barrel. Which I don't get. You guys said you were looking for a drowning victim, so when Cole reported finding her here, I assumed the body was floating in the stream. But instead someone dragged the barrel all this way and filled it up with water from the stream . . . that's some sick shit."

"Yeah." Nathaniel thought of Robin's latest session. The little girl playacting the murder. A toy drowning another toy in a Play-Doh container, headfirst. If he'd had any doubts before, they were now gone. Kathy was definitely reenacting murders.

"We found very dark bruises on her ankles. He held her down. I hope it was fast."

"I doubt it," Nathaniel said. Dark bruises indicated the murderer held her down forcefully. For a while. She was still alive and conscious when it happened. "Did the ME note any missing hair?"

"Missing hair?" Lopez frowned. "Her hair is tangled with mud. Can't really say anything about it."

"We should tell him to check when he does the autopsy. Previous victims had missing clumps of hair. We think the killer is keeping trophies."

Lopez jotted something in his notebook. "One more thing." He stepped closer to the barrel and pointed at the ground, where another evidence marker was placed. "What do you make of this?"

Nathaniel examined the mud. Three symmetrical round holes were easily noticeable, the distance between them the same, forming a perfect triangle.

"A tripod," Nathaniel hazarded.

"Exactly." Lopez grunted. "Bastard was taking photos."

"Or filming," Nathaniel said.

"Yeah." Lopez turned around and spat into the bushes. "I'm driving over to notify her parents. They reported her missing a few days ago."

"Why did they wait so long?"

"What do you mean?"

"I believe this woman was murdered at least two months ago," Nathaniel pointed out.

"No, she wasn't." Lopez flipped the pages in his notebook. "I talked to the detective who was investigating the missing person report. She showed up to work six days ago."

"I . . . that makes no sense."

"The body is in relatively good condition," Lopez pointed out. "I haven't discussed it with the ME, but I can tell you for sure it hasn't been there for months. Besides, in this area, any body would have attracted scavengers. They would have eventually dragged her out of that damn barrel."

A chill ran down Nathaniel's neck. Lopez was obviously right, but . . . "I have a witness who saw this woman murdered. A few months ago."

"Well, you should have a long talk with your witness, because that's impossible."

Kathy had been found six weeks ago. Nathaniel had assumed all the sessions Robin had with the girl were about the time before her return. When she was in captivity. That was the theory—the killer had abducted Kathy sixteen months ago, and during the time she spent with him, she'd witnessed his murders.

But if Mandy Ross had been killed a week ago, that theory didn't work anymore.

Could Kathy have witnessed the murders after she returned? No, of course not. Haley Parks, Gloria Basset, and Cynthia Rodgers all died before she returned.

It could mean this murder wasn't related to the other murders.

Except he couldn't believe that either. It had been so accurately depicted, it was impossible for the girl to imagine it. She'd seen it for sure. Could she still be in touch with her kidnapper? Suppose the kidnapper had been a family member. Maybe Kathy had been with him even after she was found. And then she'd seen this woman murdered. Except . . .

"Hang on," Nathaniel said slowly. "You said she showed up to work six days ago. When was that exactly?"

"Last Tuesday, that would be June seventh. She works in a bar in Logansport."

Nathaniel shook his head. It was impossible. He took out his notebook, making sure, even though he already knew the dates by heart.

Robin's last session with Kathy, in which Kathy showed her the drowning in the barrel, had been on June 6.

At least a full day before the murder had happened.

Chapter 35

Robin wasn't sure how she'd feel during Kathy's next session. Kathy was no longer just a traumatized child, needing her help to heal. She was now also a survivor, a witness. The one who could shed light on a series of murders. Now, after Robin had heard from the cops about the horrendous acts of violence the child had seen, after she'd seen *photos*, she was doubly anxious about what Kathy would show her next.

What she wasn't prepared for was the tiny leap of happiness in her heart when she opened the door for Kathy.

The girl stared up at her with her big, attentive eyes, a quirk of a smile on her lips, the same shoebox of props in her hands.

"I'll be back in an hour to pick her up," Claire said. She seemed distracted.

"Sure, no problem," Robin said.

Kathy handed the shoebox to Robin and hugged her mother. Then Claire left, and Robin led Kathy to the playroom.

As always, Kathy approached the art table first. She poured red paint on the page and ran her hands through it.

"The red paint is all over your hands," Robin said, standing above her. "Only you decide where the red paint goes."

Kathy finally stopped and straightened up. Robin prepared herself to follow the girl to the bathroom, when to her surprise, Kathy tentatively touched Robin's hand. A smear of red paint stained Robin's finger.

"The red paint is on my hand too," Robin said. Very gently, she pulled her hand away from her clothes. The paint was water based, and she was pretty sure it could easily be cleaned . . . but she liked her pants too much to risk it.

Kathy now grabbed Robin's hand, her touch sticky. She tugged at her hand, pulling it toward the page.

"You want me to touch the red paint too?" Robin asked.

Kathy nodded, worry in her eyes. The girl was already preparing herself for disappointment.

Robin knelt and placed both her palms on the red paint. She moved them all over the page, as Kathy had done. Her hands were much larger than the girl's, of course, so she had much less space to work with.

"I'm getting red paint all over my hands," Robin said.

For a few seconds she simply moved the hands in circular motions through the paint. It was mesmerizing. The paint represented blood for Kathy. Robin was running her hands through blood. She swallowed, kept moving her hands, though she was suddenly overcome by the desire to snatch them away.

Kathy put her hand on Robin's and pulled it. The page clung to Robin's palm, and she had to pry it off with her fingers.

"My hands are all sticky," Robin said.

Kathy grinned at her. And then she intertwined her tiny fingers through Robin's. For a few seconds they stood there, looking at each other.

Then Kathy pulled Robin to the bathroom. She turned on the water.

"We can wash all the red sticky paint away," Robin said.

She waited for Kathy to wash up first, but Kathy pulled her hand to the faucet, so Robin cleaned her own hands. Then Kathy joined her, the two of them washing their hands together. Kathy managed to clean her hands much quicker than Robin and then tried to help Robin by rubbing off some stubborn spots. At one point, Robin was forced into a cumbersome angle because of their cramped position, and the water splashed on both of them, getting them wet.

Kathy shrieked in laughter.

Robin joined her after a second, surprised at the girl's carefree joy. She finished washing her hands. Then she handed Kathy the nail file from the cabinet. Kathy cleaned the paint from under her fingernails, then looked at Robin.

"Do you want to clean mine? Or should I do it?" Robin asked.

Kathy nodded, motioning with the nail file.

Robin spread her fingers, offering them to Kathy. Very gently, Kathy scraped the paint spots under Robin's fingernails with the nail file. Once done, she smiled at Robin warmly, handing it back. Robin placed the nail file in the cabinet. They stepped out of the bathroom.

In the playroom, Kathy took Robin's hand again. She led her to the shelves of toys. Without hesitation she handed Robin the figurine of the girl and the Wonder Woman toy. Kathy took the lady baker. Following Kathy's lead, Robin took the toys she was handed and placed them in the house. She put the girl in the children's room and Wonder Woman in the living room.

Kathy placed the lady baker in the room with the girl. She looked expectantly at her. What did Kathy want her to do? Robin briefly considered going to get the Joker figure, then decided against it. Instead, she put the little girl on the tiny wooden rocking horse.

"The girl wants to play on the rocking horse," Robin said.

Kathy nudged the girl gently, and the horse rocked, the girl bobbing back and forth. Kathy grinned in delight. Then she took the Wonder Woman toy and traipsed it into the kitchen.

"The tall woman wants to make lunch for everyone," Robin said. "Maybe she should make some peas and carrots."

Kathy shook her head emphatically.

"No. They don't like peas and carrots. She'll make pasta."

Kathy grinned at her and handed her the Wonder Woman figurine. Robin took the plastic woman and acted out an elaborate imaginary cooking sequence, with Wonder Woman going to the cabinets to get the pasta, putting water in a tiny pot, putting the pot on the stove. For a while Robin let a part of herself enjoy the game as she would have all those years ago. Or as she would have now, as a mother and not as a professional. The dollhouse was so intricate, it was easy to lose herself. She kept mirroring her own actions, and Kathy's actions, as the girl reenacted with the other toys. A tiny happy family, living in their beautiful home.

But Robin caught Kathy glancing a few times toward the shelves. She knew what the girl was thinking.

The killer lurked on the other side of the room.

And then Kathy put the little girl in bed, placing the baker lady next to her. She crossed the room and picked up the evil clown figure. This time, Kathy didn't take Robin with her.

This part of the game was still only Kathy's.

All the joy had seeped away from the girl's face. She carried the figure in her fist and thrust it into the living room, propping it against the couch, in front of the plastic TV. The murderer's den.

"The scary man is sitting in front of the TV," Robin said. "Do you want to put him in jail again?"

Kathy didn't seem to hear. Instead, she turned to the shoebox. Lifting the lid, she rummaged inside it, coming up with what Robin initially thought was another Play-Doh container. But then she saw it was one of those obnoxious slime things.

Kathy pried the lid off, and then, to Robin's dismay, emptied the entire container into the miniature bathtub in the bathroom.

Robin cleared her throat. "The—"

A loud banging interrupted her.

Kathy leaped in fright, dropping the empty slime container. She hurried to Robin's side, hugging Robin's waist, trembling.

"Nothing happened," Robin said. "It's just someone knocking on the door."

The doorbell rang. Then came more banging. In a different room, Menny barked.

"I'll go see who it is," Robin said. "Okay? You can stay here."

Kathy shook her head.

"Kathy, nothing can hurt you here," Robin said. "I'll go see who's at the door and tell them to go away."

Kathy still didn't let go.

"It'll only take a minute. And then we can start again. Do you want to practice blowing bubbles while you wait?"

After a few seconds, Kathy gave a tiny nod.

Robin got a new bubble wand from her cabinet and handed it to Kathy. "Here. Let's see if you can do more than twenty."

Once Kathy began blowing bubbles, Robin left the playroom, shutting the door behind her. Someone rang the doorbell again. Menny stood in front of the front door, barking angrily.

Robin peeked through the peephole. Then, annoyed, she opened the door.

"Mr. Stone," she said. "We're still not done."

Pete Stone stood in front of her, red faced, breathing heavily. "You're definitely done. Kathy! Let's go, we're leaving."

Menny growled at Robin's feet. Pete took a step back. "Kathy!"

"Mr. Stone, you're scaring your daughter," Robin said, softening her voice. "If you want to end the session earlier, that's no problem. But let's talk outside for a moment."

Menny barked again.

"Menny, quiet!" Robin snapped.

Menny gave her an offended stare and huffed.

"Fine," Pete spat.

He took a step back, and Robin joined him outside.

"You seem angry," Robin said. She used the same voice she did when talking to frightened or aggressive children. Soft, but steady. A voice in control. Someone who called the shots and kept you safe.

"Of course I'm angry," Pete snarled. "You've kept on doing these sessions behind my back."

Robin blinked in surprise. "I didn't know you wanted these sessions to stop." Now she knew why Claire kept canceling their joint guidance sessions.

"I told Claire! I wanted you to cooperate with the police, let them ask Kathy questions and get the information to finally get the bastard who took her. That way, she would have closure, and she would never need to think about those awful experiences again."

"Mr. Stone, questioning Kathy during these sessions would have had a terrible effect on your daughter's well-being—"

"Fine!" He raised his hands in exasperation, in a manner that made Robin realize he'd heard that before. "That's what Claire said, over and over again. Then if she can't be questioned, there's no reason to dwell on those violent memories at all. But instead of letting our girl act like a normal person, you force her to act out these violent memories, for no good reason! How is she ever going to leave that behind her if you keep making her relive it?"

"Like I told you before in our session, in order to get better, Kathy needs to learn to handle these memories. I'm not making her relive them. I'm doing the opposite. Right now she's reliving them every time she recalls them. But with time and work—"

"Why does she need to recall them at all?" Pete's voice twisted, anguished. "She shouldn't! If Claire and I help her get back to a routine, make things as they were before, she won't have to."

"I understand what you're saying. But—"

"The *only* reason to bring up the past is to help the police grab her abductor. Until she's capable of doing that, I prefer she doesn't think back at all."

"These traumatic memories are triggered by everyday occurrences. You must have seen—"

"I have shitty memories!" Pete raised his voice. "I bet you do too. So what? We don't dwell on them. We don't fixate on them. Not like you're forcing Kathy to do."

"I'm not forcing her to do anything," Robin said gently. "And Kathy's experiences aren't simply shitty memories. They are traumatic experiences. And her brain is wired to replay them whenever something triggers her. I'm trying to change that."

"You are keeping us stuck in the past. My girl needs to go back to school. She needs to start meeting friends again. She needs to stop drawing freaky things and reenacting murders with dolls." Pete let out a sob. "And then she will start talking again. She was a happy girl. She can return to being the same wonderful, happy girl if you don't interfere."

The core difference between Pete and Claire was now obvious. This was why Pete didn't want these sessions. "Pete, you can't go back in time. Whatever happened to Kathy is a part of her now. You are right, she can be a happy girl, and go on and live a great life, but it won't be by undoing what has happened. It should be by healing and *overcoming* what happened."

He clenched his jaw. "You're wrong. And these sessions are done."

Walking forward, he brushed past her and entered the house. He ignored Menny, who ran after him, barking furiously. Opening the playroom's door, he said, "Kathy, let's go. We need to go home."

Robin watched helplessly as Kathy and Pete left the house hand in hand, Kathy's eyes wide and anxious.

"Bye, Kathy," Robin said, forcing a smile onto her face. She waved goodbye.

Kathy hesitantly waved back.

Robin stepped back inside, shutting the door behind her. Then she trudged to the playroom.

Kathy had left the shoebox behind. Robin would have to call Claire and return it. The slime container was discarded on the floor, and Robin picked it up. Then she walked over to the dollhouse, hoping she could manage to clean the slime up without leaving any stains on the miniature bathtub.

She paused in front of it, swallowing.

The Wonder Woman figurine was submerged in the bathtub, covered in the orange slime, only her feet protruding.

Chapter 36

Strangely, being a psychologist didn't really help when Robin had to deal with her own psychological crises.

This wasn't anything new. You'd *think* it would help. After all, if she were a car mechanic and her car wouldn't start, she'd pop the hood and find out it was a faulty carburetor or whatever. And then she'd fix it and drive merrily to her shop, where she fixed other people's cars. So ideally, if she felt her brain didn't work properly, she could say "Aha, I'm under stress, which, fueled by my childhood memories, is driving me to perceive reality in a twisted manner." And then she would just . . . fix it, and all would be well.

How happy all psychologists would be if that were the case.

But it wasn't. Therapists couldn't treat themselves. The majority of therapists went to therapy, because they *knew* they couldn't treat themselves. Robin had been to therapy too. It was a great experience. Because being a damn good psychologist herself, she knew exactly what was expected of her. So they had some great talks, and Robin supplied just the right stories and memories to keep her therapist engaged, to make her feel like they were making progress. Robin wanted to make her therapist happy. Of course, there was no actual need to delve into memories and complex uncomfortable emotions to do *that*.

Long story short: she'd stopped therapy after a while. Her therapist was sure she'd made huge progress. She'd actually made none.

She rationally knew that if an adult patient had told her for the past two months they'd been sleeping on average three hours a night, and that they were in the midst of the worst fallout with their narcissist mother they'd had ever had, less than a year after their father died, and after their divorce, and that they were treating a child who might have been the witness to horrible murders, and they constantly had to struggle with what they morally should do with it, and *then* they were accused on social media of being unprofessional, after which the aforementioned child's father blamed them for harming his daughter . . . she would have some solid advice for them. Because it sounded like they were under a lot of stress. Maybe they should take a break. And see a sleep specialist. And there were a lot of things they could do to separate what was within their control from what wasn't. And maybe, if they really needed to, they could take some mild sedatives. They *definitely* had to come for regular sessions because there was a lot there to unpack.

However, when it came to *her*, what she decided to do was to ignore it and do some bookkeeping instead. After all, it wasn't like the IRS cared she was going through shit. Taxes needed to be paid.

It almost worked. She was pleased with herself, how collected and focused she was. She was handling it.

And then she accidentally tipped her half-full coffee mug onto her receipt book, and it spilled on the receipts, and on her pants, and she *lost* it.

She screeched and threw the coffee mug against the wall, where it shattered, leaving behind a splash of brown. Menny, who was slumbering in the corner, bounced to his feet and fled from the room. She swept all the papers on the desk onto the floor and stood up and kicked the desk, which was stupid because she was wearing slippers.

And then she cried.

It was a long crying fit, sitting on the floor in the corner of her room, clutching her aching toe. She felt miserable and lonely.

Menny came back and sniffed at her worriedly, so she scratched his ear and told him she was sorry she'd scared him. She couldn't stop sobbing, tears clogging her throat and running down her cheeks.

The doorbell made her pause.

She decided to ignore it, but it rang again and again.

Maybe it was Claire, who'd come for Kathy's shoebox. Kathy could be freaking out about her missing shoebox right now. It wasn't something Robin could ignore, no matter how sorry for herself she felt. If it was Claire, she would hand her the shoebox and shut the door, and that would be it. And if it was anyone else, they could come back another day. Or never.

She went to the door and looked through the peephole. It was Nathaniel.

She cleared her throat. "Sorry, now's not a good time."

"Hey, Robin, I really need to talk to you about something," he said through the door.

"I told you to call if you wanted to come over."

"I did. Three times."

"Oh. My phone is on silent." Her voice was laced with accusation, as if it was *his* fault that her phone was on silent. Well, a lot of things were his fault at the moment, as far as she was concerned.

"Can you please open the door?"

"I . . . it's really not a good time, Nathaniel."

His voice became lower, and she could hardly hear him through the door. "Robin . . . there's been another murder. It's him."

Shit. She shut her eyes and inhaled. "Okay, give me a few minutes."

She went to the bathroom and examined herself in the mirror, aghast. Red nose; bloodshot, swollen eyes; her red hair a tangled mess. This was a nightmare.

She took a quick shower, all the while very much aware that Nathaniel was on her doorstep. Maybe, if she was lucky, he would lose his patience and leave. That done, she quickly dressed in fresh clothes, dumping her coffee-stained pants and tear-stained shirt in the laundry. The state of the laundry basket—brimming to the point of spilling over—would have sent her over the edge again if she didn't know Nathaniel was still waiting for her.

Finally she returned to the door, yanking it open.

"Sorry," she said throatily, her voice still cracked. "I'm just . . . I'm not feeling very well."

In the pandemic era, the words "I'm not feeling very well" were usually enough to make anyone leave. But Nathaniel didn't seem as if he was about to go anywhere. He gave her a long, steady look and said, "No problem. I wouldn't have bothered you if it wasn't important."

"Come in."

She led him to the kitchen. "Um, do you want anything to drink? Cookies?"

"I don't drink cookies."

She gave him a tired look.

He raised his hands. "Sorry, dumb joke. Water is fine."

"I'm having tea."

"Tea's good too."

She made them both tea, collecting herself as she did so. She would explain that Kathy's father had just let her know Kathy's sessions with Robin were done. And therefore, Robin was no longer relevant to the investigation. And that was it. It would be the last time she would have to talk to Nathaniel.

Why did she feel a sudden pang of sadness at that?

"So." She sat in front of him, handing him his mug. "You said there was another murder?"

"A woman named Mandy Ross was found in the Frances Slocum State Forest," Nathaniel said. "The murder . . . matches one of Kathy's imaginary games."

"Matches how?"

"I'm not sure how many details you want to hear."

Robin gave it some thought and clenched her jaw. "By this point, I guess I'll end up imagining the worst, so you might as well give me the details."

"She was drowned in a water barrel. It matches your description of the . . . Monopoly Man thing."

Robin swallowed, recalling how Kathy had rattled the Monopoly Man in the barrel. As if he was struggling. "Could it be a coincidence?"

"No. This girl is missing a clump of hair. This is the killer's standard signature. His trophy."

"So we found another one of the murders Kathy had witnessed," Robin said quietly.

"Not exactly." Nathaniel took a sip of his tea. "Mandy Ross died less than a week ago. *After* the session with the uh . . . Monopoly Man."

"Then it can't be related." Robin frowned.

"It's definitely related."

Robin gawked at him. "Are you suggesting Kathy can somehow predict the future? That her violent games are . . . What? Psychic?"

Nathaniel raised an eyebrow. "No. Of course not. One explanation is that this isn't the first murder in a water barrel that this guy did. Kathy saw the previous one."

Robin exhaled. "That makes sense."

"Sort of. The profiler from the bureau doesn't think it's likely. I'm not a fan of that theory myself."

"You have another explanation?"

Nathaniel stared at his mug. "What if Kathy didn't see the murder? In fact, maybe she didn't see any of them. What if the murderer had told her about his plans?"

"His plans?" Robin frowned. "You think he told her he was going to drown this girl in a barrel? And that's why she's showing it to me?"

"Something like that. You see, according to the profile, the serial killer is acting on fantasies. So let's say this guy has this very vivid fantasy of drowning a woman in a barrel. He talks about it nonstop.

Kathy has been his captive for more than a year. She heard him talk about it. Again, and again. Enough times that she can almost imagine it happening. And now, these memories of his deranged monologues are what she's showing you."

Robin sipped her tea, thinking about it. It sort of worked . . . but not quite. "I don't know. These moments she's playacting . . . she's acting out little details she couldn't imagine by herself. Like with this murder, she had the toy struggle as he was being pushed into the water barrel. That's not a detail a nine-year-old would come up with."

"Well, if he was really ranting about his fantasy, he could be specifically talking about that struggle. It could be an important part of his fantasy."

Robin shuddered. "I don't know. I guess it's possible."

"It would be better for the girl, right? I mean, it would mean she didn't see all those horrid murders."

Robin shrugged. "Even if she didn't see them, they're incredibly vivid. But maybe it would help her down the line, in her treatment."

"Did Kathy show you anything during your last session?" he asked.

"We didn't have a lot of time, but she did reenact something. I wasn't in the room to see it. She did it while I was talking to her father outside." She told him about what she'd found in the dollhouse when she returned—the toy drowned in the slime within the bathtub.

"So . . . we have someone drowned in the bathtub," Nathaniel summarized, jotting it down. "Second drowning victim."

"Originally, there had been six toys she played with, in addition to the one representing the murderer," Robin said. "Like I told you before, whenever one of them dies, she buries it in the sandbox and won't play with it again. Now we're down to two."

"So you think she has only two more murders to reenact?"

"Maybe. Or maybe one. I got the sense the little girl figure represented Kathy."

"Okay, I guess we'll have to wait for the next session to see."

Robin cleared her throat. "There won't be another session."

Nathaniel put down the mug. "Why not?"

"Kathy's father doesn't want me to treat her anymore." Robin's voice trembled slightly. "He came during the last session and picked her up."

"Oh. I see." Nathaniel watched her carefully. "Why?"

She eyed him. "Well, for one thing, he wanted me to let the cops question Kathy during the session, which was an impossible request."

Nathaniel blinked guiltily. "Oh, damn, Robin. I never thought . . . that wasn't exactly what I suggested—"

Robin shook her head. "Never mind. That's not even the main reason. My approach is that we have to face what Kathy went through. We have to heal her wounds to get her better. But Mr. Stone doesn't want that. He wants to turn the clock back. He believes that if you arrest her abductor and Kathy stops thinking about what she went through, life will return to the way it was."

"I can see the allure of that," Nathaniel said.

"Yeah. If I could wave a magic wand and undo all that happened to Kathy in the past year and a half, I would. But it's impossible." Robin bit her lip. "Kathy needs help to get over this. But I won't be the one helping her."

"I'm sorry to hear it. I got the impression you were doing a good job. Her father is an idiot."

Robin took another sip from her tea. Nathaniel's unwavering gaze made her feel strange. Vulnerable, but also . . . understood. His eyelashes were long, and beautiful.

"He just wants to do what's best for Kathy," Robin finally said. "He . . . he's completely heartbroken. I could see how desperate he was for Kathy to get all better."

"Well, I guess he's a well-intentioned idiot."

Robin let out a small, wavering laugh. "It's hard being a parent."

"I guess so. My parents always made it seem straightforward. It sounds like yours did too."

"Mine?" Robin asked, startled.

"What you told me? About your mother returning home and talking with you and your sister about her radio show? That's good parenting. She made you feel like a part of her life. And all that quality time. Most kids don't get that."

"Yeah," Robin said hollowly. She raised her eyes to meet Nathaniel's. His stare was soft, full of sympathy. She felt like a fraud.

"There's more to that story," she finally whispered. "About my mom."

"Oh?"

"Like I told you, she had that radio show. It would end at five in the afternoon. So she'd get home at about five thirty, and my sister and I would wait for her. It went on for about three years. But then they, um . . . they moved her slot. Well, frankly, I think they wanted to kill the show altogether, but she threw a scene, so they shifted it instead. To midnight. They called it *Nightly Conversations with Diana Hart*."

She took another sip from her tea. It was lukewarm, but she needed a pause. Nathaniel didn't say anything.

"You probably think, Oh, that sucks, because we didn't have our quality time anymore, right? But that's not how my mother works." Robin smiled a broken smile. It was the first time she'd ever spoken about this to anyone besides Melody. Someone from the *outside*. She hadn't gone even *near* this in therapy. "First night the show came on, we were asleep. Of course we were. I was eleven, my sister was thirteen. It was *waaaay* past our bedtime. So she came home after the show, and I woke up to some shouting. My parents were arguing. My mother was practically screeching. And my dad kept telling her we were asleep. That we had to sleep."

Robin got up and opened a drawer. She rummaged inside and found the cigarette box she knew was there. "You don't mind, right?"

"No, feel free," Nathaniel said.

"I only smoke two a day," Robin said defensively. She put the cigarette between her lips, lit it, and took a long drag. "The next two weeks were . . . it's hard to explain. You don't know my mother. She can make your life *hell*. Just with words. These aggressive little comments. It can get petty, and vicious, and it was aimed at all of us. My sister and me, and my dad . . . we were all her enemies. And it never stopped. *Never*. Whenever she was around, it was a nonstop barrage of toxicity. I finally couldn't take it anymore. So next time her show came on the air, I set the alarm clock. Woke up at five minutes to midnight. Went to the kitchen and turned on the radio. Set the volume low, so I didn't wake up my dad. And I listened to the show. And then I waited for her. And when she got home and saw me, she was so happy. And we sat up and talked about the show. Just like we used to."

Robin dropped some cigarette ash into her tea mug, then took another drag. "Next day, it was like a miracle. I wasn't a target anymore. My mother still behaved like shit to my dad and Melody . . . that's my sister. But I was the best daughter ever. I told Melody what I did and suggested that she join me, but she wouldn't. She told me I was crazy if I thought she would wake up at night to listen to my mother's show. So I kept doing it alone. After a few more weeks, my mother stopped her attacks on my sister and my dad. It was like I saved the family."

Robin dropped the cigarette stub into the mug. She shut her eyes. "Then one night I didn't wake up. I was exhausted. I was eleven and was getting up three nights a week in the middle of the night, staying up for almost two hours each time. Anyway, the next day, my mother is treating me like trash. Worst daughter ever. Not Melody, she was in the clear. But *I* was the one who wouldn't even wake up to listen to her show. So after a few days of *that*, I got up to listen again, and all was forgiven."

Robin sailed on the waves of her own memories, the words flowing, unstoppable. She'd almost forgotten Nathaniel was there. "Her midnight show went on for four years. Three times a week. I was constantly exhausted. Dad behaved like he didn't know . . . but you know what? I think he knew. There were a few times when I felt like he was about to say something. But he never did. Sometimes I wouldn't wake up, and the result would always be the same. My mother would lash out. Finally, when I was fifteen, the show was canceled. And that was that."

She opened her eyes. At some point, while she was talking, Nathaniel had moved his chair closer to her. He was now sitting beside her. She let out a shuddering breath, realized she was trembling.

He took her hand in both of his, holding it until it stopped shaking. "I'm sorry."

"It's fine now," she said. "I mean . . . usually. But when I'm under a lot of stress, I jolt up in the middle of the night, and I think I'm a kid again and that I didn't hear the alarm clock. And that I missed her show. So I wake up completely, and then I can't go back to sleep. And lately it's been happening more, so I'm a little tired."

"Okay," Nathaniel whispered.

Robin drew closer to him. His hands were so warm and firm around hers. "I never told that to anyone."

"How do you feel now that you did?"

"I don't know. Exhausted." A tear trickled down her cheek. "Better. Much better."

He gently wiped the tear from her face. "I'm glad."

She looked at his other hand, which still clasped hers, large and strong but still soft and warm. She imagined dissolving into his arms, letting him envelop her, keep her safe. Surprised at her own reaction, she nearly pulled away, but part of her wouldn't let go, and she kept still, soothed by his touch.

Chapter 37

Robin sat in her bedroom, brushing her hair slowly.

Nathaniel had left soon after they talked. He'd said repeatedly he wished he didn't have to leave, that he had a task force meeting that he had to attend. That if it was any other day, he would have stayed, but at this point in the investigation—

She'd interrupted him then and assured him it was all good, that she was fine.

And it was. The past few hours had been such a rushing roller coaster of emotions that she was glad to be alone. To process her feelings, to take them apart and think them through. Which was part of the reason she was brushing her hair. What was it about the act of brushing that made thinking that much easier? It was as if the faint tugging on her scalp loosened the sticky thoughts from within, letting them tumble freely in her mind.

She'd enjoyed Nathaniel's touch and presence. She would like to see him again, without his serial-killer case standing in the way. That much was clear to her. She dared herself to imagine how it would feel to kiss him. His height forcing her to tilt her head back, as if kissing the sky. His arms around her.

Her mind shied away from the things that had happened before Nathaniel soothed her. His theory about the murderer telling Kathy his plans unnerved her. And the way Pete stormed in before that, interrupting her session with Kathy, still felt too raw to examine closely.

Her phone rang. She put the comb aside and glanced at the screen. It was Claire.

Robin sighed and answered the phone. "Hey, Claire."

"Hi, Robin. Um . . . I heard what happened. I'm so sorry."

"Don't worry about it."

"He had no right to . . . I mean . . . it's my fault . . ." Claire's voice was tight, frustrated. "Listen . . . can I come over?"

Robin preferred doing this on the phone. "My house is a bit of a mess."

"That's okay. Actually, no, I really want to talk to you face to face. Outside. Is it okay if I pick you up?"

Robin groaned inwardly. "Yeah, sure. I can also meet you at Jimmie's or—"

"No, I'll come over and pick you up. I want to show you something."

"Okay, see you in a bit."

Robin hung up and sighed again. Claire had sounded like the girl Robin remembered from their high school days. Not the broken, traumatized mother from before. But the girl who organized parties and club meetings and always had opinions about everything. Who wouldn't listen to other perspectives because she knew best. Robin had always found her exhausting. And this was a perfect example of that behavior. Robin didn't want to meet, but Claire had to have her way, and Robin ended up agreeing.

Still, it was a good sign for Kathy. Her mother was healing from the past year and a half. And Kathy was getting her old mother back. Strong and opinionated. Kathy needed a powerful parent by her side. A mother that would give her the sense that she was safe. That she was protected.

By the time Claire called from her car outside, Robin had changed her shirt and put on her boots. She wasn't sure where Claire wanted to go, but she assumed a café or pub, so she went for a casual-but-classy look.

"You look nice," Claire told her as she stepped into her car.

"Thanks." Robin eyed Claire, who was dressed in yoga pants, a loose T-shirt, and sneakers. "Where are we going?"

"You'll see," Claire said mysteriously, starting her car.

As they drove down the street, Claire cleared her throat. "I really do want to apologize again. I don't know what Pete told you exactly—"

"He said he didn't know I was still seeing Kathy," Robin said.

"Yeah, but I saw how angry he was when he came home. And I imagine he wasn't nice about it."

"He wasn't. He interrupted the session, which wasn't ideal. *And* from what he said, you two never agreed I could talk to the police if I had any information, like you told me. *He* said he told you that if I refused to include the police in my sessions, he wanted to stop them."

"Well . . ."

"You lied to me."

"I didn't lie to you." Claire pursed her lips. "It was an argument. And it was never resolved. We left it hanging at a point where it wasn't clear what we agreed on. And I chose to interpret it as if we'd reached an agreement. Didn't you ever do that with Evan?"

Robin thought about that for a second. "I guess so, but I didn't pull other people into our fights."

"Fair point."

"And let me remind you Evan and I got divorced, so I don't know if we're a good example."

"I don't know if Pete and I are a good example either."

Robin didn't know how to respond to that.

Claire frowned. "I shouldn't have done this behind his back. But the thing is we can't agree on *anything* since Kathy came back."

"It's a very complicated situation. It's understandable that—"

"We always saw eye to eye before," Claire said tightly. "You know? We were that annoying couple who would constantly say the same thing together. We almost never argued. We would roll our eyes when we'd see other couples fighting, because we couldn't understand why anyone would stay in a relationship with so much friction."

"Must have been nice," Robin said sardonically.

Claire gave her a brief, tired smile. "It was. But when Kathy disappeared, we coped in different ways. Almost in opposite ways, really. Both of us changed. And now that she's back, it's like we can't sync anymore. So that night, Pete said that if the police couldn't sit in during the sessions, he wanted to stop them. And then *I* suggested you could tell the police if anything important came up. He said that wasn't good enough, and I said it was good enough for me. And then I think Kathy had a bad dream, so I went to her bed. And I decided not to pick up the argument where it left off. It was easier to act as if he'd come to see it from my perspective. Obviously, I knew that he didn't."

Robin shook her head. "But eventually he would have found out. You knew that, right?"

Claire shrugged. "Who even cares about *eventually*? I'm working my hardest just to get through the day."

"I know what you mean." Robin glanced out the window. They were leaving town. "Claire, where are we going?"

"It's just a bit farther," Claire said.

Robin had figured out their destination before they got there. A tiny dirt road, hardly noticeable, leading into the thick trees on their right. Claire slowed down to a crawl and gently drove down the road until they got to its end. In front of them stood a chain-link fence and a padlocked gate. And beyond it, the decrepit, abandoned house in which the police had found Kathy's shoes all those months ago.

"This is a good example of how different Pete and I became," Claire said softly. "When Kathy was gone, he couldn't stand to even drive by this place. But I couldn't stay away from it."

"I was sure they demolished it a few months ago."

Claire nodded. "They wanted to. I begged them not to. It was my last link to Kathy. I thought if they tore it down, I would lose any chance of ever seeing her again. A grieving, half-demented mother is hard to say no to. Especially when she won't stop calling. So they fenced it instead."

She got out of the car, slamming the door behind her. Robin followed suit, looking around her. It was a dismal, creepy place. The house was a wreck—half its roof gone, the front door a rotting mess, the walls tagged with various graffiti scrawls. It said something about Claire's state of mind at the time that *this* was the place she'd felt connected her to her missing daughter.

"Hang on," Claire told Robin and took her phone out. She dialed and put it to her ear. A minute later, her tone frosty, she said, "Hi, it's me. Yeah. I called to make sure Kathy is okay. I know she's . . . Can you take a look and tell me she's okay? Yes, right now."

Robin watched Claire in silence. The woman was rigid with tension.

"Thanks," Claire finally said. "I don't know when I'll be back. Bye." She hung up and pocketed the phone.

"I can't really get away from Kathy for long without getting anxious," she told Robin, circling the car. "So I need to call Pete and make sure Kathy's fine. Even when I'm furious with him." She opened the trunk and, to Robin's surprise, took out a six-pack of bottled beer.

Slamming the trunk, Claire glanced at the house. "Come on, let me give you a tour," she said in a sarcastic tone mimicking a proud owner of a new home.

Robin hesitated. There was a line you didn't cross with clients, a certain distance a therapist had to maintain. The six-pack and the creepy house tour definitely crossed that fine line. But then again, Robin wasn't sure if Claire and Kathy were even clients anymore. And part of her wanted to know where this was going. She ended up following Claire.

"I saw this place in photos. Evan once did a photo shoot here," Robin said.

"Oh, I remember that," Claire said distractedly. "A sort of pretentious series of shots with the sunlight filtering through the windows, right?" When she reached the fence, she began walking along it, running her fingers along the metal wires.

Robin grinned. "That's right. I think it was supposed to show you can find beauty anywhere. Or maybe something about nature reclaiming civilization."

"What a jackass," Claire said.

Robin let out a snort. "That's a perfect description."

"You know, he did a photo shoot of Kathy for us once, a few years ago."

"I didn't know that."

"He said she was the perfect model. The photos are beautiful. During the time she was gone, I looked at them more times than I can count."

"Well, he knows his job," Robin allowed.

"Still a jackass."

"Oh, yeah, definitely still a jackass."

They circled the fence until they reached the back of the house.

"I asked them to give me the key to the padlock," Claire said. "But I guess my persuasive skills only went so far. So I made my own gate." She reached a portion of the fence that had been cut and pulled it aside.

Robin bent and entered through the hole in the fence. Claire followed her. She led Robin to the front door and pushed it open, the hinges creaking in the manner expected of haunted houses or Transylvanian castles. Inside, it was even worse. Graffiti and garbage everywhere. Holes in the walls. In one corner, the leftovers of a campfire. The smell of urine permeated the air. Robin spotted a used condom on the floor. Who would find this place even remotely arousing?

Claire stepped inside and walked over to a corner of the room.

"One of Kathy's shoes was found here," she said and pointed to the opposite wall. "The other one was found under a wet cardboard box over there."

"Did they show it to you?" Robin asked, horrified.

"No, of course not. Not at first. But after I went to the police station day after day, after day, they finally relented and showed me the crime scene photos."

"I heard they found some other things here. Uh . . . a rope, or a knife—"

"That's just the finest of Bethelville's gossips making shit up." Claire snorted. "They only found the shoes."

She stepped through the house, Robin walking in her wake. They paused at the ruins of a bathtub, rusty exposed pipes everywhere. The walls had once been tiled, and leftovers of the ceramics still spotted them here and there. Additional tiles were scattered on the floor and inside the grimy bathtub, broken and jagged.

"Once the police found Kathy's shoes here, the entire investigation shifted," Claire said. "They brought the dogs to search the woods. And they interrogated some rough teenagers who sometimes came here. They thought a local pervert grabbed her and took her here."

Robin cleared her throat. "I thought they assumed it was someone close to her."

"At first, yes. Because there were no signs of struggle—it looked like she voluntarily entered his car. But that investigation didn't lead anywhere. Then they found her shoes here, so they figured he'd have to know about this place, right? It's not like you can see the house from the road. Even the path is hard to spot. But most people in the area came here at one time or another, or at least knew someone who came here."

"I never came here."

"Really? I was in this dump a couple of times during high school," Claire said. "A bunch of us came here to drink."

Robin decided not to point out she'd never been invited to any of those gatherings. "So they thought it was someone local? Who stalked her or something?"

"Yeah. They investigated a few registered sex offenders in the area, but it didn't pan out either."

Robin stepped into the room, accidentally kicking a broken tile. It made an unpleasant grating sound as it slid across the uneven floor.

"After Kathy disappeared, I came here about once a week," Claire said softly. "Looking everywhere. Searching for a hint that the police or I missed. Maybe a clue in the graffiti, or something hidden under a piece of junk. Trying to imagine what happened to Kathy here and where he'd taken her afterward."

Robin shuddered. She could easily picture what Claire had imagined in this sordid place. Nothing good. She followed Claire outside, relieved to be able to breathe without feeling like she was inhaling other people's excretions.

Claire stepped over to an old tree that stood close to the hole in the fence and placed the six-pack on the ground. She took one of the bottles, opened it, and offered it to Robin.

Robin hesitated, then took it from her. "Thanks."

"Thanks for letting me show you this place," Claire said, opening another bottle for herself. She leaned against the trunk and took a long swig. "I haven't been here since Kathy returned. What a shitty dump."

"It really is." Robin sipped from her bottle.

"After . . . after a while I gave up on finding any clues about Kathy. But I still came to this place. Stood right here. Got drunk, stared into the woods."

"It must have been awful."

"It was."

Robin took another swig. "Don't take this the wrong way, but . . . why *did* you want to show this place to me?"

Claire looked embarrassed. "Frankly, I mostly just wanted to get away from Pete. And to see this place now that Kathy's back. And to apologize to you . . . face to face. It's really important to me that you keep seeing Kathy. I wanted to ask if it's okay."

"I can't see her behind Pete's back."

"Oh, yeah, of course. I'll convince him, I promise. But once I do, you'll see her again? You've helped her so much. Pete doesn't see that; he keeps saying she's still not talking. But I see the rest. She's sleeping better. She's smiling more, even laughing. She's playing games . . . a lot of that is thanks to you."

Robin smiled at her. "I appreciate it. That means a lot to me. Sure, I'll be happy to see Kathy again. She's a wonderful kid."

"She really is." Claire gave her a broken smile. "Thank you so much."

She took a very long swig, emptying the bottle. Then, turning, she tossed it at a nearby boulder. The bottle smashed on the rock, its shards peppering the ground. Other, older glass shards were scattered everywhere. Robin got the sense that this was Claire's own ritual.

"I think I also wanted to take someone here. And talk about that time, before Kathy came back," Claire said. "Back then, whenever I tried to have a conversation with my friends or my family, I could see that look in their eyes. They thought Kathy was dead and that I had to face it. So I stopped talking to people about her. And I didn't tell people about coming here. It sounded like another crazy thing I was doing to avoid facing the truth."

"I don't think it's crazy," Robin said softly. "It was a coping mechanism."

"Says the therapist." Claire gave her a lopsided smile, opening another bottle. She drained half of it in one long sip. "But to regular people it might sound crazy."

"Maybe just a little," Robin allowed.

"And now, people don't want to talk to me about the time when Kathy was missing," Claire continued. "Whenever I mention it, they quickly say, 'But now she's back, you must be so happy.' And of course I'm happy, but that's not the point."

"You need to process the past year and a half from your new perspective," Robin suggested.

"Yeah, exactly."

Robin finished her bottle. "And maybe you wanted to process it with someone professional." She grinned at Claire.

"Well, maybe . . ." Claire's mouth dropped open. "Oh, God. It sounds like I tried to get a free session for myself. I'm so sorry, that wasn't my—"

"Don't worry about it, I'm just messing with you." Robin laughed. "Though it's not a bad idea for you to talk to a professional."

"I know, I know."

Robin aimed and threw her bottle at the rock, missing by at least a foot.

"Amateur," Claire said, throwing her own bottle. It shattered on the rock. "Stick with me, I could teach you my ways."

"I think I'll pass." Robin eyed Claire as the woman fished for a third bottle, already wavering slightly. "And I think I'll be driving us home."

Chapter 38

A noise woke Robin up.

Was it a door creaking? Something dragging along the floor? She wasn't sure, but it was inside the house. Probably Menny, on one of his nightly walks. But still, she couldn't ignore the nagging feeling that it wasn't her dog. It was something different.

She got out of bed and silently walked to the edge of the bedroom. Down the corridor, the door to the playroom stood ajar. She always shut it, otherwise Menny would wreak havoc on the toys inside, particularly the plastic stethoscope. Had she forgotten to shut it? Was that the noise? Menny chewing on her expensive playroom toys?

She crossed the hall to the door, peeking inside. No, Menny wasn't there. But something lay in the middle of the floor. She entered the room and crouched to pick it up.

It was the plastic TV set, the one Kathy had taken from the cheap dollhouse and placed in the larger one. What was it doing on the floor?

She went over to the dollhouse and placed the tiny TV back in the miniature living room. As she did so, her hand brushed against something sticky. She took a step back and glanced at the back of her hand.

It was smeared with red.

The red sticky paint is all over your hand.

She peered closer at the dollhouse living room, and her breath hitched.

Red paint coated everything. The tiny, precious miniature sofa, the small square rug, the grandfather clock.

The figurine of the little girl lay on the floor of the dollhouse, face-down, amid a puddle of red paint.

Robin suppressed a scream. Someone had come into her house and done this. Whoever it was, they might be inside right now. It suddenly occurred to her she didn't know where Menny was. He hadn't barked. She whirled around, her eyes scanning the dark room. There was more. A tipped over plastic toolbox. The toys on the shelves in disarray. An open cabinet.

She needed to call the police. She turned to the door, took a step toward it, then froze.

A movement in the hallway. The intruder was just outside the playroom.

Very carefully she backed away from the door. She could lock herself inside the bathroom. But the door could be unlocked from outside with a simple screwdriver. No, she needed protection. She scrutinized the shelves.

And saw the headless doll.

It was a baby doll that some of her patients loved to play with. Its head had been ripped off and placed beside it. And next to it lay the Wonder Woman figurine, both her arms torn off.

Robin stumbled over to the plastic table. Drawings covered it, horrific drawings of screaming figures, tortured women, red-eyed monsters . . . she ignored those and grabbed the scissors. Then she crept to the side of the room. She could hide there, could stay silent until he was gone.

She crouched by the sofa, hiding in its shadow, where he wouldn't be able to see her. The sofa. What was a sofa doing in the playroom? She examined her surroundings. Oh, right, she was in the dollhouse. She was hiding in the dollhouse. He would never think to search for her there. She looked around her at the furniture, now at full size. The rug, the plastic TV, the yellow drapes Kathy had made, the grandfather clock.

The figurine of the girl lay beside her, but it wasn't a toy at all. It was Kathy.

She shook the girl, and to her relief, Kathy slowly moved. She was alive. She raised her face, pale, haunted, smears of blood all over her.

Robin placed a finger on her lips. Kathy blinked. Silence was her natural state.

A shadow in the doorway. Not the playroom's doorway—the dollhouse doorway. Someone in the dollhouse's kitchen. A tall, thin figure. A terrible pasty face, an unnatural grin.

The killer clown had come for them.

Robin grabbed Kathy's hand and ran to the stairs. They ran up as fast as they could, his insane laughter following them, the stairs creaking with his weight as he got closer. They reached the children's room, and she tried to blockade the door with furniture, but they were just tiny toys, they couldn't stop him, he opened the door, the miniatures tumbling all over the place.

They were running again, blazing through the rooms, and the clown was getting close.

And then she glimpsed Nathaniel through a window. Looking around the playroom, searching for her. She had to call him.

She couldn't. She had no voice.

She knelt by Kathy, pointing at Nathaniel. The girl would have to call out to him because Robin couldn't. But Kathy shook her head violently, and now Robin knew the truth. It was what the killer did. He robbed people of their voices. He had stolen Kathy's, and now he had taken hers.

They were running again, and they'd managed to get out of the dollhouse—they were in the sandbox—but it was a trap. A graveyard of toys. Their limbs protruded from the sand. She was sinking in the sand herself. Beside her, Kathy was already gone. And the clown was getting closer, grinning, eyes shifting. And Nathaniel, pacing the room, clueless. If only she could call him. But no matter how hard she tried, she had no voice. And the clown was upon her.

Robin woke up, drenched in sweat, breathing hard, her fingers curled, as if she was about to rake the face of an assailant. She looked around her bedroom, at Menny slumbering in the corner.

"Oh, shit," she croaked.

She turned on the light, just to make sure she was truly awake. She checked the time. Quarter past three in the morning. For once, she had no interest in going back to sleep.

Leaning back in bed, she breathed deeply, trying to calm her thudding heart. She still remembered the dream as vividly as a real memory. She could recall herself inside the dollhouse, looking around her as if she were a toy, all the furniture full size. All those pieces of furniture her mother had accumulated for the house. And all those things Kathy made.

Like the drapes.

Robin took a long breath.

The drapes.

Chapter 39

Matchbox, twine, cotton ball, marbles, plastic dog.

Robin's fingers rummaged through the assortment of knickknacks, searching for something, *anything*, that would make sense.

Wooden cubes, LEGO bricks, purple stickers, cloth squares.

Over the past weeks, Kathy had accumulated a lot of small trinkets that were presumably props for the dollhouse. Most of them remained unused, but that didn't mean they weren't connected.

A stick, screws, pebbles, a piece of green glass.

If she could make sense of it, then maybe . . . maybe—

The doorbell rang.

Robin marched to the door and opened it without even checking to see who it was. Nathaniel stood on the doorstep, holding two paper bags.

"Hi," he said, smiling awkwardly. "I'm glad you called. I was about—"

"Good," Robin said. "You're here. Come in."

She turned away and walked back to the playroom, not bothering to see if he was following her. In her mind, she was still shuffling through the items she knew were there. A seashell, a coin, a plastic ruby.

"I meant to call you this morning," Nathaniel said behind her. "You just called me first. I feel like yesterday I left in a bit of a rush. But it was because I had a status meeting. I wanted to stay longer."

"It's fine." Robin returned to the table with the shoebox and turned to look at him. He seemed flustered. She smiled. "You said all that yesterday."

"Right." He examined the room. "So this is your playroom, huh?"

"Yup. What do you think?"

"It's cool. Ten-year-old Nathaniel would have given a kidney to play with all these toys, let me tell you that. Oh! I got us some coffee and cinnamon rolls from the local café." He put the bags on the table, and took out a paper cup, handing it to Robin. "I wasn't sure what kind of milk you take . . . but the guy at the counter said there was only regular milk. And then I got a lecture about the dairy industry. Anyway, I told him no milk."

"Perfect, thanks." Robin grinned, taking the cup.

"You said you wanted to show me something important?"

"This is the dollhouse Kathy plays with when she comes here." Robin gestured.

Nathaniel peered at it closely and whistled. "It's incredible. I didn't know they made them so realistic."

"They normally don't. This is sort of an antique. It belongs to my mother. Anyway, you see the living room down here?"

"Yeah."

"Anything strike you as weird?"

"The TV set. It doesn't match the rest. It looks like a shitty plastic toy."

"That's because Kathy put it in there. My mother's Victorian doll-house doesn't have a TV set. But Kathy clearly needed one there."

"Why?"

"I'm assuming because the house she was held in had a TV set. It's a crucial part of her memories. There are other things she added. Like the blanket here, see? I think this is the blanket she had over there. And this rug . . . these are all things she custom made for this house. To make it fit her memories."

"Okay," Nathaniel said. "That's definitely interesting."

"It gets better," Robin said. "Kathy made these yellow drapes in the children's room too."

"Okay." Nathaniel frowned. "So we have yellow drapes."

"You said that if Kathy shows me any clue that could help you find the guy who took her, I should tell you," Robin said. "Drapes can be seen from the outside."

Nathaniel nodded slowly. "That's . . . that's good. It's not a lot. But you're saying it could be a house with yellow drapes on one of the windows."

"You could look for it, right?" Robin said. "You think she was held in Jasper, so you could check the houses there."

"Robin . . . there are thousands of houses in Jasper. And yellow drapes are not exactly rare. They are not conclusive evidence either."

"I know. That's why I asked you to come. See all these?" She pointed at the mess on the table. "These are Kathy's props. Well . . . I think they're props. Some might be things she decided to keep as a souvenir. But I thought if we could look through them, we could figure out what they're meant to be. And maybe there are additional things that could be seen from outside the house. Like . . . I don't know. A scarecrow. Or a dog kennel. Or something. So if we find a few of those, it will make it easier to find."

"Okay." Nathaniel looked skeptically at the pile of junk.

"Look, I already got started. This pile has things whose purpose I already know." She pointed at the Play-Doh container, the bracelet, and the rest of the props Kathy used in the previous games. "They won't help us."

Nathaniel pried the plastic tree from the pile and squinted at it. "I see."

"This pile here are obviously things for inside the house. See? Dolls' clothes and blankets, and I'm pretty sure this thing is supposed to be an electric fan. So these are probably irrelevant too. Now we need to figure out the rest."

"Robin, I don't think we can really use this. I mean, do you want me to get some officers to drive around Jasper and look for a house with a big LEGO brick on the lawn? Or a . . ." He slowed down and picked up an item from the pile.

"Just give it half an hour. Use your imagination. Maybe there's something you can use here." She glanced at what he was holding—a ring taped to a paper square. "Yeah, I think that's like a sort of hat or something. I'm not sure."

"It's a basketball hoop," Nathaniel said. "See? She even drew that orange square on the board. And there's some tape on the back. It looks like it was taped to something . . ." He picked up a long plastic stick and pressed the square to it, taping it back.

"You're right," Robin breathed. "It's a basketball hoop. That's definitely something she could see in the yard, right? Some places have hoops in the driveway."

"Sure, if they have kids. Do you think whoever held her had kids?" Nathaniel sounded doubtful.

Robin shrugged. "I don't know anything about criminal psychology. Could be."

Nathaniel placed the basketball hoop by the dollhouse. "How do we know the basketball hoop is something related to the house and not to one of the murders, like the tree over there?"

"We don't," Robin said. "But if we get enough of them, you could have something to work with, right?"

"Right." Nathaniel sifted through the trinkets. "Lots of stuff here."

"She'd been collecting it for a while. Claire told me it's one of the few things Kathy was really focused on. They went together to buy supplies in a crafts shop, and Claire taught her how to sew." She gently moved a few plastic poles aside. "Some of these took a lot of work. The blankets and clothes she made are really well done."

He picked up an orange marble. "So if that thing is a basketball hoop, this could be a basketball, discarded in the yard."

"Could be," she said slowly. "But there are five of those. And she drew stuff on them, see? This looks like a face."

"Maybe they buy a new basketball every time the old one runs out of air. Some people do that."

"Maybe . . ." Robin quickly plucked the other four from the pile. "But if we imagine it's something that could stand in a backyard . . ." She placed them together next to the dollhouse front door. She took the fifth from Nathaniel and placed it there as well.

"What is that?"

"My dad loved to decorate for Halloween," Robin said. "He loved it more than Christmas. He'd get us these really corny skeletons, and he had a large ugly plastic spider . . . and those." She pointed at the marbles.

"Pumpkins," Nathaniel said.

"Plastic pumpkins. Some people never get around to storing them back in the garage when the holiday is over."

"That indicates kids again. The profiler we consulted with said in all likelihood the killer lived alone."

"Wasn't there a really famous killer who had a family? Um . . ." Robin frowned, trying to recall if she'd seen it on a documentary.

"BTK," Nathaniel said. "That's true. Okay. Basketball hoop, pumpkins, yellow drapes. What else?"

"What about the twine?" Robin asked. "It could be something."

"It could be a rope. That's murder-related, if anything."

"It could be a hose. Or laundry lines."

Nathaniel raised an eyebrow. "You're reaching. We need to ignore false positives. It's bad enough that we don't *really* know any of this is related to where she was kept."

"Okay, okay," Robin muttered.

They sifted through the items, back and forth, trying to find other similarities. Nathaniel picked up a yellow clay shape, saying it looked like a fire hydrant. Robin argued against it—she had assumed it was supposed to be some sort of food. Eventually Nathaniel announced he was right, and she was wrong, which annoyed her to no end.

"What's this?" He picked up a red cutout. It was a sort of trapezoid.

"I don't know," Robin said tiredly. The coffee and sugar rush had dissipated. She was feeling the lack of sleep. She'd been rummaging through tiny knickknacks for the past few hours, and spots danced in front of her eyes. "It looks like a hat."

"You think everything is a hat."

"Everything *is* a hat. Look." She balanced a cube on her head.

"Very nice. Looks good on you. I think it's taped together." Nathaniel gently unfolded it. He was right. It wasn't a trapezoid. It was a red hexagon.

"A stop sign," Robin said.

"Doesn't say *stop*."

"Kathy has some verbal difficulties, remember? It's very hard for her to write words." Robin found another plastic rod and taped the hexagon to it. "It's a stop sign. We have a fire hydrant and a stop sign in the street, nearby the house."

"So now you agree it's a fire hydrant."

"Whatever," Robin muttered.

Nathaniel rubbed his eyes, and then leaned forward, plucking something from the props that Robin designated belonging inside the house.

"Don't touch that, you're making a mess," Robin muttered.

"You said it's irrelevant!"

"It's a blanket. You can't see it from outside."

"It's the American flag."

"Yeah? Oh." Robin blinked. "My family was never the type to put a flag outside."

"She even sewed it so you can put it on a small pole, see? Hand me that thingy over there."

She found the tiny metal shaft and handed it to him. As he reached for it, their fingers brushed again. She didn't let go. Their heads were close together, hovering above the pile of knickknacks. She could smell him, the scent reminding her of a rainy day in the woods. She raised her eyes and met his. Her breathing slowed down, becoming deeper, huskier. He leaned forward, and his lips touched hers. She pressed herself against him, the taste of coffee and man intermingling, sending her into a short, thoughtless bliss. Finally, after what could have been seconds or minutes, she pulled away. All the nervous energy and anxiety she had stored inside her had evaporated. Her face was flushed.

She still held the small metallic rod between her fingers. She stared at it, trying to remember why she was holding it. Oh yeah. She handed it to Nathaniel. "Here," she whispered.

He took it from her, his eyes intent on hers. Then he picked up the small cloth that Robin had mistaken for a doll's blanket and slid it over the rod. "That's a pretty decent flag." He placed it next to the rest of the trinkets they'd figured out.

"It is." Robin wondered if he was as breathless as her. Suddenly, watching him was too much. She looked away, down at the assortment of toys. A flag, orange pumpkins, a stop sign, a basketball hoop, a fire hydrant. And the yellow drapes from before. Would it be enough?

They halfheartedly tried to find more, their eyes constantly meeting and glancing away. It took all of Robin's willpower to keep away from Nathaniel, knowing she needed to take it slow, to think it through, but *wanting* something else entirely.

They found no other props. After half an hour of additional rummaging, they agreed it was time to stop. Nathaniel took the tiny trinkets with him. And then, before leaving, he kissed her again.

Robin fell asleep on the living room couch soon after, the taste of that kiss still on her lips.

Chapter 40

As a kid, Nathaniel could easily tell anyone what his favorite top five movies were. They were, in order, *Lethal Weapon, Lethal Weapon 2, Lethal Weapon 3, Lethal Weapon 4,* and the first Star Wars movie. *Star Wars* made him want to own a lightsaber. The Lethal Weapon movies made him want to be a cop because it seemed incredibly exciting. He used to have a clear picture of what his cop career would be. He would show up to work, get in the car, get into a car chase, shoot down the bad guys (whose cars would explode), leap from his car onto another, kill the bad guy with the diplomatic immunity, then have a hilarious snarky conversation with his partner before being called to disarm a bomb with a big red LED timer with only ten minutes remaining.

He was glad some of these modern cop shows, like *The Wire* and *Bosch,* were a bit more realistic. Quash kids' dreams when they're young, and you won't have bitter, disappointed cops in the future.

For example, today, instead of leaping at the last moment out of a warehouse full of explosives, he was driving through Jasper, looking for yellow drapes. And pumpkins, basketball hoops, and flags.

It would have been frustrating if it weren't for the memory of Robin's smile. Of Robin's soft lips. Of the feeling of her in his arms.

He hadn't met anyone special for almost two years. Not since Imani left him and broke his heart. He had had a few dates that went nowhere and one regretful night with Imani, when they were both lonely and drunk. But other than that, no one. And while he should probably not get his hopes up, he was feeling quite smitten.

"What are *you* smiling about?" Burke, his partner, grunted from behind the wheel.

"I'm just glad to have you back at my side." Nathaniel grinned at his friend.

"Yeah, yeah." Burke shook his head. He had been reassigned to the Basset murder case, now that it turned out to be related to a case someone actually cared about. "See that basketball hoop on the right?"

"I see it." Nathaniel marked the house. "Slow down, let's check the windows."

They slowed to a crawl.

"I don't see any drapes," Burke said. "Just shutters. But there might be drapes on the windows in the back."

"We'll check it from the back when we go up Fourth Street."

Nathaniel struggled with the map, refolding it. It was an enormous sheet of paper, one out of twelve he got from the local police station. It was a high-scale map, showing each house in the city.

His radio crackled. "Delta-Five-Two, this is Delta-Seven-Four-One."

He pressed the mic button. "Go ahead."

"Delta Five-Two, we found another plastic pumpkin patch."

"Copy, Delta-Seven-Four-One."

"I'm letting you know, so that you don't get surprised when we kick your ass."

Nathaniel grinned and pressed the mic button again. "We'll see. We just saw a bunch of flags."

"Flags aren't pumpkins, Delta-Five-Two."

"You know," Burke told him, "they *are* kicking our ass."

Nathaniel had managed to get two IMPD cops to help with the search. Naturally, to make it interesting, they turned it into a bet. Flags were worth three points, basketball hoops five, and yellow drapes eight. But plastic pumpkins, being the rarest of all during June, were worth a whopping twenty points. By the end of the day, the losing team would buy the winning team dinner.

"Slow down," Nathaniel said.

"We need to work faster if we want to win," Burke pointed out.

"You drive this fast, we're bound to miss a few drapes."

Burke slowed down. "You gave them all the good streets. It's pumpkin kingdom over there on the west side."

Nathaniel reopened the map, trying to figure out a way to fold it so he could see the surrounding area. "I gave them the low-priority area. If we find the place, it's bound to be on our side."

They hadn't gone into this blindly. Kathy Stone was found at the corner of East Fifteenth Street and Cherry Street, at a quarter to four in the morning. According to her bleeding feet, she'd been walking for a while. However, if she'd been walking the streets before one in the morning, she would have probably been seen pretty quickly. Around midnight, the streets still had some traffic, the occasional group of teenagers, or someone returning late from work. So it was safe to assume she'd escaped sometime after one a.m. A barefoot, undernourished nine-year-old would be walking at an average of two miles per hour, perhaps even less in the pouring rain. So she would have been able to walk six miles tops before that guy found her. More likely three or four. When drawing possible routes from the corner she was found at, it was easy to estimate the area she had come from. That's the area Nathaniel assigned to Burke and himself.

It looked like it would end up being a bust.

Sure, so far, they'd found houses with flags, or hoops, or whatever. But no house sported more than two of those things. The closest was a house spotted by the other team, which had both a flag and a basketball hoop. But it didn't have a stop sign or a fire hydrant nearby. And Kathy would have had to take a seven-mile trek through the busiest areas in the city to get from it to the location where she was found.

Nathaniel had to admit this lead was one of the flimsiest he'd ever followed while investigating a murder. Did he really believe this idea, that the girl's shoebox props identified the house she had been kept in? Had he just gone along with it, because it was Robin's idea, and he was interested in all things Robin-related at the moment?

"Oh!" Burke suddenly said. "Flag . . . and drapes. That's eleven points, baby."

Nathaniel raised his head from the map, alert. "Where?"

"Not the same house," Burke said. "See? Drapes on our left, and the flag over there, ahead on the right?"

"Gotcha." Nathaniel sighed. He looked at the house with the drapes—a second-story window. The house didn't have any of the other characteristics they'd described. It was a shitty-looking location. The yard was neglected, full of weeds, paint peeling off the exterior walls. No kids lived there, that was for sure. He examined the map, marking both the house with the drapes and the one with the flag.

Burke slowed down and stopped. Nathaniel raised his eyes to see why and saw the stop sign.

"Wait. Go back," he said, an idea grabbing him. "To the house with the drapes."

Burke turned the car and drove back. He parked at the curb, and Nathaniel hopped out of the car, walking closer to the house. Its yard was fenced. He peered at the second-story window. The drapes were definitely yellow. The house was dark. It didn't seem like anyone was home.

Nathaniel turned with his back to the house and looked at the house with the flag.

It would have been visible from the second-story window. As would the stop sign. And the fire hydrant across the street.

Excitement shot through him. He paced up and down the street slowly, until he saw it. A basketball hoop in the yard of one of the houses across the street, hidden from the road by a large tree. But it would have been easily visible from the higher vantage point of the window.

They'd been looking for the props assuming they belonged to the house where Kathy had been held in. But they weren't. They belonged to the view *from* the house.

He found the pumpkins pretty quickly after that—on a fenced-in porch on the house across the street. Impossible to glimpse from the road, but he could see them from the nearby sidewalk if he stood on his tiptoes.

Even better, he could spot other things that matched items in the shoebox as well. One of the houses had a rope hanging from one of the trees, presumably a Tarzan swing the kids used, which matched the twine Kathy had in the shoebox. A strange garden sculpture seemed similar to a clay shape neither he nor Robin had made any sense of. One of the houses down the street had a purple Frisbee on its roof, and he recalled the round purple stickers, their purposes unknown.

This was it. This was the house. Kathy must have watched the street often from that second-story window with the yellow drapes. Perhaps the room beyond that window was the one she was held in.

What now? Nathaniel wasn't sure. He wanted to find out who lived there. He needed to get a warrant to search the place. Did he have enough to convince a judge? In any case it was probably better to wait. Stake out the street until the house's occupant returned. He should inform the task force.

Burke got out and approached him. "What's up?"

"That's the house," Nathaniel said, feeling on edge. "I'm sure of it."

"Okay, then what . . ." Burke frowned. "You hear that?"

"Hear what?" Nathaniel asked. Burke's hearing was much sharper than his.

"I'm not sure . . . it sounds like it's coming from the house."

Nathaniel opened the house's gate, its hinges squeaking. He crept toward the house. Yes, he could hear something. Music? Or something else?

He put his ear to the door.

And, beyond it, heard a woman's muffled scream.

Chapter 41

Another scream followed the first, long and twisting, a screech of agony. No time to think it through. A quick assessment of the door—it opened inward; the locking mechanism seemed cheap. Pulling his gun from its holster, Nathaniel took a step back and slammed the door with his foot, his heel hitting a few inches to the left of the doorknob. The thing rattled, wood crunching, but it stayed shut. Behind him, Burke was radioing for backup, already circling the house, checking for a back door or an open window, making sure there weren't any surprises in the backyard. Nathaniel gave the door a second kick, and it flung open.

Dark hallway. Gun aimed ahead, Nathaniel stepped in. Open doorway to the right. He turned, scanning an empty kitchen, eyes alert for movement. Dirty dishes in the sink, a mug on a small table, no visible hiding spots, no one in the room. Clear. He moved. Music somewhere in the house. And another scream. Without the front door to muffle the sound, it was clearer, sharper, and it sounded different.

Three steps down the hallway; two closed doors. Somewhere in the distance, a siren blared. Maybe it was their backup. No time to wait. The screaming was behind the door in front of him.

He kicked it open.

The room was dark, but the familiar light of a TV set flickered on the bare walls. The screaming and the music came from the damn TV.

It was some sort of horror movie, a teenage girl screeching as a masked man pursued her, a hook in place of his hand. Nathaniel looked away, scanning the room. The couch in front of the TV was empty.

A scuffling of steps behind him. He whirled, saw Burke in the hallway. A quick nod, and they both shifted closer to each other.

The TV was on, which meant someone had been watching it. Had they heard the cops at the door and quickly hid somewhere in the house? Perhaps run to grab a weapon?

Only one other door on this floor, and a staircase to the second floor.

Nathaniel and Burke flattened themselves against the wall. Burke trained his gun at the staircase while Nathaniel opened the door abruptly, his weapon ready. Bathroom. Two steps inside, checked the bathtub.

"Clear!" he called.

A jar of pills on the shelf above the kitchen sink. A quick glance at the label—prescribed to someone named Jonas Kahn. No time to look more closely. He moved out.

Only the stairs were left. Burke went first, Nathaniel at his back. The siren sounded much closer now. Probably the other team.

The top floor had three doors, all shut. Without discussing it, they split up, each taking a different door.

Nathaniel darted to the door to his right. Behind him, he heard a door slamming open, Burke shouting, "Clear!"

He turned the door's knob, kicking it open. It was a bedroom, double bed. Large closet. He moved inside, back to the wall, quickly checked behind the bed, then under it. Nothing, no movement. Below, the noise from the TV still blared. Now it sounded like a chainsaw. More screaming, dramatic music. He yanked the closet open, his finger tightening on the trigger as he saw something that looked like a man inside . . . but it was only a coat.

"Clear!"

He exited the bedroom and crept toward the last door on the floor. Burke was already there, flattened against the wall. The door was different from the rest. It had a deadbolt on it, on their side. Whoever had placed it wanted to keep someone *inside*.

Nathaniel yanked the door open, Burke already aiming his gun inside.

A girl's room. With a bed made with pink sheets. Some toys scattered on shelves. Burke moved in, checking the bed, looking around him.

"Clear," he said.

Nathaniel relaxed his tight grip on the gun, tension seeping from his body. The house was empty.

He stepped inside the room and approached the window, which was framed by the yellow drapes. He peered outside through it. He could easily spot the pumpkins, the basketball hoop, and all the rest. All those things Kathy had in the shoebox.

This was where he had kept her. In this room. Nathaniel checked the window's frame. A thick metal pin was drilled into it, preventing it from being opened. Even if Kathy had decided to risk jumping from the second story, she wouldn't have been able to do it.

As he watched, the squad car with the other team screeched by the curb. The two officers leaped from the car, guns ready.

"Tell them to check the yard again," Nathaniel said. "And the street. Maybe he heard us and managed to make a run for it."

Burke stepped out of the room, talking on his mic.

Nathaniel paced heavily in the room. With the bed in it, there was hardly any room to walk. Three steps to cross the room from one side to the other. Had Kathy been in this room for the entire time she'd been missing? How did it feel, for a little girl, to wake up every morning in this bed, alone, knowing she would stay there for the entire day?

He felt nauseated. Downstairs, the music shifted. More screams; a deranged laugh. Nathaniel gritted his teeth.

Burke stepped back into the room. "The backyard is a shit show. Full of junk. And there's a shed there."

"Did you check if he's inside it?"

"It's padlocked from the outside."

"Do you think he bolted?"

Burke shrugged. "Windows are shut. No back door. It's possible . . . but if he ran, he was very stealthy. In any case, our guys are canvassing the street, and we have a Jasper police squad car assigned to us, who are looking for him as well."

A crash reverberated from the TV downstairs. More screams. A roar.

Nathaniel clenched his fists, the noise making it difficult to concentrate. "We missed him."

Chapter 42

The day of the disappearance

Robin wished she'd had sessions that morning. Or that she'd met with Melody for breakfast. Or that Dad would drop by and visit.

Anything to push away the feeling of loneliness that stifled her.

She usually didn't feel lonely. Not even during the quarantines. Not even when Evan went on weeklong photo shoots. She had the kids she was seeing, she had her family to talk to, she had Menny to slobber on her shoes as she scratched his head.

But that day, with Kathy gone, the entire town searching for her, she felt an immense sense of solitude.

It was strange, how similar loneliness was to fear. The same pit in her stomach. The same breathlessness. The same need for someone to hold her. To talk to her.

She put her hand on her belly, trying to reassure the child within. Could they feel her torrent of emotions? Did it cause them discomfort? She hoped not. How would it feel for your child to vanish? The question shot a jolt of anxiety through her. She had formed a strong bond with her own child, yet unborn. And Kathy was already eight, the bond between her and her mother probably so much stronger.

There was nothing worse.

Robin had gone to the sheriff's office earlier to see if she could help. But she was terrified of going inside, knowing that in such a small space, even though everyone wore masks, there was a chance of catching COVID. She couldn't afford to, not now, during her pregnancy. So she stayed outside, doing her best to listen in. Feeling distant from the rest of the town's residents. Alone.

When the meeting ended and they'd stepped outside, she'd noticed Melody. She waved at her, and her sister came over, told her they'd been given areas to search. Robin wanted to help, but Melody assured her the entire town was already covered. That there was nothing Robin could do at the moment.

So she went back home.

She took Menny to the park, part of her imagining he would catch a scent. Suddenly howl and bolt into the bushes, as if possessed. Chasing him, she would find him sniffing Kathy, who was somehow unconscious but unharmed. And everything would be all right. But of course, all he did was bark at a squirrel, pee, and sniff one specific tree for five minutes.

And she was terrified of being there alone. Because something malicious had come to Bethelville. And she could imagine all sorts of horrible things that could happen to her there.

So she went back home. She called Evan, and he was short with her, as he was prone to be lately.

And then she sat in the living room. With her loneliness. That felt very similar to fear.

Chapter 43

In the main bedroom, Nathaniel opened the dresser's bottom drawer. Socks and underwear. He rummaged through them carefully, looking for those things people sometimes hid among their underclothes. Drugs, porn, a weapon. He didn't know why it was always underwear and socks that were chosen to hide dark secrets. No one ever hid their stash of cocaine among their shirts or pants.

In this case, though, the underclothes hid nothing except dust and lint. Jonas Kahn, it seemed, kept all his dark secrets in that room downstairs.

Nathaniel stepped out of the bedroom and descended the stairs. He joined Burke in the room with the television. Burke had finally muted the damn thing, the bloody images of the horror movie still flickering on the screen.

"Anything?" Burke asked.

"Nothing upstairs," Nathaniel said. "What about you? Any details?"

"We managed to get some basic details from the neighbors," Burke said. "He's a Caucasian male in his twenties or thirties, black hair. He was driving a green Honda Civic, and we got a partial license plate, so I have people in the task force working on that. Neighbors say that he was often gone for days. None of them ever talked to him, other than exchanging greetings. One neighbor said he didn't seem friendly."

"Okay, any info from the task force?"

"Nothing so far. No immediate info on anyone named Jonas Kahn in Jasper."

"Maybe it's not his real name."

"Maybe. They're looking into it, cooperating with the staties, the feds, and the IMPD."

"It's heartwarming, how he brought us all together."

Nathaniel looked around the room, ignoring the TV. A safe stood in the corner of the room. Above it was a shelf with a few books stacked one on top of the other. A single armchair in front of the television screen. Next to it stood a small round table with a box of tissues and a bottle of moisturizer. The sticky, musky smell in the room made Nathaniel want to throw up.

"What do we have here?"

"Some weird shit," Burke said. "First of all, of course, we have this." He gestured at the television set.

"A horror movie."

"The TV is hooked to the guy's laptop, and this isn't just a regular horror movie."

"What do you mean?"

"Take a look."

Nathaniel glanced at the TV as the scene changed. A teenage boy was lying on a bed asleep, a small TV on his chest. Suddenly a gloved hand emerged from the mattress, grabbing him, pulling him into the bed.

"I know that film," Nathaniel said. "That's *A Nightmare on Elm Street*." He'd seen the movie lots of times as a teenager.

Sure enough, just as he remembered, blood erupted from the bed, defying gravity, coating the ceiling. It was gory, but also absurd, ridiculously so.

But then the scene shifted. Now it was a different film. He didn't recognize it, but the amount of blood was staggering. He stared at the screen, unable to pull his eyes from the violence . . . and then it changed again. A different movie, this time in Chinese.

"What is this?" Nathaniel asked.

"As far as I can tell it's a compilation," Burke said. "All horror-movie scenes. All quite gruesome."

"Any idea how long it is?"

"Six hours and forty-seven minutes."

"Almost seven hours? *Of this?* Who would even watch this?" The more unsettling question surfaced in his mind. "Who would *make* this?"

Burke shrugged. "Jonas Kahn, I guess."

Nathaniel scrutinized the armchair again. At the tissues and moisturizer. He was starting to get the idea. Jonas Kahn had created a compilation of all his favorite moments in horror movies. An endless cascade of gruesome, over-the-top murder scenes. And then he would sit there, watching it. Getting excited. The moisturizer bottle was half-empty. This was a regular routine.

"I didn't want to mess with the laptop too much," Burke said. "I'm leaving that to forensics. The drawers in the TV cabinet all have DVDs and . . . get this, old VHS tapes. I also found a dusty VHS in the bottom drawer. As far as I can tell, it's all horror films. I recognize some of them. He has a lot of the classics. *Friday the 13th, Elm Street, Child's Play, Jaws* . . . But most of these I never saw. *Bloodbath in Psycho Town, Antlers, Alone in the Ghost House* . . . Heard of those?"

Nathaniel shook his head.

"A real horror-movie fan."

"I don't know." Nathaniel walked over to the shelf. "I like the occasional horror movie. But this compilation isn't that. It's just the gore. There's no tension, no fear."

"It's this guy's porn," Burke said.

"Exactly. And no one watches porn for the dialogue between the pizza guy and the lonely housewife." Nathaniel's finger ran down the spines of the books. Titles like *Slasher Movies, Horror Cinema, Writing the Horror Movie.* A few biographies—Hitchcock, Stephen King, Wes Craven.

A few spiral notebooks stood against the wall behind the books. He plucked them off the shelf and opened the one on top. Spidery handwritten sentences scrawled all over the page. Dates. Notes. The handwriting was barely legible. He flipped through some pages.

"Burke, check this out."

Burke came over and looked over Nathaniel's shoulder. He let out a long whistle. "What do we have here."

"Looks like a logbook of women he stalked," Nathaniel said.

Some of the dated entries were matter of fact: *MK left with her husband at ten fifteen, returned at twelve forty-five,* or *RP stayed in room all morning, shut the curtains at eleven forty-five.* In other entries, he seemed to write entire paragraphs, the handwriting erratic and barely legible. It seemed like he was writing some of the logs in the form of a movie script.

> *EXTERIOR—HOUSE*
> *CAMERA FOLLOWS HP as she goes out at night. She's wearing a short skirt that shows her long legs.*
> *CAMERA PANS BACK and we see a man watching her.*
> *FLASH FORWARD—HP comes back with a guy she picked up. It takes her a long time to unlock the door because she is drunk. The guy is GRABBING HER ASS the entire time.*

"HP," Burke said grimly.

Nathaniel nodded. "Haley Parks. He was stalking her before he took her."

"And writing a screenplay starring her, apparently."

On some pages, Kahn had doodled in the margins, presumably passing the time. The doodles were mostly of women, tortured or dead, badly drawn. One was definitely a sketch of Haley Parks, after her murder.

Nathaniel placed the notebooks on the round table. These would have to be meticulously read later. As he was doing so, something caught his eye. He crouched, looking closely at one of the table's legs.

"Burke," he said, his eyes fixed on the leg. "Can you please get tweezers from the crime kit?"

"Yeah, sure."

Two long hairs were stuck to the leg, fluttering gently. Nathaniel didn't take his eyes off them, worried they'd drop off the wooden leg and onto the wall-to-wall rug. "And an evidence bag."

Burke crouched by his side, and gently plucked the hairs with the tweezers. "Long hair. I don't think this belongs to Kahn. His hair is supposedly black, and probably shorter. This one's blond."

"What's that?" Nathaniel pointed at the end where they clung to each other. It seemed darker, and crusty. "Is that blood?"

Burke took out a small flashlight and flicked it on, casting its beam on the hairs. "Looks like it." He dropped the hair into the evidence bag.

Nathaniel stood up and looked at the safe. The murderer had taken a trophy from each victim—a lock of hair. Were his trophies in that safe?

"We should get that thing open."

"I told forensics we have a safe here," Burke said. "But you know . . . it's probably not an accident that we found those hairs here."

Oily realization crawled up his skin. "So he sits on this armchair."

"Watching his horror porn."

"Getting all worked up."

"And sometimes, he decides to spice things up. Opens the safe."

"Looks through his trophies. Snippets of hair."

"Chooses one, takes it back to his damn chair."

"Probably has them in plastic bags to keep them intact."

"Right. He takes it out of the plastic bag, playing with it, feeling it, one hand in his pants—"

"Okay," Nathaniel said abruptly, the image too vivid in his mind. "I need some air."

He strode to the front door, holding his breath, as if the air in the house was infected by the depraved acts committed in it. Once outside he took a deep breath, already annoyed with himself. He'd seen much worse in his career. In fact, he'd seen worse in the past week. So why did he let it get to him?

Part of it was knowing that Kathy, a little eight-year-old girl, had been kept here, by this man. According to Robin, during one of the sessions, Kathy played an imaginary game where the girl toy was tied up in the living room, in front of the television. Had Kahn made Kathy watch his compilation with him, like some sort of twisted father-daughter movie night?

Nathaniel walked over to the backyard as he thought about this. There was something there . . . a detail, just out of sight. Something that would shed light on everything.

The yard was covered in junk—discarded beer cans, some rusty gardening tools, a pile of broken roof tiles, and more. A decrepit shed, its color peeling from its wooden walls, stood in the corner. The door, like Burke had said earlier, was padlocked.

Nathaniel crossed the yard to the shed and inspected it. Something drew his eyes. The shed was placed near the fence, but there was a tiny gap between the fence and the shed's wooden wall. In the gap, the bottom part of the shed's wooden wall was broken.

And the ground underneath was dug out.

Nathaniel bent and wiggled into the cramped space between the shed and the fence. He peered through the broken boarded wall into the shed, using his phone's flashlight.

The flashlight's beam shone on what looked like a dirty mattress. Next to it, a bucket.

Nathaniel swallowed, drew back. Suppose that occasionally, Kathy was transferred from the locked room above to this shed. Maybe as a punishment. And then one night, already undernourished and desperate, she managed to break a few rotten boards in the shed's wall. Then dug around it until there was just enough space for her to squirm through. He recalled Kathy's broken fingernails when they found her. And the scratches on her back—scratches she could have gotten, say, when crawling underneath the broken boards, their jagged edges tearing at her skin.

And then, after fifteen long months, she was finally free.

He took a few photos of the shed's interior and the broken wall with his phone. He needed to show this to Burke.

His partner was still in the TV room, leafing through one of the notebooks.

"Hey, Burke," Nathaniel said. "I think I found out how Kathy escaped—"

"Hang on," Burke said. "You need to see this."

"What?" Nathaniel walked over and scrutinized the page Burke was looking at. It took him a moment to decipher the erratic handwriting. Short, logged entries, each with a date and a time. Dated less than two weeks ago.

> *K stayed home all day. K went to the park. K met RH*
> *today. RH had three clients in the morning. RH went*
> *to the Café this afternoon.*

"*K* is probably Kathy, right?" Burke said.

"Yes," Nathaniel said, his heart hammering. "And *RH* is Robin Hart."

Chapter 44

Nathaniel held the phone to his ear, the ringtone seemingly endless, impatiently waiting for Robin to pick up.

It was the third time he had tried to reach her in the past hour, and so far she wasn't answering.

Knowing she was probably in the middle of a session didn't help. Ever since he'd seen her initials in that journal, he couldn't stop thinking about her. In her home, alone, unaware that a serial killer was stalking her. Possibly there right now, watching her through the window or following her as she drove around town.

He shook his head. He was being an idiot. He'd contacted the Bethelville Police Department *and* the sheriff as soon as he found out. Asked them to have someone keep an eye on Robin and Kathy. Patrol their streets. Make sure they were safe.

Meanwhile the task force was coordinating the manhunt for Jonas Kahn. They had a partial license plate and a general description. It was only a matter of time.

Still, the final page in the journal was dated three days ago, chronicling Robin as she went on a walk with her dog. It was clear from the notes that Kahn had followed her from a distance as she walked to the park. And there was no other notebook. Probably meaning the next one, the current one, was with Kahn. And if that was the case, he was out stalking.

He put down the phone, picked up one of the notebooks, and flipped through it again. In the background, the forensic team spoke with each other as they slowly went through the entire house, cataloging it.

Jonas Kahn stalked each of his victims for *months* before striking. He was meticulous and careful, but it wasn't just that. It seemed he wanted to write a long movie script for each one before moving to the next phase. With Robin, the notes covered barely two and a half weeks. Kahn had no reason to break his routine. Robin was in no immediate danger. If only she would pick up.

Something drew his attention, and he raised his eyes from the notebook, glancing at the screen. The scene playing was some sort of cannibalistic ritual, gory and obscene. He thought back to the scenes that had been playing ever since he came in. There had been several he recognized, from movies he'd seen, mostly as a teenager. But one came to mind. One scene from *Friday the 13th*.

When had he glimpsed it? About twenty, maybe thirty minutes before. He walked over to the laptop and scrolled the movie back, frames jumping before his eyes. A chopped limb. A grinning Chucky. A girl running in the woods . . . Where was it?

There!

A man in a suit . . . Nathaniel hazily recalled he was supposed to be a teacher. The teacher was lying in an alley, his face bloody. And then Jason came over, picked him up.

And drowned him in a barrel of toxic waste, holding his feet as the teacher struggled.

Just like the murder of Mandy Ross.

The scene shifted, but Nathaniel ran it back, watching it a second time. And a third. It was identical to Mandy's death, except in this scene it was a movie character in a suit . . .

Oh God. A man in a suit. Just like the Monopoly Man, which Kathy used to playact the murder. The murder that happened *after* she showed it to Robin.

Kathy hadn't witnessed Kahn drowning someone in a barrel. And Kahn hadn't told her about his plans. She'd watched this scene play out on the television.

Was this what she was showing Robin? Scenes from the compilation? Ones that she saw when Kahn forced her to watch?

No, it wasn't likely. Kathy had playacted four murders so far, and three of them matched actual murders. Four murders, if he included the drawing. This compilation had hundreds of scenes in it. It was more likely that Kahn had a different compilation on the computer. One much shorter, with only a few scenes in it. One he watched repeatedly as he planned to reenact those scenes with living victims. And Kathy had witnessed him doing that. Watching *those* scenes over and over until they were scarred into her mind.

A murder with a drill. A victim's limbs being cut off. A woman stabbed and then hanged. A woman drowned in her bathtub. No wonder Kahn's murders were so inconsistent with each other, so elaborate and monstrous. He was replicating actual horror-movie scenes.

Nathaniel whirled around, shouting, "Burke!"

Then he paused.

And slowly turned back. For the first time, he noticed the tiny LED indicator on the laptop.

The thing had been on ever since they came here, but now, as he stared at the large screen, thinking, frozen in thought, it had blinked off. And when he moved to call Burke, it turned on again.

"Oh, shit," he muttered, looking closely at the laptop.

Burke came in. "What is it?"

"Out," Nathaniel said urgently. He grabbed Burke, led him out of the room, and shut the door.

"What the hell?"

"Two things," Nathaniel said. "I just realized Kahn is killing his victims by replicating scenes from movies. That's what Kathy had seen. She'd seen him watching those scenes as he planned the murders. That's how she knew about Mandy Ross's murder before it happened."

"That makes sense." Burke gripped Nathaniel's arm. "Hang on . . . Haley Parks!"

"What about her?"

"She was stabbed and then hanged, like that girl in *Scream*, remember?"

"No," Nathaniel said, feeling sick. "I don't."

"I saw that movie a bunch of times. It's that scene for sure, I—"

"Never mind that," Nathaniel said. "The second thing I figured out is that the laptop's webcam indicator light was on. It went off when I stood still and turned on when I moved again."

Burke frowned. "Then . . . it works every time it spots movement?"

"It *records* every time it notices movement. And probably alerts the owner. Maybe sending him the feed."

"In that case Kahn knows we're here." Burke's shoulders slumped. "He won't come back here."

"If he's getting the feed accompanied by audio, he also knows everything we've said in there." Nathaniel tried to remember what they'd talked about. "And he knows we're looking for him. He'll be more careful. And more desperate."

"We need to update Claflin," Burke said.

Nathaniel nodded, taking out his phone. It rang in his hand, an unfamiliar number.

He answered the call. "Hello?"

"Detective King? Hi, it's Jeff Price. Bethelville's sheriff."

Chills ran down his spine. "Yeah, what is it, Sheriff?"

"Well, I went by Robin Hart's house multiple times, and there was no answer. She's not answering her phone either."

"I tried too. I figured she might be with a patient."

"I don't think that's the case." The sheriff's voice was tight. "Her dog was spotted by the local café, walking by himself."

Nathaniel's fingers tightened over the phone. "I see."

"And his leash was still attached to his collar."

Chapter 45

Robin's head was pounding, her gut clenching, waves of nausea washing over her. Had she drunk too much? She must have, she'd practically drunk a whole bottle with Melody. But no, wait, that night was a while ago. What happened? Was she ill? She was cold, her body hurt. She shifted in her bed—

Something was very wrong.

It wasn't her bed. And her hands were somehow tangled in something. She couldn't move them from their unnatural position behind her back.

She blinked, the world rocking violently. It was dark, she needed to turn on the light. But she still couldn't move her hands. She shifted slightly, and her ankle banged against something. What was going on? And what was that horrendous noise? It was like a roar . . . it sounded familiar, but she couldn't quite pinpoint it.

She needed rest. Already she was floating away.

That roar was rain on a tin rooftop. That's why it sounded so familiar. When she was a girl, her bedroom window was by the shed in the backyard. She would sometimes lie awake at night, listening to the rain pouring on the shed's tin roof. Was she back in her childhood bed?

No, her dad took that shed apart. There was no shed, or tin roof. Or Dad.

She tried to sit up, but it was hard without moving her hands. Her head banged against something. What the . . . frightened, she shifted around, banging her head again, then her legs . . . she was in some kind of cramped space, and she couldn't move her hands.

The rain poured on the tin roof, just above her. What was going on?

She remembered bits and pieces now. She'd gone on a walk with Menny, hadn't she? She got out earlier than usual, because of the ominous sky. A quick walk. She recalled striding, leaves squelching under her shoes. The park. A light drizzle. She kept trying to tug Menny back, but the dog had sniffed a squirrel or something, and then . . .

Something grabbing her? Covering her face? A chemical smell . . . She was so dizzy and tired.

The rain kept pouring on the shed's tin roof. She huddled in her bed. She didn't feel so well, maybe she was sick. She would tell Mom and Dad: tomorrow morning she won't go to school.

The darkness enveloped her.

Chapter 46

Nathaniel parked his car by the sheriff's pickup truck, killing the siren. He had driven as fast as he could, but it still took him almost three hours to get to Bethelville.

Too long. Way too long.

He got out of the car and hurried down the muddy path leading into the park, the rain drenching him within seconds. He followed the sound of talking, of a radio crackling, until he located them. The sheriff and two uniformed cops.

"I'm Detective Nathaniel King," he called out, striding over to the sheriff.

The sheriff nodded and offered his hand. "Jeff Price. Glad you could make it."

"This is where you found her phone?"

"Yeah." Price pointed at a nearby bush. "We followed the location we got from the cellular company. When we called her, we heard it ringing from that bush over there."

"Any idea when she disappeared?"

"According to the cell data, she left her home at about three thirty. It's a fifteen-minute walk from there to here. Her dog showed up at four forty-five at the local café. I'm guessing whatever happened to her happened around four."

"No witnesses?" Nathaniel felt sick. She'd been gone for too long. Much too long.

"It's a pretty secluded part of the park, and by four the rain was getting stronger, so the regular joggers and bike riders that go through this area weren't around." Price motioned Nathaniel to follow him. He led him aside and pointed at a few muddy boot prints brimming with water. "See here? The boot prints come down the track, but over here they are much deeper. So it looks like the guy with the boots came over here and then later left, carrying something heavy."

"You think he attacked Robin and then carried her body from here." Nathaniel looked around him, picturing it. A bitter taste filled his mouth.

"Tracks lead back out to the road, and we have fresh tire tracks in the mud there."

"Identified the tire tracks?" They would probably belong to a Honda Civic.

"We sent photos to the lab."

"Did you check her home?"

"I have a guy looking there right now. Robin's sister had a key. She opened it for us."

"Any blood? Marks of a struggle?"

"Not that we could find."

"Forensics on their way?"

"Yeah, I talked to your contact, Claflin. There are a bunch of people on their way. Feds too."

Thunder rumbled above them. It seemed the rain was getting even worse. Here, under the cover of the trees, Nathaniel was out of the pelting rain, but heavy drops fell from the foliage, splashing on his head.

He took out his phone and dialed Burke.

"Hey," Burke answered. The sound of his car's engine in the background. Burke was driving. "Did you get there?"

"I'm here right now." Nathaniel wiped the rain from his face. "She was taken from the park. No apparent witnesses."

"I'm on my way to Indianapolis. Joining the task force. I'll be there in twenty minutes."

"Good. Give me a heads-up as soon as you get there."

"Okay," Burke said. "So I was looking through Kahn's journals. He first mentioned Robin about four weeks ago. He was stalking Kathy and followed her and her mother to Robin's house. Three days after that he was already stalking Robin. It looks like he was dividing his time between Robin; the girl; and Mandy Ross, our latest victim."

"Right."

"But once Mandy Ross was gone, it was only Robin and Kathy. And the most recent entries are *only* Robin."

"He was losing his interest in Kathy," Nathaniel said. "And once Mandy Ross was gone, he was focusing on his next murder. His next target."

"That makes sense," Burke said. "But listen . . . there are about twenty different women mentioned in the journals. And we assume he only killed four of them. And he took his time. He followed each of his victims for months, learning their routines. He hasn't been following Robin for that long. It seems like a shift in his MO, right? Is he getting careless?"

"I don't know. Could be."

"Maybe something about Robin made him act faster," Burke suggested.

"No." The blood drained from Nathaniel's face. He leaned closer to the tree. "It's us. He wasn't planning on acting. Not yet. He was watching her, like he had been lately. But then he got notified by his security app."

"Oh shit, maybe you're right," Burke said. "So Kahn's stalking Robin, just another day at the office. Then he sees the footage of us in his home. He realizes we know who he is and that he doesn't have a lot of time left."

"And then he gets desperate," Nathaniel said. "It's now or never for him. So he grabs her and takes her. And he'll kill her as soon as he can."

"I mean . . . he could kill her right there at the park."

"But he wants to do his thing." Nathaniel's mind churned. "Reenact the horror scene, right? We know of at least one scene we think he hasn't done yet. The one where he drowns a victim in the bathtub. So this is what he wants."

"I don't think he wants to drown her in the tub," Burke said.

"Why not?"

"I fast-forwarded through his sick compilation, trying to find the matches for the murders and for those things that the girl showed Robin. So here's what I have. Haley Parks's murder was, like I said, from *Scream*. And you were right about Mandy Ross, that's the scene from *Friday the 13th*. Cynthia Rodgers matches a scene from *Sin City* that he has there. Limbs cut off, the whole thing. And Basset is from something called *The Driller Killer*. But there's only one scene with a bathtub in the entire compilation."

"Okay," Nathaniel said impatiently. "So what—"

"It's from a movie called *Acid Bath*."

Nathaniel shut his eyes, clenching his fists. Now was not the time to let his emotions get the better of him. He needed his wits. Robin needed his wits.

"Okay," he said. "That's a good thing."

"A good . . . Are you serious? Did you hear me? Do you want to know what happens in the scene? I'm not going to be able to sleep at night."

"I think I understand the gist of it," Nathaniel said. "But remember, we're assuming he wasn't prepared to kill her yet. He'll need a bathtub, right? And acid. It's a complex murder. That's why it's a good thing."

"Right," Burke said. "He can't use the tub at his own place."

"And he didn't go to Robin's," Nathaniel said. "The police are there already. So he'll need somewhere else. And he'll need acid. We need to figure out where he could get the acid. And the tub."

"Okay, I'll work on that with the rest of the task force. You know . . . it's possible he plans to kill her differently. There are a lot of scenes in this damn compilation."

"This is the only one Kathy showed Robin we don't have a match for."

"Yeah, but . . . maybe there's a murder the girl hadn't told Robin about."

Nathaniel had had the same thought. Robin had told him that initially, Kathy had six dolls, including the figure of the little girl. One by one, Kathy reenacted the deaths with the toys. By now, only two remained. The little girl and the woman with the cake. One murder was still unknown, and it could be anything.

"If we're lucky," he said. "We'll find him before he manages to act. We have staties and feds looking for him throughout the area. But if not . . . the bathtub and the acid is the only lead we have."

"Yeah," Burke said. "I'll let you know as soon as we have anything."

Nathaniel hung up and pocketed the phone. It'd been more than four hours since Robin disappeared.

Chapter 47

Robin's eyes fluttered open. Her shoulders hurt from the uncomfortable position of her arms. She struggled for a few seconds, trying to release them, felt the bite on her wrists. Her hands were tied behind her back.

Panic slammed in, sharpening her senses. She let out a scream, her feet thumping into the walls that closed around her. She screeched for an eternity, still kicking, desperately trying to get out, escape from wherever she was. She was trapped. Writhing, she banged her head on something, and the sharp pain blinded her.

Exhausted, she slumped, whimpering.

She vaguely recalled waking up before. But she'd been too out of it, had probably lost consciousness again. There was no chance of that now. How long had she been here? Where was she?

The rain still poured above her on the tin roof. No, it wasn't a tin roof.

It was the lid of a trunk.

She was in the trunk of a car.

She forced herself to calm down, to breathe. Slowly, she managed to focus. She still trembled, cold and afraid. But at least she could think clearly.

Cars these days had safety handles inside the trunks, didn't they?

She fumbled around, searching, feeling the trunk's walls with her fingers. It had to be there. It had to . . .

There! She could feel something. Maybe a handle. She tugged at it. The thing didn't budge.

She tugged harder. She tried gripping it and pushing herself with her feet. The handle creaked but didn't move.

The blackness of her surroundings was overpowering. It was getting harder to breathe. She screamed again, tears running down her face, kicking, her shin slamming into something.

The trunk popped open.

For a second she thought she'd managed to move the handle. The rain poured down on her as she blinked, staring at the inky cloud-covered sky.

A dark figure stood above her. He was the one who'd opened the trunk.

"Oh, good. You're awake. Not much longer now, I think it's almost ready."

He leaned forward.

She kicked him in the stomach.

He let out a surprised grunt, stumbling back. Robin was already maneuvering herself up. She balanced herself with her hands behind her as she sat, feet out of the trunk, standing up.

His fist slammed into her face. Her cheek exploded with pain, her head whiplashing back, hitting the trunk lid. Her vision doubled. A weak whimper escaped her mouth.

"Okay." He was still breathing hard. "Let's try this again."

A burning pain in her scalp. He pulled her up violently by her hair. "Try anything like that again, and you'll regret it. You got it?"

She sobbed.

He shook her head back and forth by her hair. "I asked if you got it?"

"Yes!" she screamed.

An iron grip on her arm, one hand still holding her hair. He pushed her forward, away from the car. She was drenched by now. Drenched and freezing. For a moment she floated away, sinking into unconsciousness, but a vicious tug on her hair woke her up.

Where were they? It was impossible to see clearly in the rain. In front of them, she could glimpse a light. A structure. A lightning bolt lit up the sky. She spotted the outline of treetops. They were in the woods somewhere.

He kept pushing her, leading her toward the light. Something was wrong with his foot—he was limping—but his grip on her arm remained tight. They entered the structure. A small house, its walls crumbling, the roof broken. The floor was wet, water trickling from the ceiling everywhere. She blinked as she saw the graffiti on the walls.

It was the ruined house she'd been to with Claire. The place where the police had found Kathy's shoes.

He kept manhandling her, pushing her through the rooms to the back, the house's bathroom. A large spotlight lit the room with harsh white light. The bathtub had filled with rainwater, a few inches of muddy sludge. The man pushed Robin toward the tub.

She knew who he was. She knew what was about to happen. He would drown her in the tub, like Kathy had shown her.

She jerked and tried kicking his bad leg. He easily moved his foot away, then let go of her arm, clenching her throat instead. Squeezing.

No air. Her vision turned cloudy, darkening. She tried to struggle, but she had no more energy. He pushed her, forcing her into the tub. It would all be over soon.

Then, he let go.

She inhaled, wheezing, coughing, thrashing in the muddy water. It was only a few inches deep. It soaked through her clothes, chilling her to the bone.

The man moved back and turned away in disinterest. Robin kept coughing, her vision spinning. She scrambled in the slippery tub, trying to prop herself up. It was almost impossible, but finally she managed to lean on the edge of the tub, her head just above the rim.

The man was fiddling with some sort of camp stove. A large pressure cooker stood on top of it. The stove was lit, the fire roaring underneath the pot. Next to it stood a tripod with a large video camera. He examined the cooker for a few more seconds, then checked the camera.

Robin tried to think. Her mind was foggy, traces of whatever drug he had used to knock her out fragmenting her thoughts. He hadn't killed her yet. She wasn't that far from her home. She needed to buy time. Maybe the cops would find her. Maybe someone would drive by, see the light from the collapsed house and wonder who was there.

Maybe she could get him to talk. Explain himself to her. He was clearly being driven by a twisted bizarre obsession. And many people with obsessions loved to elaborate about them.

She had to start with something specific. Something that would make it clear she already knew much about him.

She took a long shuddering breath. "Was Cynthia Rodgers the first person you ever killed?"

He gaped at her, his body rigid. She had caught him by surprise, knowing the name of one of his victims. Good: she needed him unsure, off his game. She wanted him to need to know more. Lure him in. Giving the police the time they needed to find her. She met his stare, clenching her teeth, willing her lips to stop trembling. There was something vaguely familiar about this man. Had she seen his photo when she was in the police headquarters in Indianapolis? No, that wasn't it.

"How do you know about that?" he asked.

She needed him to worry. Wondering how close they were on his trail. "The police told me."

His lips shifted, eyes skittering as he processed the information. What was going through his head right now? How desperate was he becoming? Could she use that?

"Do you know my name?" His voice became raw.

His name. Did she know it? She still couldn't figure out where she'd seen him before. She hesitated. She didn't want him to realize they didn't know who he was yet. "They didn't tell me that. I'm just a consultant."

He smiled at her, baring his teeth. "My name is Jonas. Jonas Kahn."

Fear froze her gut. There was no hesitation there. He would never have told her that if he didn't intend to kill her very soon. She tried to think of a response, her mouth numb.

He frowned at her. "So if they didn't tell you my name, what *did* they tell you?"

Keep him talking. She needed more time. "You . . . you k . . . killed some other women. Haley Parks. G . . . Gloria Basset. Uh . . . Mandy Ross." Her teeth chattered, partly from the cold, partly out of fear. "Why did you kill them?"

He checked the pressure cooker, inspecting the dial temperature. She couldn't see what it showed.

"You're the shrink," he said. "Why don't you tell me?"

"I d . . . don't know. Can you t . . . tell me?"

He snorted. "Is this the scene you think we're acting out? The heroic secret agent, trapped, with the villain telling her all his secret plans?"

She stared at him. What was he talking about. Scene? Secret agent? He was talking about a movie. Did he think they were in some sort of TV show?

"You have it all wrong," he continued, speaking faster, excited, one word tumbling on the heels of the other. "This is not a James Bond movie, or *Mission: Impossible*. This isn't an action movie at all. It's a different movie we're in. You should know what sort, right? If the police told you about the others, they must have told you about the movies too."

Chapter 48

Nathaniel stood in the sheriff's office, eyes intent on the large map hanging on the wall. The numerous roads surrounding the town crisscrossed the map, a mazelike grid of possibilities. Which way had Kahn taken Robin? If he went up or down US 421, he would have been spotted by the cops. They had a dozen cars and two choppers canvasing the highway by now, searching for Kahn's vehicle. There was no way Kahn would have made it through there. Not unless he switched cars. And Nathaniel doubted he had had the time to do that.

But of course, that wasn't the only road he could take. The entire area was covered with small roads and paths. A man who was familiar with the area could get almost anywhere without using the main roads.

So which way had Kahn gone?

His phone rang. With the noise around him—the constant radio chatter, people shouting, office phones ringing—he couldn't even hear it. But it buzzed in his pocket, and he whipped it out, answering the call.

"Hello?"

"It's me." Burke's voice in his ear.

Nathaniel plugged his other ear to muffle the noise around him. "Yeah, what do you have for me?"

"I still don't have any idea where he could go," Burke said. "We figured he might go to a motel somewhere, so we're checking motels in the vicinity."

"Okay, what about the acid?"

"So here's the thing, I don't think he'll use some sort of hard-to-get acid. Hang on, I'll let you talk to this fed here, he can explain it better."

Nathaniel waited, hearing as Burke talked to someone else.

"Hello," a different voice said. Gritty and sharp. "This is Agent Armstrong."

"I'm Detective King," Nathaniel said. "My partner said you had some info about the acid. I was planning on checking chemical factories in the area—"

"Yeah, no, you're not looking for a chemical factory," Armstrong said. "Detective, do you know who Santiago Meza López is?"

"No."

"He was a cartel member. About fifteen years ago, he was on our most-wanted list. His nickname was El Pozolero—"

"Agent, the clock is ticking. What's this guy got to do with Kahn?"

"Well, El Pozolero translates roughly to *the stewmaker*. This guy apparently disintegrated about three hundred bodies for the cartel."

Nathaniel shut his eyes. "Okay."

"You know what this guy used? Lye. Mix a few pounds with water and heat it up enough, it can dissolve a body. It'll take some time, and if Kahn's not careful, he'll get some serious skin burns, but I suspect that's how he'll do it."

"Lye," Nathaniel said.

"It's not too difficult to get."

"No, it definitely isn't," Nathaniel said. "Thanks, Agent Armstrong."

He hung up and turned around, grabbing a nearby deputy who was talking on the phone. He pointed at the map. "Where are the nearest hardware stores?"

Robin watched Kahn carefully. He tried to act detached, calm. But when he questioned her, he clenched his fists and his eyes narrowed.

She'd been wrong. He wasn't interested in talking about himself at all. He wanted to know how much she knew. Probably wanted to know if the police were close on his trail. She could work with that, keep answering his questions. Maybe she'd manage to make him nervous enough to make a mistake.

She suddenly realized where she'd seen him before. He was the man Mom had nearly run over when she drove up to Jimmie's Café. Robin's heart lurched. Had it only been a coincidence? Or had Jonas Kahn been stalking her back then, more than a week ago?

"Well?" he asked again, his voice shrill. "Did they tell you about the movies?"

The movies. Her eyes flickered to the camera. He was filming this. And he'd said they weren't in an action movie. Each of his previous victims had been killed in different complex, gory methods. Of course.

"Yes," she whispered. "They did. Horror movies."

There. The clench of his jaw, the shift in his eyes. There was something he was worried she knew. What was it? What had Nathaniel told her about the investigation? It was hard to concentrate with this man towering above her, the ominous pot behind him. She turned her face away, toward the wall, her eyes locking on the grimy clay tiles.

The tiles.

She recalled the last time she was here, with Claire. Back then she'd noticed a few of the tiles had broken off, their shards in the bathtub. Now, because the tub was a few inches full of muddy rainwater, it wasn't possible to see them. But unless this guy had seen them and removed them, they were still there. Sharp tile shards.

"Look at me," he growled.

She looked back at him, her hands behind her back, fumbling at the bottom of the tub, searching. "Cynthia, Haley, Gloria, Mandy . . . they were all in your horror movies, weren't they?"

"So they figured that out."

"And now you're making another one."

"I guess I am."

"The police know about it. They know you want to drown a woman in a bathtub."

He grinned. "Is that what they think?"

She gritted her teeth. Had she been wrong? But then the thought dissipated as her fingers brushed against something. There! She thrashed in the tub, acting as if she was losing her balance, and made a grab for what she'd felt. A broken tile. Her fingers ran along its edges. It wasn't sharp enough to be used as a weapon.

But given enough time, maybe it could cut through rope.

"What I don't understand," she blurted, "is why did you cut their hair?"

His grin widened. "Haven't you ever heard of merchandise?"

And then, to her horror, he pulled a large knife from his belt and took a step toward her.

"Yeah, sure, there was a guy here, he bought some drain opener," the hardware store clerk said slowly. "Insisted on this brand. I tol' him, I said this brand was more expensive and I had something better, but he didn't want to hear it. He said that it had to be one hundred percent lye."

"What did he look like?" Nathaniel asked urgently.

The clerk licked his upper teeth thoughtfully. "Young, I guess. He was really soaked, because of the rain. Wore a coat."

Marvelous. "What about his hair?"

"It was short. Black, I guess, or brown. I didn't really get a good look at it."

"Did you see his car?"

"Yeah, sure. It was parked just across the street. A Honda. Green. I noticed, because my mother-in-law, she has a car just like that one, and I'm trying to help her sell it. Anyway, I offered to help him carry the stuff, on account of his leg, but he said he could carry everything himself."

"His leg?"

"Yeah, sure, he was limping, and he was bleeding all over the place. I told him, I said, you should go to a hospital with that dog bite, but he said it wasn't too bad."

"He had a dog bite?"

"Yeah, sure, his pants were torn, and there was a big bite. Bleeding all over the place. I had to clean the floor after he left."

That was probably Menny's contribution. Good dog. "Did you see where he went?"

"Yeah, sure. He went to his car."

Nathaniel curbed his impatience. "And which way did he drive?"

The clerk blinked. "I don't know. I was busy cleaning the mess from his blood. That's unhygienic, that is."

Nathaniel felt desperate. This was useless. "How long ago was he here?"

The clerk licked his front teeth again. "A few hours, for sure."

Nathaniel turned to leave. This guy was no help. Maybe someone in the adjacent shops saw something. Then he paused.

"How much lye did he buy?"

"Just a couple of them bottles. Two pounds each."

"You said he told you he could carry *everything* himself. Did he buy anything else?"

"Yeah, sure. He bought a backup power generator, and gas for it, and bolt cutters." The clerk licked his front teeth again. "And a flashlight. And batteries for the flashlight."

"Did he tell you why he needed all that?"

"I asked, but he said he had some problems with the electricity in his house. So I told him, I said, you have a clogged drain and electricity problems in your house, that sounds like your house isn't in great shape. And he said I didn't know the half of it, that it was falling apart."

"Did he tell you anything else?"

"Well, we talked about the lye, and I asked what he needed it for, and he said to open the drain. And I said some people use lye to make soap, and he thought it was funny."

"I bet he did," Nathaniel said darkly. "Thanks."

He exited the store and took out his phone. He toggled the flashlight app and pointed the light beam at the sidewalk. The rain had washed away everything, but he still found what he was looking for. A few brown splatters by the store's doorway, where the rain didn't reach it. Dried blood. The clerk hadn't exaggerated. It looked like Kahn had been bleeding quite badly. It had to hurt like hell.

He wouldn't have gone too far. Not with a bite like that.

Nathaniel knew what Kahn needed the lye for. But why the generator? And the flashlight?

Wherever he was going, it had no electricity and no light. But presumably it had a bathtub. Unless Kahn had decided to go significantly off script. A generator would mean noise, so wherever it was, it had to be secluded enough so that no one could interrupt him. And somewhere nearby. A scrapyard? Maybe. God knew there were numerous scrapyards in horror movies. Kahn would probably find that alluring. It would explain the bolt cutters too.

Nathaniel massaged the bridge of his nose. Kahn had been in Bethelville, stalking Robin, like he'd done for the past few weeks. He hadn't been planning on killing her. Not today. But then he got a notification on his phone. The security app. He checked the feed, saw the police were in his house. He had to move fast. So he decided to grab Robin and finish her like he'd been planning for a while.

But Menny had bitten him, and the police were after him. Would Kahn really go bumbling through a scrapyard at night, in the pouring rain, searching for an intact bathtub? No. He'd go somewhere out of the rain. Somewhere nearby. A place he knew. A place with a bathtub but with no electricity. A place he needed bolt cutters to enter . . .

"Oh, shit," Nathaniel muttered, already yanking his car door open.

He said I didn't know the half of it, that it was falling apart.

Nathaniel had seen photos of the place, back when he was looking through Kathy Stone's abduction case file.

Kahn had gone to the place he knew from all those many months before. To the ruined house where he had taken Kathy after kidnapping her.

Robin screamed and struggled as Kahn knelt over her, raising his knife. His other hand shot forward, fast as a snake, grabbing her hair. And then, with a sharp tug, he cut a thick swath of it.

"Good thing you reminded me." He grunted, shaking the wet hair in his fist. "I wouldn't be able to take it once I'm done with you."

Robin was shuddering, her breath erratic. For a few seconds, she'd thought it was over. Now, it turned out she still had some time left.

Frantically she tried to position the jagged edge of the broken tile in her hand against the rope. It was almost impossible. It would have been difficult enough as it was, but her fingers were frozen stiff, and she still felt weak and nauseated from the drug Kahn had used on her earlier.

"So . . . what else did the police tell you about me?" Kahn asked. He had shoved her hair into his pocket and was now checking the pressure cooker again, his back to her.

Robin gritted her teeth, wedging the shard between her wrists, the jagged end against the rope. If she could only run it back and forth, she could eventually cut through her bindings. But there was no way to do it. Her only option was to apply enough pressure on the rope with the shard. And then, maybe, she would be able to sever the rope. It didn't feel very thick. She leaned against the bathtub's surface, forcing the rope onto the jagged tile. This made the rope bite into her skin harder.

"Um . . . ," she said. "They . . . they said you held Kathy captive. All those months."

"Did *they* say it? Or did the girl?"

Whatever she did, she had to keep him away from Kathy. "Kathy doesn't talk."

"Oh, believe me, I know. But I thought she talked to you."

"She doesn't talk to anyone." She was getting nowhere with the shard. She forced it deeper between her wrists, hoping that somewhere along the serrated edge, there would be a sharper spot. Then, counting to three, she leaned against the tub's surface again, pushing with her feet, all her muscles screaming with pain.

"So she didn't tell you anything?"

"Kathy doesn't talk," Robin repeated, her voice tense with effort. "The cops figured it out all by themselves."

"Are you trying to protect her from me?" He grinned mockingly.

Robin swallowed. "I'm telling you the truth."

He shrugged. "It doesn't matter. I couldn't care less about the girl. She was just a stupid mistake. But tell me this. If she doesn't talk, why did the cops talk to you in the first place?"

Robin paused, breathing hard. "They . . . they were hoping I could get her to tell them something. I couldn't. But it doesn't matter. They know enough."

He shook his head. "No, it doesn't sound like it. They don't know the half of it."

What was he talking about? There was something he was worried they knew. That was why he'd questioned her. But it wasn't the four murders, and it wasn't Kathy's abduction. It was something else.

It had to be his final victim. The one Kathy had left for last—the figurine of the woman with the cake.

Kahn opened the pressure cooker's lid.

Noxious fumes filled the room. Before, the fumes that had escaped through the valve hadn't been too bad. With the enormous hole in the roof, they'd simply wafted outside. But now the entire room filled with the poisonous vapors of whatever was in there.

Robin's skin prickled. Her throat burned. She coughed and retched.

"Well, I think it's ready," Kahn said, his voice cracking.

Robin recalled what Kathy had left for her in the dollhouse in that final session. The Wonder Woman figurine in the bathtub, covered in slime.

He was about to pour that thing on her.

Frantically, Robin leaned against the ropes, forcing them onto the shard.

Kahn grunted as he lifted the large pot, turning to face her. His eyes were half-shut, probably to avoid the stinging fumes.

"The police know *everything*!" Robin shrieked. "They know about the other person!"

That made him pause. He put the pot down and crouched in front of her.

"What about the other person?" he snarled.

"They . . . they know. After you kill me, there is one left. One you still intend to kill. And they'll stop you. They know everything."

He stared at her, still crouching, his eyes boring into hers.

And then he threw his head back and laughed hysterically.

"You almost had me there!" he shouted. "The girl didn't tell you anything. That bitch! She got away." His laughter was maniacal, desperate, the laughter of a man on the edge.

Robin pushed against the tub's edge with all her strength, feeling the rope as it bit into her skin, scraping it, pressing against the jagged edge of the tile.

And it snapped.

She had one chance. She flung herself over the tub's lip. And grabbed the steaming, noxious pot.

She tried to fling it in his face, but it was a lot heavier than she'd thought. All she managed to do was to tip the thing. Some of it spattered on Kahn's face. The rest splashed all over Kahn's legs.

And his laughter morphed into agonized shrieks.

The engine roared as the car hurtled down the dark road, the silhouettes of trees closing in from both sides. Nathaniel gripped the steering wheel, his fingers tight, his jaw clenched. His siren shrieked, the emergency red and blue lights flickering, warning other vehicles to keep out of his way.

He tried to keep his mind on the road, on the instructions he had gotten from the sheriff. If he let his mind wander, it filled with what he might find when he got to the decrepit house. Kahn had bought the lye hours ago. That meant Robin could already be . . . already be . . .

No, he couldn't let himself fixate on that. He needed to focus. The dirt path that led to the ruined house could easily be overlooked in the darkness.

The sheriff and the local cops were on their way as well, of course. But Nathaniel had radioed them when he was already underway. He had a few minutes' head start. And right now, a few minutes might be the difference between life and death.

Or not. Maybe he was already too late, Kahn already long gone, Robin's remains floating in the broken bathtub.

He gritted his teeth, pushing away the errant thought. The taillights of a vehicle loomed ahead, getting closer with alarming speed. He was driving fast. Too fast.

He didn't slow down.

A sharp turn of the wheel and his car veered to the opposite lane. The headlights of another car straight ahead. He frantically returned his car to the proper lane, wheels whirring on the gravel at the road's edge. Struggling with the steering wheel, he managed to get his car back to the road, leaving the honking cars far in his wake.

He had to believe every second mattered.

Because the alternative was so much worse.

Robin stumbled out of the bathroom, Kahn's horrifying shrieks of pain behind her. She was coughing and retching, the noxious fumes of the burning liquid stinging her throat. Her eyes were watering as well, her vision blurry.

The skin on her hand burned horrifically. Drops of the liquid had spattered the back of it when she tipped the pot. It felt like someone had set her hand on fire.

She grunted, stumbling through the dark room, reached the front door, and crashed into it. Once out of the house, she slipped on the muddy ground, falling, and her back slammed onto the ground, the air rushing out of her lungs.

Rain was pouring all over her. She held her trembling hand up to wash it, but it didn't help at all—it still burned.

It was almost a relief that it was too dark to see it properly.

And then, behind her, noise. She propped herself up and glanced back.

In the light coming from the doorway of the bathroom, she saw a shadow. Kahn. Lumbering after her, making inhuman noises, growls born of agony and rage, slurred, unintelligible words.

She scrambled to her feet. She had to get away.

The fence was barely visible in the dark. She floundered toward it, her feet squelching in the mud. She reached it, her fingers tightening around the iron links. She had to find the hole through which she and Claire had entered last time. Where was it?

She could barely concentrate with the screaming pain in her hand. How was Kahn even still walking?

Lightning flashed above her, illuminating the fence, the house to her left, trees everywhere . . . she couldn't see the missing section in the fence. She would run alongside the fence until she found it. It couldn't be—

Thunder rumbled above her, so immense its tremors ran through her body. She paused, paralyzed with fear.

Where was Kahn?

She turned around, couldn't see him. The still rumbling thunder and the pouring rain made it impossible to hear anything else. Kahn could be anywhere.

Step after step, she advanced alongside the fence, trying to ignore the throbbing agony in her hand, her throat rasping as she breathed. Something grabbed her ankle and she shrieked, but it was just a branch. She kicked it away, kept going . . .

Another flash of lightning illuminated the world. And there was Kahn, mere feet away from her.

As the glow from the lightning dissipated, her mind registered the open, dripping sores on his cheek, parts of his skin dangling. And his legs . . . oh God, his legs. How could he still be standing? Walking?

Running.

She turned and fled, Kahn just behind her, shouting his unintelligible, garbled curses. She stumbled against something, fell, got up, kept running. Another lightning bolt. She saw the boulder, the one that had been near the hole in the fence. If she could only get to the hole . . .

Her foot sank into a watery hollow, and she crashed into the mud. She tried to stand up, but her ankle couldn't support her, and she fell again. Crawling now, on her hands and knees, as fast as she could, toward the boulder. And Kahn behind her, letting out a sound that might have been a laugh, demented and twisted and wrong.

She reached the boulder, knowing Kahn would catch up to her in seconds. Her fingers fumbled around her, sifting through the slimy mud. Come on, where was it . . .

A hard, smooth surface. There it was. The broken bottle from the night with Claire.

Something grabbed her foot. Her fingers tightened, and she twisted around, swinging the broken bottle in a large arc, screaming as she did so.

It slashed his face, and he shrieked, letting go, stumbling back. Hands now covering his ruined face.

More lightning. Kahn, stooping, one hand still covering the remnants of his cheek. And still, through all that blood and loose tissue and ruined skin, one eye, unblinking, focusing on her.

He raised his arm, the outline of a knife above her. All she could do was crawl back as he hurled himself at her.

An explosion, and a flash of light.

Kahn crashed into the mud, facedown. Then lifted himself, still holding the knife.

Another explosion.

And Kahn dropped.

Robin stared at the monstrous man, breath shuddering. She raised her eyes.

A silhouette stepped closer. Lightning illuminated him. Nathaniel, his gun still trained on the unmoving Kahn.

Chapter 49

Robin shifted in the darkness. Her entire body hurt. What had happened?

The memories stormed back, a confused jumble of horrific images. And Kahn, he was still out there. Where was she? This wasn't her bed. She fumbled around her in the darkness, searching for a weapon, something she could protect herself with—

"Robin? Robin!"

Melody's voice pierced the wave of terror that gripped Robin's body. She gasped, clutching at the cloth that covered her.

"What?" she rasped. "Where—"

"You're in the hospital." Melody's voice trembled. "You're safe."

"What's wrong with me?" Robin whispered. Talking hurt, a scraping in her throat.

"You were exposed to sodium hydroxide fumes." A warm hand touched Robin's wrist. Robin had to force herself not to pull her arm away.

"My eyes. I can't—"

"It's just bandaging. Your eyes were exposed as well, and they need to rest, but the doctor said they'll be fine. They'll take the bandages off in a few hours."

"Are you sure they're fine?" Panic clawed at her. "I can't see."

She felt Melody squeeze her hand reassuringly. "Trust me. The doctor assured me. I didn't let him leave the room until he agreed to give me a *very* detailed explanation."

Robin nodded blindly. She'd seen Melody in action once when Amy was hospitalized with a severe ear infection. A nurse tried to wave Melody away with vague assurances, and Melody nearly took the hospital apart with rage until two doctors sat down and gave her a full report about her daughter's well-being.

"My throat hurts," Robin mumbled.

"That's the sodium hydroxide. They said those are very light burns. You did get some on your hand. You have a nasty burn there. They treated it, but you'll have a scar."

Robin let that sink in. Her memories were still jumbled. "Kahn . . . the man who took me—"

"He's dead."

"I don't think so." Robin swallowed. "I remember. He went after me. I couldn't stop him."

"He's dead, Robin. Detective King said so. Actually, he said he was *very* dead, whatever that means."

Robin relaxed a little. Her sister gently caressed her arm.

"What time is it?" Robin finally asked.

"It's . . . half past four in the morning."

"Oh. What are you doing here? You should be at home."

Melody snorted. "Are you kidding? I wasn't about to leave you alone here."

Robin tensed. "Menny! He was in the park—"

"He's at my house, sleeping in Amy's room. Trust me, she's delighted about it. I suspect she let him on the bed. He showed up all alone at Jimmie's." Melody's voice broke. "I was terrified. I went to your house and opened the door for the police, and you weren't there. And they found your phone . . ."

Melody let out a sob. Robin fumbled for her hand and grabbed it. "I'm okay."

"Yeah," Melody whispered. She sniffed. "I should tell Detective King you're awake."

"You can wait until morning," Robin said.

"Well . . . he's waiting outside in the visitors' lounge, so I should probably tell him now."

"Oh."

Melody let go of Robin's hand and stood up. Robin heard her footsteps as she walked away. A door opening and closing. And Robin was alone.

The fear crawled back almost immediately. She was alone in an unknown room, her eyes bandaged, her body hurt. Anyone could get to her right now. She wouldn't be able to stop them.

Kahn was dead, she reminded herself. He was *very* dead.

Her heart thrummed. The hell with it, she had to get away from here, had to get somewhere safe—

"Robin?"

Nathaniel's voice.

She exhaled, her breath trembling. "Hey."

"It's good to see you're all right," Nathaniel said softly.

"Melody said Kahn's dead." Robin swallowed. "Are you sure?"

"Yes," Nathaniel said. "I'm sure."

"Okay." Robin tried to calm her still beating heart. "There was something . . . when he was about to kill me, he said . . . I think he was still hiding something. It was important. I think it was another woman that he planned to kill."

"Well," Nathaniel said, "he's not going to hurt anyone ever again. Forensics are going through his stuff. If he was hiding anything else, we'll find it, I promise you."

Robin swallowed. "Does Kathy know?"

"Kathy?"

"Kathy Stone. Does she know he's dead?"

"No . . . not yet."

"You should tell her." Robin curled, hugging herself, exhausted. "You should tell her the evil clown man is gone for good."

Chapter 50

Robin opened the passenger door of Nathaniel's car and took a deep breath, bracing for the pain that was about to follow.

"Let me help you," Nathaniel said, already leaping out from the driver's side.

He quickly circled the car, going over to the passenger door, and offered her his hand.

He had volunteered to take her home from the hospital. Melody had intended to do that but was then summoned to the summer camp—Liam had gotten into a fight, and she had to pick him up. She intended to return to the hospital as soon as that was done, when Nathaniel assured her he could do it. Robin told her it was totally all right. In fact, she insisted, she could call an Uber. Both Nathaniel and Melody stared at her as if she was insane when she said that.

By now, she was relieved she had someone to help her. She hadn't realized how much everything hurt. She'd sprained her ankle when she tried to get away from Kahn, and now every second step shot a jolt of pain up her leg.

She took Nathaniel's hand, and he helped her stand up on the sidewalk. She bit her lip as she delicately put her injured leg on the ground.

"Okay." She breathed. "Now I need my bag from the trunk."

"Don't worry about that," Nathaniel said. "Let's get you inside, and then I'll get the bag."

"All right."

She leaned on him as she walked. He took his time, utterly patient as she limped with him to the door. She was breathing hard by the time they got to the front door.

"Oh, shit," she muttered. "The keys are in the bag."

"Melody gave me her spare." Nathaniel fished a key from his pocket. "Hang on."

He unlocked the door and helped her inside. He escorted her to the couch, and she crashed on it, relieved.

"Thanks." She shut her eyes, her ankle still pulsing with pain.

"Let me get your stuff," he said.

He stepped out, shutting the door behind him.

The house was silent. The hallway was dark, the doors shut. After a whole day in the hospital, with people there all the time and the incessant sounds of machines bleeping, the silence felt overpowering. Stifling. Without distraction, the fear that had been lurking at the edge of her mind came crawling back, its insidious tentacles wrapping themselves around her. Her breathing turned erratic. She tried to tell herself she was home, she was safe, but it was like nonsensical babble.

Flashes from the day before came to her. Kahn with his knife. The pain as he hit her. The terror as he still stumbled toward her, malformed, his one good eye unblinking—

"Hey." Nathaniel was by her side. "Are you okay?"

"Um." Robin swallowed. "Yeah, I . . . no. I'm not totally okay."

"I think that's understandable."

"Yesterday was, um . . . traumatic."

Nathaniel nodded, taking her hand. Squeezing it.

"Most people use that word without even knowing what it means," Robin said, her voice trembling. "You know. Like, 'I was stuck in traffic two hours, it was so traumatic.'"

"But you know what it means."

"I know what it means. I know how to treat it. But it doesn't . . . it doesn't help *me*, you know? It's like . . . I read the manual, so I know all the theories about how the brain works. I know that right now my amygdala hijacked my brain. But, um . . ." Her lips trembled. "I still feel like . . ." She couldn't finish her sentence. Tears clogged her throat and clouded her eyes.

Nathaniel leaned forward, taking her into his arms. She buried her face in his chest and sobbed, shaking.

After what felt like a few minutes, she pulled away, wiping her eyes. "I'm sorry."

"You have nothing to be sorry about," Nathaniel said gently.

"It's stupid, but would you mind . . . not leaving for now. I don't want to be alone. Not yet."

"It's not stupid. Besides, I wasn't planning on leaving just yet. I was about to make lunch."

That got a tiny smile from Robin. "You don't need to do that."

"It's no problem."

"I don't really have anything you can cook here. We can order something. There's a good Thai place nearby, or we can get burgers, or pizzushi—"

"I'm sorry, what now?" Nathaniel gaped at her with astonishment.

"Pizzushi. There's a new branch of Bill's Pizzushi nearby. It's this thing where they roll a pizza like a sushi. It's a whole new thing."

"Is it . . . any good?"

Robin considered it. "No. Not really. It's pretty bad."

Nathaniel stood up. "It sounds like it. No, I'm making lunch. I already got the groceries here."

Robin realized there were two paper bags on the floor. "When did you get those?"

"This morning, when you were in the hospital."

"You planned this?"

"Well . . . I planned on eating some chicken and green beans, and I was hoping you'd join me as well."

"Okay." Robin's heart made a tiny leap in her chest.

"So if you don't mind, I'll show myself to the kitchen and start making lunch?"

"Yeah, okay. I'll go take a shower."

Nathaniel looked at her for a moment. Was he about to ask her if she needed help? She wasn't even sure how she'd respond if he did.

But then he said, "Okay, call me if you need anything."

"I will." She smiled. "Thanks."

Nathaniel brought the bags into the kitchen. Robin stood up gently and limped to her bedroom. For some reason, the pain wasn't as bad as before. Perhaps just being in her home, and being taken care of, took some of the pain away.

She shut the bedroom door. Then, hesitating, feeling the fear lurking in the corners, she opened it, just a crack. She could hear Nathaniel in the kitchen. She wasn't alone. She was safe.

The mirror in the bathroom was unforgiving. Robin had a large bruise on her cheek. Her nose was red and her eyes bloodshot from crying. She could easily see where Kahn had chopped off a large swath of her hair. She clenched her jaw. She'd been considering a short haircut for years. It was as good a time as any to do that.

Gently, she peeled the bandage from the back of her hand. The lye burn looked awful. A dime-size blotchy spot, the skin completely malformed. It made her nauseated looking at it. The doctor had said once it healed, simple plastic surgery could make the scar almost nonexistent.

"You should have seen the other guy," she told her reflection in the mirror. And then let out a shaky laugh.

She closed the bathroom door, leaving it open, just a crack, like the bedroom door. She was acting like a child. If Nathaniel realized she was showering with the bedroom and bathroom doors open, she would be mortified.

But she kept the door open. And listened, reassuring herself that he was in the kitchen. She heard a repetitive tapping sound. He was chopping something.

The shower was pure bliss. She could almost feel the scalding-hot water washing the pain away. It was tricky to stand for long on her ankle, but she forced herself to take an extralong shower, shampooing her hair four times, until she couldn't feel the remnants of Kahn's fingers on it anymore.

She put on the tight-fitting black shirt she had bought in the beginning of the spring and the plaid skirt Melody had gotten her for her birthday. That done, she went to the mirror and put on some makeup, mostly hiding the bruise on her cheek. Letting out a long breath, she limped out of the bedroom.

The house smelled incredible, the scent of cooking beckoning from the kitchen. Nathaniel waited there, the table already set. His eyes widened slightly as she entered the room, and Robin's confidence returned, bit by bit. She wasn't that broken thing she'd seen in the mirror. She was the woman she saw reflected in Nathaniel's gaze.

"This looks . . ." She stared at the dishes on the table. "Incredible. When you said chicken and green beans, I pictured something, uh . . ."

"Dry?" He grinned.

"Yeah. I mean . . . healthy and all, sure, but this looks really good."

"Well, it *is* chicken and green beans. Cooked in a skillet with lemon garlic butter."

"Oh wow." Saliva filled her mouth.

"And sprinkled with parsley."

"Parsley, huh?" Robin sat down.

"It has a lot of vitamin K. That's what my mother always said."

"What's vitamin K?"

Nathaniel shrugged. "No idea. But I bet it's vital. Hang on, I'll get the wine. I put it in the freezer, so I hope it's already properly chilled."

Robin looked at him as he bent and took a bottle of white wine from the freezer. She couldn't tear her eyes away.

"The corkscrew is in the left-hand drawer," she said, her voice huskier than she'd intended. "And, uh . . . the wineglasses above in the cupboard."

He found it and popped the cork. Then he poured them each a glass. The bubbling of wine being poured was a sound full of promise.

Nathaniel handed her a glass. She took a tiny sip, savoring the chilly taste of the wine. She put the glass down, then cut a piece of chicken, speared it with some green beans, and took a bite.

"This is so freaking good," she said after swallowing.

He grinned at her. "Better than hospital food?"

"What do you think?" She took another bite.

They ate in silence for a few minutes. There was something so relaxing in sitting there, eating a meal that this man cooked for her, thinking of nothing beyond the question of whether the next bite should be chicken or beans, or maybe both.

She finished her glass of wine and decided she needed a refill. The bottle was still on the counter, so she got up, momentarily forgetting her ankle injury. Hissing in pain, she leaned against the table.

"Are you okay?" Nathaniel asked, alarmed.

"Yeah," she blurted. "I just . . . stepped wrong, that's all."

"You know what, I should have served you in the living room, with your leg elevated," Nathaniel said, approaching her.

"Don't be ridiculous, I—ow!" She shut her eyes. "Okay, you know what, can you help me to the couch for a moment? Maybe you're right, I should lie down."

"Sure." He let her lean on him and slowly escorted her to the couch. "Here."

She lay down on the couch and elevated her foot. Then she bent her knee, massaging it carefully.

"Does that help?" Nathaniel asked.

"A bit." Robin winced.

"Here, let me." He sat beside her and gently took her foot, straightening it. He pressed her sole lightly. "How's that?"

"Um." She shut her eyes. "That feels really good."

"Okay. Let me know if I'm hurting you, okay?"

"Yeah."

His fingers massaged her heel, then the arch of her foot. Warmth spread through her entire foot, then her leg, the throbbing ankle almost forgotten.

"That's really good," she whispered.

He moved his thumb in a circular motion on her sole. "That doesn't hurt?"

"No." She breathed deeply. "It's really helping."

"How about this?" He touched her ankle softly.

"Yeah . . . really gently, please."

"Okay." His touch was like warm silk.

"Maybe a bit higher," Robin murmured, shutting her eyes.

"Here?" He massaged above her ankle.

"Yeah . . . a bit higher."

His hand shifted, reaching her calf, his palm softly massaging her. She felt like she was melting.

"Maybe . . . just a bit higher."

Two hands now, on her thigh.

"Here?" he asked, his voice low.

"Yeah." She let out a small groan of pleasure. "That's so good . . . for my ankle."

His hand kept massaging her, caressing her thigh, up and down, under her skirt, a single brush against her panties.

She grabbed his arm, pulling him on top of her, her fingers running up and down his back, underneath his shirt, his skin smooth and warm, his muscles shifting under her touch. His lips touched hers. The pain she'd felt before was completely forgotten.

Chapter 51

Robin had seen Mom react to crises more than once. When Melody had given birth to Liam, she'd suffered from postpartum hemorrhage. A few hours after the birth, she started bleeding, and it didn't stop. Her blood pressure dropped alarmingly fast. The medical staff took their time figuring out what was going on, and even more time until they actually explained it to Fred, Robin, and Mom.

Mom's reaction was to yell at random doctors and nurses. Then she had a fainting spell in the hospital. Then, after Dad managed to get her home, she got on the phone and repeatedly called Fred and Robin to angrily demand updates. At some point she talked to Robin about funeral arrangements for Melody. Fred and Robin, who were supposed to dedicate themselves to Melody and her newborn son, had instead found themselves spending hours managing Mom.

It was an extreme example, but one of many, and it had led to an agreement between Melody and Robin. During a crisis of any sort, their mother had to be kept in the dark.

Which was why Melody didn't tell Mom about Robin's violent encounter with Kahn. Sure, she'd called Mom when Robin disappeared, just to check if she knew where Robin was. But once she ascertained that Mom was clueless, she'd ended the call, telling her that Robin was probably in the middle of a session. And that was that.

Robin hadn't given it much thought. Until, three days later, she got a message from Mom.

I just found out my own daughter was violently assaulted, and everyone knew about it but me. I really hope you are okay. If I had known, I could have helped.

Robin reread that message about a dozen times. It seemed almost like that optical illusion of a drawing of Sigmund Freud, where if you look at it long enough you realize it's also a naked woman. Was this the message of a worried mother who was also hurt at not being told? Or of a narcissist mother, aghast at not being told but also a bit worried for her daughter?

Whatever it was, Robin knew the more she postponed talking to Mom, the worse it would be when they finally met. So she went to Mom's in the afternoon, anticipating an exhausting visit.

"Hello?" she said, opening the front door. "Mom, it's me."

For a few seconds there was no response, and then a frail "Robin?" emanated from the bedroom.

"Yeah. Um . . . I called you, but there was no answer." Robin slowly limped inside. Her ankle didn't hurt as before, but it was still swollen and tender.

"I was . . . asleep." Mom sounded weird. Zoned out.

Robin reached the bedroom doorway, and leaned on it, giving her foot a rest.

Mom was in the bed, looking deathly pale. She wore no makeup and was in her nightdress, which absolutely never happened in the afternoons. She took very special care with her wardrobe.

"Are you okay? Are you sick?"

"No," Mom whispered. "I just . . . took a sedative."

"Oh." Robin stepped inside and sat at the edge of the bed.

"I was so scared, when I heard." Mom's chin trembled. "*Glenda* told me. She said this man grabbed you and took you somewhere in the trunk of his car."

"Mom, I'm fine—"

"I've already lost your father. Do you know what would happen if I lost you too? A mother can't lose her children." Tears misted Mom's eyes. "It would shatter me."

Robin swallowed, a lump in her throat. "The cops found me in time. Nothing happened. Really."

"And after that," Mom murmured, "not even a single phone call. To tell me you're fine. Melody didn't tell me to come to the hospital. You know . . . when you were a baby, you had a severe ear infection, and you were in the hospital for a whole week. I stayed with you in that room for the entire time. The doctors couldn't make me leave. One of them told the nurse that with a mother like me, you would never have anything to worry about. *He* understood."

Robin cleared her throat, already drained. "I didn't want to worry you. That's why I didn't call."

"Glenda was so surprised I didn't know. I must have sounded like a fool."

"I'm sure she understood."

Mom's eyes fluttered. "You once had a terrible ear infection. When you were a baby. You were hospitalized for a whole week."

"Mom . . . are you okay?"

"They couldn't make me leave the room. The doctors were so impressed. One of them told the nurse I was such a good mother."

She was completely out of it. Robin had never seen her so unfocused before. She was staring at the wall, looking confused. Her headstrong dominating mother, suddenly so fragile. All the venomous corners were smoothed out by the meds. Robin squeezed her hand, her heart throbbing.

"I'm all right," she said.

"I would have been shattered," Mom whispered.

"I know, but I'm really fine."

"I . . . I realize sometimes I'm a bit hard on you. But you have to understand that I always only wanted the best for you."

Robin wiped a tear. "Yes, I understand—"

"And you were always *so* disappointing."

Robin stared at her in shock.

"No matter how much time and energy I gave you," she carried on. "You did nothing right. That's why I'm so hard on you."

Robin let go of her mother's hand. "I see."

"Maybe now, after this terrible experience, you'll finally get your act together," Mom said, her tone becoming lighter, hopeful. Her eyes were shutting; she was slipping away into sleep.

"Could be," Robin said, standing up. "Diana, I'm going to make some tea. Do you want anything?"

Mom looked at her through half-shut eyelids. "What did you do to your hair?" she slurred. "Why did you cut it so short? It looks awful."

After a few seconds, she began snoring lightly.

Robin went to the kitchen and fixed herself a cup of tea. Then she rummaged in her bag, finding her cigarettes. She'd already smoked two today. She really shouldn't have a third.

She thought of Mom as she lit it. How she would step into the kitchen later and smell the cigarette smoke. Her mother detested smoking. Robin inhaled the smoke into her lungs and then blew it, turning her head left and right, watching the smoke cloud as it curled and rose, filling the room.

No ashtray of course. Robin opened the cupboard with the best china, took out one of the golden-rimmed cups that Mom treasured so much. Sitting back down, she took another cigarette from the box. Fourth one today. She lit it from the one she was smoking and stubbed away the half-smoked one in the china cup.

She shut her eyes as she inhaled from the cigarette. Already planning her fifth cigarette.

And after today, it was time to quit.

Chapter 52

For the past few days, Nathaniel had been walking around in a sort of daze. He tried to tell himself it was mostly the result of the Kahn investigation. He'd put an end to the murder spree of a horrific serial killer. This was one of those cases that made him feel good about being a cop, and God knew those were few and far between. Not to mention, it was probably a good case for his career.

So yeah, he was satisfied with it. But he also knew that this airy feeling that permeated his day had a completely different reason. Robin.

They talked every day. He had gone to her place once more and had spent the night. It had been years since he'd felt like this about anyone. It was incredible. And scary. Because at some point she'd realize a relationship with a cop wasn't the best deal ever, just like Imani had. Sure, it was a good thing when one was being kidnapped by a serial killer. But the rest of the time?

There was a reason the divorce rate of cops was so high.

But for now, he would enjoy what he had. So when he walked into Vernon Horowitz's lab, he had a smile smeared on his face, thinking about his latest text exchanges with Robin.

"What are you smiling about?" Vernon grunted.

"Nothing, I'm just in a good mood."

"A good mood, huh? I think I had that once." Vernon was doing one of his exercises, alternately crouching and standing. He spent the entire day in the dark lab, mostly in front of the computer, and would often explain how bad that was for his health. He cycled through various methods that were aimed at negating that.

"I saw your email," Nathaniel said. "So you're done with Kahn's laptop?" The forensics on Kahn's house had become less urgent after his death, so it had taken longer than it would have otherwise.

"Yeah." Vernon leaned on the desk and stretched one of his legs. "A lot of what he had on it was just video snippets from horror movies. He used those to make his weird compilation video. He had a few versions of that one."

"Okay," Nathaniel said. "Anything interesting there?"

"Well, some are longer, and some are pretty short. The shortest one is only five video clips."

Nathaniel sat down on one of the office chairs. "Five video clips? Let me guess. One from *Scream*. One from *Friday the 13th* . . ."

"You got it. Each of them corresponding to one of his murders."

"So there wasn't a sixth one," Nathaniel said, thinking of Robin's words about the other victim.

"Nope. Just five."

That was probably the compilation he had watched during the time Kathy was held in his house. The one she playacted with the dollhouse. "Okay, good."

"I think that was his main use for his laptop. I went over his documents, found some things he did during college, a few years back. Also found some lists of horror movies. A big Excel sheet that sorted them according to subgenres, murder types, nudity, amount of goriness, that sort of thing."

"What a fun hobby," Nathaniel said dryly.

Vernon sat down. "He was generally a fun guy. His browser history was a trip down creepy lane. He'd repeatedly obsess about some aspect of horror movies and dig into it. So for example, in the first week of April, he spent five whole days searching and watching videos of people drowning in quicksand. And he had a brief fixation with plague-infested rats. And a thing with eyeballs—"

"Okay." Nathaniel raised his hand. "I get the picture. You said you found some things he did in college?"

"Yeah. I gather he studied cinematography?"

"He started a BA in cinema and media studies but dropped out two years ago," Nathaniel said.

"Right. So I found a few of his assignments. I don't think he was particularly invested in it. They seemed mostly copy-paste jobs from Wikipedia."

"They probably didn't delve enough into horror for his taste."

"So that's all that was on the laptop. Now we can talk about the thumb drive."

Nathaniel took a deep breath. That was the main reason he was there.

When forensics opened the safe in Kahn's home, the first thing they found were his trophies. Four snippets of hair, matching his four victims. Those matched the hair Burke found in the room and other hairs forensics managed to locate later. It indicated Kahn occasionally took the hair out of the safe. The profiler from the bureau explained the reasons for that quite graphically, and Nathaniel wished he could bleach that knowledge out of his brain. Knowing a fifth snippet of red hair was found on Kahn's body during the autopsy made it even worse. He liked Robin's new short haircut, which made her look like a cute pixie. But he hated knowing the reason for it.

In addition to the hair, they'd found a password-protected thumb drive. Vernon had finally managed to decrypt the thing.

"There are four videos on the thumb drive. Snuff films." Vernon's voice trembled slightly. That was unusual. As a computer forensics expert, Vernon had seen a lot of awful stuff. It took something bad to unsettle him.

"You watched them?"

"Yes. Partly. Once I realized what they were . . ." Vernon cleared his throat. "It's one thing to watch this guy's collection of horror-movie videos. It's another thing completely when it's . . . uh . . ."

"Real," Nathaniel said.

"Yeah."

"Can you show me?"

"I can put them on . . ." Vernon hesitated. "And would you mind if I take a walk? It's good for my back if I walk every couple of hours."

"Sure."

Vernon opened the folder on his computer. "There. Four files. I'll be back in a bit."

Nathaniel took a deep breath. He had already watched the raw footage they'd retrieved from Kahn's camera, from the night he took Robin. It had been nauseating to watch as Robin struggled for her life. Though he did feel a surge of pride as he watched her freeing herself, dumping the boiling lye mixture on Kahn.

This would be worse. Part of him considered walking away. Kahn was dead. He would hurt no one else. They knew who his victims were; their bodies had been retrieved. He did not need the memory of these videos in his mind.

But he owed the victims and their families to see this to the end. Perhaps one of the victims had said something their family would want to know about. Or maybe he would see something that would shed some light on the whole thing, earn the families some piece of mind. Probably not, but he had to take a look.

He clicked the first video. It was the earliest one. Cynthia Rodgers.

It was fortunate that he'd only drunk coffee for breakfast, because when he threw up in the middle of the video, it didn't make too much of a mess on the floor. He got some paper towels and cleaned it up as best as he could.

No wonder Vernon couldn't wait to get out of there before he watched the videos.

Compromising with himself, he decided to watch the rest of the videos with the sound almost muted, just enough to be able to hear Kahn, and his victims, in case they said anything important.

Next came Gloria Basset. He was gritting his teeth so hard by the time it was over, he almost pulverized them. Two down, two to go.

Mandy Ross was the third. He was already deeply regretting his decision to do this. It would haunt his nights. He was glad Kahn was dead. He was especially pleased *he* was the one who had pulled the trigger.

Haley Parks came last. After that he was done. He would go home and shower, and—

Hang on.

He rewound it, watched it again. Just the beginning. Kahn was struggling with Haley, knife in hand, and then . . .

He watched it a third time. Oh, shit.

When Vernon came back, Nathaniel was sitting in front of the paused video, lost in thought.

"Hey," Nathaniel said. "Would you mind watching something with me?"

"Um . . . I prefer not to."

"It's not . . . one of the more terrible parts. And we can mute the video. I need another pair of eyes."

Vernon seemed pale as he sat down. "Okay."

"Watch the trees in the background." Nathaniel unpaused the video.

Vernon watched with him. "Oh. Oh!"

Nathaniel nodded. It was impossible to see if you only looked at Kahn and Haley, struggling. They were moving too fast, motions jarring and violent. But if you kept your eyes on the motionless trees on the right side of the frame you saw that . . .

"The frame moved," Victor said. "The camera isn't on a tripod."

"Someone is filming this. Kahn wasn't alone that day. Someone was helping. And look . . ." Nathaniel fast-forwarded it. "See? It happens again."

"Yeah, I see it."

"I was thinking . . . Haley Parks was murdered when Kathy Stone was held by Kahn. Could *she* be the one holding the camera?"

Vernon leaned forward, rewinding the video, looking at it carefully. "Well . . . I'm no expert, but I don't think it likely. The camera is *very* stable. We can hardly see when it shifts. And also . . . the angle would be different if it was held by a little girl, wouldn't it?"

"Probably. Unless she stood on something," Nathaniel suggested.

"Yeah . . . I mean, I guess it's possible, but it sounds very unlikely. But that means—"

"It means Kahn had an accomplice."

Chapter 53

Here's something Claire hadn't told anyone, not even her new therapist. Washing the dishes filled her with dread.

A year and a half ago, all it had taken was a few minutes of inattention, washing a pan, and Kathy disappeared. Now, whenever she did the dishes, she made sure Kathy was in the same room with her, and Claire never took her eyes off her. She broke a few plates because of that, but it was the price that had to be paid. She only baked with disposable cake pans, so she wouldn't have to clean them. She generally avoided cooking anything that was difficult to clean. And suggesting Pete do the dishes had opened a long discussion that infuriated her so much that she decided to drop it.

And if doing the dishes was difficult, how much worse was it to be away from Kathy for a few hours?

Much worse, it turned out. It was relatively easy if Pete was with Kathy. Like she'd done that night with Robin, she simply called Pete to make sure Kathy was all right. But when Kathy had gone to Robin's for a session, Claire would grit her teeth and let the panic attacks wash over her, wait for them to dissipate.

Her therapist told her it was part of the healing process. Claire obviously knew she couldn't be with Kathy every second of every day for the rest of their lives.

Still, she already regretted going on this dinner date with Pete.

It had been his idea. He said they needed some time together, just the two of them. At home, every minute they had together was about Kathy. Even at night, when Kathy was asleep, they could still feel that tension between them, which often boiled over to disagreements, to hissed arguments, to anger.

So, Pete suggested an evening out. And they agreed, this evening, not to talk about Kathy. Not to discuss if she was going back to her sessions with Robin, not to talk about school next year, not to argue about whether Claire was coddling her or if Pete was ignoring her emotional scars.

This was about Claire and Pete, trying to figure out if they could still love each other, if they could still be a family.

Claire had planned to see Kathy before she went to bed, but when her therapy session ended, she saw a new message from Pete. Kathy had fallen asleep early, so it was better if they met outside the house. That made sense. Even a tiny sound could wake Kathy up, and if she woke up scared, they would probably have to postpone their date. Still, Claire wished she could have seen her daughter for just a minute. And that she could have showered, for that matter.

Now they entered the restaurant, and the hostess beamed at them.

"Hello, do you have a reservation?"

"Yes," Pete said. "Pete Stone. Table for two. We're supposed to be in the—"

"In the gazebo," the hostess said. "Of course, follow me."

She led them to the back of the restaurant and opened a side door, and Claire stepped in after Pete.

"Oh wow," she whispered.

The small gazebo outside overlooked the river. Vines covered the gazebo walls, its interior lit with a string of lights lining its roof. The table was covered in rose petals.

"I wanted this evening to be special," Pete said.

"I didn't even know this place had a gazebo," Claire said.

"Nice, right?" Pete glowed. "Evan knows the owner, so he organized this for us. It was his idea that we come here this evening."

◆ ◆ ◆

Robin was cleaning the playroom after a busy day. Donny, her fourth session, had been particularly energetic and seemed to want to play with *all* the toys. She was now slowly putting them back on their shelves. She was tired, and her ankle was throbbing.

She picked up toys from the floor, where Donny had positioned his "army of monsters." A dragon, a troll, a shark, the Joker, and a squirrel had formed the army together for villainous purposes. Robin put them all on the shelf until only the clown remained in her hand. She stared at the figure, and not for the first time in the past week, contemplated if she should throw it in the trash.

She hated this figure. His red smile now unnerved her, sometimes making her mind go back to that night. The only reason she hadn't gotten rid of it yet was because she hoped Kathy would resume her sessions. Claire said she intended to convince Pete to agree to it. And if Kathy came back, she might need this toy, a vessel for her memories of Kahn.

But maybe Robin could store this plastic clown in the cabinet for now, until Kathy came back.

Her phone rang. She glanced at the screen and smiled, her heart giving a tiny skip, as Nathaniel's name flashed on the screen.

"Hey," she said. She was almost embarrassed by how she sounded when she answered the phone. Who *was* this Robin who sounded like a schoolgirl in love?

"Hi," Nathaniel said. She could hear her smile mirrored on his side. "How are you?"

"I'm okay. It was a busy afternoon."

"Yeah, here as well. I know I said I'll be at your place for dinner, but I don't think I'll make it."

"Oh," she said, disappointed.

"I'll do my best to get there later," he said apologetically. "Maybe we can watch some Netflix together or something?"

"Okay. Is something wrong?"

"Uh, not exactly. There's been a development."

"A new case?"

"No, this is still the Kahn case."

"What is it?"

"Nothing, I . . . don't worry about it."

"Was it another victim, like I thought?" She swallowed.

"No, no, we just think someone might have helped him in some of the murders."

Robin swallowed. "Another murderer."

"Yeah, maybe. We're interviewing a couple of guys he hung around with during his cinematography studies. See if one of them fits the profile. It would make sense for the accomplice to be interested in films as well."

"What about . . ." Robin's voice trembled. "Me? And Kathy?"

"We have no reason to believe the other guy knew either of you," Nathaniel said. "As far as we can tell, he was involved only in the Haley Parks murder. Kathy never showed you anyone else working with Kahn, right?"

Robin looked at the clown figure in her hand. It almost seemed as if his smile was stretching. "No."

"And when Kahn followed you, we're pretty sure he was alone. But if anything changes, I'll let you know."

"Um . . . when you're done . . . can you come over in any case? Even if it's really late."

"Sure," Nathaniel said. "I'll be there as soon as I'm done."

Claire sipped from the red wine, looking at the man in front of her.

It was like looking at a stranger.

The Claire that had fallen in love with Pete Stone, who'd agreed to marry him after dating him for six months, was someone from the distant past. Claire still recalled that other Claire as if she was recalling a childhood friend, one that in time, she'd lost touch with.

When Kathy had been kidnapped, Claire had been shattered. But she'd picked herself up and for endless months forced herself to act, to save her daughter. In that time, she'd become someone else. And then, after all those months with no news, she'd been shattered again. Spent the time without her daughter in a haze. During that time, Pete had tried to help her, but it was like they didn't even speak the same language anymore. And then Kathy returned, and she needed her mother, and Claire rebuilt herself a second time.

But, as the nursery rhyme went, all the king's horses and all the king's men couldn't put Claire together again. Not the way she was before.

She was still figuring out who she was. Maybe, in time, she could learn to like this man, the one that another Claire had chosen to marry. But she doubted she could ever love him.

He was talking about the future. About giving them a fresh start. He wanted to make these decisions together. If she didn't want to move to Indianapolis, that was fine by him; it was something they could discuss. He was so glad she was getting back on her feet. He believed they were a better family now. Stronger. They knew how to work together.

She listened to him, bewildered by how differently they perceived everything. Even this gazebo. After the initial shock wore off, she couldn't figure out why he thought this was a good idea. This was a place for a young man to propose. Not for a couple to decide if they still belonged together.

Her phone rang. She took it out, and Pete frowned, as if annoyed that she'd let the thing interrupt his impassioned speech.

It was Ellie, Kathy's babysitter.

Claire answered immediately, her breathing already quickening. "Hello?"

"Claire?" Ellie's tone was teary, panicked. And Claire instantly knew her gut feeling had been right. She shouldn't have left Kathy.

"What happened?" she blurted.

"I don't even know." Ellie sobbed. "She was *fine*. We were playing with her Barbies, and . . . she saw something . . . someone. Outside the window. She screamed and locked herself in her room, and wouldn't open the door . . ."

Claire was already standing. "We'll be home in ten minutes. I can calm her down. It happens sometimes—"

"She's not here!" Ellie said.

"What do you mean?" Claire's heart plunged down, down, down.

"I finally got the door to her room open. She climbed out the window. I can't find her anywhere."

Chapter 54

Robin elbowed her way into the sheriff's office, a dark twisting sense of déjà vu coiling in her gut. The office was full of town residents, all looking serious and tense. The room hummed with the sound of whispered conversations—snatches of sentences. ". . . through the window . . ." ". . . thought he was dead . . ." ". . . long gone by now . . ."

It was Bethelville's worst memories, happening all over again.

Robin had come after Melody called her, telling her what had happened. Kathy had disappeared. The sheriff was organizing a search party. Robin had also talked to Nathaniel, who was now on his way.

She spotted Ellie, her face smeared with tears, and jostled her way over to her.

"Hey," she said in a low voice. "What happened? Melody told me Kathy is missing?"

Ellie's lower lip trembled. "It's all my fault. I was looking after her. And . . . and . . . there was something outside. A shadow or something. Kathy saw it, and she freaked out."

Robin swallowed. She could imagine the girl's eyes widening as her traumatic memories flooded her yet again, triggered by who knew what.

"She, um . . . locked herself in her room. And I tried to talk her out of it, you know? Tried to calm her down through the door. It was so stupid of me. If I only didn't waste time—"

"What happened?"

"I finally unlocked the door . . . she has one of those locks that can be unlocked with a kitchen knife or a screwdriver . . . you know the kind. But she was already gone. Her window was open. She must have crawled out. I looked for her . . . I called out to her, but she wasn't there." Ellie stifled a sob. "What if she's hurt somewhere? Or . . . or . . ."

"She's just hiding," Robin said, trying to reassure her. "She'll turn up."

"Yeah." Ellie's voice faltered. "You know . . . back when she was first abducted . . . I always wondered. There was something I maybe could have—"

"There was nothing you could have done," Robin said. "And it doesn't matter now. We have to focus on what happens tonight."

Ellie blinked. "You're right. We need to find her."

Robin didn't voice her own fears. Kahn had had an accomplice. And he could have been the shadow Kathy had seen outside her window.

Claire listened hollowly as the sheriff instructed people where to look. The police had barricades on the main roads leading out of town. Claire repeatedly told herself that those barricades were just a precaution. After all, the man who had kidnapped Kathy was gone. There was no reason to think history would repeat itself.

Pete had dropped Claire off at the sheriff's office and driven straight home in case Kathy returned. Claire now regretted that they hadn't done it the other way around. Kathy would surely come back home once she calmed down, and she would need her mother waiting for her there.

Her phone rang. It was Pete. Claire answered the phone, her heart leaping. Had Kathy returned?

"Hey." Pete's tone made it obvious that wasn't the case.

"No sign?" Claire asked.

"None yet. I'm sure she'll return eventually."

"Yeah," Claire said hollowly. "I just don't understand. She has been doing so much better lately. And there was no problem when we left, right?"

"No. Nothing serious."

A shift in his tone there. "Pete," she said, her voice sharpening. "You said it went smoothly."

"It did! Sure, Kathy seemed a bit frightened to see me leaving. But we expected that, right?"

Claire shut her eyes. She should never have trusted Pete. If Kathy had already been frightened when he left, it wouldn't have taken much to drive that fear to a full-blown anxiety attack. She hung up the phone, sickened.

"Claire." Sheriff Price approached her, his expression gentle. "You should wait for Kathy at home with Pete. We have this under—"

"No," she blurted. The idea of going home and *waiting*, like she'd done for months on end, was unthinkable. Even worse would be waiting there with Pete. "No, I'll join the search. If Kathy doesn't return home, she'll go somewhere she knows, right? I should go with someone, look for her in the places we went to."

Price seemed hesitant. "Well . . ."

Her eyes scanned the room, locked on a familiar face. "Evan!" she called.

Evan turned around, starting when he saw her. He came over. "I just got here. I only just heard . . . I'm sure Kathy will turn up in no time."

"Can I ride with you?" Claire asked, ignoring his words. "I need someone to drive me to places Kathy might hide in."

Evan's eyes shifted. "The sheriff said I should go check the area around the school. Maybe someone else can—"

Claire grabbed his hand. "Please. I don't want to look for Kathy with a stranger."

"I'll send someone else to look around the school," Price said.

Evan exhaled. "Okay. My car's out front."

"Thanks," Claire said, her mind already churning with the places she and Kathy had gone to in the past weeks. "We should start at the park near our home."

◆ ◆ ◆

Robin drove slowly down the street, her eyes jerking left and right, searching desperately for Kathy's tiny figure hiding somewhere, scared and alone.

The sheriff had asked Robin to search in the southern part of town, close to her own home. But the more she drove around, the more she became certain she wouldn't find Kathy. Not like this.

Robin knew Kathy well. Even if the girl was terrified out of her wits, she would search for a place she perceived to be safe. The most likely thing she'd do was go back home.

Unless she had been taken.

Robin swallowed, thinking of that unknown accomplice. What if it was someone who *did* know Kathy? Who knew Kathy could still identify him? To someone like that, Kathy posed a risk. Maybe he had just waited for things to calm down a bit before deciding to strike himself.

It occurred to Robin that maybe Kathy didn't escape through her window at all. Maybe she was *taken* through the window. After all, it made no sense for Kathy to leave the house when she saw something that terrified her outside. It was much more likely she would lock herself in the room and hide there.

She should go back to the sheriff's office. Talk to him. Get Nathaniel involved.

But first . . . if Kathy *had* run away, there was one place Robin knew she thought of as a safe place. Robin's playroom.

She would swing back home, make sure Kathy wasn't there. And then drive to the sheriff's office.

She hoped Kahn's accomplice didn't have Kathy. She hoped he was nowhere nearby.

Claire looked out the passenger window. She felt detached, as if she was a helpless spectator, watching something that was doomed to fail. The mother looking for her daughter. She knew the role well; she knew how it went. First the urgency, then the desperate actions, the dwindling hope, and then . . . the nothingness, consuming all in its path.

They drove around the park, looking, searching. There was no one there other than them. The other volunteers were searching the rest of the town. The cloudy night had turned the street much murkier than usual, the streetlights fighting a hopeless battle with the dark.

Evan had been quiet for the entire drive, his hands clutching the steering wheel so tightly, they turned white. Now, he pulled the car aside, stopping at the curb, and killed the engine.

"Why did you stop?" Claire asked hollowly.

He turned to look at her. His eyes were wide. Haunted.

"Claire . . . I'm sorry."

Robin knew something was wrong the moment she set foot inside her house. Though the house was dark, and she couldn't hear a sound, she could feel it, a tremor in the air. An empty house felt a certain way. Her house wasn't empty.

Where was Menny?

She crept inside, holding her breath, her heart thrumming in her chest. Fear threatened to overwhelm her. Memories invaded her mind: of being trapped in a trunk, of being tied up in a broken bathtub while Kahn prepared his lye concoction, of fleeing his mangled body in the rain.

342

She shut her eyes, forced herself to breathe shallowly as she took another step inside.

A sound from the playroom.

She crossed the hallway and peered inside.

Kathy was inside the dark playroom, standing by the dollhouse, calmly playing with the toys.

Robin breathed out a long, shuddering exhale. She opened the door slowly and examined the room. Noted the open window through which Kathy had entered. Ah, and there was Menny, in the corner of the room, happily chewing on the plastic stethoscope. As he noticed her, he paused, giving her a guilty stare.

"Hey, Kathy," Robin said softly.

The girl raised her eyes and smiled at her. She didn't seem scared. In the playroom, she felt safe.

Robin stepped inside. "Your mom and dad are looking for you."

Kathy blinked, then turned back to the dollhouse.

"I'm going to call them, okay?" Robin said. "Tell them to come over and pick you up?"

At that, Kathy stiffened. She turned to Robin and shook her head violently, her jaw clenched.

Robin looked at the dollhouse. The three remaining figures were all there. Kathy had placed the evil clown figure in the living room. The little girl and the woman with the cake were in the tiny kitchen.

"I know your mom told you that the evil clown man is gone," Robin said. "He is dead. And he will never hurt anyone ever again. The little girl is safe."

Kathy mulled this over. She picked up the figure of the little girl, holding it in her hand.

"He can't hurt the little girl anymore," Robin said.

Kathy turned her back to the dollhouse and looked around. She crossed the room to the box where Robin kept all the toy trucks and cars and rummaged inside it, finding a red convertible. The plastic car used to be controlled by a remote, but the batteries had run out, and the remote was lost, as inevitably happened with that kind of toy. Kathy returned to the dollhouse, car in hand. She placed the little girl in the car, then added the woman holding the cake by her side. And she drove the car away from the house.

"That's right," Robin said. "The little girl and the nice woman can drive away. The evil clown man can't hurt them anymore."

Claire stared at Evan, confused. "You're sorry? What are you sorry about?"

Evan looked at her, his face pale. "I . . . this is all my fault. I talked Pete into it. He didn't want to leave Kathy alone with a babysitter. He said she wasn't ready yet. But I thought it was a good idea for you and Pete. And if I hadn't . . ."

"Evan," Claire said through clenched teeth. "I don't give a damn about your guilty conscience. Right now, I just want to find Kathy."

"Um . . . right. That's why I stopped the car. I figured we should cross the park on foot. See if we can find her."

"Okay." Claire opened the passenger door, getting out of the car. It was as good a plan as any. "Let's go looking."

Chapter 55

Kathy drove the tiny red car back and forth along the table's edge, the figures of the woman and the girl sitting inside.

"That's right," Robin said gently. "The bad clown man is gone. The girl and the woman are free to drive away."

Kathy tightened her grip, her eyes intent on the car.

"I'll call your parents now, okay?"

Kathy shook her head, her jaw clenched. She moved the car back and forth, faster, faster, her eyes wide, body trembling.

"The little girl and the woman are safe," Robin said patiently. She took out her phone and wrote a quick text to Claire. I found Kathy, she's okay. I'll bring her back home.

Kathy let out a sob, a tear running down her cheek. She drove the car intently yet again.

Robin put the phone down and stared at what Kathy was doing. She'd spent a lot of time processing what this girl had accomplished over the last two months, and she knew Kathy put a lot of attention into details.

She was driving the car with its front facing the dollhouse. The clown figure still sat inside the living room. Robin had told her he was gone forever, but Kathy hadn't put it away. Hadn't placed him on the shelf or buried him in the sandbox. It was possible Kathy didn't believe he was really gone.

"The bad clown man is gone. I saw it with my own eyes," Robin said. "Do you believe me?"

Kathy looked at her and then nodded.

"Then we can put him away."

Kathy shook her head again. She drove the car again to the house, then paused it. She took the two figures from the car, holding them together so they seemed to be holding hands, and then marched them to the house.

"The bad clown man is gone," Robin repeated. "He can't . . ." Her voice dissipated as she stared at the toys.

Kathy wasn't showing her something she was afraid would happen. She was showing her something that *had* happened.

She was showing her the day of her own abduction.

Robin swallowed. They had assumed Kahn had kidnapped Kathy. After all, she'd been held in his house. But there was no evidence of it. In fact, there was evidence to contradict it. Robin remembered the drive with Claire to the abandoned house, where Kathy's shoes had been found. The path to the house was nearly invisible. Easily overlooked by someone who didn't know it was there. Someone who didn't live around town, familiar with the house where teenagers used to camp out and party.

And Kahn took grown women and killed them. He'd never shown any interest in taking young girls.

Robin recalled Kahn's words when she talked about another person being involved. At the time she'd thought there was one other victim they didn't know about. Kahn had seemed nervous when she mentioned the other person, but then, when she said it was a victim . . .

The girl didn't tell you anything. That bitch! She got away.

Robin had assumed he was talking about Kathy who got away. But that was a strange thing to say in retrospect. Kathy had been long gone. He was talking about someone else who had gotten away. His accomplice. Who had gotten away with it, staying free even after the police knew about him.

Throughout the sessions, Robin had always assumed the figures were of the victims and of Kathy. But the figure of the woman with the cake wasn't one of the victims at all. Now that Robin thought about it, in every session, Kathy always placed the girl and the woman together. A mother figure . . . and a warden, making sure Kathy didn't escape.

Someone local. Someone who spent the past years out of town, living with Kahn and Kathy in his home.

Kathy placed the figures in the car again. Driving them back and forth. Glancing at Robin, trying to make her *understand*.

Why would Kathy flee her room through the window if she saw someone threatening *outside*? Kathy was a bright kid. She would have stayed in the room. Made sure the window was locked, like the door.

Unless the danger wasn't outside. Unless she was running away from someone inside the house.

Ellie.

Who had lived out of town for the past two years and had come back only recently.

Who'd just claimed to have seen something on the day Kathy had been abducted, while she was supposedly away at college.

Robin recalled that day at the café, Jimmie telling them about Ellie's college degree. What was it? Something about her writing screenplays and filming artsy movies.

Ellie had studied media and cinematography. Like Kahn. And she was away from Bethelville for two years, ostensibly working on her college degree. She'd returned only a few weeks before Kathy reappeared. Had she met Kahn there? Dropped out of college and moved in with him?

And that day in the supermarket. Robin and Ellie were together when Kathy walked in with Claire. Kathy had been awash with fear, and Robin had assumed it was the experience of meeting *her* outside the playroom. But it wasn't. It was seeing Ellie.

Like Claire said, the police had assumed someone who was close to Kathy had kidnapped her, since there was no evidence of a struggle. Almost as if the girl had entered the abductor's car of her own free will. Her babysitter's car.

And tonight Claire and Pete left Kathy alone with her old babysitter. The woman who'd kidnapped her. What Ellie said was partially true, most likely. Kathy had locked herself in her room and then escaped through the window. Not outside, into the arms of a supposed threat. But *away* from the threat.

"Kathy," Robin said, her voice croaking, pointing at the woman in the girl's hand. "Is *that* Ellie? Your babysitter?"

Kathy nodded, her chin trembling.

"Okay," Robin whispered. "Okay. Don't worry. I'll take care of this."

She turned on the phone's screen. It was time to call Nathaniel.

A knock on the door. Robin raised her eyes, Kathy clutching her.

"Don't worry," Robin said. She'd check the door in a minute. First—

The doorbell rang. And then a voice, calling out. "Robin?"

Ellie's voice.

Robin's trembling finger tapped on the screen hurriedly.

The front door opened.

Chapter 56

Nathaniel thought of Robin as he drove toward Bethelville. Her voice, tense and worried when she called to let him know Kathy had run away from home. He hoped they would find the girl quickly. A sliver of unease crawled through his gut. Kahn's accomplice was still out there.

The interrogations he conducted that day hadn't turned up much. Two guys who'd studied with Kahn in college before he dropped out. Neither of them raised any red flags, and Nathaniel suspected they were both dead ends. One of them hazily remembered Kahn dated a girl that studied with them, though he couldn't remember her name. He would follow up on that—

His phone rang. Robin. He tapped the screen, smiling.

"Hey."

No answer on the other end. Some muffled shuffling. It sounded like she'd butt-dialed him.

"Hello . . . Robin? I'm on my way, I'll be at your place in about an hour. Hello . . . Can you hear me?"

Nothing. His finger hovered above the hang-up button.

Then he froze. There was something on the other side of the call.

The sound of erratic, terrified breathing.

◆　◆　◆

"Hello? Robin?" Ellie's voice, high pitched, friendly. The voice of a young woman no one would suspect of anything.

The front door shut, then the sound of hurried footsteps. Robin stood frozen at the edge of the playroom, the door to the room ajar. It opened.

Ellie stood in the doorway, her nose pink, her eyes still bloodshot from crying.

"Hey," she said. "I thought you were home. I saw your car."

"Yeah," Robin said hoarsely. "I . . . I swung back home."

"I guess you had the same idea as I did," Ellie said.

"Um, maybe. What idea?"

"That Kathy might come here. I mean . . . the poor girl was so frightened by whatever she saw . . . I thought she might go somewhere she felt safe."

"Oh. Right. That crossed my mind. So I figured I should check."

Ellie nodded, looking around. She wiped her eye. "I keep thinking," she said, her voice trembling. "If I'd only opened the door to her room sooner, none of this would have happened."

Robin stared at her, amazed. She could almost believe she'd been wrong in her reasoning. Ellie seemed so earnest. So sad.

"You can't think that way," Robin croaked. "It's not your fault. I'm sure they'll find her soon."

"Yeah," Ellie whispered. She glanced at the open window.

"We should go help with the search," Robin said. "You go on, I just need to grab something warm from the bedroom."

"Yeah." Ellie approached the dollhouse, looked at it closely. The figure of the little girl and the woman with the cake lay by the house, forgotten. Ellie picked the figures up.

Robin swallowed. She didn't dare move from where she stood, between the bathroom door and Ellie. "So?" she said. "Shall we?"

"Hello?" Nathaniel said. "Robin? Is everything all right?"

He increased the volume, listening carefully. He could definitely hear breathing by the phone. Quivering, laced with the hint of tears. And very faintly, hardly audible above the sound of the car's engine, he could hear conversation.

"Robin, I'm on my way, but I have to know. Are you safe?"

A shudder. A sob.

"Robin, are you—"

"No." A tiny voice. "Not safe."

It wasn't Robin at all. It was the voice of a little girl.

"Who is this?" Nathaniel asked.

Another sob. Breathing. He knew who it was.

"Is this . . . Kathy?"

"Yes," the girl whispered.

"Where are you?"

"Robin's house." Kathy's voice trembled. "Please . . . help us."

Nathaniel grabbed the police mic and pressed it. "Dispatch, this is Delta-Five-Two."

The radio crackled. "Go ahead, Delta-Five-Two."

"There's a ten thirty-five in Bethelville. Require immediate police assistance."

"We should really get moving," Robin said.

"Didn't you say you were grabbing something warm?" Ellie asked.

"You know what? It doesn't matter. It's not that cold."

"It's actually pretty cold outside," Ellie said. "Which is why I'm wondering . . . Why's the window open?"

"I like to air the room in the evening after all the sessions. You know, with the pandemic and everything. Say, I was wondering . . . earlier you said you'd seen something. The day Kathy was taken."

"What?" Ellie asked distractedly, her eyes skittering, scanning the room. "What had you seen?"

"Oh. Yeah. I thought I saw Evan with Kathy . . . What's there?" Ellie pointed at the bathroom door.

"That's just the clinic's bathroom." Robin shifted, blocking the door. "It's a mess. This kid today had some stomach problems, and—"

"What if Kathy is there?"

Robin waved her hand dismissively. "I checked. She isn't. You said you saw Evan—"

"I want to check myself." Ellie rummaged in her handbag.

"I really feel uncomfortable with you seeing it. Like I said, it's a—"

A gun materialized from Ellie's handbag, barrel pointed at Robin.

"Like I said," Ellie said. "I want to check myself. Move."

"Ellie," Robin said, eyes locked on the gun. "What are you doing?"

"I'm not going to ask again," Ellie snarled. "Move. *Now.*" She gestured with her gun.

Robin shifted away, holding her breath in terror. The gun followed her as she moved to the corner of the room. She glanced at Menny, who'd stopped chewing the stethoscope and was looking at them both in confusion.

Ellie grinned, a maniacal smile. "Menny," she cooed. "Come here."

Menny stood up and waddled over, wagging his tail. Ellie crouched and scratched behind his ear, the gun still trained on Robin.

"Who's a good boy?" she asked. "Who's a very good boy?"

Menny shut his eyes and rolled to his side, hoping for a belly rub. Robin stared at her useless dog and at the deranged woman holding her at gunpoint.

Ellie stood up and, with the gun still pointed at Robin, slowly walked over to the bathroom. She tried the door handle. The door was locked. Sighing, she rummaged in her purse with her free hand, coming up with a small screwdriver.

"Learned my lesson from earlier," she said.

She stuck the screwdriver in the lock and twisted it, and the lock clicked open. She opened the door and glanced briefly inside.

"Hey Kathy," she said, warmly. "Come out from there."

Ellie waited. Robin held her breath.

"Kathy." Ellie's voice sharpened. "You know what happens to girls who don't do what they're told."

Robin considered jumping Ellie now, when her attention was elsewhere, but Ellie's eyes kept skittering in her direction, the gun never shifting an inch.

Kathy stepped out of the bathroom, shivering.

"There, that wasn't so hard, was it?" Ellie smiled. She pulled a small cloth doll from her bag. "Look what I have here. The second doll I gave you. You thought you'd lost her, didn't you? But I kept her for you."

Robin recalled the doll that Kathy had held when she was found—the one she'd brought to her first session. This one looked similar. Both were handmade. Had Ellie made them for Kathy?

Ellie held out her hand, and Kathy stepped forward and took it, her eyes wide with terror.

"We're going on a little trip," Ellie told Kathy cheerfully, handing her the doll. She began leading her slowly out of the room, gun still trained on Robin.

Robin stared helplessly, her mind whirling. She had to stop them from leaving. Talk. Make the woman talk. Ellie *loved* talking. She loved giving her side of the story. Enjoyed her imagined moral superiority. That was the core of all her arguments with Jimmie at the café. Robin could use that.

"Why take her now?" Robin blurted. "You've left her before."

Ellie paused, her face hardening. "You have no idea what you're talking about."

"Don't I?" Robin asked. "You took Kathy from her home and held her prisoner in Jonas Kahn's place—"

"She *wasn't* a prisoner. She was . . . she is my daughter. I took care of her."

So that was what it was all about. Ellie perceived herself as Kathy's replacement mother.

"You took care of her?" Robin repeated, lifting an eyebrow. "You left Kahn a month before Kathy got free of that place, didn't you? Abandoned Kathy with that twisted monster—"

The gun twitched in Ellie's hand. "You didn't know him. He's not what you imagine."

"He locked her in a *shed*, Ellie."

"Well, what was I supposed to do?" Ellie snarled. "She stopped talking to me! Just sulked all day in her room. I sacrificed *everything* for her, and she didn't even bother to *speak*."

Robin now had a full grip on the conversation. She knew who Ellie was. Robin had been raised by someone similar. And she could do these conversations in her *sleep*. Don't argue too much; that would only make her lose her temper. Reel her in, give her the occasional compliment. Let her tell the story as she perceived it.

"I imagine your feelings were hurt," Robin said.

"You don't know the half of it. You're not a mother. I cooked her meals, I read her bedtime stories. I played with her. Jonas . . . he could be difficult sometimes, and when he got angry, I would keep her safe. And *this* is how she repaid me. You know what the problem was? She took me for granted. So I figured I'd give her a couple of months without me. She'd see everything I gave her."

"But she ran away before you came back."

Ellie nodded, frustration etched on her face. "I thought Jonas could do the basics. But all that man really cared about were his movie projects."

His movie projects. Robin felt nauseated. "And she managed to get back to her mother—"

"*I* was her mother! Do you have any idea how many times Claire whined about Kathy to me when I came to babysit?" Ellie changed her tone, mimicking Claire's voice. "Kathy's been a real handful today, Ellie. It's so hard to raise a child during lockdown, Ellie. I wish I had a moment to myself, Ellie. Is *that* how a mother should talk about her daughter?"

"And you figured you'd be a better mother."

"I *was*. Claire would let Kathy play in the yard all alone, with no one watching her. So I decided if she cared so little about her girl, I could let her off the hook. Take Kathy and raise her myself."

And that's how Kathy disappeared that day from the yard. Robin imagined Ellie as she drove by, stopped her car. Motioned Kathy over. Of course Kathy approached her babysitter's car.

"They found her shoes in that abandoned house."

Ellie smirked. "That's right. I met with Jonas there, and we decided to leave a little something for the cops. So that they'd assume the local drug addicts were to blame. Guess whose idea that was."

With narcissists, rhetorical questions weren't necessarily rhetorical. "Yours?"

"That's right. Mine."

"It was a clever idea," Robin said. "Worked like a charm. Kahn wouldn't have thought of that."

"No," Ellie said victoriously. "He wouldn't."

"And that story about Evan you mentioned?"

Ellie shrugged. "At the time I wanted a scapegoat. Someone the police would go after. Evan didn't have an alibi. I knew that. Saw his updates on social media. And the police always look at people who knew the victim, right?"

"But you decided not to point a finger at him?"

"It would have drawn too much attention to me. I shouldn't have been here, I was in college, right? The cops would have wondered why I happened to be in Bethelville. In the end I decided to go with the shoes. And like I said, it did the job. We had Kathy to ourselves."

"You had Kathy. You could be her mother," Robin repeated. She had to keep Ellie talking. "So why didn't it work out?"

"It did! I was the *perfect* mother. Never complained. My entire day revolved around her. But Jonas wasn't really father material. He wasn't ready. So yeah, a few times he let her watch his video compilations. He loved horror movies as a child, and he figured she'd like them too."

Robin recalled the session in which Kathy chained the little girl figure to the couch in the living room. She suspected Kahn did a lot more than just "let" Kathy watch those videos.

"I told him not all children like those things, but he said it would toughen her up. I wanted my girl to be tough. The world is not a good place, Robin. COVID, global warming, wars . . . anyone growing up now should be ready for life to become difficult." Ellie's eyes seemed to drift, as if she was recalling the past. "And at first, it was fine. But then one day Kathy sneaked out of her room while Jonas was working on one of his projects. That Rodgers girl."

Cynthia Rodgers. The one they found dismembered in the forest. Kathy's first session—drawing the screaming person and the blood covering everything. And her ritual blood cleansing. Robin swallowed. Kathy was a bright girl who'd had a lot of time to think. That must have been when she realized the movies Kahn watched over and over weren't just movies.

"I caught her in time," Ellie said, her voice sharp. "She hardly saw *anything*. And anyway, it was *her* fault. She knew she wasn't allowed to leave the room on her own. So I took her back to her room and stayed with her until she calmed down. It took *hours*. But instead of thanking me, she began to talk less. And after a while, she stopped talking entirely."

Robin identified her cue. "It was also Kahn's fault," she suggested.

"Right!" Ellie beamed. "I told him not to work on his projects in the house. It wasn't good for Kathy. But sometimes it was impossible to get through to him."

"You were a good mother," Robin said. "But the circumstances were difficult."

"Exactly. I was a great—"

Ellie suddenly screamed, stumbling back. Kathy bolted away, ran across the room, and hid behind Robin, clutching at her.

"You little bitch!" Ellie snarled.

Her hand was bleeding. Robin looked down at Kathy and saw that she was holding the nail file they always used when she cleaned the red paint from her hands. She must have taken it while in the bathroom. Its tip was crimson with blood.

Ellie raised the gun. Without thinking, Robin shifted, getting Kathy behind her, protecting the girl with her body.

"You see what she does?" Ellie snarled. "After everything I gave her."

"You're better off without her," Robin said. "You can leave by yourself."

Ellie snorted. "She's my *daughter*, Robin. A mother doesn't desert her kid. And I'm not stupid. If I leave her here, I won't have another chance to take her with me. Kathy, come here."

Kathy clutched at Robin tighter. Robin put a hand on Kathy's, reassuring her.

"Ellie, you should leave."

"Not without my girl," Ellie said hoarsely. "I'll shoot you if I have to, Robin."

A sound from outside. A siren. Red and blue lights flickered through the window. The police were here. Robin exhaled. Nathaniel must have understood she was in trouble. He'd called them here.

Ellie's eyes flickered to the window. "Fuck."

"It's over," Robin said gently.

Ellie narrowed her eyes. "You think they'll believe you?" she snarled. "The psychologist who everyone knew used a girl for her own professional needs? If you tell them about this, I'll say *you* took Kathy. Because you wanted to keep doing your weird experimental therapy on her."

"You think they'll buy that?"

Ellie snorted. "I'm a good person. Everyone in town loves me. Do you really think they'll take your word over mine? It's not like the girl will say anything." She slowly put the gun back in her purse. "I'm getting out of here. I don't need this."

She turned and walked away. Robin exhaled and looked at Kathy. "Are you all right?"

Kathy nodded.

Robin listened as the front door opened and closed.

"Where's my phone?" she asked.

Kathy lifted her shirt and took it out of the waistband in her pants, where she must have hidden it. Robin took it. The phone call to Nathaniel was still ongoing.

She put her phone to her ear. "Nathaniel?"

"Robin! Are you all right?" he said, relief in his voice.

"Yeah. Did you hear all that?"

"Every word."

"Okay." Robin took Kathy's hand. "I'm going out to talk to the cops before Ellie drives away."

Chapter 57

Robin stood in the street and stared at Menny impatiently as he investigated a fire hydrant. He was thoroughly fascinated by it, as if he had never sniffed anything so captivating.

"It's a fire hydrant," Robin told him. "You've smelled one of those before. In fact, you smelled *this one* before. Is this some sort of canine art exhibit? Or did a celebrity dog pee on it?"

She gave his leash another tug. He let out an offended huff and kept sniffing.

Robin sighed. It was the end of their walk, and she wanted to get home. At least, despite the long walk, her ankle didn't hurt. In fact, the only thing that hadn't healed completely by now was the burn mark on her hand. She'd talked to a plastic surgeon the day before, and he was quite confident he could make it look "as good as new."

Plastic surgeons, Robin reflected, did what she could never do in her work. They covered the imperfection, fixing the external layer.

The scars inside her would be trickier to heal.

She was getting there. Today she'd managed a record of a three-minute walk with Menny in the park before the silence of the woods around her became ominous and every shadowy tree seemed like it could hide someone. Tomorrow she'd try to go for four minutes. She wouldn't let Kahn ruin her walks.

Finally, Menny obliged, and they walked back.

Jimmie's Café was closed, as it had been for the past month. But today, she glimpsed Jimmie inside, sweeping the floor. She hesitated, then stepped over and rapped her knuckles on the café's glass door. He raised his eyes and blinked a few times. Then he put his broom aside and shuffled to the door.

He seemed old. For Robin, Jimmie had always been ageless, his gruff demeanor and Geppetto-like hair keeping him in a constant status quo. But today that wasn't the case. His movements were frail and tired.

He opened the door, the doorbell jingling, and smiled at her. "Hi, Robin. I'm afraid we aren't open."

"Yeah, I know. I just wanted to say hello and to check in on you."

"That's nice of you." He grunted and glanced at Menny. "You, sir, seem thirsty."

"It's a hot day," Robin said.

"Hmph. Well, let's do something about that." He turned and stepped into the café. "Come in, I'll get him a bowl of water."

Robin and Menny followed Jimmie inside. There was an aura of neglect in the place. A thin coat of dust on the tables and chairs. The air felt stale. Was today the first day in the past month that Jimmie had been here himself?

Jimmie came back through the back door, a bowl of water and a dog biscuit in his hands. Menny hoovered the biscuit from Jimmie's hand, leaving behind a dollop of saliva, and then proceeded to slurp noisily from the bowl.

"Can I get you something? A glass of cold water?" Jimmie asked.

"No need, thank you."

"I never got to talk to you after that night," Jimmie said gruffly, looking at Menny. "I'm really sorry about what my niece did to you."

He didn't distance himself from Ellie. He could have easily called her by name, instead of referring to her as his niece. And he could have just as easily not said anything at all.

"It wasn't your fault."

"Well, whose fault it is can be a very long discussion. And one which I already had with myself, and with several members of my family, a bunch of times." Jimmie frowned, his shaggy eyebrows scrunching. "I'd rather not repeat it again."

Robin nodded. "Are you going to reopen soon?"

Jimmie frowned. "I don't know. It's difficult, Robin. Whenever I step in here, I start thinking back. You know, in the past few years, before Ellie came to work here, I sometimes had local teens working for me. And I sometimes worked alone. And it was *okay*. But when she was here . . ." For a moment his voice dissipated into nothing. Then he cleared his throat. "I know she's a bad person. But it was really nice to have family around. To have *her* around. She's so opinionated, and full of life. I actually imagined giving her half of this place. Turning it into *our* business. A family business." He shrugged.

"I'm sorry," Robin said gently.

"I visit her in prison," Jimmie said. "I went two days ago. And I told her I'll come next week. Her parents . . . my sister . . . they don't want anything to do with her. You think it's right? For a mother to abandon her girl like that? Even if she did something so horrible, like Ellie did?" Tears shone in his eyes.

"I think there's no right answer to that. It depends on the mother. Or the father. Maybe they're angry now, and they'll change their minds later. It must be difficult for them."

"I've never been a parent," Jimmie said. "But I imagine that's where it really counts. How you act when things get difficult."

"I think the everyday stuff is just as important."

Jimmie let out a heavy sigh. "My sister used to give her a hard time. Ellie kept getting into trouble at school. My sister said she kept lying about it, trying to weasel out of problems. I always stuck by her. Now I'm wondering if my sister was right all along. Maybe Ellie did lie all the time. Or maybe she became this way because her parents didn't have her back . . ." His voice broke.

"Does it matter?"

"I guess not. It is what it is."

"Yeah."

"You know, maybe all this would be easier for me if I stopped visiting her. At least for a while. Distance myself." Jimmie shook his head. "But I can't. When I leave her there, and she asks me when I'll come next, I just . . . I feel like I can't let her down."

Robin knew what he meant, better than he could imagine. She gave him a little smile. "Family's sometimes like that. Whatever there is between us and them . . . they're still family, right?"

Jimmie let out a small, sad chuckle. "Yeah. I suppose so."

She leaned forward and gave his arm a squeeze.

"Anyway," Jimmie said, turning back and grabbing his broom, "I don't know if I can really open this place anytime soon. But I can't afford to keep it shut for much longer. So maybe I'll let someone else run it for a while. Just so the locals have a place to sit down and have a warm drink."

"Yeah," Robin said brightly. "That's not a bad idea. Let some youngster manage the place for a while, until you get your bearings."

"Uh-huh," Jimmie said, looking uncertain.

"Maybe they can serve some modern drinks around here, get us a taste of the big city. I went with my boyfriend to Starbucks last week and had chai tea with vanilla syrup, almond milk, and pumpkin spice topping. It was fantastic. Could be nice to have something like that here."

Jimmie stared at her, aghast.

"Or iced coffee with toffee syrup and some cold soy milk foam," Robin said dreamily. "Like I had every week during college."

"Now look here . . ."

"Oh! I once had a caramel macchiato—"

"Sit down," Jimmie snapped, gesturing angrily to one of the chairs. "And don't you start talking like that here. This is a respectable establishment."

Robin demurely sat on one of the chairs.

Jimmie went behind the counter, shaking his head. He turned on the coffee machine. "I'm going to make you some coffee," he grumbled. "*Good* coffee. First cup is on the house. Just to make sure you still remember what *that* tastes like."

"Black, please," Robin called.

"Yeah, yeah." He was tinkering with the machine, muttering to himself. His motions became smoother, the tiredness gone from his face.

Robin leaned back in her chair contentedly. She could do with some of Jimmie's tar-colored coffee right about now.

Chapter 58

One of the exercises that Claire's therapist had her doing was to try and measure her anxiety on a scale of one to ten, which was pretty limiting. Because when the anxiety hit hard, it didn't feel like a ten. It felt like a thousand. Or a million. But maybe that was the point.

Right now, at Melody's house, drinking chilly lemonade, watching Melody's boys grappling with each other on the lawn, her anxiety was about a four. It wasn't lower because Kathy wasn't in her line of sight—she was in Amy's room. And also, she was worried one of Melody's boys was about to dislocate his shoulder.

"How's Pete settling in?" Melody asked, sipping from her own glass. Her lemonade was spiked with rum. She'd suggested some for Claire, but alcohol didn't mix well with Claire's medication.

"It's hard to tell," Claire said. "We don't really talk about it when he calls. We mainly talk about Kathy."

"I guess that makes sense."

Claire suspected Melody knew how Pete was doing better than her. After all, he and Fred were still friends, right? Then again, she was never sure how much Pete shared with his friends. Claire knew he'd furnished his new apartment, including a room for Kathy, for when the three of them agreed Kathy was really ready to sleep at his place. And Claire had seen him post something on Facebook—a photo from work, and there was this one woman who seemed to stand unusually close to him. Were they becoming a thing now? And was it bizarre that it bothered her?

"Maybe the boys want some lemonade," she suggested.

"Nah. They'll come drink some when they've exhausted themselves," Melody said.

"Right," Claire said, her plan foiled. What should have happened was that Melody would say yes and then would call the boys for lemonade. And then Claire would innocently suggest checking if the girls wanted lemonade too. Because it made sense to check, since the boys were already having some. It was only fair. And then she could see Kathy was still all right.

She wasn't even sure who she was trying to fool. Melody, who saw Claire peek into Amy's room every fifteen minutes? Or Kathy, who was getting tired of her mother constantly hovering around her?

Or herself?

Her therapist said she was progressing remarkably well. Claire hoped so. She was exhausted. She probably *was* doing better. She was just getting impatient with herself. Claire was ready to move the hell on.

"Do you think Kathy's ready to go back to school?" Melody asked.

"Yeah," Claire said. "You know, it's weird to realize how fast she caught up with all the material she missed. It makes you wonder what they're doing with them all day at school."

"Absolutely nothing," Melody said. "The teachers can't get the kids under control. Not to mention that after the quarantines, some of these kids have been completely left behind."

"It's awful," Claire said. "This generation of kids were the ones hurt the most by the pandemic. They'll be carrying the remnants of it for the rest of their lives."

"Tell me about it. They say they'll address the steps they're taking at the next parent-teacher conference, but they never get anything done there."

"We can *force* them to take steps," Claire said. "This is important, right? It's the future of our children."

She was talking the talk, settling into the same old conversations. Melody didn't give her those looks anymore, as if she was worried Claire would implode at any moment. And yesterday, when she went to Jimmie's, she didn't see anyone having hushed conversations while glancing in her direction.

She was doing better. And the people around her were doing better too. And maybe her anxiety wasn't really a four right now.

It was three and a half. A one-to-ten scale was way too limiting.

Chapter 59

"Can you hand me that marmalade jar?" Robin asked, pointing at the jar on the top shelf.

"Sure thing," Nathaniel walked over behind her, raised his long arm, and plucked the jar from the shelf as if it was low-hanging fruit.

Robin used the opportunity to lean back into him. He hugged her with one arm as he handed her the jar.

"There you go," he said, his voice low. He kissed the back of her neck.

"Mmmm . . ." She took the jar. "Tall men have their uses."

"We're irreplaceable."

"Oh, trust me, tall men are easily replaceable. With a ladder or a chair."

"Could a chair do that?"

"Get your hand away from there. I have a session in fifteen minutes."

He pulled away. Robin shut her eyes and exhaled slowly. She could get used to that. She *was* getting used to that, to be honest. Nathaniel had slept over at her place five nights in a row. He kept saying he'd sleep at his own apartment the next night. The drives were long, traffic was killing him, his captain was getting annoyed with his tardiness at work. And then, come evening, he would call to ask if it was okay for him to come over that night.

Because Robin, it seemed, was worth the long drives and horrendous traffic and disgruntled captains. Which made her feel . . . incredible. Not to mention the happiness that filled her whenever they were together. And he could get the jars on the top shelf, so it was really a no-brainer.

She spread some butter and marmalade on her toast and sat down at the table, Nathaniel across from her, drinking his morning coffee.

"Melody invited me to dinner this Friday at her place," Robin said. "Would you come with me?"

"Sure." Nathaniel sipped from his mug. "Do you want me to make anything?"

"If you have time."

"I can make my zucchini casserole."

Robin's mouth was already watering. "That would be amazing."

Nathaniel kept warning her that relationships with cops were a complicated business. The job wasn't easy; it often invaded their private lives. But he also said that he wanted to set some clear boundaries between his job and their relationship. Because he loved her. Robin was prepared to face that difficulty together with him.

A knock on the door interrupted her rumination. She checked the time. "That's probably my eight o'clock." She stood up, cramming the last of her toast into her mouth.

"They're early," Nathaniel grumbled. "I'm out in a few minutes."

"Okay." She circled the table and leaned down to kiss him. A kiss of marmalade and toast crumbs, mixing with his coffee. The perfect romantic breakfast. "I'll see you tonight?"

"Maybe. I might stay in Indianapolis tonight. I need to get to bed early for one night, at least."

"I can come over to your place," she suggested.

"Yeah." He brightened up. "Maybe that would be better."

His apartment was much smaller, and the young neighbors above him often partied late, so it definitely wouldn't be better. But being with Nathaniel was worth small apartments and noisy neighbors. "No problem. Let me know."

She ran her hand along his shoulder and went over to the front door and opened it.

"Hey." Claire smiled at her.

Robin smiled back and looked warmly down at Kathy. "It's good to see you. Let's go inside."

"I'll pick her up in an hour," Claire said and kissed Kathy on the cheek. "Bye, sweetie."

Robin led Kathy to the playroom. "We'll have to start meeting in the afternoon, starting next week. School's starting, right?"

Kathy nodded.

"So . . . what do you want to do today?" Robin asked.

Kathy glanced at the dollhouse. It stood there, the rock of contention between Robin and her mother. Every time they talked, Mom would demand that Robin return it. Robin would remind her she'd agreed to give it to Robin. Or she would tell her she would in a few more weeks. Or she'd change the subject. She was resolved to keep the dollhouse in her playroom. Where actual kids could play with it. For Robin, its presence was therapeutic.

"You want to play with the dollhouse?" she asked Kathy.

Kathy looked at her, then back at the playroom.

"I want to play at the nurse's station today," she finally said.

"Sure," Robin answered. "In this room, only you decide what we'll play."

ACKNOWLEDGMENTS

"Listen," I told Liora, my wife, as I barged into my home after an hour-long jog. "I have an amazing idea for a book. I need to talk to you about it."

"Wouldn't you rather shower first?" she asked, twisting her nose.

"No! We need to talk about this now."

And we did, the first brainstorm of many, which might explain why, first and foremost, this book would never have been written without Liora's help—brainstorming even when I was stinky, helping me out with problematic chapters, and fixing all the horrible mistakes in my first draft.

My editor, Jessica Tribble Wells, received my draft and cracked her knuckles. She helped me make the beginning of the book more engaging, developed Robin's character with me, and was instrumental in finding the killer's voice.

After writing nine books about cops and feds, writing one about a child therapist was . . . challenging. Therapists, it turns out, do not inhabit crime scenes or investigate forensic evidence. In fact, it's almost like they're not interested in capturing serial killers at all. Luckily for me, I know a few therapists. Christine Mancuso was one before she became a brilliant writer, and she read my draft and gave me a bunch of notes—more about pacing and character development than therapy. Then my parents and my sister Yael, all psychologists, read the book, too, and each gave me their own notes. My mom gave me that wonderful scene where Robin guides Claire and Pete. My dad removed some moments of questionable actions by Robin. Yael helped make each of the sessions with Kathy and the other kids more believable. Atara Beiserman, a wonderful friend and a great child therapist, also gave me a lot of advice. Without all of them, Robin wouldn't have turned out to be what she inevitably became—a wonderful therapist and one of my favorite characters ever.

Kevin Smith, my developmental editor, helped me get the final draft to a great shape. It's always a tricky tightrope act to create the perfect mystery—scattering the clues while distracting the reader with those dastardly red herrings. Kevin helped me fine-tune it until it was perfect.

Elyse Lyon received that final draft and spied all those inevitable mistakes that are bound to happen, because for me, timelines are somewhat flexible, character names change midparagraph on a whim, and adjectives fall out of order on a regular basis.

My agent, Sarah Hershman, cheered me on in this book. When I sent her my synopsis, she told me that it legit gave her chills, and that's what a thriller writer really wants to hear.

Stacey Mann has been a huge help to me, shepherding me as I bumble and stumble on social media, and I'm incredibly lucky to have met her.

And of course, thanks to all my wonderful readers, who read my books, write me lovely emails, and are the best readers a writer could ask for.

ABOUT THE AUTHOR

Photo © 2017 Yael Omer

Mike Omer has been a journalist, a game developer, and the CEO of Loadingames, but he can currently be found penning his next thriller. Omer loves to write about two things: real people who could be the perpetrators or victims of crimes—and funny stuff. He mixes these two loves quite passionately in his suspenseful and often macabre mysteries. Omer is married to a woman who diligently forces him to live his dream, and he is a father to an angel, a pixie, and a gremlin. He has a voracious hound that wags his tail quite menacingly at anyone who dares approach his home. Learn more by emailing him at mike@strangerealm.com.